Laurene

RACING PASSIONS

"Come back to bed, Zeke," Abbie told him softly. "You
know how I hate storms. Come and hold me."

The rain started pelting the roof then and he came back
beside her. Both were naked, for that was the way they
always slept. He moved in beside her and she pulled the
buffalo robe over them, snuggling close to him, finding
perfect shelter from the storm that frightened her. She was
afraid of nothing when he was beside her. He was like a
rock, indestructible, strong, hard, never afraid. She lifted
her face to his. Then his lips covered hers and she had no
defense against the way he had of enticing her, as if his
manliness and his touch were not enough. His lips moved
down over her throat. He gently kissed and caressed the
scar around her breast where he had once removed an arrow
from her when she was only fifteen. But now she was a
woman. Yes, she was most definitely a woman—alive and
warm and pleasing to a man!

SAVAGE DESTINY #3:
RIVER OF LOVE

BY F. ROSANNE BITTNER

ZEBRA BOOKS
KENSINGTON PUBLISHING CORP.

ZEBRA BOOKS

are published by

Kensington Publishing Corp.
475 Park Avenue South
New York, N.Y. 10016

Third printing: December, 1989

Printed in the United States of America

With grateful acknowledgment to authors whose works have both inspired me and taught me: Donald J. Berthrong, *The Southern Cheyennes*; Will Henry, *The Last Warpath*; Dee Brown, *Bury My Heart at Wounded Knee*; and to authors and/or establishments whose books were of valuable resource: St. Stephen's Indian Foundation, Wyoming, *The Wind River Rendezvous* magazine; the Language Research Department of the Northern Cheyenne, *English/Cheyenne Student Dictionary*; Ronald P. Koch, *Dress Clothing of the Plains Indians*; and the Time/Life series, *The Old West* and *The Civil War*.

Throughout this novel the reader will find reference to Utah Territory, Nebraska Territory, New Mexico Territory, and Kansas Territory. For clarification, portions of these territories comprised what is now Colorado, Nebraska, Wyoming and South Dakota. So that the reader understands specific locations, the major part of this novel is centered in present-day Colorado. The Arkansas River, the major territory of the Southern Cheyenne, is located in southeastern Colorado, as is Bent's Fort. Fort Laramie is located in southeastern Wyoming.

The meeting place of the Cheyenne/Sioux for the Sun Dance Ritual is in the southwest corner of South Dakota.

If you love someone, you will always be loyal to him no matter what the cost. You will always believe in him, always expect the best of him, and always stand your ground in defending him. . . .

There are three things that remain—faith, hope, love—and the greatest of these is love.

1 Corinthians 13: 7 and 13

Introduction

It was called the Treaty of 1851. Some called it the Big Treaty, the Fort Laramie Treaty, the Horse Creek Treaty, and sometimes the Fitzpatrick Treaty, after the famous scout-turned-agent Thomas "Broken Hand" Fitzpatrick, who had been instrumental in bringing the tribes together that year for the "big talk."

Never before and never again would so many thousands of Indians of so many different tribes gather together in one place. And there, for the first time, a boundary was drawn by the Great White Father for a Plains Indian tribe—the Cheyenne/Arapahos. It was a vast piece of land, situated in the heart of what was then Cheyenne country—a large section of what would one day be Colorado.

By 1853 the original treaty was being butchered with amendments, so that the final wording would bear little resemblance to the original pact to which the Cheyenne had agreed two years earlier. Promised supplies and money had not been awarded, and disease and thinning buffalo herds brought on by more and more white settlement were making the Indians impatient and angry. The "savages" were becoming restless, their pride wounded, their honor betrayed. Such things were enough to make young warriors thirst for a good fight, and it became increasingly difficult for soldiers and agents to keep them calm.

Thus, by 1853 the problems of a land about to burst with growth were many, for it was also a lawless land, filling with riff-raff from the East who were themselves fleeing the law, mingling with others sniffing for gold, prostitutes and out-

9

laws, land magnates and investors backed by Eastern money. Already the scheming was in motion to get the Indians out of the way, with false or exaggerated stories being fed to Eastern newspapers about the "savage, brutal Indians"—with white raiders posing as Indians and stealing cattle and horses and burning homes, raping and pillaging and blaming it all on the Indians; with illegal whiskey traders who introduced the red man to the sugared fire-water, trading a penny's worth of whiskey for a five dollar robe.

As a forewarning of what was to come, perhaps nothing is more accurate than the words of Broken Hand Fitzpatrick himself, when he wrote in his report for that year that "mineral wealth likewise abounds in the sands of the water courses, and in the gorges and canyons from which they issue; and should public attention ever be strongly directed to this section of our territory, and free access be obtained, the inducements which it holds will soon people it with thousands of citizens, and cause it to rise speedily into a flourishing mountain State."

He was talking about principal Cheyenne Territory. He was talking about what would one day be—Colorado.

One

The log cabin sat quietly on the north bank of the Arkansas River, the great, granite Rockies to the west of it, and broad, endless plains to the east. Blue smoke curled up lazily from the embers of the dying fire in the great stone fireplace, and the morning broke with its usual combination of chores and beauty for Abigail Monroe. The beauty was life itself, and the love she shared with her man and her children. She didn't mind the chores. It was just one form of love.

She turned to see the other half of the bed empty, which was to be expected. It could not really be called a bed, for her half-breed husband preferred sleeping on an elkskin-covered mattress stuffed with leaves and straw, with skins and buffalo robes for blankets. A mattress of feathers or one with springs was much too soft.

Abbie smiled and rose, straightening the robes and slipping on her Indian tunic, preferring its exquisite doe-skin softness to the stiff stays of undergarments and the coarse binding of cotton dresses with high necks and long sleeves and too many slips. Indian women were practical and knew how to dress for comfort, and, other than her white skin, Abigail Monroe was an Indian—in spirit and in heart.

She walked into the main room of the cabin, stirring the coals of the fire and adding wood to it before climbing the ladder to the upper loft, where the children slept. Little Kseé, Young Girl, slept quietly in her cradle. Abbie lightly touched the child's blond curls, almost laughing aloud at

11

what little resemblance the child bore to her half-Indian father and dark-haired mother. But she was theirs, nonetheless, for no man but Cheyenne Zeke had ever touched Abigail Monroe, and the thought of being his woman continued to bring the pleasant warmth to her blood, even after eight years of marriage. But little Young Girl had the blond hair and blue eyes of Abbie's mother and older sister, now long dead, and it was amazing to think that she was the product of Zeke and Abbie's sharing of bodies and life.

She turned to check on her other daughter, Blue Sky, called Moheya in the Cheyenne tongue. All three children had Cheyenne names, for the Cheyenne were an important part of their lives, and Zeke's Indian relatives were all the family Abbie had, her own family having all died on a wagon train going west. Little Blue Sky was an exact opposite of Young Girl. There was no mistaking Blue Sky's Indian blood, and without a closer look one would never dream the girl had any white blood at all. But a second glance would reveal that she was actually the best of both, a child with the rare beauty given only to those of mixed blood. Blue Sky would some day be an extraordinarily beautiful woman.

Abbie glanced at her son's bed and sighed. There was no use checking on that one, for his bed would most assuredly be empty, just as Zeke's side of their own bed was every morning. Father and son were as two peas in a pod, their Indian blood forcing them up before the sun and dragging them out for their habitual early morning ride. It was important to drink the wind, to straddle a painted pony bareback and breathe deeply of the life source and welcome the Great Sun Spirit who brought them a new day.

Cheyenne Zeke had a special love in his heart for his son, his firstborn, who was called Little Rock, Hohanino-o. The boy was only six years old, but he could ride as well as any Cheyenne warrior, seemingly a part of the animal he straddled with his little brown legs. Raised in part by his Cheyenne uncles, Swift Arrow and Black Elk, the child was proud and sure, learning the Cheyenne tongue, learning about weapons and hunting, learning to be a man. For six years old, the child's shoulders were unusually muscular,

12

and his skin was deep brown. His glossy black hair was straight and hung nearly to his waist. He was a fine son, a source of great pride to his father.

Abbie straightened when she heard the warcry in the distance. They were coming! She climbed back down the ladder and set the coffee pot on the grate over the fire, then went to the door. Her heart swelled with pride and love. Zeke needed his family. He was happy now. For many years he had lived with the hell of having seen his first wife's raped and tortured body, a white girl he had married back in Tennessee, who had been murdered by white friends for running off with a half-breed. The saddest part was that they had also killed Zeke's little baby boy. Abbie was glad to be the woman who had come into Zeke's life to bring him happiness again. He loved his daughters fiercely and would die for them in a moment, but Abbie knew without his saying that their firstborn son would forever hold a special place in Cheyenne Zeke's heart.

Father and son rode hard in the distance, side by side, racing and laughing, both with long black hair flying out behind them. The horses' manes also flew up from the wind, man and boy as wild and free as the animals they rode.

Then she smiled to herself. "No, the animals are tamer," she muttered. She waved to Dooley, a good friend and hired hand who was exiting his own shack. "We'll have breakfast in about a half hour!" she called out to him.

The man nodded and headed for the corral where Zeke's Appaloosas were kept, while Zeke and Little Rock rounded the corral gate and galloped past the cabin to a cottonwood tree, the "finish line." The horses were nose to nose, and Little Rock laughed his tiny laugh, insisting he had beat his father.

"I think perhaps you did this time, but you tricked me, Hohanino-o!" Zeke told the boy. "You picked the fast mare I told you about yesterday. I was not ready for that one!" He grabbed the boy from the horse and threw him over his lap, and Little Rock screamed. Zeke grasped the child's ankles and held him upside down for a moment, while Little Rock laughed delightedly, screaming "I tricked you!" to his

13

father. Zeke touched his horse's flanks with his heels and urged it forward, carrying his upside-down son over to Abbie, who reached out and turned him up to set him on his feet.

"I beat him!" the boy told his mother.

"That is questionable," Zeke put in, grinning handsomely at Abbie, his eyes roving her body, taking in the soft roundness of her breasts beneath the tunic. She put her hands on her hips and tried to give him a chastising look.

"The bed was empty again this morning," she told him. "I think perhaps I married the wind. One moment I feel you and the next moment you are gone, and I never know when there will be a breeze."

He laughed and slid agilely off the horse. "It is more fun being married to the wind, and never knowing when the breeze will touch your body, Abbie girl," he told her, leaning down and kissing her cheek. "Little Rock and I will take the horses to be brushed and fed while you start breakfast." He touched her cheek lightly with the back of his hand, then left. She stood watching him, shaking her head over the wild streak in him that she would never tame. But then she didn't really want to tame him completely, for she loved him just as he was. She walked back inside and sat down to the table to wait, picking up a potato from several she had left out the night before so that they would be ready to peel in the morning. She began deftly carving off the skin with a small knife, and Little Rock came barging through the door.

"I am hungry, Mother!" came the expected first words from her son.

"Quiet your voice," Abbie replied. "Your sisters are sleeping. Get yourself a piece of bread and go back outside." This time they spoke in English. Zeke and Abbie used both languages with their children, knowing that to survive they would have to speak the white man's tongue, but also wanting them to never lose the Cheyenne language.

Little Rock ran to the cupboard for a piece of bread and hurried out, just as Zeke was coming inside. Zeke walked to a basin in the corner to splash water on his face. Then he

14

ambled over to sit down at the corner of the table next to Abbie. His big frame seemed to fill the small room, and he sprawled into the chair like a restless panther, ready to spring back out of it at the first hint of trouble. He stretched out a long leg and touched her knee with his own. She stopped peeling the potatoes and met his dark eyes, feeling a pleasant warmth at the way he looked at her.

"What's for breakfast, woman?" he asked, grinning the handsome grin that always stirred her blood. His face was finely chiseled, a beautiful mixture of Cheyenne and white, the cheekbones high, the nose straight and sharp, the eyes large and dark, showing much emotion at times—and sometimes showing anger that would frighten away the worst of men.

"Potatoes and pork," she replied, "thanks to being able to pick up that pork at the fort. It will be good to taste bacon. It's been a long time." Zeke leaned forward and grasped the back of her neck, gently pulling her forward and kissing her hungrily.

"And what about dessert?" he asked.

Her cheeks turned pink, for he had a way of rousing her with his eyes and with a gentle flick of his tongue against her lips that always made her blush. She looked down at the potato she was peeling and returned to her work.

"Since when do we have a dessert after breakfast—or after any meal, for that matter?" she replied curtly. "There is little time and not enough of the right ingredients for making desserts. But the wild berries should be coming out soon. I'll make you some pies."

He grinned. "It isn't pie I'm talking about, woman, and you know it," he replied.

She gave him a feigned disgusted look. "In the morning?" she replied. "I just got out of that bed, and you weren't there. Now you want me to just turn around and get right back into it?" She turned her eyes back to the potato she was peeling. "Of course, since the damage is already done and I'm pregnant again, I suppose you can have your dessert whenever you want it." Then she grinned. "A woman would be a fool to deny you your dessert."

15

He laughed lightly. Then he whipped out his infamous knife, fifteen inches long from the end of its buffalo jawbone handle to the curved tip of its blade. He picked up a potato and had the skin peeled off almost instantly, for he was good with that knife, and the blade was razor sharp.

"Our son rides just like a warrior, Abbie girl! He sits on that mount like he was born a part of it."

"I saw," she replied in a worried tone.

He put down the potato and grasped her wrist to stop her work. She met his eyes again, and hers were full of fear for her son.

"He'll be okay, Abbie girl."

"He's all Cheyenne. What kind of future will that bring him?"

"At least he'll be proud and brave. He'll be a man."

She closed her eyes and put her hand over his. "Zeke, you know I want that just as much as you do. You know how I love the People. No matter what happens, I want always to be with them, to help them. I have no other family now. But when I think of what the future might hold for them, and then consider my own son being a part of that—"

"A man does what he has to do, what is right, no matter what the cost, Abbie girl. We'll teach Little Rock right from wrong, teach him courage and skill and honesty, and the rest will be up to him. That's all we can do. He'll have every right to live in the white man's world, because he's only one-quarter Cheyenne. But already I can see where his heart lies. Next year I'd like to take him on a buffalo hunt with Black Elk, just to let him watch. And I'm going to start carving out a bow for him."

She studied the dark eyes. "And the knife? Will you teach him to use a blade the way you do?"

Their eyes held for several seconds. Then he nodded. "Out here it's a good thing to know how to use. Perhaps he'll be as good as his father—perhaps not. Some things come more naturally to some than others. But I'll teach him what I know, Abbie. That knife has saved my skin many a time—and saved yours, too."

She smiled softly. Yes, he had used the knife to defend

her—and probably would again. His left cheek still bore the long, thin, white scar, put there by a Crow warrior years before in Zeke's fur trapping days in the Rockies, before he had met and married Abigail Trent.

"The frightening thing, Zeke, is that you're so right in teaching Little Rock how to ride and use weapons and to be proud. But he also has to learn tolerance, Zeke. He has to understand what is happening out here in this land, that he has to get along with the white man as well as the Indians. He can't be all Indian, Zeke. It isn't good for him to want only to be Indian, even though that would make my heart most proud."

His eyes clouded, and he pulled away from her, getting up from the chair. He shoved the knife roughly into its sheath. "He'll be what his heart tells him to be!" he said flatly.

She put down the potato and wiped her hands on her apron, rising from her chair. His back was to her. She walked over to face him, putting her arms around his waist and resting her head against his broad chest, breathing in the sweet scent of man and open air, rubbing her cheek against the soft buckskin shirt.

"Don't be angry," she told him softly. "You know how I love the Cheyenne—that I don't feel white myself anymore. But these are my babies, Zeke. I get so afraid."

He hugged her tightly, kissing the top of her head. "I get afraid, too, Abbie girl. But I refuse to let it stop me from making my son proud to be Cheyenne. The white man might come here and destroy our freedom, but I'll be damned if they'll destroy our very heritage, our pride and courage, our very manhood! We might all go down, but we'll go down fighting, and we'll go down Cheyenne and proud of it!"

He held her so tightly she could barely breathe, and she could feel him trembling. He rested his cheek on top of her head. She was still small in his arms, and to him she was still the little girl he had broken into womanhood—the young, loving, sweet and lonely girl from the wagon train—the girl he had tried to forget but could not. He grasped her long, dark, lustrous hair and leaned back slightly, forcing her to look up at him.

"You get more beautiful with every year and every baby," he told her. She saw the wild need in his eyes, the need to prove to himself that in spite of what was going on around them, they could still be together, that none of it would interfere with their love. For he was certain that without Abbie he would not even be able to breathe.

"Zeke, Dooley says they're building a fort now at the junction of the Republican and Kansas Rivers—and another one at Walnut Creek—forts and soldiers and—"

He covered her mouth with his own to stop her talking, kissing her savagely, possessively, almost hurting her. Then his lips moved to her neck.

"Let them build their goddamned forts!" he groaned. He moved to her lips and kissed her again, pressing her tight against him and moving his tongue over her lips hungrily. He finally left her mouth and kissed her eyes. "Leave the potatoes, Abbie girl," he told her softly. "I'll tell Dooley to keep our son outside. The girls are still asleep. And I want my white squaw."

She began to blush again. "Zeke, Dooley will know what we're doing!"

He smiled the fetching smile and dropped his eyes to her full breasts. "So what? With three kids and a fourth on the way, is it something new?" He tousled her hair.

"But I'll be embarrassed at breakfast!"

He gently grasped one breast, feeling its full softness through the velvety doeskin tunic. It was heavy with milk for Young Girl. "You'll just look prettier. You always look even prettier after we've made love."

Her roused nipple made a small point through the tunic, and her cheeks felt hot. She met his eyes for a brief moment, blushing more, then pulled away from him and walked to the bedroom. She heard him go outside and talk to Dooley. She closed the curtain to the bedroom and pulled off her tunic. There was no arguing, and she had no objections anyway. When he came back inside and into the bedroom, she was lying on the bed of skins.

She curled up defensively when his eyes scanned her white nakedness. "My waist is getting thick again already," she said bashfully. "I feel funny when you look at me. I'm not sixteen years old anymore."

His eyes were liquid with love. "Don't talk like an old woman. You're still young, and you're much more beautiful than when you were sixteen," he answered, pulling off his shirt. At thirty-three, his body was still hard and strong, his broad chest revealing the scars from suffering the Sun Dance ritual to test his manhood. "And you're the most beautiful when you're carrying my life in your belly," he added. He removed his weapons belt and unlaced his leggings, and soon that part of him that brought out her wildest desires was revealed. He came down to her, and her slim, white thighs parted for him.

"*Ne-mehotatse*," he whispered, his lips gently tasting her breasts before he pushed himself inside of her.

She gasped and arched up to him. "And I love you!" she moaned, her eyes closing in ecstasy.

He came down closer, and the room was warm and sweet, their lovemaking as tender and beautiful as that first time, out on the prairies of Nebraska, when she was only fifteen.

Outside, Little Rock let out a warcry as he played with his little toy bow and arrow, dreaming of some day being an honored dog soldier, like his uncles, Swift Arrow and Black Elk. He shot at a scarecrow in the little garden Abbie kept behind the cabin, pretending it was a nameless enemy and pretending the arrow had pierced the enemy's heart. Yes! He would be one of the great *Hotamitanui!*

Henry Page spread out the map for Zeb Crawley, a robust, bearded mountain man turned scout. There was no longer any money in trapping, and Crawley supported himself by helping Easterners find their way around in the new territory. Crawley knew the land between the Mississippi River and the Pacific Ocean as well as he knew the back of his hand.

Both men leaned over the homemade table, which consisted of two planks of wood laid over barrels. They were a sharp contrast—Zeb Crawley a burly, buckskin-clad man who survived on open air and hard ground and game that he killed himself, and Henry Page a modestly built man who wore a neatly cut suit and sported a fine, curled mustache and hands cleaner than any Zeb had seen in quite some time. The government agent was smooth and educated, with neat brown hair and soft brown eyes that were hard to read. Zeb wasn't certain of the extent of Henry Page's plans for the land along the Arkansas River area, and he didn't mind helping point out a few things on the map for Page. He was being paid well for this job, and he did not truly believe the government would ever actually build a railroad right through the heart of Cheyenne country. If they wanted to be foolish enough to come out here and do some surveying, Zeb didn't mind helping. He needed the money.

Page carefully smoothed out the drawings as Zeb watched, growing impatient with Page's obvious concern for neatness. Zeb leaned on his rifle and wondered if Henry Page would ever be ready to ask whatever it was he intended to ask. It was a warm spring day, and it was getting even warmer inside Page's canvas tent.

"There now," Page finally spoke up. "Come around to this side and look."

Zeb sighed and set his rifle aside, walking around to the other side of the table. "What is it you want from me?" he asked Page.

"Here—right here," Page replied, running his finger along the Arkansas River. "I want to ride through this country, with you as a guide. Most of this land is unoccupied. I'll be making notes—finding out who owns what—determining how easy it will be for the government to claim most of it for building the railroad. Will you guide me?"

Zeb stood staring at the drawing, then folded his arms in front of him and turned to face Page, towering over the much smaller man. "Mister, a lot of that is Cheyenne country—land your government gave to them in the Treaty of 1851."

Page averted his eyes and leaned over the map again. "Poppycock! Indians don't own anything—and that treaty

20

still hasn't even been ratified. I'm told there will be some changes to it. Besides," he stood up straighter again, "even if the Indians keep it, that doesn't mean we can't put a railroad through there. That won't bother the Indians."

Zeb grinned and shook his head. "You greenhorns are all alike," he commented, walking around to the other side of the table. He took a chunk of chewing tobacco from a pouch at his waist and stuck it between his cheek and gum.

"I don't need such remarks, Mr. Crawley," Page replied coolly. "I only ask your services as a scout. You may keep your opinions to yourself."

"A railroad would destroy the Indians," Zeb answered. "It would chase away the wild game and the buffalo—and it would bring in more whites."

Page frowned. "I hardly think one railroad track is going to make much of a change," he answered. He grinned a little. "You actually sound like you're defending the Indians."

Their eyes held. "Maybe I am. Some of my best friends is Indians, Mr. Page. I've been livin' around them for a good many years. I'm fifty years old, and I come out here when I was fifteen. Ain't never gone back to civilization since. But my fur trappin' days is over, and I just got word that my sister back East just lost her husband and still has two kids at home—one of them bad sick. She's runnin' out of money. So I'll do your scoutin' for you—for the money—so's I can send her some. If I really believed you'd succeed in gettin' a railroad through that country, I'd not help you. But you'll never do it."

Page grinned more. "You underestimate the government, Mr. Crawley." He leaned over the table again. "Be that as it may, I'm only out here to do some very early and very secret surveying. Plans for a railroad haven't even been formally announced yet. In the meantime, tell me what you know about some of this property. Any of it privately owned?"

Zeb walked outside a moment to spit, then returned to the map. He ran a soiled finger along the river, then stopped at a piece about sixty miles west of the new Bent's Fort, which had just recently been rebuilt by William Bent near the site of a heavily wooded area called the Big Timbers—"Hinta Nagi" to the Cheyenne.

"Here's a piece you'll never touch," he told the man.

"Why not?" Page asked.

Zeb grinned a little. "Belongs to Zeke Monroe—a half-breed."

Page smiled triumphantly. "Indians can't own land, Mr. Crawley. Not even half-Indians can own land."

Zeb suppressed a chuckle. "It ain't in his name, actually. It's in his wife's name."

Page shrugged. "So? A squaw can't own land either."

This time Zeb did chuckle. "This squaw is white," he replied.

Page lost his smile. He paled slightly in surprise. "White!"

Zeb nodded.

"Married to . . . a half-breed?"

Zeb nodded again.

Page walked to a corner of the tent, retrieving a pipe from the pocket of his overcoat. "How low can a woman get?" he mumbled.

Zeb Crawley bristled. "Mrs. Monroe is one of the finest ladies in this territory, Mr. Page. You insult her again in my presence, and you can find yourself another guide."

Page's eyes widened in surprise. "I . . . I'm sorry, Mr. Crawley."

Crawley scowled at the man. "Zeke and his wife claimed that land some years back, five hundred acres. William Bent helped them draw up the papers. Zeke raises Appaloosas on it. It ain't such a big piece; not all five hundred acres can be used. It's partly just rock. But it's all damned pretty, and it's close to the Cheyenne, which is the way Zeke wanted it. He only settled there so's his white wife could have a regular house. They lived with the Cheyenne 'fore that. Mrs. Monroe herself lived in a tipi a good many years before Zeke built them a cabin and settled there on the Arkansas. The man takes pride in his little ranch and that Mrs. Monroe is a damned good woman. They got kids now. You don't need that land, Mr. Page. You can work around it."

The scout stepped back then, walking back to the tent entrance and spitting again, while Page straightened his lapels and proceeded to stuff his pipe with tobacco.

"Perhaps if enough money was offered—"

"Money don't mean much to people like them," Zeb replied. "They like that piece of land—like bein' close to the Cheyenne. Mrs. Monroe is probably more Cheyenne herself than white. She loves them people as much as anybody."

Page frowned and lit his pipe, puffing it for a moment. "The government has ways of getting what they need, Mr. Crawley. If we need it and this Zeke Monroe won't bargain, we'll just have to use other tactics."

Zeb scowled at first, then began to grin. Then he began laughing with robust humor, while Page puffed his pipe more and felt his anger rising.

"What's so funny?" he finally asked impatiently.

Zeb just shook his head and scratched his bearded cheek. "Mister you don't know Cheyenne Zeke!"

"Cheyenne Zeke?"

"That's what most folks out in these parts call him. I did some huntin' and trappin' with the man myself years back. His people call him Lone Eagle, and I'll tell you right now, he ain't a man you want to mess with. I expect he can't even remember how many men he's killed, and I guarantee that if you try to take his land, he'll add you to his list. You might be able to go in there and run his place over, but Cheyenne Zeke would make damned sure you met your Maker before it was over with. Ain't no doubt in my mind. He carries a blade bigger than any you ever saw, and you go in there and threaten him, and your liver will be breathin' fresh air!"

Page felt a chill, but he calmly puffed his pipe. "Well, then, perhaps we'll see what we can do about going around Mr. Monroe's property," he replied. "But only out of consideration for his white wife, not because of any threats some worthless half-breed would pose."

Page leaned over the map again, studying the tiny piece of land owned by Zeke Monroe and his mysterious white wife.

*   *   *

23

Black Elk sat by the fire of his tipi, honing a sharp edge to his tomahawk with a stone, while his father, Deer Slayer, sat watching quietly as he puffed on a pipe. Black Elk's new wife, Blue Bird Woman, only fourteen, sat behind her adored warrior husband, afraid of his going to war with the Pawnee, but proud of him also. There was Cheyenne honor to defend and hunting grounds to reclaim. Pawnee scalps would be taken!

Black Elk set down the tomahawk and took one more piece of meat from the pan beside the fire.

"If not for Zeke, we would not be eating this venison tonight," the young man told his father bitterly. "What little buffalo we had for the winter has long been gone, and the filthy Pawnee have stolen that which should be ours! The game grows more scarce every year. Zeke says this is the first deer he has seen in many, many weeks."

Deer Slayer nodded, proud of his half-breed stepson's loyalty to his Cheyenne family. "Zeke is a good man," he replied, speaking as his son had, in the Cheyenne tongue. "He should have kept the meat for himself and his family, for Abigail carries life in her belly again and soon there will be yet another mouth to feed."

"The white squaw has done well for Zeke. She gives him many children. After what happened to him in that place called Tennessee, it is good that he has found another woman and has his son and daughters."

Young Blue Bird Woman listened quietly, hoping she would also bear many children, for Black Elk wanted sons, and he was a good husband to her. The thought of the things he had been teaching her in the night brought a warmth to her blood and a blush to her cheeks, and she never turned her new husband away, for she intended to make his life take root in her womb as quickly as possible so she would please him even more.

"It is too bad Gentle Woman did not live to see Zeke's happiness with his white woman—all the grandchildren Zeke and Abbie would have given her," Black Elk continued, "but at least she was still alive when Zeke first brought his wife to us. She saw the joy in his face and the goodness in Abigail. My mother always had a special love for her half-breed son."

Deer Slayer's eyes saddened, and he stared at the bone in his hand. "That is because Zeke's white father stole him away from Gentle Woman when Zeke was only a very small boy," he told his son. "Your mother mourned for many years for Zeke until he came out to find her after he was grown. I remember the many times she cried for him, even after you and your two brothers were born to us. I tried everything to keep her happy after I rescued her from that stinking Crow warrior Zeke's white father had sold her to. I made her my wife and showed her much love, but always there was an emptiness there that only Zeke could fill." He turned the bone around in his fingers. "I miss your mother, Black Elk. It is unwise to speak of the dead, but I cannot help thinking of her. I am like a shell without her."

Black Elk watched his father for a moment, his heart paining him. The cholera had taken Gentle Woman sooner than she should have had her life taken from her. He looked back at the fire. "At least she did not live to see Red Eagle worship the brown whiskey bottle!" he grumbled. "Maybe it is best she lived just long enough to see Zeke again, but died before one of her other sons became such a drunkard! It would break her heart to see that he cannot even rise in the morning without first swallowing some of the evil spirits. I am ashamed of Red Eagle! His warrior society has disowned him—and then he had to go and try to rape another man's wife. I do not understand why Yellow Moon stays with him. Now they have been banished, and how do we know if he is taking care of Yellow Moon and his son? She should not have gone with him!"

"Yellow Moon loves your brother. She is loyal. Perhaps one day her love—and the love he has for his son—will help him turn away from the firewater and be a man again."

"That will never happen!" Black Elk said bitterly. "Once he was a proud warrior, but the firewater has reduced him to a woman. Just as it has done to many of the others. They think it makes them strong, but it makes them weak!"

The young man cleaned off the bone he'd been chewing

25

on and laid it in a clay bowl where bones were collected for possible use as utensils. Seldom was any part of an animal wasted in the hands of the Indian, especially the buffalo, from which nearly all clothing, shelter and utensils were made. Whatever he needed, the Indian had found in the earth and the animals. But now the earth was being ravaged, and the animals were disappearing.

"I keep praying that my son will change," Deer Slayer said sadly. "But at least I have pride in you, my son—and in Swift Arrow. I miss your brother who rides in the north now."

Black Elk sighed and picked up his tomahawk again. "I miss him also, my father. Perhaps he will ride with us against the Pawnees. When we leave, we will go north first and get help from our northern brothers with whom Swift Arrow rides. I think they are the smart ones. The northern Cheyenne and the Sioux make no treaties with the whites, and I am tired of our chiefs saying we must make peace." He ground at the tomahawk's blade angrily. "All of our bad luck is because of the whites. Swift Arrow's wife and son died of the spotted disease, leaving him a bitter man. My own mother died of the hated cholera—another white man's disease. Now they come—by the thousands—swarming over our land like bees, destroying the water, chasing away the game. Because of the white man's whiskey my brother is a drunkard, and the rest of us are starving because there is no game. Now the Great White Father does not care for the Eastern tribes as he promised them, and they make war on us, trying to take what we have left. We will show the Pawnee what still belongs to the Cheyenne!" He held up the tomahawk.

Deer Slayer, in his aging years, wanted to tell his son that he feared such wars would be of no use, that he saw the white man coming to take everything away—from Pawnee and Cheyenne alike. But Black Elk was young and proud. He needed his revenge, for he was Cheyenne, and it was the way. Deer Slayer would not take this moment from his son. The Pawnee had been raiding into Cheyenne Territory. It was time to remind them they did not belong there.

26

Two

Yellow Moon rode quietly on the pack mule behind her husband, Red Eagle. She clung tightly to their little two-year-old son, Laughing Boy, who got his name from his happy personality. The child smiled often, giggled easily, and seldom cried. He was a good boy, a strong and healthy boy, an open and loving child.

Yellow Moon already missed the People and longed to go home. But they could not go back, for Red Eagle had shamed himself and his family because of his drinking. But Yellow Moon still loved her once brave and respected husband, and she was convinced that one day he would stop drinking the firewater and would return to his honorable ways. Always, after he had done something bad because of the drinking, including hurting her physically, he would beg for forgiveness and swear his love, and always she took him back, forgiving him and giving him another chance to mend his ways. For she was Red Eagle's woman, and there was a time when it was good between them—a time when she had danced the blanket dance for him before they were married and had chosen him to sit with her and touch her secretly beneath the blanket. That was when Red Eagle was younger, before the whiskey had taken hold of his mind and his soul, controlling his every move.

Now they had no home and no honor. But he had clung to her in the night and had begged her to stay with him—to go away with him to find a new home. She did not like this barren land they had come to south of the Arkansas. It was hot and dry and rocky, and they did not know the Indians here. They were past Comanche territory, closer to Apache country. She did not know the Apaches, and she had heard tales of bandits and outlaws who roamed this land. She prayed to the Spirits to protect them and wondered what Red Eagle would do when he again needed more whiskey. He had sold everything they owned, and now he had only one horse—the one he rode. They no longer even owned a tipi, for he had sold that to traders at Bent's Fort who wanted the skins. Red Eagle had used all the money for more whiskey.

She wished he had gone to Zeke and Abbie first. Surely Zeke would have let them live somewhere on his land. Still, Zeke and Red Eagle had been born of the same mother, and Zeke's heart and proud spirit were Cheyenne. He, too, would have been ashamed of Red Eagle, just as Black Elk and their father, Deer Slayer, were ashamed. Perhaps even Zeke would have turned them away.

Now they were forced to wander homeless, to find shelter wherever they could, usually in a cave; but often they slept in the open air without shelter. Yellow Moon was hungry most of the time, as was their son, and she sometimes thought of turning back without Red Eagle and going home. Surely she could find the way. If not for her son, she would do so. But if an enemy should capture her, they would capture her son also. She was safer with Red Eagle, in spite of the fact that he was drunk most of the time. Even now he lifted the bottle again, seemingly unable to breathe without the hated firewater. And she wondered what he would do if she destroyed his supply.

It was something to consider. Perhaps if she destroyed the whiskey while they were out here in this strange land, he would learn to get along without it. For he had nothing left to trade, and there was no one with whom to trade anyway. Yes! Perhaps that would be a good way to help her husband end his drinking! She smiled and kissed the top of Laughing Boy's head. She would help her man. She would destroy the firewater and he would learn to live without it!

There was no sound but the occasional yelping of wolves

28

somewhere in the foothills of the great, silent Rockies, now black shadows standing stark in the bright moonlight. All was quiet inside the little cabin on the Arkansas, until the faint rumble that led to the louder sound of thundering hooves. Zeke leaped up from the bed of robes, quickly pulling on his leggings and grabbing his knife and a rifle. "Stay inside!" he ordered as Abbie sat up, rubbing her eyes.

He disappeared, and Abbie was instantly fully awake. She hurriedly pulled her tunic over her head and climbed to the loft of the cabin, grabbing Young Girl from her cradle on the way and taking her up to where the other two children slept. Little Rock and Blue Sky did not stir. Abbie quietly went to the window of the loft and opened the wooden door that covered it, peeking out through the opening that still had no glass in it.

Below she could see Zeke's Cheyenne half brother, Black Elk, and a painted war party of Cheyenne, their voices angry.

"If you try to make war against the Pawnee, the soldiers will come after you!" Zeke was arguing.

"We do not make war! It is the Pawnee who have made war against *us*!" Black Elk replied. "Let the soldiers come! We will still have Pawnee scalps! We leave now, at dark time, so soldiers do not know. We will brave the spirits of the night for secrecy. I come to tell you, my brother, because I want you to help us. If soldiers come to ask you where your Cheyenne brothers have gone, you tell them we only go to hunt buffalo. You will do this?"

Zeke folded his arms, secretly longing to accompany the war party himself. But that way of life was over for him. "You know I will, Black Elk. How is our father?"

"He is well. He stays with the women and children this time. He takes care of my Blue Bird Woman." Black Elk's voice softened when he spoke the name of his new wife.

"Black Elk will kill many Pawnee quickly," one of the other braves spoke up with a grin. "He wishes to get back home to his tipi and his new young wife who waits inside it."

The rest of the half-naked warriors grinned and some snickered, and Black Elk turned dark eyes on the one who had made the joke. "Perhaps Big Horse would like to challenge Black Elk and see if his new wife has made him soft!" he sneered.

Big Horse sobered. "We will save our strength for the Pawnee."

Black Elk grinned and nodded. He turned back to Zeke. "The Pawnee will regret moving into our land and taking our game."

"The Pawnee have rifles." Zeke warned them. "Many more than the Cheyenne own. And they have the help of the Eastern Indians who have been pushed into Pawnee country and who have learned the white man's ways and have many rifles. The Sac and the Fox and the Potawatomis will help the Pawnee."

Black Elk's horse snorted and jerked its head. Black Elk yanked on the reins and the animal pranced in place nervously.

"We go and find small Pawnee hunting parties—get many scalps!" the young man replied, using the English his mother and half-breed brother had taught him. "Then we talk to our other allies—the Kiowa and Arapaho and others—and we make plans! We will ride against the Pawnee for what they have done. Many of our friends have been killed, my brother—your friends, too. We have little land on which to hunt, and the Pawnee try to take it from us. We will not let them. We attack them now—and many moons from now we surprise them by attacking again when they think we are done with them!"

"You've signed a treaty agreeing to end the warring between the tribes," Zeke reminded him, afraid an attack on the Pawnee would only make more trouble for the Cheyenne in being allowed to keep what land the government had awarded them.

"Treaty!" Black Elk spat. "The Great White Father lied to us! He said we would get a lot of money—'for the next fifty years,' he tells us!" He sniffed haughtily. "It has been two winters since the treaty, and they tell us some things will now be changed—that the Great White Father still has not decided if he agrees. First he makes the offer—then he

30

thinks maybe he should take it back! Where are our supplies? Where is the money?" He waved his hand angrily. "Our wives and children starve and the Great White Father does not care! Now the Pawnee try to take our hunting grounds. The Great White Father does not stop them. There is no more treaty. If they come with something to sign, we shall not sign it. We go now—show the Pawnee they should stay out of Cheyenne country!" He whirled his painted pony in a circle. *"Nohetto!"* he shouted, signifying he was through talking. "Go and see our father soon—be sure my Blue Bird Woman is well, my brother. I entrust them to you."

"Wait, my brother!" Zeke called out. "What about Red Eagle? Why is he not with you?"

Their eyes held and Black Elk sneered. "We both know why," he grumbled. "The whiskey has made him too weak to fight!" His horse pranced and whinnied. "But it is worse than that, my brother. He drank so much one night that he could not even find his own lodge. He entered another, and when he saw the strange woman inside, he went to her and attacked her, trying to force himself on her. It was Flat Foot's wife. Flat Foot found her struggling with him and began beating on Red Eagle and kicked him out of the lodge. He has been banished from the village, Zeke—from all Cheyenne and Arapaho villages. And I am not sorry. He was becoming a disgrace!"

Abbie heard as she sat up in the loft. She closed her eyes and held the baby closer. "Oh, dear God," she whispered. "Poor Yellow Moon."

"What about Yellow Moon?" Zeke was already asking.

"She had the choice of going back to her Arapaho family. But she chose to stay with Red Eagle. They are gone now. I do not know where they are going, except that they went south."

Zeke sighed and clenched his fists. "You shouldn't have let her go with him!" he growled.

"She is Red Eagle's woman!" Black Elk barked back. "She made the choice herself. I did not want her to go any more than you. But she has always been a loyal woman to

31

him. She *wanted* to go."

"The country south of here is too dangerous!"

Black Elk's eyes narrowed. "All country is dangerous now. Even this place the Great White Father says belongs to us is invaded by white outlaws and by Eastern Indians who come now and try to take it. We are going now to stop them." He let out a war cry and held up his lance, then galloped off, with nearly fifty men riding after him, yipping and calling out more war cries.

They thundered away, and Abbie could feel Zeke's worry. The once happy and carefree Black Elk was becoming more and more rebellious, just like their brother in the north, Swift Arrow. Their anger over the bungled Treaty of 1851 was boiling, and the whites' destruction of the forests and streams and precious buffalo were adding fire under the kettle. For now they would take their anger out on the hated Pawnees, who were trying to move in on what little good hunting territory was left. But how long would it be before that volcano of anger would erupt against the whites?

She knew the same thoughts were rushing through Zeke's mind, as he stood there looking after them. He looked so lonely, and she blinked back tears. If not for her, he would probably ride with them, for it was in his blood to hunt and make war and ride free.

She turned back around to check the children, surprised to see Little Rock awake and standing behind her. It startled her, and she saw with sudden reality just how "Indian" he was, for he had walked up behind her so quietly that she did not know he was there.

"I want to go fight, too!" he said with puckered lips. His large, dark eyes at that very moment did not look like a little boy's, but more like a vengeful man's. It was the same look she had seen in Zeke's dark eyes before he killed men who had tried to harm her. It was a Cheyenne look—a warrior's look—a wild, savage look. And she was afraid for her son.

"No, Little Rock!" she said softly. She put her arms around him, and for a moment he stood there stiffly. Then he put his little brown arms around her neck, and he was

32

her little boy again.

Yellow Moon drew on her inner strength to stay on the mule as Red Eagle led the animal onward in an aimless search for someone—anyone—who would have whiskey to trade. The day had been long, for her beaten, weary body had found it difficult to withstand the pain and agony of wandering about beneath the hot, relentless sun, her cut lips cracking from the heat. Her side ached fiercely, and she was certain a rib must be cracked or broken. She had thought it such a good idea to destroy her husband's whiskey, sure he would understand that she was only trying to help him. But his anger had been worse than anything she had expected, as was the beating he gave her for being such a "bad wife." He had beaten her before, but never like this.

Laughing Boy sat in front of her, his tired little head hanging in a half sleep. Yellow Moon wished only for the day to end, so that she and her little son could sleep and her wounds could heal more. She was not certain how much longer she could ride, but Red Eagle continued on like a crazed man, his eyes wild with his need for the firewater against his tongue.

Such a changed man he was from the proud warrior she had married! What a terrible thing the whiskey had done to him, and to many others like him. What was it about the strange, burning drink in the brown bottles that turned brave, strong men into weak women? Surely it was an evil spirit, somehow captured by the white men and sealed with a cork, there to wait for a red man to remove the cork so that the evil spirit could leap out and possess him. Still, she clung to the hope that after a few days without the whiskey, Red Eagle would become his old self again. He would be sorry for beating her and would again prove his manhood to the others and rejoin the People, where they could be happy again.

But then they heard voices and laughter. Red Eagle halted his horse and only sat and listened for a moment. The

33

sun had already set, and Yellow Moon had been hoping he would stop and make camp soon. She was half asleep herself when the mule came to a halt, and at first her heart gladdened that finally he would stop and make camp. But then she heard the voices, too, coming from somewhere over the next rise, and it frightened her. Surely her husband would not be foolish enough to ride right into the camp of strangers in this unknown land!

Yet now he seemed to perk up like a dog that has spotted a piece of fresh meat. She knew what he was thinking—that where there were voices there might also be whiskey. He sat a little straighter on his horse and kicked his heels into the animal's flanks, jerking on the reins of the mule as he proceeded forward.

"Red Eagle, you must be careful!" she warned. "Use the caution you learned from the dog soldiers."

"Be still, woman!" he barked. "I have heard enough from you!"

She closed her lips and swallowed, her fear building as they crested a rocky cliff and looked down on an encampment below. A group of men sat around a campfire, playing cards and passing around a bottle like so many others Yellow Moon had seen. She recognized the men as mostly white men and some Mexicans. She clung more tightly to Laughing Boy, her mind racing with tales she had heard of white outlaws and Mexican slave traders.

Red Eagle watched, his body shaking from his need for the firewater, his lips dry, his throat screaming, every muscle in his body crying out for the needed alcohol. His heart secretly hurt for what he had done to his beloved Yellow Moon, for he had hit her many times when he awoke to find his supply of firewater all destroyed. But she deserved the beating for being such a traitor to him!

He would not turn to look at her and see the bruises on her face and the cut on her lip. Perhaps now she would think twice about again destroying his whiskey! He watched the Mexicans below, his mind racing with how he could bargain with them for some of the whiskey, his body sweating and in pain. He could almost smell the whiskey they passed among

34

themselves, and finally he could no longer resist at least trying to get at least one bottle from them. They were probably just whiskey traders anyway, willing to take a pretty blanket for one bottle. Just one bottle! That could hold him until he could reach a fort or a town where he could get more. He would steal it if he had to!

He turned his horse and started down a rocky escarpment, leading Yellow Moon behind him by the reins of her mule. She hung her head in despair, for she knew that he would buy more whiskey now and again become drunk from the evil spirits. She had been foolish to think she could cure him. She heard the laughter of the men below, and her chest tightened, for she did not like strangers. She clung to little Laughing Boy and threw a blanket around herself so that her legs would not show.

It took several minutes to reach the bottom. Small rocks tumbled down ahead of them, and one of the men rose at the sound, pulling a gun when he saw the two of them approaching. "Who goes there!" he commanded.

"Just one man and his squaw," Red Eagle shouted in reply. "We are lost and wish your help in directing us to the nearest fort—and perhaps we can camp with you for the night."

The men eyed each other and one of them grinned. "Did he say squaw?" the grinning one asked quietly.

"I believe so," the leader replied. "Come on in!" he shouted to Red Eagle. "And don't try to trick us, redskin, or you'll be a dead man, your woman dead also."

"I do not trick you." Red Eagle answered, hopeful of being offered some whiskey.

They approached cautiously, and when they came close, Yellow Moon stayed on the mule. She did not like the way the men looked at her. Laughing Boy roused awake and peeked out at them from under the blanket and smiled.

"Welcome to our camp!" the leader told Red Eagle with a smile. "I'm called Nick Trapper and these are my men. We're, uh, traders, you might say. Are you hungry? We have food."

Yellow Moon thought the man overly friendly, and she

still made no move to get off the mule. The men seemed to be making a point now of not looking at her, as they slapped Red Eagle on the back and welcomed him in a friendly fashion.

"I . . . I am in need of some . . . whiskey," Red Eagle answered. His near begging reply made Yellow Moon feel ashamed. Nick Trapper's eyebrows arched and he laughed. He looked around at the others.

"The man wants whiskey!" he said jovially. They all laughed, and Trapper picked up a bottle and handed it out to Red Eagle, then jerked it back. "I don't even know your name," he told Red Eagle.

Red Eagle licked his lips, his eyes glued to the bottle. "I am Red Eagle . . . a Cheyenne," he replied.

"Cheyenne! Ah, the Cheyenne are great warriors, and their women beautiful, no?" Trapper answered.

Red Eagle grinned and nodded. "Ai! We are great warriors, and our women are beautiful. I . . . I would like some whiskey now, please. I will pay you." His body was beginning to shake violently, but Trapper held back the bottle.

"And how will you pay us, my Cheyenne friend?" he asked.

Red Eagle swallowed, wanting to scream for the whiskey. "I . . . I have a blanket or two left . . . pretty ones. And I have a good horse, friend."

The other men sat watching with quiet humor as their leader teased Red Eagle with the whiskey, keeping it just out of reach. Yellow Moon could hardly believe Red Eagle was offering his only horse for a swallow of whiskey. If it were not so dark, she would jump on the horse herself and ride away quickly, for she did not like this place and these men.

"I am afraid I don't need blankets or a horse, Red Eagle," Trapper teased the man. He glanced up at Yellow Moon, and he could tell even with the blanket around her that she was lovely and young. Cheyenne women were usually prettier than other Indian women. But perhaps she was Arapaho. The Cheyenne often intermarried with the Arapaho, with whom they lived and hunted closely. But that would not matter, for the Arapaho women were just as pretty as the

36

Cheyenne. "There is only one thing I need, Red Eagle."

"What ... what is that?" Red Eagle asked, his eyes almost bulging as they stared at the whiskey.

"I would not mind sleeping with a pretty woman tonight."

Red Eagle froze, and finally he tore his eyes from the whiskey bottle and met Nick Trapper's leering eyes. Yellow Moon's heart pounded with great fear, and she pressed Laughing Boy closer to her breast.

"No!" Red Eagle replied quickly. "She belongs to Red Eagle. I will not trade her!"

Trapper shrugged. "Suit yourself. She looks like the only thing you have to offer that is worth anything." He turned and sat down with the rest of the men, taking a long slug of whiskey while Red Eagle watched. "You may eat some of our food, though, my Cheyenne friend. Feed your squaw if you wish. Then be on your way!"

Red Eagle stood there hesitantly, almost ready to weep in his need for the firewater.

"Let us go, Red Eagle, quickly!" Yellow Moon spoke up in a tiny voice. "Please!"

The man turned to look up at her, and the others eyed one another slyly. They could see her face was bruised and they knew her husband must be desperate for whiskey. Red Eagle stared at Yellow Moon pleadingly, as though he expected her to offer herself and take the responsibility from his own shoulders, just so he could have some of the whiskey. Her eyes widened in anger and terrible grief at what she saw in his eyes.

"Let us leave now!" she repeated. "Do not shame yourself this way, my husband!"

He walked up closer. "It is your fault!" he growled. "If you had not destroyed my whiskey!" He stood there shaking and wringing his hands. "Your fault! It would be good punishment for you!"

She felt a scream rising in her throat, and for the first time all of the love she had for him left her soul.

"Red Eagle!" she groaned. "How can you say such a thing!"

Red Eagle glanced back at the men and the whiskey. They

continued to drink and play cards, pretending they did not notice the conversation. Red Eagle looked back up at Yellow Moon. What harm would there be in letting this Nick Trapper sleep with her for a night? She would still belong to him, and how could sleeping with another man harm her? It was not as though they wanted to kill her or hurt her. It was not such a terrible price to pay to stop his chills and shaking, to stop the awful pain in his body and in his head. He could not think clearly. He could not function. He had to have the whiskey, or he would die before the night was over, he was certain.

"Get down!" he growled.

Her eyes widened, and her breath came in short gasps. "No!" she whispered.

"You were a bad wife! You poured out my whiskey! Get down!" he ordered again.

"If you do this, you will burn and scream in the under-world of evil spirits forever when you die!" she told him bitterly. "Your soul will never know peace. Your mind will never know rest. And I shall never forgive you, my husband. Never!"

Red Eagle looked back at the whiskey again. It was a good brand, he could tell. His tongue felt swollen and his whole body felt as though it would explode. Suddenly he turned and grabbed her arm, jerking her down from the mule viciously, causing Laughing Boy to fall off. The boy began to cry for the first time in many moons, and Yellow Moon struggled to put the blanket back around her while at the same time trying to pick up Laughing Boy. The men watched then, all looking hungrily at the slender legs that had been exposed, the pretty face shrouded by the long, thick hair. Her breasts were full, for Indian children often fed at their mother's breasts until three and four years old. She was lovely to behold, and now Red Eagle was pulling her crying son from her arms and shoving her toward them.

"Be still!" he barked to Laughing Boy. The child immediately quieted, afraid of his father since he had seen him hurt his mother that morning. The child plunked down on the hard earth, sniffling and afraid, for he knew his mother was going to be hurt, but he was not old enough to understand what was really happening.

Red Eagle shoved Yellow Moon into the firelight. "She was a bad wife to me last night!" he told the men. "She broke all my whiskey bottles. For this I beat her. Now she will pay by giving her body to you, Nick Trapper, so that I can have some whiskey! Look at her. She is worth more than just one bottle."

Trapper grinned, scanning her with his eyes. Yellow Moon stood still, her head hanging. She knew it would do no good to fight, for they would only kill Red Eagle and perhaps kill her son. She would be quiet so that her little boy would not cry and be afraid. She would have to be still if she was to live now for Laughing Boy.

Trapper was nodding. "I'll give you five bottles for one night with her." He rose and walked to a wagon, reaching inside and returning with five full bottles in his arms. He set them on the ground in front of Red Eagle, one by one. Red Eagle hesitated again for a moment, glancing at the shaking and frightened Yellow Moon. He tried to remember the time when she had danced for him—so young and innocent and so much in love. He tried to bring back that feeling—to draw on his Cheyenne pride and courage. But they were gone. His courage lay in the brown bottle, and there was no pride left. She would never love him again now anyway. It was done. He looked at Trapper, whose grin was broad and evil. He was a big man, wearing many weapons and dressed entirely in black.

"Do not hurt her," Red Eagle said quietly, reaching out for the bottles. Yellow Moon felt her heart shatter at the words, and she felt as though she might faint with fear and horror as Trapper stepped closer, towering over her. He pulled her to him and ran his hands over her breasts. "I assure you, my friend, hurting her is the last thing I will do." He chuckled and picked up a blanket, then shoved Yellow Moon toward a wagon, pushing her around behind it out of the light of the fire.

Red Eagle watched the darkness for a moment. He heard no sounds of protest or pain. He turned and went to sit

39

beside his son, who stared at his father with frightened eyes. Then Red Eagle uncorked a bottle and took a long drink, swallowing nearly half the whiskey in one gulp. It tasted wonderful! Then he thought he heard a faint whimper. He listened for a moment and could hear Nick Trapper's grunting, but there was no more sound out of Yellow Moon. His whiskey was being well paid for. He took another swallow.

Then Yellow Moon cried out, but Red Eagle did not notice. He was in such bad need of the firewater that it quickly affected his blood, bringing on a drunken stupor very rapidly. Everything became blurry as he opened a second bottle. The world and the campfire swirled around him, and Laughing Boy crawled away from his father, who now sat grinning and swaying. The boy crawled into the darkness to try to find his mother, and a moment later Red Eagle was flat on the ground, the second bottle half empty and still in his hand. He was totally oblivious to anything going on around him, and to the fact that Trapper had finished with Yellow Moon—for the moment. The man came back into the firelight, buttoning his pants.

"She's a good one," he told the others. "I'll let you all have a turn with her. Then we'll take her and the boy to the Lady Z. She'll buy them for the slave market."

The others nodded, one of them rising and rubbing himself between the legs. "Let me go next," he told Trapper. "Is she a fighter?"

The big man in black grinned. "I think she'd like to kill me. But I tied her wrists to the wagon wheel. She'll give you no trouble. I think she's smart enough to know she'd best lay still and take it." He glanced over at the passed-out Red Eagle as the second man went behind the wagon.

"No!" Yellow Moon whimpered. "It was to be only the other man!" The second man laughed, and they heard a hard slap. There were no more protests from Yellow Moon. There was only a soft whimpering.

"Find the boy," Trapper told one of the others. "Maybe he's worth money, too."

The other man nodded and went to search for Laughing

Boy, who had crawled out of the firelight. "I don't like stinking, crying kids," he grumbled.

Trapper shrugged. "If he gives us trouble, we'll get rid of him."

"Lady Z will pay us well for the woman and child," one of the Mexicans spoke up to Trapper. He took a drink of whiskey and listened to Yellow Moon's whimperings, eager for his turn. "We will all have a good time with this Arapaho woman tonight," he continued. "But all of us know what Arapaho woman we would rather be with, no? The Lady Z! To get between that one's legs is the dream of every outlaw south of the Arkansas River. It is no wonder she is our leader and we are the followers!"

They all laughed, passing some more whiskey.

"And who carved his initial into the lovely Lady Z's face?" another asked Trapper. "You are her favorite, Nick. Has she ever told you?"

Trapper rubbed his chin, contemplating memories of bedding his "boss," the beautiful but evil Lady Z, who had a way of putting all men under her spell to do her bidding.

"She told me just once," he replied. "She was very drunk and wanted to talk." He took a slug of whiskey while the rest of them waited for him to finish. There was a long moment of silence as he stared at the flames of the night fire. "Zeke," he finally told them. "Cheyenne Zeke. That's who she says put those Zs on her cheeks. But when she said the name, even though she said it with gritted teeth and bitterness, there was something else behind those dark eyes of hers. He was once a favorite of hers, I could tell. Maybe she even loved him, if that one is capable of loving. But something happened, and he must hate her very much to carve his initial into that beautiful face."

"Ah, but who cares about her face when he is ravishing her body, huh?" someone else put in.

They laughed again, and Trapper took another slug of whiskey while a third man headed toward the wagon from which the second man who had raped Yellow Moon was now approaching, grinning broadly.

"Ha! You were right, Nick!" the second man exclaimed,

his brow damp with sweat. "She is very good. Lady Z will be pleased with this one!"

Nick Trapper did not reply. He stared at the fire, wondering with immense curiosity what this Cheyenne Zeke was like, and why he had branded Lady Z, infamous leader of outlaws and slave traders.

Abbie turned in her sleep, vaguely aware that the room seemed close and full of tenseness. She dreamed that a spring storm was about to come, the air still and quiet, all living things silent and hiding, the horizon black and ominous. Then she thought she heard drums, war drums, beating rhythmically, and groaning voices. In her dream she saw men dancing by the light of an eerie fire, shaking rattles and jingling bells and blowing on bone whistles. Some were bleeding where skewers were forced through the skin of their breasts. Their mouths were open but they did not cry out, for they were men suffering the agonies of the Sun Dance, proving their courage and searching for a vision. The drums grew louder and louder, pounding, sending a message to the birds and the animals and the earth.

"The People are dying," they seemed to be saying. "The People are dying." Women were weeping and holding dead children, and finally the drums grew so loud that she started awake, gasping and sitting up, her body clammy and trembling. A clap of thunder hit again, and she realized an approaching storm had been the background of her dream. Lightning whitened the night sky and lit up the room, where someone had opened the shutters to let in the stiff mountain breeze.

He stood there, a tall, dark shadow against the white lightning, gazing out the window, standing still and quiet, the wind blowing the long unbraided hair back from his shoulders.

"Zeke?" she asked in concern.

He turned, his broad shoulders outlined as lightning struck again. He was silent and tense, and she thought for a moment he would turn and jump out the window and run

42

away like an animal just let out of its cage.

"You wanted to go with them, didn't you?" she said quietly. "You wanted to go with Black Elk and hunt buffalo and ride against the Pawnee and even take scalps. It's in your blood. But I keep you caged here."

He stared at her silently for several long seconds.

"No one cages Cheyenne Zeke. I am where I choose to be, Abbie girl."

"Are you truly?"

He came toward her as another clap of thunder rolled down off the mountains and shook the little cabin. In the next moment he was on his knees beside the bed of robes, kissing her gently.

"I can remember the first time I saw you," he told her, "the night I offered to scout for your father's wagon train." He put a big hand to the side of her face. "This house is no cage. And your love is no chain."

She grasped his wrist. "Why were you at the window?"

He rose again, obviously restless and disturbed. "I feel something. I thought I heard someone cry out. Something is wrong, but I have no way of knowing what it is. I am worried." He walked back to the window and looked out again. He thought for a moment of how he'd been promising Abbie he'd put glass in the windows some day, but somehow the thought of it gave him a closed-in feeling, as though he would be shutting out the wind spirits and the sounds of the birds and the animals.

"It's easy to worry," she replied, "with Swift Arrow riding in the North with the Sioux, and now Black Elk somewhere out there on the Plains searching out the Pawnee. But I'm most worried about Red Eagle and Yellow Moon. He never should have taken her south, Zeke."

He sighed. "I know." There was another long moment of worried silence.

"There's nothing you can do about any of it, Zeke. I . . . I had a dream. Cheyenne women were weeping and holding dead children. Sometimes I feel like . . . like they're all destined for something we can't stop or control. Some kind of nameless, ominous threat. And our own destiny will be

43

marked by what happens to the People. Do you feel that way, Zeke?"

He turned to look at her again. "I feel it in my bones. I know it's so because I know that no matter what happens I can never completely desert them, Abbie. I hope you understand that."

"I understand. I'll never desert them either. Your people are mine. I've told you that. My family is gone and Tennessee seems a million miles and a million years away. You and the Cheyenne are my family."

Thunder boomed around them again and his wild, dark eyes were lit up by more lightning, and she was sure she could hear rattles and bone whistles again. Why did she love this man whom she had seen savagely rip open men with his infamous knife; this man who worshipped spirits that were foreign to her and who bore the scars on his chest from the Sun Dance ritual? Perhaps it was his gentle side that she loved, the side few besides herself knew was there. Perhaps it was the loneliness in his eyes and the tortured memories he bore from a childhood of growing up a half-breed among people who scorned him. He was, after all, a man, who needed love and a woman and family like any other man. And when she had been hardly more than a child, left without family in a strange and savage land, it was Cheyenne Zeke who had comforted her, protected her, stood fast by her side and even saved her life more than once.

"Come back to bed, Zeke," she told him softly. "You know how I hate storms. Come and hold me."

The rain started pelting the roof then and he came back beside her. Both were naked, for that was the way they always slept. He moved in beside her and she pulled the buffalo robe over them, snuggling close to him, finding perfect shelter from the storm that frightened her. She was afraid of nothing when he was beside her. He was like a rock, indestructible, strong, hard, never afraid. She kissed his chest.

"Zeke, I started teaching Little Rock today how to read and write a few simple words." She sighed. "I had a terrible time keeping his attention. He squirmed so badly you'd have thought he had ants crawling over him. And as soon as I told him he could go, he flew out the door and jumped on his horse to go and find you. You'd have thought I'd been torturing him or something."

He chuckled and pulled her close. "It's the free spirit in him, Abbie girl. The Indian in him would rather be out learning about the land than learning about books. Back in Tennessee my father and stepmother used to beat the hell out of me to get me to school, then the white kids would beat the hell out of me at the playground and the teacher would beat me again once we got inside because I'd always be staring out the window. I'd look out at those Tennessee hills and crave to see what was beyond them, long to come West and find my real mother again. I knew I'd never know myself until I found the Cheyenne and knew that side of my life again. And there was a need in me—a need to touch the earth and hear the birds and feel the wind on my face. It was like, I don't know, kind of like a secret happiness deep inside that was being stifled by day-to-day routines and hard benches and itchy clothes—and rules, so many rules."

"We have to have rules in life, Zeke. They help us learn right from wrong."

"Do they? Some of the kids who grew up by those rules back in Tennessee are the same ones who killed my Ellen and our son. The whites have a strange set of rules, Abbie girl, and no son of mine is going to play by those rules. A man learns right and wrong from living in and off the land— from fending for himself, surviving the elements, sleeping with the deer and the elk, knowing Escheheman, Grandmother Earth, and knowing himself, his inner spirit. That's how Little Rock will be. He's alive with spirit and a hunger for life and freedom, Abbie girl. Don't get too upset with him."

"But he needs to learn, Zeke. It will be important to him later—to know how to read and write. Blue Sky is already doing so well and she's two years younger. He's so bright, Zeke, but he just doesn't seem to care. Promise me you'll talk to him. He listens to anything you tell him."

He sighed and kissed her hair, chuckling again. "All right, woman. But I wouldn't expect any schooling miracles out of that one. What he'll be good at is riding a fast horse, tracking and hunting. And out here those are the things a man has to learn if he's to provide for himself and his family, and protect them."

She ran her hand over the scar at his side where he'd taken a bullet protecting her once. How well she knew he was right. But she also knew that by the time her son was grown it might be essential that he know reading and writing. Her concerned thoughts were interrupted by her husband's big, gentle hand moving over her hips.

"I'm wide awake now, Abbie girl," he teased, moving his hand around to the inside of her thigh. "No sense both of us lying here worrying about things that haven't happened yet. Lord knows we've got our share of things to worry about." He kissed her eyes as his hand touched secret places that made her feel warm and alive. "Let's shake away the bad dreams and enjoy the here and now—this quiet little cabin and you and me lying here together with the sweet sound of rain on the roof and the smell of the mountain air moving over us."

His lips covered hers and she had no defense against the way he had of using lovely words to entice her, as if his manliness and his touch were not enough. His lips moved down over her throat and chest to taste the full nipple of one breast. He gently kissed and caressed the scar around her breast where he had once removed an arrow from her when she was only fifteen. The thought of almost losing her to death then dredged up the memory of how it had felt when he thought she might die. It was the one thing that had made him realize he loved her and must make her his wife if she lived.

And she had lived. A better wife no man would find. She sighed and arched up to him now. Yes, she was most definitely alive—alive and warm and pleasing to a man! He moved on top of her and invaded her with the fullness of his manhood; and as thunder rolled outside and lightning flashed to reveal the passion in his dark eyes, he seemed to

46

her an extension of the storm that tore through the skies outside the window, himself a man of thunder and lightning, a piece of the elements put into human form, structured perfectly, powerful and commanding. Commanding until she opened herself to him and took him inside herself. It was at that moment that his tiny, quiet wife became the ruler of his wild, untamed blood.

Three

The canvas-topped wagons were lined up so far down the street that Lieutenant Daniel Monroe could not even see where the line ended. The City of St. Louis, in return for the trade and tremendous growth it had realized from the westward emigrants, had allowed its new and impressive courthouse to be used by the travelers as a gathering point, aiding them by holding meetings to explain what to expect on their journey, help them make final arrangements, find scouts, and in general provide needed guidance for their journey into the "big sky" country. The prominent citizens of St. Louis felt it was the least they could do, for their city was, after all, the gateway to the West, and many of its citizens had realized great monetary rewards from supplying the wagon trains.

Thousands of emigrants passed through the courthouse every spring now, on their way to Independence, the "jumping off" point. The lieutenant turned to go up the wide marble steps of the courthouse, now crowded with people, mostly excited children waiting for parents who were still inside. Barefoot girls with long hair and gingham dresses and barefoot boys in cotton pants and suspenders chased and played, their shrieks and laughter adding to the noise of clattering wagons and the bustle of a booming city.

Lieutenant Monroe shook his head. How little these people knew of the Great West—how big it really was, and how dangerous. They were all in for a surprise, no matter how much they learned this day at the meetings. No one could imagine what it was really like west of the Missouri

48

River. He had been in their shoes once, a young buck private from Tennessee who had volunteered for the army and the Mexican War as a way of surviving out there while he searched for his half-blood brother, Cheyenne Zeke.

That had been eight years ago. Fate and intelligence had brought him rapidly up the ladder of rank, and at twenty-seven he was an officer at Fort Laramie in Nebraska Territory. Now he was in St. Louis to do some recruiting. It wasn't easy finding good men to serve in Western outposts. Duty was lonely and dangerous, in areas totally remote from the kind of civilization that existed in cities like St. Louis. Too often only rabble and outlaws volunteered as a way of escaping the law. But Danny was good at picking out the good from the bad, and the good men were usually quickly advanced in rank to give them incentive to continue their service in the West.

That was the case with himself and he had developed a special love for the prairies and a keen respect for the Indians. But he knew without a doubt that the vast numbers of people milling about the courthouse now were going to be the source of a great deal of trouble for men like himself, who would be pitted between the innocent emigrants, whom he was there to protect, and the alarmed and angering Indians, whom he was also supposed to be protecting. With the thousands of new settlers moving through this city on their way to the Rocky Mountains and the golden coast of California, the problems could only grow worse, for many of these people would never go all the way to California or Oregon. They would settle in Nebraska Territory, Kansas Territory, Utah or New Mexico Territory, in the heart of Indian country.

Monroe carried his tall, striking physique through the doors and into the great rotunda. Several women turned to look at him, for his blue dress uniform, six-foot frame, soft blue eyes, and thick blond hair gave him a commanding appearance. The gold epaulets at his shoulders made him look even broader, and the silver bar of rank on his collar, as well as the medal he had won for bravery in the Mexican War, all revealed him to be a man who commanded honor and respect.

He walked to a desk where a small man wearing thick spectacles sat writing something in a logbook.

"Excuse me," Danny interrupted him.

The man looked up, arching his eyebrows at the striking man before him. "What can I do for you, sir?"

"I'm looking for a Major Epcott. I was to meet him here."

"Major Stanley Epcott. Yes." The man came around from behind the desk and pointed down one of the many hallways that led out from the rotunda. "Go right down there, mister. At the end is a stairway. Go up one floor and there's an office right at the head of the stairs. You'll find him there."

"Thank you." Danny nodded and walked toward the hall. The rotunda was alive and echoing with voices that filtered up to its great dome and were magnified by the acoustics of its tremendous height. It seemed impossible that so many people could be heading West and that there could still be anyone left in the East. It seemed the population was exploding like shot out of a cannon, and Danny Monroe felt restless, for there was much talk now about railroads. The Appropriations Act had been passed, and money would now be provided for surveying and construction of rails West, once it was decided just where it was best to lay track. It was exciting but also frightening, for railroads through Indian territory could only bring yet more trouble.

His boots sounded loud against the limestone floor. The elegance and progress that was the City of St. Louis were a striking contrast to where Monroe had been for the past several years. It always amazed him that there could be such a vast difference in ways of life, with the East and the West seeming to him as two totally different worlds, separated only by a thousand miles of almost vacant land, wide skies, and beautiful silence.

He climbed the striking spiral staircase, his hand running along polished, hand-grained woodwork. He looked back down to see the rotunda filling up with more and more emigrants, some also beginning to climb the stairs to spill out into the balcony above, where they would listen to experienced scouts tell them about the West. He had to grin.

Zeke and Abbie could tell them some tales, he thought. If Abigail Monroe could be here and tell them about her first trip West and what happened to her wagon train and her family, perhaps many of these people would turn around and go back home. He grinned again at the thought of his sister-in-law, a woman of true courage and beauty.

He reached the top of the stairs and walked to the first door, knocking lightly. When it opened, a surge of pleasant surprise flowed through the young man's veins as he looked into the lovely face of a very young woman, with auburn hair piled beautifully on top of her head and eyes as green as the green checkered dress she wore.

"How do you do!" he said with a quick, handsome smile. "I . . . uh . . . I expected a Major Epcott to open the door. Perhaps I'm in the wrong place."

She blushed and smiled sweetly, and his eyes dropped to the disturbing way her full breasts had of filling out the bodice of the high-necked dress.

"You're in the right place, she said softly. "Major Epcott is my father. You must be Lieutenant Monroe?"

Their eyes held a moment as he nodded. "Yes, ma'am." He could smell a sweet perfume. "I . . . I didn't know the major even had a daughter. This is a pleasant surprise."

She blushed more. "Thank you. Do come inside. I was just leaving." She stepped aside and ushered him to an inner doorway. Their eyes held again before she opened it. "I'm . . . very honored to meet you, Lieutenant," she told him softly. "If not for you, my father would be dead now, and I'd be an orphan. My mother died about a year ago."

He frowned. "I'm sorry."

She stepped back a little, feeling small and nervous so close to his towering physique. "I've often heard the story of how you threw yourself in front of my father and saved him from a bullet during the Mexican War. I'm glad it didn't kill you, and I have prayed for you often. It's truly wonderful to finally meet the man who saved my father's life."

He blushed a little and smiled. "Most brave acts are done

51

without forethought, Miss Epcott," he replied. "I saw the flash of a gun and I had a feeling where the bullet was headed. I guess I'll never know exactly why I did what I did."

"You did it automatically because you're a good person—good soldier material, as my father puts it."

They both smiled and she admired the reddish tan on his fair skin and the full blond mustache over the fine line of his upper lip. She suddenly felt too warm and she hurried to the outer door.

"I must be going now. Father is right inside there. Just knock." She hesitated at the door. "It really is good to finally meet you, Lieutenant. I've heard so many stories about you. Is it really true you have a brother who is part Cheyenne?"

He nodded. "His mother was Cheyenne. We share the same father."

She frowned. "It must be very strange, having a half-breed for a brother. Indians frighten me terribly. I don't think I could ever live out there among those savages like you do. You must be very brave."

He studied the curious green eyes. "They really aren't savages, ma'am. In fact, one term for the Cheyenne is the 'Beautiful People.' Some of them truly are. You might learn to like some of them, Miss Epcott."

She sighed. "Perhaps." Then she brightened. "If we meet again, please call me Emily. That's my name."

He nodded. "It's a very pretty one. And if we meet again you can call me Dan."

She smiled and started to leave. "Miss Epcott—I mean, Emily—" he stopped her. She turned back to look at him. "I have three weeks left here. Rather than wondering if we will meet again, perhaps you would allow me to take you to the theater, or perhaps a concert?"

She dropped her eyes. "I would be honored, Lieutenant." She moved partway through the door. "But you will have to ask my father first." She met his eyes once more. "Thank you. And I must repeat it's a great honor to finally meet you, Lieutenant Monroe."

"Dan. Remember?"

She smiled sweetly. "Of course. Good day, Dan."

"Good day, Emily."

She hurried through the door, and Daniel Monroe realized he had been away from civilization for much too long. A very accommodating prostitute had satisfied his most urgent needs when he'd first arrived in the city, but he had a greater need, a distant longing for more than just a woman to romp in bed with. He listened until her light footsteps disappeared into the crowd, then turned and knocked on the inner door.

"Come in," came the commanding voice. Monroe went through the door into the high-ceilinged, stark room decorated with only two paintings, one of President Washington and one of President Jefferson. The major rose from a chair behind an oak desk and returned Monroe's salute, then put out his hand to the younger man. "Good to see you, Dan!" he said with a grin. "It's been a couple of years. Have a seat, son."

"Thank you, sir." Dan moved to a red leather chair and sat down, enjoying its coolness and the cool air that filled the large room sheltered from the hot Missouri sun. This spring day was unusually warm.

"You met my daughter as she was leaving?"

"Yes, sir," the lieutenant replied with a grin. "She's beautiful, sir. I didn't even know you had a daughter."

The man chuckled, sitting down on the front edge of his desk near Dan. "Be honest now. I heard you asking her out."

Monroe blushed. "I didn't know you could hear us, sir. But since you did—"

"Of course you can take her to a concert, or anyplace else for that matter. I can't think of a finer man for my daughter to be with. Good Lord, son, you saved my life once. The least I can do is let you see my daughter. You're a gentleman and an officer."

The young lieutenant shifted in his chair. "Thank you, sir. You compliment me too much, Major Epcott."

"Nonsense! In fact, what you did for me is part of the

53

reason I asked you here today, Lieutenant. I still feel a need to repay you somehow, and I have finally been able to do something about it."

Monroe frowned. "I don't understand, sir. Your daughter?"

"No, no. I'm not talking about Emily. I'm talking about your half-blood brother, Zeke Monroe." He rose and walked to one of the tall windows of the office, sitting down on its ledge, while the lieutenant waited for an explanation. "Lieutenant," he continued. "I've managed to get your brother's name cleared in Tennessee. He is no longer a wanted man there."

Danny Monroe's heartbeat quickened with surprise and joy. He rose from his chair. "Are you serious, Major?"

The man smiled. "Very serious. I have connections, Lieutenant—good ones. I explained to the right people what really happened thirteen years ago—the atrocious things those eight men did to your brother's first wife and their little son. I made them understand the horror and hatred a young, twenty-year-old man would feel at such an act, and I also explained the hell your brother had already been through being a half-breed and always persecuted for his Indian blood." He moved away from the window and came closer to Danny. "It's been thirteen years, son. Your brother may have killed men since then, but it hasn't been in Tennessee. And now he has a wife and children. It's time they should be able to stop worrying about some bounty hunter coming to find him and drag him back for hanging— if it's possible for any man to capture Cheyenne Zeke in the first place. I have a feeling that would be quite a project."

Their eyes held and Danny put out his hand again. "I don't know what to say except thank you, sir. This is wonderful news. I'll get word to Zeke as soon as I can. Abbie will be very, very happy. She's always worried about him being wanted for murder and all. It . . . it's just that he's a man of vengeance, sir. He had to do what he did or go crazy."

The major shook his hand firmly. "Perhaps. But the fact remains, Lieutenant, that he shouldn't have taken justice into his own hands."

54

Danny's eyes clouded with sorrow. "I'm afraid that's the only thing left to a man like Zeke, sir. There is no justice for the Indian, or even a man who's only half Indian. So Zeke deals out his own justice, and God help the man he's after."

The major thought about the stories he had heard of how Cheyenne Zeke had wreaked his revenge on the eight men who had raped and murdered his first wife. They had been left hanging by their heels with their torsos split open—one by one—at different times, in different places, but each dying the same way, left alive to hang and bleed to death. A chill moved through his body in spite of the warm day.

"Yes. I'm sure having Cheyenne Zeke for an enemy would be very uncomfortable," he replied with a frown. "I am going to have to meet this half-savage brother of yours someday, Lieutenant. I can't imagine how a white woman as lovely and gentle as you describe this Abigail can be married to such a man."

"She loves him, sir. And he loves her. He's very good to her. They're quite happy, in spite of the hardships of their life. They've been through an awful lot together, saved each other's lives. Abbie has no family left. They all died on the wagon train she first took West. That's where she met Zeke. He was their scout."

"Hmmm." The man rubbed his chin and moved around behind his desk. "Well, be that as it may, he's a free man. One of the wealthiest men in Tennessee happens to be my brother-in-law, Emily's uncle, brother to my late wife. When you saved my life eight years ago, my lovely wife felt very indebted to you, and my brother-in-law has always known I've wanted to do something for you. Handing you money seemed, I don't know, kind of crude. I wanted to do something more than that. I thought a lot about this brother of yours, how fond you are of him, how badly you felt about what happened to him back in Tennessee. So, we came up with getting him off the hook and wiping the slate clean. I guess you'd say it's being done in my wife's memory. She'd have wanted us to do something like this."

Danny's heart swelled with joy. "I'm deeply grateful, sir. It's a magnificent gesture, the best thing you could have

55

done. Please thank your brother-in-law for me. Now I'm the one who feels indebted. I know Zeke will, too."

"Nonsense. I'm not even going to tell you who all was involved in the pardon. Neither you nor your brother need know. That will make it easier for you—and help keep the secrecy. This is being done very quietly, Lieutenant. Sort of an 'illegal' family favor, you might say. So mention it no more. It's done, no strings attached. In fact, I order you to feel neither guilt nor indebtedness, and to never again even bring up the subject." He sat down behind his desk and motioned for Dan to also sit again. "Now, let's change the subject. Tell me how things are out on the prairies around Fort Laramie, Lieutenant."

Danny sat down again, sighing as he settled into the chair. "Restless, sir. Especially the Sioux and the Northern Cheyenne. They're a peaceful people, sir, truly, other than some warring that goes on between tribes. Those things have been going on for hundreds of years. But they pretty much leave the emigrants alone. They really do want peace, sir. They want to be left alone. But they're scared, too. They're dying off left and right from our diseases. Their ability to hunt has become inhibited, and game is getting scarce. A lot of them are starving, sir, and they blame it on the white people who come out here and kill the game for just a couple of pieces of meat and leave the rest; people who strip the forests just for firewood and leave excrement and dead animals in the streams. They need assurance that certain lands will be theirs, places where the whites won't be allowed to enter, where they can roam and hunt freely."

"Washington is doing what it can, Lieutenant."

"But they move too slowly, sir. They make promises but they don't follow through, and they aren't clear on anything they say. In the meantime, besides disease and destruction, some whites are coming out there now and killing off buffalo just for sport. I've even seen people from other countries out there, wealthy fools from England, France, you name it, out there for what they consider the big kill, which is a farce. The Indians are furious, sir, and I can't blame them. The buffalo is the most vital commodity to their existence. When I try to explain that, the whites say the Indians ought to quit chasing buffalo and settle into one place to live like the white man. But that's like taking a fish out of water and throwing it into the desert sand and telling it to swim. It simply can't be done, sir. They're born to hunt and roam. Freedom of movement is as important to their welfare as breathing. And if we don't give them some kind of assurance that certain lands are theirs, and we'll stop slaughtering their game and destroying the trees and fresh water, there will be *hell* to pay! I feel it in my bones."

The major sighed and leaned forward. "I wish I could give you that assurance, son. But I can't. You saw the crowd downstairs. That's just a drop in the bucket, Lieutenant. People are moving out there by the thousands, looking for more space, some running from the law, some thinking maybe there's more gold out there, some just going after a vague dream and not even realizing what they're asking for by going out there. What's happening is called progress, Lieutenant, and it can't be stopped, no matter how badly the Indian might like to see it stopped. This country is growing at an astounding rate, and people have to have room to spread out. There's only one direction they can go in. 'Manifest Destiny,' they call it, the right and duty of Christian Americans to claim, settle and rule the virgin land west of the Missouri River. That's where good men like yourself come in, to keep the peace between the two factions." He held the young man's eyes, studying the sorrow in them. "I have confidence in you, Danny. But don't get your priorities mixed up, son. You have a half-blood brother and a deep respect and affection for these Indians. You're a good friend to Zeke's full-blood brother, Swift Arrow. Don't let those feelings interfere with your purpose out there—to protect the emigrants. You are first and above all an army man, Lieutenant, and your blood runs pure white. Don't ever forget that."

Danny's chest tightened, and he felt an odd depression. "I won't, sir," he replied quietly. For some reason the vision suddenly came to Danny's mind of a tiny Sioux girl he'd seen in the last throes of death from cholera, and he knew in that moment there was no future for the red men of the plains and prairies. It would not be the emigrants who needed protection in the end. It would be the Indian.

"Oh, by the way," the major was adding, "when you get back you can get word to the Cheyenne that the Treaty of 1851 is close to being ratified, with a few revisions, I'm afraid, but ratified nonetheless. Some basic provisions will be sent out later this year, as well as a few things for the Sioux and Northern Cheyenne. They should understand that the government is not totally callous toward their problems, Lieutenant. But it would help if they obeyed the rules. The Northern Cheyenne should be down in the lands awarded them in the treaty, not up in the Black Hills. Perhaps you can make them understand that."

Danny gave him a patronizing nod. "I'll do my best, sir. But I have a feeling none of the Cheyenne cares to go along with the Treaty of 1851 any longer. They feel betrayed, and it's getting a little difficult to reason with them."

The man waved his hand. "They'll calm down when they get their supplies," he answered, totally unperturbed. "Now, I'll draw you a map of how to get to my house, Lieutenant. I insist that you come for supper this evening. We can talk some more about these things and you can get to know Emily better. She'd be delighted."

Danny sighed, anxious to continue the conversation about Indians right then and make the man understand the seriousness of the situation. But he could see the major did not care to discuss it further at the moment, and the man had been kind enough to get Zeke cleared of the murders in Tennessee. This was not the time for arguing, and he wondered if stressing his point that evening again would make any difference. Perhaps he should just set aside his concerns while he was in St. Louis and just enjoy his stay there, in the company of the lovely Emily.

The vision of the dying Sioux child disappeared as he walked around the desk to study the major's drawing.

58

Maybe for these three weeks he could forget about the Indians, and the dead, rotting bodies of the buffalo he had seen on the prairies.

Abbie put another spoonful of potatoes on Zeke's plate when they heard the strange thump at the door. She stepped back and Zeke was on his feet in an instant, his hand resting on the handle of his wicked knife while Dooley grabbed a rifle. The children sat and watched in wide-eyed wonder as Zeke went to the door.

"Who's there?" he commanded.

"Zeke. Zeke, help me," came the weak reply.

Zeke frowned and glanced at Dooley, who cocked his rifle and waited as Zeke unlatched the door. Red Eagle stumbled inside and fell to the floor.

"Dear God!" Abbie exclaimed, setting down the potatoes and kneeling down beside him as Zeke turned him over. His body was dusty and cracked-looking, his eyes ugly red from too much whiskey and too little sleep. Abbie rushed to the door as Zeke helped Red Eagle sit up, taking his cup of water from the table and holding it to Red Eagle's lips.

"Zeke, I don't see Yellow Moon and Laughing Boy anywhere!" Abbie said with concern. She turned and knelt back down beside Red Eagle, who was pushing at the cup of water.

"Whiskey! Just give me . . . whiskey!" he grumbled.

Zeke's eyes blazed, and he pulled the man to his feet, forcing him to stand. "You'll get no whiskey from me, my drunken brother! Not until you tell me what has happened to Yellow Moon and Laughing Boy! Where are they?"

The young man's eyes teared, and Abbie thought to herself that he was only young in age, for one would have thought him much older to look at him. The whiskey had turned his eyes to red slits and his body had lost its hardness and shape. He had turned from a powerful, respected warrior to a weak, cowering old man in the eight years she had watched the whiskey destroy him. Now he began to cry like a child, and even Zeke felt a pull at his heart in spite of his anger.

59

"They are—gone!" he whimpered. "My . . . Yellow Moon and my son! Gone!" He wept harder and Zeke shook him.

"Where! Gone where, damn it!"

The young man wiped at his eyes. "Promise me . . . you will not kill me, my brother! For I am already . . . a dead man . . . inside. Do not kill me for what I have done. I . . . I came here . . . rode hard . . . stole a horse to get to you . . . so you could help."

Zeke pushed him into a chair and sat down next to him, while the children watched in total silence.

"What have you done with Yellow Moon and your son?" Zeke demanded.

"I . . . I needed whiskey. You know . . . how I must have my whiskey . . . or go crazy. She . . . destroyed all I had. She was . . . a bad wife . . . doing that." Abbie turned away, feeling ill at the sight of him. "I . . . had to have the fire-water," the man repeated. "We came across some traders . . . far to the south, in the land of Apaches and Mexicans. They had whiskey . . . good whiskey."

There was a long moment of silence, and Abbie jumped when Zeke grabbed the man up from the chair and threw him against the wall. "You *traded* her, didn't you? You traded her for whiskey!"

The man covered his face. "I . . . did not know . . . what I was doing!" he wailed. "I did not know! I have . . . suffered enough, my brother! Do not kill me!"

Zeke turned away, breathing hard, while Red Eagle slumped to the floor. "I . . . I wish that . . . that you could go after her, Zeke. Find my Yellow Moon."

Abbie's heart tightened. She could have shot Red Eagle then and there for what he was asking, for to go after Yellow Moon would be dangerous, and it was Red Eagle's job. But Red Eagle wasn't fit, and Zeke would do it, she knew already, for that was the kind of man he was. Her chest pounded with dread.

Zeke grasped the back of a chair, his knuckles white with the strain of trying to stay in control and not beat his brother to death.

"Where did it happen?" he asked gruffly. A wave of despair moved through Abbie and she blinked back tears. Zeke watched her as she stood there with her back turned. He knew what she was thinking, and he did not want to leave her any more than she would want him to go. But this had to be done and he was the only one to do it. No soldier would see fit to go riding off into outlaw country just to save an Indian woman, nor would any white lawman. The Cheyenne couldn't do it. They had enough troubles already with soldiers and with just finding enough game to keep their bellies full.

"Far to the south," Red Eagle whimpered. "Even south of the Cimmarron, in the place . . . where there is only desert . . . and rocks. I . . . I did not know, Zeke. I thought I was trading her with just one man . . . for just one night. But when I woke up the next day . . . they were gone . . . all of them. Even my Laughing Boy." He choked in a sob, fully realizing now what the whiskey had done to him, horribly ashamed to be weeping in front of them and crawling to his half-blood brother for help. "But . . . that is not the worst, my brother."

Zeke turned to look at him. "What do you mean?" he seethed.

"I . . . I remember . . . hearing them talk. I was . . . drunk, Zeke . . . lying there so drunk I could not move . . . yet I could hear them . . . their voices floating . . . their laughing and joking." He swallowed and raised his eyes to meet his brother's. "They . . . they spoke of a woman . . . an Arapaho woman, who was their leader . . . a woman who deals in buying and selling other women. They . . . they called her . . ." he swallowed again. "They called her . . . Lady Z . . . and spoke of . . . of the symbol 'Z' carved into her cheeks."

Abbie turned. "No!" she gasped, her face paling alarmingly. She grasped a chair and stared at Zeke, who in turn stood staring silently at his brother. His jaw flexed in hatred and anger.

"Are you sure, Red Eagle?" he hissed. "Are you *sure*?"

"Yes, my brother. Who else could it be . . . but the one

61

we once called Dancing Moon? Who else would have the 'Z's in her cheeks?"

Abbie shivered and sank into a chair. Zeke glanced at her, worried now about the fact that Dancing Moon, now apparently called Lady Z, still lived. He could hardly believe it himself, for he had left her for dead many years before, the only woman he had ever wanted to harm, for she had been more animal than woman.

"They said . . . they would take my Yellow Moon . . . to the Lady Z," Red Eagle continued. "You must find her and help her, my brother! I can think of no one else . . . better able to find her . . . no one else with more reason to see that evil Dancing Moon dead. She will . . . hurt my poor Yellow Moon . . . when she realizes who it is. She is . . . evil. She hates the People . . . because we banished her many years ago . . . for being loose with all the men . . . and for attacking your white woman."

Abbie unconsciously put a hand to her side, where Dancing Moon, once Zeke's lover, had stabbed her in a vicious attack of jealousy the first time Zeke had brought Abbie to the Cheyenne as his new bride.

Zeke closed his eyes. "I will find her for you, Red Eagle," he said in a near whisper.

"It is . . . a promise?"

"It is a promise," Zeke replied. He turned to watch Abbie, and it seemed she was withering before his eyes. The thought of having to leave her for such a dangerous mission angered him all over again, for it was his drunken brother's fault. He whirled in rage and grabbed the man up, dragging him to the door and throwing him out, kicking him down the steps.

"Leave my land, my drunken brother! Don't ever set foot on it again," he roared, "or you will feel my blade across your throat!" He stormed back inside and glared at Dooley. "Go out there and make sure he gets off this place!" he growled. "I don't want to be responsible for killing my own brother, which I am about ready to do!"

Dooley sighed. "Sure, Zeke." He brushed past the man on his way out, then stopped at the door. "I'm sorry, Zeke.

It's a real shame. You do what's best. If you have to go, I'll make sure the wife and kids are looked after."

Zeke sighed and nodded. "I appreciate it, Dooley."

The man left, and Abbie remained turned away. There was a long moment of tense silence until Zeke finally walked over to kneel in front of her. He touched her face with a big, strong hand.

"It will be okay, Abbie girl."

She met his eyes and shook her head. "You can't go!" she whimpered. "It's too dangerous! Her men almost killed you once before, Zeke!"

He put on a smile for her. "They got the drop on me. I had no idea they'd be waiting for me. But this time I'm the one who'll be pulling the surprises. Hell, you know me, Abbie. I'm too goddamned mean to get myself killed."

She could no longer control the tears of fear and dread. She threw her arms around his neck and wept.

"Oh, Zeke, I can't believe that horrible woman is still alive!" she sobbed.

He stood up with his arms tight around her, lifting her feet off the floor. "Abbie, my poor Abbie," he whispered, kissing her hair. "Life's been so hard for you."

The children sat watching curiously, and Little Rock's mouth puckered in anger and disappointment that his father might be going away.

Four

Abbie stood behind the others, her eyes closed, her body swaying and an urgent desire to wail aloud building in her throat. Red Eagle was dead. The whiskey and the fact that he had sold his wife and child for it had been more than he could bear. He had shot himself in the head.

Cheyenne women crouched around Red Eagle's death platform, where the body that had been tortured and enslaved by the white man's firewater finally lay at peace. The women's keening and chanting seemed to epitomize the hopelessness the future appeared to hold for the People. Red Eagle's destruction by the firewater was only one link of the ever-lengthening chain that was tightening around not only the Cheyenne, but also the Sioux, the Arapaho, the Crow, Shoshoni, Kiowa, Apache, Comanche and Navaho, and all the others. So many others!

Little Rock and Blue Sky stood on either side of their mother, holding Abbie's hands. Behind them Young Girl sat playing with wildflowers, oblivious to the grief that was taking place. Her blond curls were totally out of place there among her dark-haired relatives. But Little Rock and Blue Sky looked no different from the full-blood Cheyenne children present.

Little Rock stared hard at the burial platform, realizing that some kind of tragedy had befallen his uncle, Red Eagle. He sensed in his little heart that the white man had in some way tricked his uncle into doing something bad. It was the dirty whiskey traders who frequently visited Indian territory and sold the bad firewater that had made his uncle weak

64

and mean. Somewhere a little voice told him he should never be a part of the white man's world when he grew up, even though his own mother was white. He would be a brave warrior like his father and uncles, Black Elk and Swift Arrow, and he would some day fight against the white man who seemed to always be bringing problems and disease to the Cheyenne.

Blue Sky held her mother's hand tightly as she watched the Cheyenne women wailing and crying. It frightened her. She did not like this thing called death, nor did she like the strange talk about invading whites. Always there was talk of fighting, and it frightened her. Everything frightened her, except when she was holding her mother's hand or when she was snug in her father's arms. Seldom did she let either one of them out of her sight. The only other person she would go to was Tall Grass Woman, her mother's good Cheyenne friend.

The wailing of the Indian women continued, and a great, choking sob rose in Abbie's throat as she watched Zeke pull off his buckskin shirt. She knew what would come. Outsiders would shudder and gasp at what she witnessed then, but Abbie watched with total understanding and aching love. Deer Slayer, father of Red Eagle and stepfather of Zeke, began slashing at his own chest, wanting to bleed for his lost son, hoping that some kind of sacrifice would save Red Eagle's soul from the pit of evil spirits—that his pain and bleeding would somehow make amends for the shame of Red Eagle's suicide. Tears streamed down Abbie's face when Zeke took out his own famous blade, gripping the buffalo jawbone handle and slitting his forearm in sacrifice, falling to his knees and letting the blood flow freely.

She had expected it. And she knew that if Black Elk and Swift Arrow were present, they would do the same or worse. For it was the way of the People—a fitting sacrifice—a sign of mourning and an offering to the Spirits to take a dead man's soul on the long walk up Ekutsihimmiyo, the Hanging Road, the bridge between heaven and earth along which the dead departed. Perhaps Maheo would understand why Red Eagle had taken his own life—that it was a sacrifice for his

65

great shame. Perhaps the Spirits would remember what a fine and brave warrior he once was and would accept him.

Deer Slayer had placed all of Red Eagle's good luck charms and weapons on the scaffold, along with a new pair of moccasins to wear on his journey to the Spirits. Now the old man wept and bled for his son.

But then, death was something the Cheyenne understood well. Death came often to the People of the Plains—more often, now that the white man had come and was polluting their water with white men's germs and cutting off their food supply by chasing away the buffalo and taking away their land. Death would be a familiar partner in the future. But it had always been close by. The People's understanding of this was exemplified in the ancient Shahi-yena prayer that some of the keening women now chanted.

> "Nothing lives long,
> Nothing stays here,
> Except the earth and the mountains."

Abbie knew the song. She swayed to the chant, joining in the singing, using the Cheyenne tongue. She wore her best doeskin tunic, and her hair was braided, and at first glance, one could not have been certain she was a white woman.

They sat astride their mounts, perched high on a mesa that gave a broad view of Zeke Monroe's ranch below. They were father and son, looking almost exactly alike, except that one was broad and towering, and the other was still a small boy. Both were nearly naked, wearing only loincloths, for it was a hot day. But Little Rock did not care about the heat, nor did his father. There was something else to be more concerned about. Cheyenne Zeke was going away.

"I do not understand about this woman called Lady Z, Father," the boy pouted, toying with the mane of his horse. "Why did you make scars on her face? You would never hurt my mother that way, would you?"

Zeke stared at the peaks of the Rockies that were just

barely visible behind a humid haze far, far off on the horizon. "No, son. I would never hurt your mother that way. People like your mother are incapable of deliberately doing anything wrong. They have too much good in them. But Lady Z . . ." he sighed, turning to look at his son. "Little Rock, Lady Z is an Arapaho woman. Her name used to be Dancing Moon, years ago when she still dwelled among the People. She was bad, Little Rock. She was a trouble-maker and a trickster, and she was loose with the men and often caused quarrels between husbands and wives. Do you know what I mean?"

The boy squinted and nodded. "I think so."

Zeke patted his horse's neck. "I know it's hard for you to understand right now, but you will as you get older. Some-times, son, when you grow to be a man you feel a certain . . . need . . . for a woman. And if you don't have a wife, you turn to the loose squaws, the ones who come free and easy, until you're ready to take a wife and the respon-sibilities that come with that. I, like many of the other men in camp, turned to Dancing Moon, because she was always willing and eager to give a man satisfaction, and she didn't care if a man loved her or not."

Little Rock mimicked his father in petting his horse's neck. "Did you love her?"

Zeke looked back out over the ranch below. "No. Oh, I had a little bit of feeling for her at times, but I never loved her. No man truly loves a woman like that." He sat staring silently for a moment while Little Rock waited for him to continue. Finally Zeke turned his eyes back to his son, and there was a hatred beginning to smolder in them. "When I brought your mother to the People as my wife, Dancing Moon was jealous," he went on. "Even though she liked to give favors to all the men, she in turn sometimes got angry if one of her lovers showed an interest in someone else. She wanted to own them all. But she couldn't own me, and she hated your mother because she was my wife and I wouldn't be needing Dancing Moon any longer. That was when we found out how bad Dancing Moon really was. She attacked your mother, tried to drown her, then stabbed her. Your

67

mother was pregnant at the time and she lost the baby. She almost died on me, Little Rock. That is when I learned to truly hate Dancing Moon."

"Is that when you put the symbol 'Z' on her cheeks?"

Zeke studied his bright, inquisitive son, seeing the boy's fear and concern that his father would leave to search out the mysterious Dancing Moon. "No, son," he answered. He dismounted, coming around and reaching up for Little Rock and lifting the boy to his shoulders. He walked to a large, flat rock, where he swung the boy around and set him down, then sat down beside him, putting an arm around his shoulder. The horses waited quietly, bowing their heads and nibbling at bunch grass. "Dancing Moon ran away that night," Zeke proceeded. "She was banned from all the tribes for what she had done. She apparently headed south after that—got mixed up with bandits and Mexicans—got involved with gun running during the Mexican War. I didn't know what had happened to her until I ran into her again quite by accident. The first year your mother and I were married, there was a run on the banks because of the war, and I lost a lot of money I had been saving for a long time. A man offered me a job to drive some wagons to Santa Fe, so I left your mother with Swift Arrow and the rest of my family and took the job. I talked a friend of mine, a white man, into helping me out, because there were two wagons to drive. But we never made it to Santa Fe. We were attacked by outlaws, and they murdered my friend in cold blood. My life was spared, but only because the leader of the outlaws turned out to be none other than Dancing Moon, who wanted to save me for torture. She had a burning hatred for me because of her long-smoldering jealousy."

The boy looked up at the man he worshipped. "Didn't you use your knife on those men?" he asked curiously. "You can kill many men with your knife. That is what Black Elk says, and Mr. Dooley."

Zeke nodded his head. "I have been in fights against many men and won, Little Rock. But all circumstances are different. In this case they got the drop on me. There were simply too many, and all had rifles pointed right at me. I moved fast and got two or three before one shot went off and side-swiped my skull, knocking me from the wagon. The next thing I knew Dancing Moon was there, ordering me stripped and beaten. Her last order was to have me thrown into a dark pit where there were many rattlesnakes." He tensed and took his arm from around his son's shoulders. "That is when my hatred for Dancing Moon grew even deeper, and she became as much an enemy as a Crow or Pawnee warrior," he continued, his voice ringing with bitterness. "To me she became an equal, deserving of any pain I could give her. Before they threw me into the pit, I had seen her do things . . . with her men . . . ugly, filthy things. She'd become an animal, a vicious, evil she-devil."

The boy frowned and studied the big man who sat beside him. "The snakes did not bite you?" he asked in surprise.

Zeke reached over and ran his hand over the boy's hair. "That's where finding your inner self and trusting the spirits can help you, son. I was half dead when they threw me in there. Luckily I landed on a rocky ledge instead of going all the way to the bottom. And even though I was in great pain and was naked and shivering, I knew I must lie very still and not move. I must breathe as little as possible. It was getting dark then, and I had to wait until the morning sun would light the shaft above me so that I could see where the snakes were and how I might escape." He picked up a rock and turned it in his hands. "It was the most horrible night of my life, Little Rock. I still have nightmares about it. I can hear the hissing, feel them crawling over me."

He gritted his teeth on the last words and tossed the rock viciously. Little Rock watched it sail far out over the valley below before it began descending to the ground.

"That was when I knew that if I escaped that place I would find Dancing Moon and end her life so that she could never hurt anyone again! I prayed. I prayed so hard, Little Rock, singing the Cheyenne death song, drawing on the power of my inner spirit to be strong and brave, reminding myself I had suffered the Sun Dance and I was a man, and that my intelligence was that of a man, which meant I had the power to rule the snakes. I was in their kingdom, their domain. But they would learn that a man can conquer anything. And when the sun lighted the shaft above me, it shined down on my knife!" He drew out the big blade and held it up, letting it gleam in the sun. "Dancing Moon had thrown it into the pit also, laughing that every warrior should be buried with his greatest weapon. But little did she know I would *not* die that day!" His eyes gleamed now and he grinned wickedly. "I climbed out of that pit, inch by inch, ever so sowly, talking to the snakes, going through the worst hell a man could ever experience, never knowing when one might strike out at me and fill my blood with his hated venom! I killed one, proving I was faster than the snake, but his blood and venom squirted out on me and it still gives me bad dreams."

Little Rock listened in an almost hypnotized state, enjoying, as he always did, listening to his brave father tell his stories. This was one he had never told before, and never had the boy seen such fire in his father's eyes, such a gleam of hatred and vengeance.

"I reached the top!" Zeke said victoriously. "I climbed out and rolled on the ground, glorying in the feel of the warm dirt and rocks on my body, the ecstasy of the hot sun on my skin, the joy of breathing fresh air and knowing I was alive!"

The boy's eyes sparkled with pride and excitement, and to him his father was suddenly invincible. "Some day I will be as strong and brave as you, Father!" he told Zeke with all seriousness. "I will seek a vision and know how to be strong inside like you."

Zeke turned to face his son and lowered the big knife. Their eyes held. "You will find your inner self, Little Rock. Of this I am sure. You will have a vision."

The boy straightened, studying the fine, white scar on his father's cheek and envisioning the fight with the Crow warrior who had put it there. Dooley and Zeke's Cheyenne relatives had told him many stories of Zeke's prowess with the knife. "How will I know, Father? How will I know when it is time?" he asked.

"I can't tell you that. It is different for all men."

70

The boy looked down at the knife Zeke still held in his hand. "You found that bad woman after you got out of the pit of snakes?"

Zeke gripped the knife tighter. "Yes, I found her. And I . . ." he hesitated and sighed. "I was so full of hatred that I wanted her to suffer, Little Rock, even though she was only a woman and hurting or killing her would bring me no honor. I had never before and have never since hurt a woman." He shoved the knife back into its sheath. "But Dancing Moon had become my bitter enemy. All I could think of was my poor Abbie suffering at that woman's hands, and the night I spent in the pit of snakes. I wanted Dancing Moon to feel Abbie's pain, so I cut my initial into her cheeks and let the blood flow, just as Abbie's blood had flowed. And I wanted her to know the horror and fear of a rattler on her skin, so I tied her and stripped her and laid a sack on her belly that had a rattler inside. I left her that way in the desert, sure she would die slowly as she had expected *me* to die!" He stood up. "But somehow she must have lived," he hissed, "to become a leader of men who raid and deal in the slave trade. The one called Lady Z must be the same woman. There is no other answer. I should have sunk my knife into her heart that day!"

A gentle breeze ruffled the coup feathers in Zeke's braid, and Little Rock watched him as he struggled against his own tears, for a boy should not cry. "I am afraid for you to go after that woman," he told Zeke. "What if you do not come back? Who will ride with me and teach me to hunt? And who will . . ." the boy stopped and swallowed, looking down at his lap. Zeke turned and knelt in front of him, taking the boy's hands.

"If I never came back, my son, I would still always be with you," he told the boy. "We are all a spirit, Little Rock. Spirits walking around in bodies. The spirit can never die, and mine would always be with you. When you ride in the mornings, I will be riding with you. When you hunt, I will talk to the animals and tell them to offer themselves so that your belly might be full. When you make war, I will put speed and accuracy into your weapons. And my love will

71

warm you in the night. I will never be away from you, Little Rock." He smoothed the boy's stick-straight, glossy hair. "But you should not worry that I won't come back. I must come back . . . to this land, to my little daughters, to my Abbie." His heart was torn at the sight of the tears in his son's eyes. "And to my son. Nothing in the world can keep me from coming back to you. There is no evil strong enough to keep me from winning, Little Rock. My power is greater, my spirit stronger. Maheo will be with me."

The boy reached out and squeezed his father tightly around the neck. Zeke grabbed him in a firm hug.

"While I am gone, Little Rock, you must be the man," he told the boy. "You must watch out for your mother and sisters. I give that responsibility to you. I will bring Deer Slayer to be with them, but he is an old man. He will need your help."

"I will help grandfather take care of them," the boy sniffed. "I . . . did not want to cry, but we have never before been apart."

Zeke grinned and pulled back from him. "There is nothing wrong with crying, son. Do you think I have never wept?"

The boy blinked. "Have you?"

"Many times," Zeke replied, wiping at some tears that spilled down his son's cheeks. "All men weep. Maybe not as openly as women, but they weep, Little Rock. Life brings both joy and tears. There is no shame in crying, Little Rock, when there is just cause. The only shameful tears are the tears of a coward."

"Am I a coward for not wanting you to go away from us?"

Zeke smiled softly. "No. You are just showing how much you care about me." The boy hugged him once more, and Zeke stood up with the child in his arms and carried him back to his horse. He set Little Rock on his mount. "We'd best get back, son," he told the child, turning and mounting his own horse with ease. His big frame seemed almost too large for the animal. He picked up the reins, then turned to Little Rock again. "You'd better not tell your mother about our talk of vengeance, son. I only tell you these things to teach you about survival, and I wanted you to understand why I did what I did to Dancing Moon. But sometimes that talk upsets your mother, even though she understands my own need for vengeance when someone I love is harmed. Your mother's white blood is much tamer than mine, and she thinks it is more important that you learn schooling than to learn about vengeance and fighting. But out here certain things are more important than an education, because out here survival is not easy. I hope you understand why I must go and find poor Yellow Moon and save her from that evil woman and the men she rides with."

"I understand, Father. And I will not tell my mother of our talk. Sometimes she gets angry with you when you teach me about these things. But she has the soft heart of a white woman. She does not always understand like we do." He grinned. "It is funny when she is angry with you, because she walks around with her mouth closed real tight and looks funny at you, but she never says anything." He giggled and Zeke laughed aloud.

"You noticed, did you?" He reached over and patted the boy's back. "You must promise me to study your letters and numbers while I'm away, Little Rock. That's important to your mother. Keep her happy."

The boy frowned. "I will try, but it will not be easy," he complained. "I do not care for letters and numbers. I would rather go and hunt rabbit." His eyes suddenly brightened. "Race me back, Father! I will beat you again!"

Zeke nodded. "Let's feel some wind on our face!" He kicked his horse's flanks and rode off, deliberately holding back just enough so that the boy would catch up and move ahead.

They sat quietly around the supper table, Blue Sky obedient and wide-eyed, aware that her father was going to leave the next morning on a dangerous journey, but unsure just what his mission would be. For some reason they had to leave the ranch and go to Bent's Fort, a three-day ride to the east, where they would live until their father returned.

73

Little Rock was secretly excited, for they would dwell in the tipi again, as they had done when he was a very small boy. He would live like his uncles, Black Elk and Swift Arrow lived—and he would pretend he was a great warrior! But his excitement was dimmed by his restless fear that harm might come to his father.

Abbie held Young Girl on her lap, feeding her pieces of potato. But Abbie did not eat. She could not eat. Even Zeke ate little, for neither of them enjoyed the idea of being apart.

Dooley ate quickly, feeling as though he were in the way. "I'll take some of the horses to the fort when we go," he told Zeke, trying to make small talk. "Bein' it's spring, I expect I can sell them right quick. Deer Slayer will be here soon. Him and some others will watch the rest of the herd till I get back." He swallowed down some cow's milk. "I'll take good care of the place for you, friend."

Zeke picked at a piece of antelope. "I'm not worried about the place, Dooley." He met the man's eyes. "Just don't go risking your neck too far just to protect the place. If it means your life, let it go. A damned good friend lost his life helping me once, and I don't intend to feel that guilt again." He put the fork down and leanrd back in his chair, rubbing his eyes.

Dooley sighed and drank the rest of the milk, getting up quickly and nodding to Abbie.

"Excuse me, Abbie. I'll go tend to things outside. There's a lot to do before we leave in the morning. Thanks for the supper. It was real good."

She forced a smile for him. "I'm afraid I could have done better tonight, Dooley. But I just wasn't in the mood to cook a big meal."

He pushed his chair in. "'Course not. It was just fine." He turned and put a hand on Zeke's shoulder for just a moment. "You get some rest tonight, and don't let that hatred keep you from keepin' a clear head, understand?" He left, and Zeke met Abbie's eyes. She returned the look with her own pleading one.

"Does it have to be you?" she asked quietly.

His dark eyes burned into hers with determination. "You

74

know it does, Abbie."

She sighed and rose, carrying Young Girl to a buffalo robe in the corner and setting her on the robe to play. She stood with her back turned for a moment, not sure what the right words were to say to him.

"Zeke, I . . . I'd rather stay here. This is our home—"

"No!" he snapped, getting up from his chair. "Once Dancing Moon knows she's got my brother's wife, she'll know I'm the one who will come after Yellow Moon and Laughing Boy. That will mean you are here unprotected. You'll be much safer at the fort. With everything else I have to do, it won't help worrying about you being out here with just Dooley to help. He's a good man but he can't fight a whole gang of outlaws, and that's what Dancing Moon will send if she knows I'm not here. I know the bitch!"

He paced nervously, restless and anxious to get started.

"You stay at Bent's Fort until I return, understand? Promise me, Abbie!"

She nodded. "I promise. I just . . . I wish it was closer. Old Bent's Fort was much closer. I don't like being so far from my home."

"With Black Elk and the others gone from the village hunting for Pawnee war parties, and Swift Arrow up North with the Sioux, there's no one to stay here and protect you."

She nodded. "I understand," she said quietly. She swallowed, wanting to scream out in her fear for him.

He looked over at her, his heart softening at the sight of her standing there, her back to him, her head hanging in despair. He knew how hard it was for her when he had to go away. They had been through this before. He stepped closer to her, and she could feel his tension and the great hatred that lay in his soul for the Arapaho woman who had once shared his bed. "Abbie, this time I will be the stalker. And this time she'll get no second chance!" he told her.

Abbie covered her face. "Oh, Zeke, poor Yellow Moon! And little Laughing Boy! What will happen to them!"

Her body jerked in a sob, and he put his hands on her shoulders, turning her and enfolding her in his strong, reassuring arms.

"And you! You shouldn't have to do this!" Abbie added.

"I'll be all right, Abbie girl," he replied, kissing the top of her head. "And I'll find them. I'll get them back."

She new he would—or die trying. For that was the kind of man he was. She breathed in the sweet, earthy scent of man and buckskins and pressed her face against the broad chest that brought her peace and comfort.

How long would he be there for her, with the kind of life he led? It was something she must never dwell upon—yet it was only natural to wonder, for always there seemed to be something about this wild land that came between them, pulling them apart when they wanted only to be together.

"What have I always told you, Abbie, about always coming back?" he said softly, kissing her hair again. "I haven't failed you yet."

She pulled away a little and wiped at her wet cheeks, turning her face up to him and reminding him of a small girl when she sniffled. "I'm pregnant with your fourth child," she whimpered. "You have to come back. It's another boy, I'm sure!"

He smiled for her, deliberately putting to the back of his mind all his hatred and vengeance. This would be his last night with her for many weeks. There would be no more talk of hatred and killing and fear.

"And I'll be here to help deliver it just like I helped with the first three," he told her.

But then his smile faded as their eyes held. For both were thinking that there had really been more than three. There had been the first one—the one she had lost because of Dancing Moon's cruel attack.

"Zeke!" she whispered.

"Don't think about it!" he answered quickly and almost angrily. "Tonight it's just you and me, Abbie girl. And we're going to make love and hold each other all night."

He bent down and met her lips, kissing her almost savagely, assuring her that she had given him more pleasure in their bed of robes than Dancing Moon had ever given him. She was his Abbie girl—the virgin child he had claimed

76

and who had imprisoned his heart so that he could not live without her, even though he'd known how unwise it would be to marry a white woman.

He pressed her tight against himself, wanting to hold her forever, wanting not to leave her. For always he felt she needed extra protection, because others would be cruel to her—people of her own blood who would look down on her and ridicule her for marrying a half-breed. Zeke knew that kind of suffering.

"I'm so sorry, Abbie girl," he groaned. "So sorry things always have to be so hard for you!" His lips moved over her cheek and down to her throat.

"I'd not trade one day of my life with you, and you know it," she replied.

He kissed her eyes and hair, pressing her face to his chest again with a big hand, his other arm about her waist. She could feel his hardness against her belly and she felt the warm flush of desire that had not lessened with time. And she knew his lovemaking would be active and close to violent that night, for there were many reasons why he would be making love to her. But the reasons would not matter. Whatever they were, she would gladly satisfy his needs.

"Maheo bless and guide you, Zeke," she told him. "I'll pray for you constantly."

"Then I'll be safe. Your prayers are strong. They saved me once from the snakepit—when your love was so strong for me that you sensed my danger, even though we were hundreds of miles apart."

He looked over at his son, who sat watching his father and somehow knowing his parents must be alone. The boy got up from his chair and took Blue Sky's hand.

"I will take my sister to bed now," he declared.

Abbie turned to look at him in surprise, then looked up at Zeke as she wiped at her eyes. He only grinned and winked. He reluctantly let go of his wife and knelt down, holding his arms out to the always frightened Blue Sky, who came running to her father and hugged him tightly.

"Love you, Father," the little girl told him.

"And I love you," he replied, pulling back and studying the exquisite beauty of his dark-skinned daughter. "You mind Little Rock while I'm gone, understand? He's in charge of watching out for you."

The girl nodded and obediently turned to take Little Rock's hand again. Father and son exchanged an understanding look, and the boy led his sister to the stepladder that went to the loft. Zeke turned and knelt down beside Young Girl, who had fallen asleep on the buffalo robe on the floor. He reached out to touch a golden curl with his dark hand.

"Does this one really belong to us?" he teased. "I can't believe there's an ounce of Indian blood in her."

"She does have high cheekbones," Abbie replied. "She'll be as pretty as my sister LeeAnn was," she added, her heart paining at the thought of her dead sister. LeeAnn had been one of Abbie's many losses on the wagon train West. But she had met Cheyenne Zeke on that same wagon train, and he had branded her with his body and changed her from girl to woman. He looked up at her now.

"Let her sleep where she is," he told her. "Put a blanket over her. I want to go to bed, Abbie girl."

Warm desire surged through her again and she blushed. "I'll cover her," she answered. "Go bolt the door. I'll clean up the table in the morning." She went to get a blanket, wishing there were some way to keep the morning from ever coming. For in the morning, he would go away. She heard the bolt slide shut, and in the next moment she gasped as he came up behind her and whisked her into his arms, carrying her through the curtained doorway to their bedroom. He set her on her feet and unlaced the front of her tunic.

"I never tire of this," he told her. "It only gets better."

She grasped his hands, so strong and sure, hands that had killed swiftly and without feeling; hands that had never brought her harm, but that had always touched her gently. He had already removed his shirt, and her eyes fell to the scar at his side where, when they had first met, she had removed a bullet from him herself, after he had saved her, against great odds, from the hands of outlaws. Her eyes

78

filled with tears, and she kissed his hands.

"Abbie, it will be all right," he repeated.

"I'm so afraid for you!" she whimpered.

He bent down and covered her mouth with his own, kissing her hard, and she returned the kiss with a terrible need to know he was there and alive, hoping against hope that when he made love to her he would change his mind about leaving. He let go of her hands and quickly pulled her tunic down over her shoulders, while their lips continued to melt together desperately. He pulled her tight against him, relishing the feel of her full, milk-laden breasts against his bare chest. He groaned with his own desperateness, for he did not like being away from his beloved Abigail.

Her face was hot and her breathing labored when he left her lips and moved his mouth over her cheek and to her neck. He continued down her body as she stood there limp and willing, wanting to cherish every touch, every moment now in this short time that was left. His lips gently tasted the tracings of sweet milk at her nipples, then moved over her belly as he pulled her tunic the rest of the way off and softly kissed her groin and the soft hairs that covered places only Cheyenne Zeke had touched and tasted.

He rose and picked her up again, laying her onto the bed of robes and deftly removing his own leggings and loincloth before joining her again. She returned the lovemaking just as eagerly, wanting to remember him—the hard muscle of his arms and chest, the scars on his chest from suffering the agonies of the Sun Dance to prove his manhood. His hands caressed her body softly as he allowed her to kiss him everywhere, for she, too, needed to touch and to remember; to fill her memory with the glory of his manhood and hold it until she could again be in his arms.

He touched her soft belly that held his life as she moved back up to greet his mouth with her own, and then it was his turn again. He moved on top of her, and she felt lost beneath him, as she always did. His long hair was loose, and it softly brushed her shoulders as she felt the rock-hard muscle of his long legs as they moved between her own legs. Almost instantly she was experiencing that most manly part of

79

Cheyenne Zeke, and she felt a sudden, horrible jealousy at the realization that Dancing Moon had once shared this man; and for one brief moment she could understand Dancing Moon's jealousy. But Dancing Moon had not loved Zeke for Zeke. She had loved him only for this part of him. And that was not love. It was only a sick, insatiable hunger—one that any man could feed. She would give him much more than that. She would give her life for him if need be, and she would give life to him by taking in his seed and turning it into sons and daughters for Cheyenne Zeke. He needed sons and daughters. She understood that about him. She understood everything about him—that vulnerable side of the half-breed who to others often appeared vicious and brutal—a man no one cared to cross. The man she took to her bed was not like that. In those moments he belonged only to Abigail—totally possesed by her, and she by him.

She opened her eyes and met his as she arched upward to meet his rhythmic movements, and his own dark eyes were lit up with fire and desire. He raised up and ran his big hands over her slim white thighs that were parted to take him in, then moved his hands up over her belly again and to her breasts, coming down and grasping her hair as he met her lips with a groan and rammed himself even deeper inside of her, wanting to cling to this moment and remember it, just as she did.

He took his time before the life finally flowed out of him and surged into her womb. They lay there in silence, their bodies heated and damp, waiting only for what they knew must happen again this precious, last night together. Minutes later he began to move over her again, his own desire to leave a lasting brand on her intense, for this was his woman, and if he never came back she must always remember who had her first.

He gently pushed her legs apart again, as his mouth tasted hers. Tomorrow he must leave her. But that was tomorrow. This was tonight. Perhaps tomorrow would never come. Perhaps they could hold this moment forever.

Five

The sight at the end of the rifle followed the outlaws silently, the Texas sun shining down hot against the steel barrel, and against the dark brown skin of Cheyenne Zeke's hands as he held the weapon steadily on his prey. There were five of them below, riding through a narrow canyon with no way out but past their silent enemy above. He had followed them for many days, tracking them from the burned-out remnants of the ranch they had attacked. The tracks had led him to a deserted stagecoach, its drivers and two passengers dead and bloated, stripped of their valuables.

The hoofprints of their horses told him all he needed to know. They wore shoes. They were not Indian ponies. They were white men, the very kind of outlaws he was searching for in the hopes they could lead him to Lady Z. But there was a flaw in his plan now, one he'd suspected since leaving the site of the plundered stagecoach. One passenger had been left alive, and now he saw his suspicion was right. The outlaws had a woman with them.

There was no longer any question about what he must do. His original plan to simply continue to follow them was out. He had to help the woman. He must be careful and accurate, for if one of them got away he would be sure to go for more men and Zeke would never get the woman to safety. So he would simply have to kill them all, and hopefully keep one alive long enough to see if he could get any information about the whereabouts of Lady Z. Surely these were the kind of men who would know about the notorious female leader. Perhaps they even intended to take their captive to Lady Z to sell her.

The woman was white. She was tied by the wrists, the other end of the rope attached to the pommel of an outlaw's saddle. She staggered as she walked, and her clothes were torn. Zeke knew she could not last much longer under the relentless sun that beat down upon her fair skin, and vengeance burned in his chest at seeing someone so innocent, so pitifully abused. All he could think of was how he would feel if it were his Abbie tied to the horse. The woman he watched below had probably already been violated. It was difficult to tell. If the outlaws thought her to be a virgin, it was possible she had not yet been touched. The virgins were usually saved, for they brought a high price on the slave market.

Either way, the woman's fate would not be a kind one. He had to do what he could to help her. He continued to follow the men in his rifle sight, as soundless and undetectable as a desert lizard. If the woman was killed in the exchange of fire once he started shooting, she would probably be better off than to suffer what lay ahead for her. But if she was lucky, she would not be harmed. He had the element of surprise on his side, which meant he could get two or three of them before they even had the chance to pull their guns and start shooting back. If he ended up killing all of them and not getting any information about Lady Z, his mission would have failed and he would have to start all over again in his search. But it was a risk he must take. The woman must come first. He could wait no longer.

There was no sound but the echoing of the hooves of the outlaws' horses grating against the canyon's rocky floor. The reverberating sound waves shattered back and forth against the steep redrock cliffs, making it sound as though there were many more men below than there really were. Yet above the sound of the hooves could be heard the woman's pitiful whimpering, as she struggled fruitlessly against the ropes at her wrists.

Suddenly the outlaw who dragged the woman behind his horse stopped his mount and yelled to the others to hold up. Zeke's hand gripped the rifle more tightly as the man dismounted and walked back to the woman, and she cringed and cried even harder as he approached her.

"Goddamn it, can't you ever shut up?" the man yelled, his words echoing up the canyon to Zeke's ears. He back-handed her hard, knocking his captive to the ground. "I'm sick of listenin' to your goddamned whimperin' all the time! Shut your trap, or I'll have at you and let my men have at you and put a bullet in that pretty little forehead! You might be worth some money, but that damned cryin' makes me wonder if I want to put up with you all the way to where we're goin'!"

He grabbed her up by the hair of the head and hit her again as one of the others rode back to the first man, dis-mounting before his horse came to a halt and storming up to the scene.

"Lay off, Jackson!" the second man growled. "You mess up that face and we lose money!"

"I'm sick of the bitch's cryin'!" the first man snapped, shoving the woman to the ground again and turning to face the second man with clenched fists. The other three men also rode back then, as the first two men began shoving each other back and forth. All sported soiled clothes and grizzly, half-grown beards, and from above Zeke could see the dark stains under the arms of their shirts from perspiration.

"She's worth a lot of gold!" the second man was yelling at the first. "You know the virgins are worth more, Jackson, let alone the pretty ones! You go messin' her up and we lose a lot of money!"

Jackson backed off, looking down at the girl and rubbing at his privates. "Might be worth the loss," he growled. "Why do we always have to sell the best ones and never get a piece for ourselves?"

The others quieted, looking first at each other, then down at the cringing woman. She was a young, fair, blond-headed thing with fetching blue eyes. But those eyes were wide and terrified now as she stared back at them. Her dirty face was stained with tears, and her mouth was bleeding. Her breath came in short gasps, and part of one breast showed through a tear in the front of her dress, while the disheveled skirt of the dress showed a good share of her thigh.

Jackson bent down and roughly ripped open the front of her dress, exposing the untouched breasts. "Why should we always give that to somebody else?" he said with a grin.

The girl's crying began all over again, as she struggled to turn away from them to hide herself. Her tears came in jerking, grunting sobs as the men began forming a circle around her.

"Who would get to be first?" one of them grumbled. "I want to be first!"

"Wait!" another spoke up. He kicked at her with a big boot, forcing her onto her stomach and holding her down hard against the ground with his foot as he bent down and threw her dress up, revealing ruffled pantaloons. He grinned and reached down, yanking the pantaloons down over her hips to her knees and exposing her bottom. The girl screamed in horror as his hands grabbed at her. "We could all have at her from this side, and she'd still be a virgin," he told the others with a victorious grin. "That's better than nothin', right?"

The others looked at each other, then began grinning and nodding. Now that they had seen enticing parts exposed to their hungry eyes, there was no one who wanted to argue the issue.

"No, God, no!" the woman begged, realizing what they intended to do with her. From above, Zeke knew also, and he knew time had run out for thinking and planning. With the woman on the ground, perhaps she would not be hit by a bullet.

He would have to aim sure and true, and the first man to go would be the bastard who sat straddled over his screaming victim at that very moment, preparing to humiliate and injure her just to satisfy his animal desires. That man happened to be the one called Jackson. He grasped at her bottom as the woman's screams were muffled into the hot gravel beneath her face, and Zeke's rifle glinted again in the sun. But none of the men noticed, all of them too excited now, too eager to watch what was to happen next.

But then there was an echoing boom from somewhere up in the rocks, and Jackson's body jerked as a bright, red hole

84

appeared in his skull. He slumped forward over the woman's body, his full weight crushing her, while a second shot opened up the chest of another of the outlaws.

All of this happened in only two or three seconds, and the three remaining men looked up in terror at the cliffs above, all of them stunned and confused. Another shot rang out before they could get their wits together, and a bullet plunged into the horse to which the woman was tied, dropping the animal to its death so that it would not spook and run off, dragging the woman with it.

The captive woman screamed in terror and revulsion, realizing the man on top of her was dead. She struggled and hunched to get the body off of her, while the other three men ran for their horses, dodging and shooting at the cliffs above, but unable to see their predator. One fell with a bullet in his back just as he got his foot into the stirrup of his saddle. His horse reared and ran off, dragging its dead master with it for several yards.

Zeke stood up then, as the remaining two men managed to get mounted, both charging away toward the only exit out of the narrow canyon. They shot at the cliffs above them, but their bullets went astray, their target elusive. Zeke removed an arrow from the quiver he wore slung over his back. He quickly placed the arrow into his bow and pulled back the rawhide string. He smiled with excitement, much preferring the use of Indian weapons to his rifle, for killing a man with an arrow took greater skill. He keenly gauged the speed of the fleeing outlaws' horses, then, with the eyes of a hawk and the calm of a stalking bobcat, he let go of the arrow, enjoying the whirring sound it made as it traveled through the air.

A second later there was a scream as the arrow pierced one rider near his hip. He fell from his mount and the horse itself stumbled, but quickly got its bearings and thundered on without its rider.

The fifth man did not look back or try to help his companion. He rode hard, his heart pounding with fear, sure there must be an entire war party of Apaches or Comanches on the ridge above, probably after their horses and the white woman they themselves had stolen. There was nothing to do now but leave both to the Indians and get out fast!

But then another arrow sang through the air. No one escaped the canyon.

The only sound left in the canyon was the whimpering of the white woman, who had managed to roll the dead Jackson's body off her own and to get herself to a sitting position. She searched the cliffs above in terror, waiting for the Indians or outlaws who had killed her abductors. Whoever it was probably had no better plans in mind for her than the outlaws had, and she prayed with all her strength for God to rescue her, while at the same time she struggled to pull up her pantaloons, getting them most of the way up in spite of her tied wrists, for her hands were in front of her body and she could at least use her fingers.

But whoever was above had already seen, and she knew it would be a miracle if a band of raiding Apaches did not appear from above and come down to take turns with her.

"Oh, God! Oh, God!" she whimpered, straining to see who had showered the deadly arrows and bullets down onto the outlaws.

Finally a figure appeared, tall and dark and shadowy, the sun's glare behind him so that the woman could not see him well. She trembled as she watched him descend the ridge almost soundlessly, his moccasined feet making no noise at all. Even his horse seemed to know it must tread lightly.

"God, don't let him hurt me!" the woman whispered as he came closer to the bottom. At least there appeared to be only one man, which was a surprise in itself, considering how quickly the five outlaws had been murdered. But he was a big man, and one or many, it was all the same for a weak, defenseless girl.

He made it to the bottom of the canyon and headed toward her, but suddenly a shot rang out, and the mysterious figure whirled and landed with a grunt on his back. The woman gasped, and her eyes darted over to the outlaw who had been shot with an arrow in the hip. The man was still alive and had managed to find his handgun. He had shot the mysterious assailant, then groaned and gone limp from pain and loss of blood.

The woman choked in a sob and glanced back at the man who had come down from the cliffs, still unsure if he was good or evil. Zeke grunted and pushed himself to his knees. Blood stained the front of his tunic at his left shoulder, and he forced himself to his feet, gripping his huge knife in his right hand. The woman watched in terror as he walked unsteadily toward the man who had shot him, who now lay seemingly oblivious to any movement around him.

Zeke came close to the man and kicked the handgun away, then took his foot and shoved the body onto its back. The man groaned, the arrow still sticking out of the side of his left hip. Zeke breathed deeply to keep from passing out, as he knelt down over the man and placed the wide blade of his infamous knife against the man's cheek.

"Where's Dancing Moon?" he growled. The man only moaned, his eyes closed. "Where is she?" Zeke demanded. "Where is the Lady Z? Do you deal with her?"

The man's eyes blinked open. "Who . . . are you? Where are the others?"

"There's only me!" Zeke hissed through gritted teeth, the bloodstain on the front of his tunic getting bigger. "Tell me where the Lady Z is, or I'll cut out your eyeballs!"

The man's eyes widened. "Take the arrow . . . out of me!" he wept.

"Not till you tell me if you know of the Lady Z!"

The man licked his lips and swallowed. "I . . . don't know. Nobody knows." He licked his lips again. "She hides . . . with just a few . . . of her best men . . . somewhere in the . . . Sangre de Cristo Mountains. No one has ever . . . been able to find her hiding place!"

Zeke grabbed the man's hair and jerked his head up, laying the knife on his cheek with the tip just beneath the man's eye. "Then how do you deal with her?" he barked. "How do you contact her?"

"A . . . little place . . . called Gila . . . where the Canadian River . . . and the Mora River meet . . . in New Mexico Territory, at the base of . . . the Sangre de Cristos. A tavern there. We . . . take our captives there . . . and someone takes a message to the Lady Z whose men come for the captive. Sometimes . . . sometimes the Lady Z comes herself."

Zeke let go of his head and the man fell back into the dirt. "The . . . arrow," the man groaned. "Take it out!"

Zeke only grinned. "I am afraid I have no use for men who buy and sell innocent women!" he replied. "You have asked the wrong man for mercy. I have another form of mercy for you, my friend. I will end your pain—forever!"

The man's eyes widened and he started to scream as the huge blade was raised above him, but Zeke plunged the instrument of death before the man could even get out a sound. For a brief moment there was the gleam in Zeke's dark eyes of the pure savage blood that coursed through his veins, and he was even tempted to take the man's scalp, an act he had performed many times before, especially in the days when he rode with his Cheyenne brothers against other Indian tribes. But this man was a coward. To take his scalp would bring Zeke no glory. He wiped the blood from his knife onto the man's shirt and struggled to his feet, his head getting dizzy from his own loss of blood. He stumbled toward the captive woman, who watched in cold horror, stunned at the savage way this mysterious man had sunk his knife into the outlaw as though the man were a piece of wild game to be slaughtered.

All five of her captors now lay dead, and the man who had killed them was walking toward her, himself wounded. He was a big man, a good six feet tall if not more, lean in build but broad in the shoulders. The woman remained speechless as he came close to her and knelt to his knees, still gripping the knife.

"Please don't hurt me!" the woman begged.

He closed his eyes, his breathing becoming labored. "I'm . . . not here to hurt you, ma'am," he said, his voice growing weak. "Put out your hands . . . and I'll cut the ropes at your wrists. I'm afraid you're . . . going to have to help me. Are you . . . strong enough to walk to a stream . . . up ahead?"

She sniffed and nodded, slowly raising out her wrists to him, her arms shaking from fear. He deftly sliced the knife through the ropes at her wrists as though they were mere butter, then shoved the knife back into its sheath.

The woman quickly pulled the ropes from her wrists as Zeke struggled to his feet again and stumbled toward his horse. The woman hurriedly pulled her pantaloons up better and grasped at her torn dress, struggling to hold the pieces over her breasts. But he had already seen them, and she was glad he was wounded. For surely this strange Indian man would try to rape her. Still, he spoke very good English, with even a bit of a southern accent. It was still difficult to tell if he was friend or foe, but he was bleeding so badly now that he did not appear to be a threat. If she knew where to go, she would have simply run away and left him there, but for now she needed him, for she had no idea where she was. She would have to hope that this strange, savage man was her savior sent from God and not another enemy.

He walked toward her, clinging to the bridle of his handsome Appaloosa. "Mount up," he told her, his big frame towering over her. "I'll show you . . . to the stream. You'll . . . have to cut a bullet out of me, I'm afraid."

Their eyes held, and she saw a sudden compassion and gentleness in his dark eyes that did not match the deed he had just performed in killing her abductors. She suddenly felt safe. Surely God had sent this man to help her. Now she must help him, for God's messengers came in mysterious packages, and it was not her place to judge this man who had just saved her.

"There's a blanket . . . tied to my saddle . . . you can cover yourself with," he was telling her. She reddened and blinked back tears, grasping her dress more tightly. He forced a smile through his pain. "Ma'am, I have a woman . . . and three kids . . . waiting for me to come home to them. I've got no desire, and right now not even the physical ability . . . to violate you. I just want to . . . get this bullet out and stop the bleeding . . . so I can live to go back

89

home. Will you please . . . help me?"

Her eyes widened in her own shame at letting him stand there for so long. "Of course!" she answered, hurrying over to take the blanket from the horse. She threw it around her shoulders. "And you must ride, sir. Not me. Tell me where to go and I'll lead the animal. You'll never make it that far walking."

She took his arm and gently urged him back to the saddle. "Are you sure . . . you can walk?" he asked her.

"Yes, yes. You ride, please!"

She noticed the saddle was not a common western saddle and it had no stirrups. She surmised it was some kind of Indian saddle, for everything else about him was Indian. He put his right arm around the base of the horse's neck, and with his last bit of energy he hoisted himself up onto the animal's back without the need of a stirrup. He lay his head down against the animal's mane.

"Straight ahead," he mumbled, "at the opening of the canyon. Just past that . . . you'll see a dropoff. At the base . . . of the embankment . . . there's a green spot . . . water . . . a couple of piñon trees for shade. Can you . . . take out a bullet?"

She started forward with the horse. "I'll do my best, sir," she answered. "My father is a doctor. I've helped him before." She led the horse past the dead bodies, and tried not to look at them. It was amazing to think that the man who had apparently saved her from these men could himself be brutal and savage. Yet now he seemed almost helpless, his own life in her hands. All her life she had been raised to do God's will, and she knew in her heart she would not have run out on him if she were able to find her own way. He had helped her. Now she must help him, whoever he was.

"Abbie?" he mumbled. She turned to look back at him, and his eyes were closed. "Help me, Abbie girl." Blood trickled down the side of his painted horse, over the picture of a yellow sun. The woman frowned, amazed that apparently his woman's name was Abbie, for he had called out for her. But Abbie was a white woman's name, not an Indian squaw's name. She shrugged and led the horse on toward the opening of the canyon. He whispered Abbie's name again, but she did not hear him this time. She only wondered how he happened to be there to help her, and who was the Lady Z he had quizzed the outlaw about. The answers would have to wait, and if he died, she would never know at all, and she herself would probably die in this desolate, unfamiliar land.

Abbie stood outside the tipi, drinking in the night air and wishing she could feel Zeke's warm strength, his welcome arms holding her, his deep, reassuring voice telling her he was there and everything was all right. But he was not there. He had been gone three weeks, and tonight she felt a cold chill, an eerie feeling that all was not well with her husband. It frightened her, for she had felt this way once before when he was gone, and had later learned it had been on the night he spent in the snakepit. She had even dreamed of snakes that night.

Their relationship was so finely tuned that she often could sense his need. She wished the Cheyenne priests could be called together to pray for him, for there was power in their prayers, a kind of spiritual strength that could seemingly be transmitted to one of their own who needed the help of the Great Spirit. But there were no priests to call upon now. Hundreds of men from the southern bands had headed out to fight the Pawnee and reclaim buffalo hunting grounds. The nearest villages to Bent's Fort were full of mostly women and children and old people. Deer Slayer had come to the fort to be with Abbie, and he had his young daughter-in-law, Blue Bird Woman, with him.

"Sweet Jesus, help him," she whispered into the darkness. "My Zeke prays to Maheo, but surely you and the Cheyenne spirits are one and the same."

Thunder rolled in the distance, and the night sky lit up with white lightning. It reminded her of the stormy night she had awakened and seen Zeke standing at the window. He had sensed even then something was wrong. His spirit was restless that night. Now she felt it was restless again, and she was troubled.

She heard footsteps behind her and turned to see Deer Slayer approaching. "You should not stand out here alone, my daughter," he told her.

She sighed and turned back around to watch the lightning flicker around the granite peaks of the great Rockies. "I'm worried, Deer Slayer. I have that bad feeling again."

"Then we should pray for him."

"We had the aid of the priests before—the whole tribe."

"It does not take the whole tribe. You have enough love in your heart to bring him the power all by yourself. Your God will hear you, and our Gods will also hear you. It is the power within oneself that counts, and you have much power. You are a good woman. The spirits shine on you and do your bidding."

She smiled softly and turned to face him. "It's Zeke who has the real power. I don't know that I'll ever have that kind of spirituality. Perhaps I need to suffer the pain of the Sun Dance ritual, sacrifice my flesh, to truly understand."

He folded his arms. "Zeke would never allow you to suffer—for any reason. Come, you should be inside. You will get chilled, and someone might come and steal you."

Abbie laughed lightly. "I hardly think so."

"Do laugh, my daughter. The land is dangerous. You know this to be true. Bent has promised to watch out for you, and I shall do the same, for you and for Blue Bird Woman, until your husband returns."

"I wish we could go back to the ranch. I'd feel so much better there."

"Zeke has forbidden this. The evil Dancing Moon might try to find you there. You are safer here at the fort for now, but some of these traders must be watched also. Stay away from them. You know how Zeke feels about the way some white men look at a white woman who sleeps with a man with Indian blood in his veins. He remembers from that place called Tennessee. Always he is afraid the same thing could happen to you that happened to his first wife."

They walked slowly back toward the tipi. "I know. It will haunt him the rest of his life."

"Many things haunt my stepson. He grew up in a place where there was no love. He wishes only to hang on to what love he has found with you and his children."

Abbie looked down at her growing belly, thinking with a flash of warmth about how that life had got there. Yes, Cheyenne Zeke was most certainly loved, and she was loved in return. That love was their strength.

"Will you pray with me, Deer Slayer?"

"I will pray with you. Young Blue Bird Woman will pray also."

Little Rock came out of the tipi just as they approached, and he folded his arms and puckered his lips. "Where do you go, Mother? I cannot watch you if you are always walking away!"

She raised her eyebrows. "Forgive me, my son. I should have told you!" she replied, trying to sound serious.

"I am to protect you!" he grumbled. "You do not think I can do it."

She smiled softly and knelt in front of him. "That isn't so, Little Rock. I am very confident you can protect me. You are already becoming a man, and I'm proud of you. Sometimes you remind me of my little brother, who died on the wagon train. He was brave and full of life like you. He was a little boy but he . . . died . . . like a man."

Her voice trailed off.

"How did he die, Mother?" the boy asked.

Her eyes teared and she glanced up at Deer Slayer, who nodded that it was time the boy was told. Abbie looked back at her son and took his hands. His dark eyes studied her curiously.

"He fell from our wagon, Little Rock, and was crushed beneath the wheel," she told the boy. "But . . . he didn't die right away, my darling. He suffered . . . terribly. His body was broken beyond repair, and his pain was a terrible thing to watch. We knew that . . . that it was only a matter of time until he died, and I couldn't bear to see him suffering. That was when your father and I were only . . . friends. He was a scout for the wagon train. And I . . . I asked your father to do something that will probably give him bad dreams for the rest of his life, for it was a terrible thing to ask of him, but something that had to be done. He did it . . . for me . . . and for little Jeremy. Your father ended his suffering," she went on, her voice choking. "Quickly and painlessly, with that big knife that he uses with such skill. Your father ended Jeremy's misery, Little Rock, and . . . he told me . . . Jeremy was brave and ready to meet the Great Spirit. Your father has great respect for Jeremy's memory."

The boy frowned. "You were not angry with him for doing this?"

Tears began to trickle down her cheeks. "No. It was a very brave thing your father did, an act of great mercy, committed out of compassion for Jeremy, and respect for my wishes. He did it even though he knew it would pain his heart and his memory for the rest of his life, for your father would die before he would bring harm to a child. It was probably . . . the hardest thing he has ever done."

Their eyes held. "Would he kill me if I was dying?"

Abbie felt the cold chill again. She grabbed her son close to her. "I can't answer that, Little Rock. I can only tell you that if something happened to you, I think your father would want to be dead also."

He wrapped his arms around her neck. "I miss him," he said quietly.

"I know, son. But he'll be back. He's gone away before, and he always comes back. Always."

She did not reveal her cold suspicion that something was wrong with Zeke. She would not cast the burden on her little son. There was nothing she could do but pray silently, and wait.

Zeke's body shook, and he moaned Abbie's name again, as the woman he had rescued tried to keep the blankets tucked around him against the chilly night air. She had done all she could do, using the Indian man's own amazingly sharp knife to cut a bullet from the left side of his chest, closing her ears to his groans and glad when he passed out completely. She found a small vial of whiskey in his parfleche and poured

94

some into the wound, then wrapped it with strips from her own slips. There was nothing she could do now but sit and wait and hope he would not die on her, for he was her only hope of finding her way back to civilization.

She took his hand as he called for the woman named Abbie again. Whoever the woman was, she was very important to this man. It must be his wife, for he had mentioned he had a wife and children. She wondered at the fine scar on his left cheek, and the many scars on his chest. The one at his side looked like an old bullet wound, but those at his breasts and upper arms were odd. She had heard tales of Indian rituals, wherein young men had skewers pierced through their flesh from which they hung until the flesh was torn from their bodies. It was some kind of test of manhood, and a means of contacting the spirits and finding one's true self. Had this man participated in such a ritual? Perhaps that was where the scars had come from.

She shuddered. She had come to Santa Fe with her preacher/doctor father to help him in his work. One of their missions was to convert the savage Indians to Christianity. Now as she watched this man and had seen how savage he truly could be, she wondered how easy it would be to make such men live the gentle life of the whites.

He held her hand tightly, and with her other hand she gently dabbed at his perspiring forehead with a cool cloth, worried that he was sweating in spite of the cold night air. No matter how hot the days were in this country, the nights were always cold, with no foliage to catch and hold the heat. She could feel an urgency about the way he held her hand, and she tried to ignore her sudden curiosity about what it would be like being married to such a powerful and savage man. What would his lovemaking be like?

She shook away the thought, actually reddening. Never had she seen a man built as this one was, nor one as skilled as he apparently was with weapons. Women back East would often whisper and giggle about Indian men and other "wild mountain men" of the West, secretly wondering what such men were like with their women and supposing they were brutal and cruel.

But she sensed this man was not cruel to his wife, or squaw, whatever she was. There was such love in his voice when he called out for her, such need in the grip on her hand. But it was not her place to wonder about him physically, for she was a Christian girl who had never even known a man yet, even though she was already twenty-five years old. There had been little time for men in her life, for her mission had been that of her father—to carry the word of God to new frontiers. Soon, though, she would be married, if she could ever get back to Santa Fe. Rodney would be on his way West now, headed for a new settlement in Indian territory north of Fort Laramie, where she had been headed to meet him when her stagecoach was attacked by outlaws. Rodney would not even know yet that anything had gone wrong, but her father must know by now and would be sick with worry.

Her thoughts turned again to Rodney, her intended. It had been understood from childhood that she and Rodney would marry. But sometimes she wondered vaguely if there wasn't supposed to be some kind of excitement and fire when he touched her. There was none. Their relationship was simply "proper." Rodney had finished his schooling in ministry now. He would come West and they would marry and work among the Northern Cheyenne and the Sioux in Nebraska Territory along the North Platte River, if she ever reached the new settlement. But as she watched this Indian man who had rescued her, she felt a strange emptiness, as though she had missed out on something in life, and she knew secretly that here lay a kind of man that Rodney could never be. She had had secret doubts about Rodney for several months, but was too shy to voice them. Now the presence of this Indian man somehow brought the doubts forward again. Again she had to shake off her "sinful" thoughts, and she surmised that this man most certainly was not Christian, for being around him brought the devil to her heart and made her think thoughts that were all wrong.

He whispered the name Abbie again, gripping her hand tightly, his mind floating in and out of consciousness because of the great loss of blood. She was sure the wound was not fatal, but it would take a day or two for his body to build up its fluids again. She reached over for a canteen and uncorked the opening, bending over him and gently lifting his head to force more water into his mouth. It was important that he have a lot of water.

He coughed and choked.

"It's all right," she told him gently. She wiped off his face again.

"Don't go away, Abbie girl," he moaned.

She studied the handsome face, its high cheekbones and the finely chiseled lips and prominent nose. He was much cleaner than she had pictured Indian men. She had seen many, but never had she been so close to one. His long black hair was silky and shiny.

"I'm right here," she answered, hoping if he thought she was Abbie it would help him through this crisis. He shivered more, and she tucked the blankets around him again, but it didn't seem to help. She knew that logically she should lie down beside him under the blankets to help keep him warm, but her puritan mind told her to do such a thing for an Indian man would be wrong. To lie beside any man who was not her husband was wrong, no matter what the reason. Yet this man had saved her from a fate worse than death, and had risked his own life doing it. She owed him.

She added the blanket around her own shoulders to those that covered him, then put more wood on the fire that burned nearby for warmth. Then she got under the blankets beside him, pulling them back around his neck and lying half on top of him, with one arm under his neck and the other around his chest. She rubbed at his arm and breathed her warm breath against his neck, whispering to him that he would be all right.

His shaking lessened, and soon his breathing seemed more rhythmic. She rested her face against his neck, and felt a strange warmth at his earthy, masculine scent. She was soon asleep herself. She was not afraid of him anymore.

Six

A lizard slithered silently past Zeke's cheek, its tail scattering a whisper of air against his skin. Zeke blinked open his eyes and stared up at the sky, the rising sun making it glow orange. He was immediately aware of the weight on his right side and warm breath against his neck.

He lay perfectly still, waiting for his fuzzy mind to clear, trying to gather his thoughts and decipher who in the world could be lying so close to him. It surely was not Abbie, for his first memory was that he had gone away from home for something. He closed his eyes, and the memory of the flash of a gun came to him, followed by a sharp pain in his upper left chest, and then the feeling of his body hitting the dirt.

There was a face—a man's—telling him how to find Lady Z. He strained to remember the words. Gila. The man had told him of a place called Gila, where the Canadian and Mora Rivers met below the Sangre de Cristo Mountains. Now he could see his knife, remembered plunging it into the man and then walking toward someone—a woman—a captive.

His eyes blinked open again. The woman. He shifted his eyes to the right, then turned his head very slowly, making no sound. She lay there beside him fast asleep, her blond hair tangled and her lips puckered. She slept hard, and he surmised she had probably not slept since she had been taken captive from the stagecoach.

Again he thought of Abbie. If only this woman were she, for no one would be a more welcome sight. How he missed her! He studied the woman's face. She was not as young as Abbie, but she was a lovely woman, obvious even through the bruises and tear-stained dirt on her face. It felt strange to be lying so close to a strange woman. He had had many women before Abbie, but no others since, nor had he even desired any other. For Abbie was Abbie, and he needed nothing more.

But he must not think of Abbie now. He must think about his present situation. The sun was making its full appearance above the distant mountains to the east. It was obviously morning. Surely then a whole day had gone by! What had happened between then and now? He was still confused.

He turned his face away and bent his left arm to rub at his eyes, but a fierce ache hit his left shoulder and he grunted from the pain. The woman started awake at the sound and movement. She gasped and sat bolt upright, embarrassed that she had fallen asleep and slept close to him all night. She was flustered and confused at first. She put a hand to her forehead and blinked, part of her torn dress falling open again to expose one breast before she realized her bearings.

Zeke had turned at the movement and their eyes held briefly, neither of them certain of the other. Zeke knew if he frightened her she might shoot him before asking questions. His eyes briefly caught sight of her breast and he looked away, rubbing at his eyes and moaning as the pain shot through him again. She realized her condition then, and she turned crimson, grabbing a blanket and putting it around her shoulders. She scooted back from him and hunched over, watching him silently, now unsure of him since he had regained consciousness and had seen her.

Zeke looked at her again and saw her eyes shift to his rifle, which lay next to his gear on the other side of the campfire. His knife was also there. He raised up with much effort onto his right elbow, prepared to dive for the rifle in spite of his pain if she made a move for it, realizing the terror she must have experienced with the outlaws and the present terror she must feel knowing she was still at the mercy of a total stranger, a man who must surely look to her to be nothing but a "savage Indian."

"It's all right, ma'am," he told her quickly. "I'm not

99

going to hurt you."

She turned wide, frightened eyes back to meet his, and he could see her trembling visibly.

"Please . . . you're telling the truth?" she asked in a shaking voice. "I . . . want to trust you, but . . . those men . . . those awful men!" She burst into tears and hung her head, hunching over more and rocking. He grunted with pain and his head swam as he sat up straighter. He forced himself to scoot closer to her, reaching out and grasping one of her arms as firmly as he could in his weak condition.

She stiffened and looked at him with terrified, tear-filled eyes. "Look, ma'am," he told her gently, "if I had wanted to abuse you, I'd have ridden down there and joined up with those men. Why would I have risked my life just to go down there and get a woman? I could have had you the easy way."

She reddened again, but he could feel her trembling begin to vanish. Her rapid breathing calmed and she sniffed and blinked. "I . . . never thought of it . . . that way," she answered.

He forced a smile for her, ignoring his pain to try to comfort her. She was struck by his handsomeness when he smiled and felt even more at ease. "Well think on it," he told her. "I came out here searching for my own sister-in-law, who was stolen by those same kind of men. My name is Zeke—Zeke Monroe. And I'm not all Indian, just half—Cheyenne."

She sniffed and put a hand over his. "I'm . . . sorry. But, the last few days—" Her voice choked again.

"I know, ma'am. Are you all right? I mean, did they hurt you bad, or rape you?"

She reddened again at his forthrightness, supposing such things must come naturally to a man of the wilderness. She lowered her head. "No," she replied quietly. "I'm just . . . bruised up . . . tired. They were . . . saving me."

"Did they mention someone called the Lady Z?"

She looked at him again. "Yes. But . . . how did you know? Who is she?"

His eyes hardened. "It's a long story. But I'm looking for her."

He squinted with pain again, and she took his arm, forgetting her own desperation and urging him back to his blanket. "You lost a lot of blood, Mr. Monroe. You must lie back down."

"I'm all right. We should get going."

"No. Not today. Perhaps tomorrow. You lost far too much blood. You won't ride a hundred yards without falling off your horse. Now lie back down here."

"How long was I out?" he asked, suddenly deciding she was right. Everything was swirling around him.

"All yesterday afternoon and most of the night," she replied. He lay back down and she rose to search for more wood, his wounded condition prompting her to ignore her own recent terror and take care of matters at hand. "The wound wasn't that bad," she continued. She stopped to wipe at her eyes again. "It was the loss of blood that made you pass out. The bullet must have hit an artery. I had a terrible time stopping the bleeding, I'm afraid I used up most of my slips on you."

He looked down at himself, glimpsing the white strips she had wrapped around his chest and shoulder. He was shirtless, and his bandages were wrapped in a professional manner.

"You took the bullet out yourself?" he asked in surprise.

"My father is a doctor, Mr. Monroe, and I am a nurse. I have helped him with operations many times. I must say, that is quite a knife you have. I think it would cut a leather saddle like it was butter." She turned to meet his eyes. "Have you killed many men with it?"

He grinned a little. "Many. All of them deserved it."

She threw what pieces of wood she could find on the old coals and stirred them. "It is not our place to judge and execute, Mr. Monroe."

He frowned and studied her. "You saying I shouldn't have killed those men yesterday? I should have let them abuse you and just sat there and watched?"

She blushed again and kept poking at the fire. "In that case, I believe God sent you to do His will. You were the answer to my prayers for help, and it was His will that you

101

kill those men. 'God moves in mysterious ways, His wonders to perform.' That's a saying among us Christians, Mr. Monroe. I don't suppose you are Christian."

She turned to face him and he met her eyes steadily. "I don't suppose I am. A man's religion is kind of a personal thing, ma'am. You talk like a preacher."

She smiled softly. "I didn't mean to be rude. But in a sense I guess I am a preacher. I am a missionary, Mr. Monroe. So is my father. He works with Mexicans and Indians in Santa Fe." She turned back to the fire. "And if you're wondering how I survived my attack, it was through my faith. As far as being able to make a camp here and remove your bullet and all, I am a survivor, Mr. Monroe. I learned a lot about these things on our trip out here. I'm not quite so pampered as most white women." A small flame flickered and the fire took hold.

"You still haven't told me your name," he told her.

She tucked her skirt under her knees and knelt near the fire, meeting his eyes again. "My name is Bonita Beaker, but you may call me Bonnie. My father is Conrad Beaker, a Methodist minister. We've been in Santa Fe for three years now."

He rubbed at his left shoulder. "How did you end up out here with those outlaws? I came across an abandoned stagecoach when I was tracking those men. Were you on it?"

She looked back at the canyon far in the distance, where the five men he had killed without feeling still lay dead. She could see buzzards circling far off, and she felt a chill. When she looked back at him, she found it hard to believe the handsome man with such gentle eyes who lay there wounded was the same man who had done all the killing.

"Yes. I was on my way north, to a settlement north of Fort Laramie, in Nebraska Territory, to meet my betrothed. We were to be married there. He has just finished his schooling in the ministry and is on his way out here. Those awful men attacked my coach, killed the others without hesitation and robbed them of all money and jewelry and. . . ." She shuddered. "They took me away with them. I've never been so humiliated and terrified in my life." She shook her head. "My father will be beside himself when he discovers what happened. I must get back to him as soon as possible. He'll be sick with worry."

"Soon as I can stay on a horse I'll see you get back."

Their eyes held. "I'm very grateful, Mr. Monroe."

His eyes took in her face and dropped over the rest of her body, creating a stir in her she had never felt before. He met her eyes again, and she was blushing.

"Why is such a pretty woman as you just now marrying?" he asked her with the handsome grin. "Out here a woman usually marries at fourteen or fifteen, sometimes younger."

Her eyebrows arched and her heart was strangely stirred when he said she was pretty. "Our work and our education had to come first, Mr. Monroe," she replied, sounding unsure of the statement. "However, I thank you . . . for making certain that I . . . I will belong only to my husband when our marriage does occur," she added. "I'm not at all sure he'd have understood if . . . if those men had violated me."

He closed his eyes again, wishing his dizziness would go away. "No real man would blame a woman for that," he remarked.

She stiffened defensively. "Rodney Lewis is a good man—a man who believes in right and wrong!" she replied, surprising him with her sudden defensiveness. "All of us have our ideas of good and bad, Mr. Monroe. And as far as my not marrying yet, that is my choice. If a squaw thinks it is right to marry at a young age and without Christian blessing, then I suppose in her mind it is right. We are here to teach what we know as right, to teach Indian women that there is more to life than just giving herself to a man as soon as her body tells her she is ready to bear children!"

She reddened more, suddenly nervous and perspiring, and he watched her curiously.

"I'm sorry, Miss Beaker. You believe your way and I believe mine. I always thought giving her man children was one of the most beautiful and loving things a woman could do for him. And I ought to tell you I'm not married to an

103

Indian woman. My own wife is white—white as you—and she's as Christian as you, and the best woman this side of the Mississippi. She's given me three children and is carrying the fourth. She was fifteen when I made her mine, and if you knew the hell she'd been through you'd understand why she married so young—why she needed me—and why I love her for it."

She caught the defensiveness in his own voice, and their eyes held again, his dark ones making her feel hypnotized. So, it was true. Of course. Abbie was a white woman's name.

She remained speechless as his own eyes were fired at the moment with a mixture of love and loyalty and a challenging look that she should suggest Abbie had done wrong. Then he sat up again. His broad, dark shoulders glistened in the morning sunlight, his biceps hard and rounded without even being flexed, his hair hanging nearly to his waist. She was suddenly jealous of his mysterious wife, for again she felt an attraction to this man she had never felt before, certainly not for Rodney. And that was the hell of it. She knew that was why she had so quickly jumped to Rodney's defense.

"I'm sorry, Mr. Monroe," she told him. "I . . . I'm not myself." She looked down at her lap. "I truly am sorry. Life is so . . . different . . . out here. And I've been through so much these last three days. I didn't mean to insult your wife."

He sighed and managed to struggle to his feet.

"Please, Mr. Monroe, you shouldn't be up."

"I have to go tend to something personal, Miss Beaker," he said rather sarcastically. "There's some jerky in my parfleche—and some pemmican." He staggered slightly. "Pemmican is Indian food, in case you don't know that. It's quite good. My wife makes some of the best. We'd best try to eat."

He stumbled off to a large boulder and walked behind it, and she blinked back tears as she walked over to his supply pack and searched for the food amid the many items in the large parfleche. She pulled out two blue ribbons that were tied into bows. She sniffed at them, and caught the scent of sweet perfume. Surely they belonged to his wife, and it was touching to know he carried them around.

She quickly put back the ribbons when she heard him returning, and she pulled out a leather pouch, opening it to see there were strips of jerky inside. Zeke half fell to the blanket and she hurried to his side, noticing a stain on the strips of cloth around his wound.

"I can't emphasize enough that you must lie still the rest of the day, Mr. Monroe," she told him. "You'll reopen the wound. And you must drink lots and lots of water to replace the liquids you have lost."

"Sure," he mumbled, lying back down.

She put a blanket over him. "Please forgive me, Mr. Monroe. I am truly ashamed. You risked your life for me yesterday and saved me from something worse than death would have been. I will never be able to repay you. My father will also be very grateful to you."

"Call me Zeke. Mr. Monroe doesn't sound right to me."

"And you must stop calling me Miss Beaker. I already told you to call me Bonnie," she replied with a smile.

He grinned back at her, and she was relieved to see that he had seemed to lose his initial angry feelings at her earlier remarks. "I thank you for taking out that bullet and stopping the bleeding, Bonnie. I saved your life, and you saved mine. We're even. And you're a good doctor, by the way."

"I hardly consider us even, Mr.—I mean, Zeke. You still have to lead me out of here and get me to Santa Fe. I will still be in debt to you. And what you've already done is much more than I did for you. You risked your life doing it."

"No risk involved when I'm angry, Bonnie. Between my temper and my knife, men don't generally escape me."

She leaned over to check the bandages and his power and masculinity seemed to radiate from the bronze body. She felt the sudden warmth again, and she moved away from him. "I think it's all right. I'll prepare something for you to eat," she said quietly. "Do you have coffee?"

"In that other parfleche over there," he replied. "By the way, my wife did all the beadwork on that one. Pretty,

105

isn't it?"

She reached over and picked it up. "Yes. It's lovely." She looked over at him. "Her name is Abbie?"

He frowned. "How did you know?"

"You called out for her when you were in pain." She fingered the beadwork. "How did your wife come to learn to do all these things?" she asked.

"Lived with the Cheyenne for a long time. We didn't have a regular house till just a couple of years ago. Lived in a tipi. Abbie knew we'd have to live with or near my people when she agreed to stay with me. I was married once before to a white woman back in Tennessee, when I was very young." He looked away. "I've seen how whites treat a half-breed, and any white woman who would marry one," he added coldly. "I can't bear the thought of Abbie being insulted that way—hurt that way—maybe even killed, like my first wife was. So we stayed out here with the Cheyenne. That's all the family my Abbie has now. Hers was killed on the wagon train Abbie came West on. I guess if they hadn't been, I'd have let her go on to Oregon and tried to forget her. But then there she was, alone and scared, with nobody. I tried like hell to—" He stopped and shrugged. "Let's just say she never got to Oregon."

He sighed and she watched him closely. "I can see that you love her very much." She made the statement rather wistfully, then reddened when his eyes met hers, realizing he was a grown man and not unacquainted with women's romantic notions.

"I do," he replied, now smiling.

She dropped her eyes and handed him a piece of jerky; then took a tin kettle to the nearby stream that was close to drying up, grateful for the opportunity to turn away so he would not see her flustered state. She managed to trickle enough water into the kettle to brew some coffee. It would be bitter and full of grounds, but it would be coffee nonetheless.

"How is it that you speak such good English, Zeke?" she asked, wanting to change the subject. He swallowed some of the dried meat before replying.

106

"I was raised in Tennessee. My white father took me there when I was four, pulled me from the arms of my screaming, begging Cheyenne mother. I never forgot her face. Soon as I was old enough to make my own way, I came back out here to search for my mother. That was after my wife was killed and I felt like I didn't have anything left to live for except to find my Cheyenne family. I wasn't wanted by anybody in Tennessee, except the authorities—for murder."

His voice trailed off and she threw some grounds into the water. She would strain the coffee through some cloth when it was ready. She knew she should be apprehensive of this apparently violent man, yet she felt calm.

"You killed your first wife's murderers?" she asked hesitantly.

He did not reply right away, but stared into the distance with eyes that suddenly smoldered. "Very slowly," he answered bitterly. He bit off another piece of jerky with more than necessary force, and she could feel his tenseness.

"You're a strange man, Mr. Zeke Monroe. A murderer, and a man who helps stranded women. A savage and a man of gentleness. With Indian blood and white blood in your veins, life must be very difficult for you at times."

"Difficult is a mild word, ma'am. You don't know the half."

"I would like to know. I would like to understand. It might help me be better at my work."

He glanced at her. "I'm afraid, Miss Beaker, that it was 'proper Christians' like you who made my life miserable back in Tennessee; who didn't want me attending school with their precious, innocent children; who would only let me come to church if I sat in the back pews, and even then I was allowed to come only because they figured my 'heathen' soul needed saving. I never learned about real love, real spirituality, until I came out here among my People. They could teach you Christians a few things."

She bit into a piece of jerky herself. "Perhaps they could." She sighed and glanced around the small valley where they were camped. "Are we safe here, Zeke?"

107

His eyes darted to the surrounding cliffs and barren hills, where rock formations jutted upward in weird shapes, silently watching the two of them.

"I doubt it," he replied. "If we're lucky there's nobody around for miles. If there is anybody around, they're probably as bad as those I killed yesterday. You hand over my rifle and weapons and get some more rest yourself. We have a long ride ahead of us. Eat up and clean up. I have a couple of extra buckskin shirts rolled up in my pack there. You can cover yourself with one. It will be big, but it's better than trying to hang on to that blanket all the time."

She pulled the blanket closer around her, suddenly realizing that this wild, half-Indian man was the only living being who had looked upon her breasts. It gave her a strange feeling, as though she had somehow betrayed her Rodney.

"Thank you for the offer," she replied quietly. She turned away again, pretending to watch the pot over the fire. But she was stirred by his raw power and open attitude. He was most certainly the strangest answer to a prayer God had ever sent her, and she could not help thinking that there was some mysterious, unknown purpose for their meeting.

The Cheyenne warriors rode into the fort like the wild and free things that they were then, calling out their cries of victory and brandishing fresh Pawnee scalps. Whites at the fort scurried inside its walls as the painted ponies thundered forward and circled the stone walls of William Bent's new fort, recently constructed to the east of old Bent's Fort, near Hinta Nagi, the Big Timbers.

Abbie came out of her tipi, which was staked near the entrance to the fort. She did not join the traders and travelers who ran into the fort, for she was not afraid. She folded her arms and smiled at the sight of the free-spirited Cheyenne men, picturing Zeke among them and aching to see him. She suspected he would have been safer riding against the Pawnee than against Dancing Moon and her vicious men.

The horses dashed by her, kicking up dirt, and then to

her great joy she saw Swift Arrow, the eldest of Zeke's Cheyenne brothers. Now twenty-five, Swift Arrow had been living in the North with the Sioux since the signing of the Treaty of 1851.

Abbie's heart quickened with joy at the sight of Zeke's brother, for he reminded her of Zeke, and she felt a special closeness to him because he had been one of those who had taught her many things about the Cheyenne ways during her first year among the People. She started to call out to him, but his horse reared and he let out a bloodcurdling war whoop, raising a pole of scalps and laughing with his fellow warriors.

Swift Arrow was the most obstinate and warlike of Zeke's brothers, and since losing his young wife and son eight years earlier to white man's disease, he had refused to remarry, wanting nothing more but to be an excellent dog soldier, and carrying a dangerous grudge against whites in general. But the man had no hatred for Abigail, for he respected her worth as a woman and as a wife to his half-blood brother. Abigail Monroe was a rare white woman, who had an open heart and the ability to understand the Cheyenne way and to accept it. He had been the last to accept the white woman as a sister, yet he was the one most ready to rise to her defense now, for Abigail was "big medicine" among the Cheyenne. She had herself killed three Crow Indians with her father's booming Spencer Carbine, and she had suffered a Crow arrow wound, as well as having saved a little Cheyenne girl from drowning that first year Zeke brought her to the People as his wife.

Swift Arrow's horse whirled then, and at that moment he saw her, smiling and waving, calling out his name. His chest tightened, and he held back for a moment, watching her. Unknown to Abbie, there was more to the reason Swift Arrow now dwelled in the North, more than the excuse he gave that the Northern Cheyenne were more warlike and rebellious, and that he wanted to remain more free than the Southern Cheyenne had now become. Although Zeke and their father, Deer Slayer, knew of Swift Arrow's special feelings for Abbie, Abbie herself remained innocently oblivious of any such feelings, considering Swift Arrow as nothing more than a brother-in-law and a dear friend.

Swift Arrow saw Abigail as a white woman of rare quality, who spoke softly and was steadfastly loyal to her man; a brave woman, much like the best of the Cheyenne women. She even wore the tunics of the Cheyenne women, and when painted for ceremonies, her white skin was exceedingly lovely. But Abigail Monroe belonged to Cheyenne Zeke, loved him desperately and totally. She had not eyes or heart or desire for any other man. And so she would look upon Swift Arrow always as Zeke's brother, never seeing in his eyes the true reason he stayed far to the north so he did not have to be near her.

The man trotted his mount toward her then. How beautiful she had become! Prettier than he had remembered. He had not intended to see her, but had ridden south only to meet Black Elk's new wife and to see his father, for he had been gone a long time in the North and missed his father and friends along the Arkansas.

Swift Arrow's plan had been to ride to the fort first with the others, where they intended to hear of any news about the still unsigned treaty. He would then circle Zeke's ranch and hope to see his half-brother alone out in the pasture, then ride on to his father's village and visit Deer Slayer and meet Blue Bird Woman. But now Abbie was very unexpectedly standing there smiling, and he was struck by how she had become more beautiful with the years, her shape still slim, her face unchanged from the way she had looked when first he saw her as a girl of sixteen. Zeke must be very pleased with her, he was sure. He watched her with a mixture of joy for Zeke and an unspoken need of his own, for her belly was slightly swollen with child, and Swift Arrow remained a man without sons.

"Swift Arrow!" Abbie called out as he came close to her. She smiled more and reached up to him. "Swift Arrow, I was wondering if we would ever see you again! Why have you waited so long to come back south!"

He reached down and she took his hand. Their eyes held for a moment, and his jaw flexed in an effort not to appear too joyful at seeing her. "I have joined the Cheyenne dog soldiers in the North. We do much raiding, hunting. I . . . came home to see Deer Slayer. I have missed my father."

"And we have all missed you, Swift Arrow," she replied sincerely. "But—" Her smile faded. "You . . . have not been to the village?"

He frowned. "No. Is something wrong? Is it my father?"

She let go of his hand and stroked the mane of his horse. "Swift Arrow, it's . . . Red Eagle." More horses thundered by, and her voice was lost amid the war whoops and yelps. She glanced at the fresh scalps on the pole Swift Arrow had slung across his mount and she grimaced slightly. "Come inside the tipi, Swift Arrow. Deer Slayer has gone out to hunt a rabbit, and Little Rock has gone with him. Black Elk's new wife is out gathering berries with our daughter. Come inside where we can talk. Zeke and I have a third child, another daughter. She's asleep inside. Come and see her!" She pulled at his horse's bridle and led it closer to the tipi. "Where is Black Elk?" she asked him.

"He is a few days behind with another band. He came to the North and urged me to ride with him." His eyes scanned her again. "It was Black Elk who made me see I should come and see my father, for he is aging. And Black Elk wanted me to see his new wife. But . . . I do not understand. Why are you here? Where is Zeke?"

"That's what I have to tell you about," she replied, holding his eyes and looking worried. She sighed. "Blue Bird Woman will be disappointed that Black Elk is not with you, Swift Arrow."

"He will be along." He frowned. "What is this about Red Eagle? And Zeke? If you are going to tell me Red Eagle has been banished from the tribe, I already know this." He slung his right leg over the horse's back and slid down. "Black Elk told me what he did. He deserves banishment! He shamed us!"

He stood close to her then, and she smelled sweet as she touched his arm in pure innocence. "Swift Arrow, Red Eagle is . . . he's dead. He . . . shot himself."

111

The malice for his brother left his eyes and he went rigid, not wanting to show too much emotion in front of a woman. "When?" he asked quietly.

"About a month ago. Come inside, Swift Arrow." She started toward the tipi, and it was then she noticed he was limping.

"You're hurt!" she exclaimed, looking down at a long tear in his leggings at the right thigh. Dried blood showed itself.

"It is nothing," he murmured, continuing toward the tipi.

"No wound is nothing!" she said worriedly. "Have you treated it?"

"I am fine. A Pawnee got too close with his tomahawk. But he is dead now, and I have his scalp."

She opened the flap of the tipi and they entered. "If you haven't treated the wound, then it is not fine!" Abbie was scolding. "Get those leggings off and let me dress it this minute."

He grinned and shook his head at her concern, then removed his many weapons, deciding it would be pleasant to be treated by this woman he had missed so fiercely. He untied his leggings and removed them, feeling no hesitation at wearing only his loincloth in front of her. She was the wife of his brother. Besides, Cheyenne men often wore nothing more than a loincloth and apron on hot summer days.

Abbie had grown used to such uninhibited habits, and it was Zeke's own freedom around the body and sex that brought the pleasant warmth to their lovemaking. He had brought out her natural abandon by teaching her that bodies and the pleasure they brought were all a part of life, for the enjoyment of man and woman. Practicality of dress, open emotions, spontaneous sex between a man and his woman, all were parts of the Cheyenne life that were so often misunderstood by the outside world as being heathen, when they were simply a matter of being joyful and free.

She wet a rag with water that had already been heated for an herb tea, then knelt near Swift Arrow and began gently

112

washing dried blood from the wound. She did not see how his eyes watched her, taking in the thickness and sheen of her long, dark tresses that glowed just slightly red in certain light. He watched her delicate hands and studied the fine lines of her lovely face, and his memory was refreshed as to how easy it must have been for Cheyenne Zeke to want her, how necessary it was for Zeke to claim her so that no other man could have her.

She scowled and fussed over the ugly wound and mumbled about how foolish it was of him not to treat it. She reached for a bottle of whiskey to pour some of the firewater over the wound, but he caught her arm. "Tell me . . . about Red Eagle," he urged.

She sighed and set down the bottle of whiskey. "It is as I said, Swift Arrow. He's dead. I'm sorry."

"But how? Why did my brother go against the Spirits by taking his own life?"

She sat back and stared at the rag in her hands. "It was the whiskey, Swift Arrow. He got much worse when we left you two years ago up at Fort Laramie. The whiskey just seemed to . . . to take full control of him. He couldn't get up in the morning without it. He couldn't talk straight without it. He got lazy and cared little about his appearance. If not for others who brought food, Yellow Moon and Laughing Boy would have starved, because Red Eagle did no hunting. He did nothing at all but lie around and drink. He . . . he began beating Yellow Moon more often . . . sold everything they owned in trade for more whiskey. And as Black Elk probably told you, he got so drunk one night he went after another man's wife. It brought such shame to his warrior society that they voted to banish him."

Swift Arrow's eyes narrowed and his lips curled. "Red Eagle was a fool! I told him and told him to stay away from the white man's demon drink! It is good our mother did not live to see this!"

Abbie nodded and reached over to rinse out the cloth. "Sometimes he tried to stop, Swift Arrow," she answered, coming back and laying the wet cloth over the wound to soften more dried blood. "But his body seemed to crave it

113

so. He was unable to function without it. When he was banished, Yellow Moon had the choice of staying at the village, but . . . she was always so loyal to him." Her eyes teared. "Like the good wife she was . . . she went with him. And a couple of weeks later, we found Red Eagle at our door back at the ranch. He . . . cried and cried . . . and he told us . . . he'd traded Yellow Moon to some slave traders . . . for whiskey."

He sat up straighter. "No! Tell me this is not so!"

She squeezed her eyes shut and a tear slipped down her cheek. "I'm afraid it's true," she answered. "He . . . felt so bad he . . . he shot himself in the head. He told Zeke he wanted to do it as soon as he'd come out of his drunken stupor and realized what he'd done, but he wanted to come back first to ask Zeke . . . to ask Zeke to try to find Yellow Moon and Laughing Boy. Both were taken, Swift Arrow. And the worst part is we . . . we think it's Dancing Moon who has them."

A heavy silence hung inside the dwelling while she wiped at her eyes. "Dancing Moon!" Swift Arrow suddenly hissed in surprise. "She is . . . alive?"

Abbie pressed her lips tightly together and sniffed. "Red Eagle heard the outlaws talking about her. Only now she is called Lady Z. We're sure it's the same woman. Somehow she survived after Zeke left her to die. The men talked of an Arapaho woman with the letter Z carved in her face. There is no doubt who it is. She has apparently become . . . some kind of leader of outlaws . . . raiders who steal horses and money . . . and worst of all, women and children."

She could not stop her tears, for she had forced herself not to think about Zeke out there searching for the wicked Dancing Moon and her vicious men. But now the reality of it overwhelmed her. He had been gone a month, and she had no way of knowing if he was all right. Swift Arrow reached out and touched her shoulder, wishing he could somehow comfort her, but not daring to hold her for fear she would suspect his feelings.

"Zeke . . . he has gone to find Yellow Moon and Laugh-

114

ing Boy?" he asked gently.

She nodded. "That's why I'm here at the fort," she replied, wiping at her tears with the back of her hand. She breathed deeply to control her crying. "He . . . doesn't want me to be alone at the ranch." She sniffed and met his eyes, taking another deep breath. "He's afraid that when Lady Z realizes it is Yellow Moon, Red Eagle's woman, she has captured, she will suspect Zeke himself might come looking for her. That would mean he is away from me. He thinks she might send men, or come herself, to try to find me and kill me. Besides that, there is always the worry of Comanche raiders and other white outlaws." She tried to smile. "I must say life certainly has not been boring out here, Swift Arrow." She sniffed again and lifted the cloth from his wound. "Mr. Bent and other men here at the fort who know Zeke well are keeping an eye out for me. And Deer Slayer and Blue Bird Woman came here to be with me also. Our good friend, Dooley, is at the ranch with part of the herd. Some of the horses are right here at the fort, with men here tending them."

Swift Arrow reached out and took her hand. "It is best you are here. Zeke was right."

Their eyes held. How good it was to see this man who looked so much like Zeke and who was such a good friend. "Will you stay, Swift Arrow? Camp here at the fort for a while? We were such good friends before you left. And we have many things to talk about. I want to know what life has been like in the North with the Sioux. And you must see Little Rock. He's all Cheyenne, and he remembers the many things his dog soldier uncle, Swift Arrow, taught him. You won't believe how he's grown! And he talks about you all the time. And little Blue Sky is so much bigger. She's so beautiful, Swift Arrow. And look!" She reached over and pulled the blanket away from Young Girl's blond curls.

Swift Arrow's eyebrows arched. He had not even realized a child slept there beneath the robe, she was so small. "Who is this?" he exclaimed.

"This is Young Girl," Abbie answered. "She is our third child. And I carry a fourth. I am hoping for a second son

115

for Zeke."

Swift Arrow reached out and lightly touched the blond curls with his dark hand. "This one will bring you heartache," he said, almost as an omen. Abbie felt a chill. "No one will believe she belongs to Zeke. How strange that he should have such a child."

Abbie shook off the eerie feeling his statement gave her. "She will look like my mother and my older sister. They had light hair, and they were much prettier than I."

His dark eyes studied her face and hair while she watched her child. "I do not think that is true," he told her quietly. "Zeke picked the prettiest."

She met his eyes and blushed. His eyes dropped to her swollen belly, and she put a hand over it bashfully. Swift Arrow smiled. "So, it is still good between my brother and his white woman," he commented.

Abbie smiled and reached over to rinse the cloth again. "We are very happy, in spite of all the hardships and dangers we've suffered out here," she replied. "Zeke works hard on the ranch, but I feel badly for him sometimes. I know he's just doing it for me, to give me a settled life. He'd rather be out riding with his brothers against the Pawnee." She reached for the whiskey bottle, and he put a hand on her arm. She looked up at him.

"I will stay," he told her. "For a little while. Besides, I want to see Zeke again, so I must wait until he gets back. If I leave, I will not sleep well knowing you are here without your man. Zeke is my brother. It is my duty. I will watch over you, as I did those many years ago when first you came to our village and Zeke had to go away."

She smiled teasingly. "You wanted nothing to do with me then, as I remember. I was a soft, simpering white woman, or so you said. Something like that."

He chuckled. "I was wrong. You proved yourself as good as any Cheyenne squaw."

She uncorked the whiskey bottle. "Well, now I am going to get back at you for some of the insults you handed me back then," she told him, suddenly dousing his wound with the firewater. He jerked and grunted, but did not cry out.

116

He shook his head and grinned.

"I did not know you could be so mean," he joked.

"I can be as mean as necessary," she answered. She reached for a stone bowl that held bear grease and dipped her fingers into the smelly substance that was the Indians' most used remedy for superficial wounds. She began gently applying the grease, and his heart swelled at the touch of her hand on his skin.

"I have always remembered what you taught me, Swift Arrow," she was saying, "about being one with the earth and sky; thinking in unison with the wild things; to feel the earth breathe. You did more than help me understand Zeke. You helped me understand life itself, the meaning of existence, the simple things that make life joyful."

He looked at her strangely, as though to say something, but his lips did not speak. He leaned away from her and rested on his elbow.

"Wrap my wound quickly if you think it needs it," he finally spoke up quietly. "I wish to go and find Deer Slayer and talk about Red Eagle. Soon I will go and see his scaffold. I shall sacrifice my flesh and perhaps help his spirit along Ekutsihimmiyo. Then I wish to visit Hinta Nagi. I miss the old places."

She reached for some cotton wrappings in a parfleche that hung near her. "I am afraid some day soon many of the old places will be forbidden to the People, Swift Arrow. They don't know just what is supposed to be theirs and what is not. The treaty still has not been ratified, and the People are getting restless and angry."

He watched her quietly as she began wrapping his thigh and waited several seconds before he spoke. "I smell death in the air, Abigail," he finally said sadly. His usual proud and arrogant air was suddenly gone. "I . . . saw something when we were out raiding the Pawnee. It frightened me. It was the first time I have ever been truly frightened. I would rather face a whole tribe of Crow or Pawnee or Utes than to see what I saw."

She frowned and stopped wrapping his thigh for the moment, studying the strange fear and sadness on his face.

117

She had never seen him look that way.

"Our human enemies are something we can touch," he was saying, staring at the earthen floor of the tipi. "They are something I can fight and defeat. But what I saw was something much more dangerous than our human enemies."

She sat back slightly, hanging on to the cotton stripping she had been wrapping his thigh with, letting it hang loosely for a moment. "I can't imagine anything frightening you, Swift Arrow," she said with concern. "What was it you saw?"

He met her eyes, his jaw flexing in an effort to control his emotions, and for the first time she saw a trace of tears in Swift Arrow's eyes. "I saw . . . a buffalo," he replied, struggling for the words. "It had been shot." He swallowed and breathed deeply. Then he looked away again. "It was so strange. Only the hide was taken," he said gruffly. "Only the hide! The bones, the meat, the fat, the blood, the hooves, the horns, the great shaggy fur of its head, the tongue . . . everything was left to rot! Everything!" He picked up a stick Blue Sky had brought in earlier to play with, and he angrily snapped it. "No Indian tribe . . . of any kind . . . would do such a thing! Not any! It is a bad omen. A bad omen!" His head jerked around to face her own stunned look. "If the white man destroys the buffalo, all of us die, Abigail! *All* of us! There will not be a red man left to walk this land if we lose the buffalo!" His teeth were gritted in anger. "Everything we wear, everything we eat, sleep on, hunt with, cook in, get shelter from—everything comes from the sacred buffalo! And there lay one out there, rotting on the prairie! Wasted!" He closed his eyes and breathed deeply, resting back on his elbow again.

"I'm . . . sorry," she said quietly, her own heart aching at the frightful future such a thing projected for the Indian. "But surely it was just . . . just one man's foolishness. There are so many buffalo—thousands—maybe millions. Surely no amount of men could kill them all."

He grunted and waved her off. "Now you talk like a foolish woman. Already the white settlers have slaughtered many for their own use, and more have scattered to places

118

where we cannot find them. You have seen how some of us are beginning to starve already. You have seen it with your own eyes! It is bad enough that the whites kill them for their own survival, but to kill one and take only the hide!" He literally shivered. "It was an omen. I am sure of it. It is only a beginning," he groaned. "I feel it in my bones. Just as what happened to Red Eagle is also a warning of the things that will happen to us because of the white man. His diseases have taken half our people, and now this! We are doomed. Doomed to be scattered to the winds!"

"Stop it, Swift Arrow!" she wispered, looking down at her lap and squeezing her eyes shut against her own tears. "I can't bear the thought of it!"

He threw the stick. "Swift Arrow is ready to fight it! I and the others are vowed to do everything we can to stop the rape of our land and the useless slaughter of the wild things! If we have to kill white men, then we have to kill them. We will fight to our last breath to keep what belongs to us! That is why I ride with my brothers to the North, who still have fight in their blood and do not always talk of peace like the Southern Cheyenne do!"

"Swift Arrow, there is much danger in the way you talk," she pleaded, a tear spilling down her cheek as she looked up at him again.

"Do you think I care about danger?" He tossed his head. Tiny beads woven neatly into two thin sections braided over the rest of his long hair made a clicking sound. "Swift Arrow welcomes danger. I spit on the day the first white man ever came across the great river!"

Their eyes held, and he found himself reaching out to gently touch her hair. "Except for you," he added, suddenly softening. "If all were like Cheyenne Zeke's woman, there would be no problems for us."

She took his hand. "It will be all right, Swift Arrow. And no matter what happens, Zeke and I will be with the People. My first allegiance is to the Cheyenne, not to my own kind. Whenever men have been cruel to me, they have been white men. And it was white men who tortured and killed Zeke's first wife in Tennessee. We know, Swift Arrow. Our hearts

119

lie here, with the People."

He nodded, then suddenly hardened slightly again, his eyes widening as though startled, and he jerked away his hand.

"Finish your wrapping," he told her. "Tonight at this fort there will be a great scalp dance! You will come to the celebration?"

She smiled for him. "I will come. But only if you let me finish wrapping this wound and promise me you'll leave these wrappings on for a few days."

He grinned then, some of his anger fading. "Bring Zeke's son. I have not seen my little warrior nephew in many moons. I will teach him about the scalp dance. Is he a brave and good boy? A true Cheyenne?"

Her smile faded slightly. "Yes, he is, Swift Arrow. He is all Cheyenne." Her heart pained, for if a sad destiny awaited the Cheyenne and other red men, then it also awaited her son, for he would surely ride as a Cheyenne until his dying day.

Outside drums began to beat, and already the braves were pounding feet rhythmically, celebrating victories over the Pawnee. Bells jingled amid chanting voices, while scalps were displayed for all to see. They seemed a people born to war, and if those wars were only with enemy tribes, perhaps it would be more bearable. But she feared a much more dangerous war—the one against whites. Few, if any of them, understood just how many whites there really were east of the "great river"; nor did they understand the powerful weapons the whites could bring against them. She forced the thought to the back of her mind and continued with wrapping his wound. This was today, and today Zeke's brother had returned to the Arkansas. She had learned to take one day at a time, for to do otherwise would be too much to bear.

Seven

Bonnie awoke to the sudden movement, to see Zeke viciously sink his huge blade into the head of a rattler. She gasped and scooted back as he plunged the knife twice more, then kicked the snake away. He stood there a moment, breathing rapidly and staring at the snake, muttering something in the Cheyenne tongue as though cursing. He bent down and quickly wiped blood from the knife onto some bunch grass, then slid the knife back into its sheath and whirled, his dark eyes gleaming frighteningly.

"The one called Lady Z once had me thrown into a pit of snakes!" he growled. "You speak of forgiveness and that men should not judge. But I do not understand such things. What I went through escaping that pit of hell will be in my mind forever. I do *not* forgive such things!"

He walked away and began gathering what remnants of wood could be found in the desolate area where they had rested. It had taken two days for him to feel strong enough to ride, but now as they rose with the morning sun, it was obvious he was anxious to be going.

Bonnie threw off her blanket and shivered, tightening the laces of the buckskin shirt she wore over her bodice. Again she felt the warm sensation of sweet desire at the masculine scent of the shirt he had given her to wear over her torn dress. It smelled of Zeke and man and leather and fresh air. Even though he was resting and healing while they were camped there, she knew he was also watching over her. Now there was proof in the dead snake. She had not known in her sleep that it was near, but Cheyenne Zeke had known.

121

She knelt down to stir the almost dead coals of the fire, then glanced over to where he stood staring out at the endless horizon ahead, a vast Texas wasteland dotted with strange rock formations. She wondered what he was thinking, and her heart tightened when she realized he was probably thinking about his wife; about the faceless Abbie whom he had called for when he was wounded. What kind of white woman had it taken to capture such a man? For he seemed as wild as a mustang, as stealthy as a preying wolf, and his skin was nearly as dark as that of his full-blood relatives. His black hair hung long and shiny in the morning sun that he now greeted, raising his arms and throwing back his head.

"Thank you, Maheo, for my life," she heard him say quietly. "Guard my family, and give me the strength I need to find Yellow Moon and to have my vengeance."

She wondered at the spirituality of the Indians she had known thus far. Even though they might be worshipping the wrong Gods, as she was convinced they were, she had to admit that their faith was strong, and some of the stories Zeke had told her of how he and other Cheyennes had been aided and their lives literally saved through prayer and through being true to rituals and restrictions had left a deep impression on her. Until their long talks over the past two days, she had not truly considered the viewpoint of the "heathen" Indians. But she was learning to appreciate their particular religion, and Cheyenne Zeke had patiently taught her about the many Spirits of the Cheyenne, the Arapaho, and the Sioux. He told her beautiful stories, about Mutsiluiv, Sweet Medicine, who in the beginning was given the Sacred Arrows by a supernatural being, and presented them to the Cheyenne. The Sacred Arrows were apparently a central object in the Cheyenne religion, and the ritual of the renewal of the arrows was a very special and somber occasion. He told her about Heammawihio, the Sky Spirit, and Maheo, the all-powerful one, who created the sun and all living things and placed his people on the Plains to live a simple and happy life, providing them with the buffalo, the only thing they needed for survival.

She had intended to talk to him more about her own God and His Son, but she found herself so fascinated by his stories, and the way he had of putting her under a kind of magic spell as he told them with his deep, mellow voice, that she had done more learning than teaching. He told her many Indian stories, about ghosts and monsters, stories that were often told inside tipis on cold winter days when the children could not play outside. And she saw through the telling that this sometimes wild and vicious man could be gentle and loving, and that surely he was a loving husband and father. Somehow she had not looked at Indians as having the same human feelings as whites. But she saw them differently now, and she was fighting her own all-too-human feeling of attraction to this forbidden man. He had a way of making her want him without even trying, and she knew that in his mind there were no such thoughts. But she could see how easily the white woman called Abbie could have been overwhelmed by this man of men.

He was walking back now with a few sticks of wood. She turned her eyes away from his long, muscular frame, the slim hips and broad shoulders, the handsome, high cheekbones and deep-set eyes. She was a white missionary, traveling north to meet her intended. She must control her thoughts and urges.

"We must ride soon, Bonnie," he told her, bending down and placing the wood on the fire. "I must get you back to Santa Fe so that I can go on to search for Yellow Moon and my nephew. We have little food left. If I see any kind of game as we ride I will try to get it with my knife. I don't want to use a gun if I don't have to. Out here a gunshot can be heard for miles, and might bring unwanted company. That's why I used my knife on that rattler."

"I see," she said quietly.

He watched her a moment. "Are you rested enough to ride?" he asked.

She met his eyes, and his face was close to hers. She nodded and looked down again, unable to look at him for too long. "Yes. I'm fine."

He put a hand on her shoulder and squeezed it lightly.

123

"I'll get you there safely. I know this country."

"What about Apaches?" she asked, nearly trembling at the touch of his hand on her.

He snickered. "I can handle the Apaches. And if we do run into any, or any suspicious-looking outlaws for that matter, go along with whatever I do or say, understand? I might have to be rough with you—make them think you're my woman or perhaps a woman I've paid for. If they think you're just an innocent woman I'm trying to rescue, they'll be more tempted to try to take you. Remember that."

She nodded, feeling a burning at her cheeks at the thought of being his woman. "I'll remember."

Lady Z strutted around the campfire, wearing a white satin dress one of her men had purchased for her in Santa Fe, as well as a ruby necklace and a fancy feathered hat. None of the items were designed to be worn together, and she wore no undergarments and no shoes. Her hair hung long and wild, making the fashionable hat appear ridiculous on her head.

"Now, do I not look as good as the white dance hall girls?" she bragged, her breasts billowing fetchingly over the satin ruffles.

"You look better than all of them put together," Nick Trapper answered.

All the men watched hungrily, eyeing the silken skin that looked even darker against the white dress. Even with the gawdy, unmatched clothes, the untamed hair and the scars in her cheeks, she was exceedingly beautiful, but it was an evil, threatening beauty, the kind that brought out a kind of lust that was difficult to control, and all of those watching her were wondering anxiously which of them would have the privilege of sleeping with their Arapaho leader that night.

She strutted up to Nick Trapper, her favorite because he was bigger than the others, and because he had once supervised a whorehouse and knew all the tricks and pleasantly exciting sexual cavorting of the white prostitutes. He had

124

taught her many new ways to enjoy a man, helping feed her voracious appetite for thrilling sexual encounters, including introducing her to the slave trade and to the pleasures of sometimes bedding her own female captives. That was something she had not contemplated but had found delightfully amusing, especially when the captives protested with tears and begging.

"You may take off my dress tonight, Nick Trapper," she purred. "For you brought me the Arapaho woman, and through her I was able to get my revenge against those Arapaho women who banished me from their villages."

She whirled and strutted again, her hands on her hips, her full lips smiling and revealing beautiful, even teeth.

"Them women was just jealous of your beauty, Lady Z," one of the other men spoke up. "You can't help it if their sons and husbands came sneakin' over to your tipi. I'd crawl a hundred miles to get between them long legs of yours and feel them wrapped around my middle."

She threw back her head and laughed. "Perhaps I should be one of those whores who gets paid!" she teased. "I would make much money, no?"

"You're making more money this way, Lady," Nick told her. "Give us your favors for free and we go find your slaves for you, as well as take the risks in gun smuggling and whiskey trading. There's a lot of gold stored away there in the cabin and more where that came from."

She sniffed and turned to him with a pout. "I am tired of this hiding in the mountains—tired of this stinking little canyon! I want to go someplace and live like a rich lady, in one of those fancy houses like the white people live in, or maybe a big *ranchero* down in Mexico."

"In time, Lady. In time. It won't be long before you'll have enough money to do just that. You don't understand how much it takes."

She kicked at a stone and ripped angrily at the expensive dress, tearing away part of the skirt to reveal a long, slender leg and most of one side of her naked hips. The men squirmed and stared, drinking in the long, voluptuous body, yet not daring to touch it without her permission. Others had tried and had been ordered whipped until they were dead.

"What good is a pretty dress when I cannot go out in public and wear it!" she fumed. She threw the torn piece of dress into the fire, then grabbed a bottle of whiskey from one of the men, completely unaffected by her partially exposed bottom. After all, she had slept with all of them at one time or another. "I think we have enough gold to split it all up and go have some fun!" she declared.

"I'd wait, Lady," Trapper warned. "These are good times for gun running and slave trade. So far there isn't enough law out here to stop us, and what's even better is we can dress ourselves like Indians and let them take the blame while we get richer. The Comanches and Kiowas and Apaches have been doing a lot of raiding. It's easy to make them look like the guilty ones. Let us keep this up a while longer, and we'll have more gold than we can spend."

She took another drink of whiskey. "I am bored." She turned to face Trapper again. "You took Yellow Moon to the whorehouse?"

He nodded. "I did. Got the gold right over there in my saddlebags. Took her to Anna Gale's place. Anna will fix her up real pretty, oil her down and all. She's a fair piece of woman. Anna will get a good price for her."

Lady Z grinned. "Yes. And I got my revenge when I touched her! She did not speak or move, but I saw the horror in her eyes," she sneered. "But the best is yet to come! Cheyenne Zeke has not yet tracked her here. But he will! And when he does, I shall have the sweetest revenge I have ever tasted!" She spat out the words through gritted teeth, her fists clenched. "I shall torture him first, weaken him! I shall make him *beg* me to let him go." She laughed again, strutting provocatively in the firelight, looking like an angel of Satan. "And I shall tell him the only way he will gain his freedom is to make love to me again, like in the old days." Her voice and eyes softened for a moment. But then she whirled, her eyes fiery. "And when I am through using his body, I shall have him castrated!" Her lips curled. "Then he will be a woman! And he will never again bed that white bitch he married!"

Her laughter echoed out into the night like a demon spirit of the darkness, and she strutted up closer to Nick Trapper. "You must all be careful of a tall, dark man with a scar on his cheek who might ask about the slave trade. Watch the shadows." She turned. "All of you—watch for him!"

"He won't come, Lady," Trapper replied. "Why should he risk his neck coming into outlaw country after one lone Arapaho woman?"

She turned back to face him. "You do not know him as I do. Perhaps he does not know I still live. Perhaps he only knows some outlaw slave traders stole her, for as you say, her husband was too drunk to hear you talk that night. But all Cheyenne Zeke needs to know is that his sister-in-law and nephew were stolen, and he will come searching."

Nick waved her off. "He wouldn't know where to begin. Besides, that Red Eagle probably died out there before he even got back home to tell anybody. No Cheyenne Zeke is going to show up."

She stared past him into the darkness. "He is a man of stubborn vengeance." She shivered and touched one of her scarred cheeks. "He will come. Cheyenne Zeke will come," she repeated. "And I do not intend to be under his knife again." She turned and moved her eyes around the circle of men. "That is why I keep so many of you with me at all times, and why I keep the guards at the top of the canyon. It is not soldiers or lawmen that I fear. It is Cheyenne Zeke. And yet I *want* him to come!"

"Relax, Lady," Nick assured her. "You're safe here."

She looked around at all of them and finally smiled again. "Of course I am! And tomorrow or the next day Boots and Charlie will show up with the Mexican gold from the stolen guns, no?" She laughed and tossed her head. "And maybe soon another captive will come to us who will bring much gold from the dealers in Mexico." She looked at Trapper. "I wish to ride again on another raid myself. I have not killed a man for a long time. I will lead the next raid."

"Fine, but it will be a couple of weeks or better. We'd best lay low for a while."

She scowled. "Then go to Santa Fe and find me a woman,

127

a willing woman. I need more than just you men to keep me busy. I want to have some fun while I am stuck here."

The men glanced at each other, amused by her odd sexual hunger. Nick leaned forward and kissed her bared thigh.

"Let me show you some fun tonight, my Arapaho woman, and then I'll go find a woman for you, if you promise to let me watch you with her."

She grinned and ran a hand through his thick, dark hair, excited by his size and his ruthlessness, and the fact that he wore nothing but black. She often teased him that his heart was as black as his appearance.

"I must be careful with you," she purred. "Or you will be the leader instead of Lady Z."

Nick grinned. "You'll always be the boss," he told her wisely, aware of how quickly she was capable of changing face and allowing her vengeful jealousy and her craving to be in command overtake her emotions. It was as easy for Lady Z to stick a knife in a man's gut as it was for her to make love to him. To Lady Z it was all the same.

Zeke led the big Appaloosa down an embankment, handling the horse with the expertise of a man who knew horses as well as he knew his own body. Rocks slid and skipped down the steep hill, but the steed remained sure-footed.

Bonnie sat straddled over the horse behind him, clinging to him with her arms about his slim waist, taking secret pleasure in the closeness, feeling sometimes a little lost behind the broad shoulders in front of her. It was odd that she could feel so uninhibited and free of all the social "do's" and "don't's" she had been raised on. But with Zeke she felt a sudden desire to abandon all prim and proper thoughts, and she smiled at how the ladies of her social circle would whisper and gasp if they saw her now, straddled behind a half-breed she barely knew, part of her legs showing from beneath her torn dress, her hair a tangled mess, her finger-nails torn and the creases of her knuckles stained from the smoky wood she handled making fires.

She knew that soon she would have to return to the old life, for it was right and fitting. But she liked to pretend it could be like this forever—this freedom and this pleasant feeling of being close to a man who was like one of nature's wild things, his long black hair sometimes brushing her face. She found herself wishing they would never get to Santa Fe. But then she would feel guilty and sinful, and in the night she would beg God to forgive her for her wanton thoughts. Not only was a man with Indian blood forbidden to proper white women, but this man already had a woman, and children. Never had her body ached for anyone more and never had she felt more ashamed of her thoughts; and the most painful realization was that Rodney had never made her feel like this man made her feel.

They reached the bottom of the escarpment; and suddenly, like ghosts, five Apache Indians appeared from behind rocks as though they had been mere vapors a moment before. Bonnie gasped and clung tighter to Zeke, who reined his horse to a halt and waited cautiously as the wily band of Mescaleros came closer, their dark eyes and haughty sneers daring Zeke to make one wrong move.

"Don't say a damned thing and don't act afraid," Zeke told Bonnie quietly.

The Apaches came close enough to reach out and touch, and Bonnie swallowed her fear as best she could. They wore next to nothing, only loincloths and moccasins. Bonepipe necklaces and breastplates adorned their dark-skinned chests, and their dull, coal-black hair hung straight and snarled. Their bare skin was covered with a light coating of desert dust, and although small in build, they were nonetheless fierce-looking and brought terror to Bonnie's heart. She had heard many horror stories about the Comanche and Apache, and now these five were looking at the whites of her legs that were exposed, as well as the array of weapons Zeke carried, and the fine horse that he rode.

Zeke began speaking to them in a mixture of their own tongue and sign language. The apparent leader of the five moved his horse forward, grinning. He motioned back to Zeke, eyeing Bonnie and the horse. Zeke shook his head vehemently, signing again and grasping Bonnie's thigh. She stiffened, but forced herself not to show shock, although she could not help the blush his touch brought to her face. He ran his hand over her leg, saying something more to the Apache and grinning. The Apache nodded. Then Zeke took his hand from her leg and patted his Appaloosa's neck. The horse tossed its head and snorted, while Zeke made more signs to the Apache. Then he removed one rifle and held it up in the air.

The Apache leader nodded and backed up his horse, saying something to his men.

"I told them you were my woman," Zeke said quietly to Bonnie. "That I stole you from some settlers and claimed you and that now you carry my child. I can only hope they respect the fact that you're my woman. They want the horse, though, and we'll die out here without it. I told them I would trade my horse and my rifle for one of their mounts if they leave my woman alone."

She clung more tightly to him, secretly relishing the thought of truly being his woman, loving him more now for his courage and his skill in dealing with these wild men of the New Mexico mountains. "Do you think it will work?" she asked quietly.

"Can't tell. Apaches have a habit of saying one thing and doing another."

The leader rode forward again, making more signs. Then he shook his head, eyeing Bonnie again.

"He doesn't believe a white woman would consent to staying with an Indian," Zeke said to Bonnie. "He wants you included in the trade—thinks I'm covering because you're worth a lot and I want to sell you myself."

"What will we do?" she whimpered.

Zeke grasped her thigh again and jerked his other arm in an outward motion, giving the Apache an absolute sign of "no deal." The leader came closer while the other four nudged their horses forward. It was obvious to Zeke that they planned to take what they wanted and there would be no more bargaining. But before any of them could gather their thoughts, Zeke's huge blade was removed from its

130

sheath and plunged with lightning speed into the breast of the leader, who had come close enough to be reached with Zeke's long arm. The startled Apache grunted and looked bug-eyed at Zeke, not having expected much resistance from one man against five. Zeke jerked out the knife and took advantage of the hesitation on the part of the other four, throwing the knife with easy accuracy into the heart of another one of them.

Bonnie screamed as two of the others removed hatchets from their mounts and headed for Zeke, who quickly knocked Bonnie from his horse and rode forward, ducking to the side of the big Appaloosa just as the two Apache men took a swing at him, both of them missing. Bonnie rolled and crawled out of the way, her heart pounding with fear for Zeke and for what would happen to her if the Apaches killed him, which they most surely would do.

Now Zeke was off his horse, rolling over to the Indian who lay on the ground with Zeke's knife still in his chest. Zeke deftly removed the knife and whirled to face the three Apaches, his knife in one hand and his hatchet in the other Now they came for him one at a time, all three of them dismounting and two of them charging over to Bonnie. She screamed as they grabbed her up, holding her arms with vicelike grips while the third man approached Zeke with his own knife and tomahawk.

Bonnie watched in wide-eyed fear as the two of them circled, Zeke now looking every bit as savage and hungry for blood as the Apache, his own skin as dark as the Apache's, his arms and shoulders too dusted with desert earth, for he wore only a vest because of the heat. His eyes gleamed and his teeth were gritted; and Bonnie thought of his wound, which was still wrapped and painful. Yet he seemed oblivious to the pain as he drew on some hidden power to rise above it and face his enemy.

The Apache swung with his hatchet and Zeke jumped back, bringing his own tomahawk down across the right shoulder blade of the Apache as the latter's arm had come around to strike. The Apache cried out, and Bonnie watched in frozen horror. Blood poured down the Apache's back, but

131

he faced Zeke again, seemingly unaffected by the wound, his eyes on fire for a victory. He jabbed forward with his knife, then swung again with his hatchet, but Zeke was agile and experienced, and his knowledge of Cheyenne hand-to-hand fighting made him alert to every probable move the Apache would make.

The Apache was panting now, frustrated and tiring from swinging and jabbing without hitting his target, and weakening from loss of blood. Zeke waited patiently, not caring to waste his energy. There would be a right moment, and it came when the Apache raised his hatchet and began to strike downward. Zeke swung out with his own tomahawk, smashing it into the Apache's raised arm, while at the same time plunging his big blade into the man's middle, ripping upward with the curved end of the blade. The movement was swift and accurately timed, and there was a sickening grunt from the Apache's lips, followed by blood that oozed from his mouth while his eyes bulged. Bonnie groaned and closed her eyes, turning her face away from the gruesome sight. The lower half of the Apache's right arm lay on the ground, his hatchet still gripped in the lifeless hand. The man managed to nick the skin at Zeke's side with the tip of his own knife before Zeke yanked his blade from the man's throat and jumped back. The Apache stared at him, trying to say something, but choking on his own blood. Then he went to his knees, still staring, until he finally fell forward and gave up his life, his eyes still open.

Zeke whirled and faced the remaining two men, who remained apprehensive for a moment. Then one of them left Bonnie's side, and she opened her eyes to see with terror that still another would challenge Zeke, who must by now be getting very tired. She saw a trickle of blood at his side, and her horror at his viciousness was replaced by the renewed fear for his own life. But then, as the next Apache approached Zeke, the one left holding her suddenly barked something at the other man, who stopped still and went no closer to Zeke. Then to Bonnie's surprise, the Apache backed away from Zeke, as Zeke watched guardedly, his arms held out in challenge, his straight, black hair blowing softly with the desert wind, looking to Bonnie as much a wild thing as a wolf or a bobcat. If she did not already know him, she would have been terrified at the vicious, menacing look on his face at that moment.

The Apache holding Bonnie spoke up again in his guttural tongue to the second man, then said something to Zeke. Zeke straightened and nodded. Then the Apache man gave Bonnie a shove and left her, going to his horse and growling something to the other man, who glared heatedly at Zeke for a moment before shoving his hatchet back into its holder and going to his own horse, apparently giving up the fight.

Bonnie watched in confusion as Zeke and the first man exchanged more words. Zeke walked over to his mount, again patting it. Then he picked up the rifle he had offered and held it out to the Apache who had stopped the fight. The man smiled and nodded. Zeke walked over to Bonnie, jerking her forward and putting one arm around her from behind, his arm firmly planted across her breasts. He grasped some of her hair in his other hand and repeated a word several times to the Apache man until he finally nodded. Zeke shoved Bonnie aside and began removing his gear from his horse.

"What . . . what are you doing?" she asked, reddening at the fact that he had touched her breasts.

"We're trading horses like I wanted to do in the first place," he replied quietly. "I convinced them to give me one of theirs in return so we can get to Santa Fe. Mine is a better horse, but we don't have a hell of a lot of room to bargain." He set his gear on the ground. "I had a run-in with some Apaches a few years back. At the time I proved myself with my knife. The one I've been talking with remembers. He was there. He respects me as a great warrior, and I'm not going to argue the issue. He says because of my skill and courage, you and I can go free, as long as I trade him my Appaloosa and give him the rifle. Considering the circumstances and the fact that they could call up a hundred more warriors if they wanted, I think we're getting off light. Be grateful. That God of yours is still watching over you."

She watched him lovingly, for he had just risked his life to save her again. "I'd say He was watching over you, too," she replied in a shaky voice. He glanced at her and grinned, then finished stripping his Appaloosa. He walked the animal to the Apaches, and the one who had stopped the fight handed him the reins to a horse that had belonged to one of his now dead comrades. He grasped the mane of Zeke's horse and jumped onto its back, giving out a war whoop of joy at his new mount. He grasped the rifle Zeke handed him and grinned at Zeke, then rode off, leading two of the riderless horses and followed by the second Apache, who led the fourth horse. Zeke stood beside the red mare they had left behind, watching them until they vanished into the myriad of rocks along the cliffs ahead of them, becoming ghosts once again.

Zeke proceeded to repack his gear onto the mare, acting as though none of it had happened, or if it had, as though it were an everyday occurrence. Bonnie watched in a kind of daze, wondering herself if any of it had really occurred; but there were three dead bodies lying in bloody heaps to remind her that it had indeed taken place. Zeke seemed not to notice them at all, as he took a large piece of the shaggy skin of a buffalo from one of his parfleches and began using it to rub off the dust from his skin, using it like a giant powder puff to clean himself as best he could in the absence of plentiful water. He said nothing as he used a little canteen water to rinse the superficial wound at his side, then proceeded with packing his gear.

"We'll have to move fast now," he was telling her, his back to her. "They'll send men back for the dead bodies, and we'd better not be here when they come."

She did not reply, and when he turned to look at her, her eyes were wide and her body trembling. He had been so involved with the fight and then getting away, that he had forgotten how traumatic the entire event must have been for her, for she had already been through torture and terror. She suddenly went to her knees, feeling faint from the heat and the realization of what could have happened to her if Zeke had not won the fight.

In the next moment Zeke was beside her, picking her up

in his strong arms and carrying her to the shade of a large, overhanging rock. He left her to go and get his canteen, returning with a piece of buckskin, which he dampened with the cool water and pressed against her forehead.

"It's all right, Bonnie," he told her quietly.

She opened her eyes to look into the face that bore the fine, white scar down his left cheek, the face of experience and a hard life, but one that had remained handsome, even with the fine lines from worry and living under the sun about his eyes.

"I was . . . so frightened!" she moaned.

"Just sit still for a minute with this cool rag on your head," he told her gently. "It's mostly just the heat that's got you. The Apache are gone now, but they may change their minds and come back for you after all. I've got to get you out of here."

She nodded, still shaking. He started to rise, but she grabbed his arm. He knelt back down as her eyes searched his pleadingly. "Hold me . . . for just a moment?" she beseeched him. "I feel like I'm going to fall into a hundred pieces!"

He sat down beside her but facing her, and he pulled her into his arms to comfort her. She collapsed into sobs of what he thought at first was relief; but she clung to him almost possessively, and he suddenly understood all too clearly the meaning behind the tears. His heart quickened with the sudden knowledge, for they had become good friends, and he did not want to hurt her or embarrass her.

He held her firmly to calm her, and she felt his strength flowing through her, but then he gently pushed her away. She looked up at him, and his eyes were gently apologizing, while hers were filled with the pain of unrequited love.

"I'm . . . sorry," she said, almost inaudibly, her face turning crimson.

He touched her hair. "Bonnie—"

She jerked away. "Dear God, I'm so sorry!" she repeated. "What must you think of me?" She put a hand to the side of her face, her eyes displaying her humiliation. "I didn't expect . . . I mean . . . I never meant . . . to reveal my feel-

135

ings. This . . . isn't like me!"

He sighed deeply and rose, feeling awkward and yet sorry for her. "Out here a woman can lose track of herself, Bonnie," he told her, hoping to make her feel more at ease. "When you're frightened and alone, you can't think straight. You tend to turn to anybody, feel dependent on them. It's all right, Bonnie."

She shook her head. "You're a married man, and I'm betrothed. And a missionary no less!" she choked out. "I've been . . . fighting my feelings for days, but I . . . I've been unable to ignore them.

He frowned and watched her as she turned away, and he suddenly wondered what Rodney Lewis was like. Surely he was not much of a man if he hadn't made this lovely woman his wife yet. It always amazed him how whites could put education and social amenities above love and honest emotion. It seemed they were always putting on a face for others and never being themselves. But not his Abbie. He suddenly ached for her open spirit and blatant passion. From the first day they had met on the wagon train when she was only fifteen, Abigail's feelings had been splattered all over her sweet, innocent face. She wanted Cheyenne Zeke to be the one to break her into womanhood, and he had obliged with no regrets.

"I'm . . . honored, Bonnie," he spoke up aloud. "I believe that a person should never make excuses for his or her feelings, whether it's love or hatred. Own up to them. They're there, and there is nothing can be done about it. You're a fine and honorable woman, and I'm flattered you'd have such feelings for a man like me." He turned toward the horse. "I'll get the mount," he added, not sure what else to say to her. "We've got to get going. It's too dangerous to stay around here."

She sniffed and nodded. He left to get the horse, returning moments later to come and stand close to her, where she still sat with her head hanging.

"No more crying, Bonnie Beaker," he told her sternly. "You cry any more and I'll think it's because you're ashamed you've got feelings for me just because I'm a half-

136

breed heathen, and not because I'm married and you're promised. We've hung around here too long and I don't aim to get caught and die now after all I've been through to get you this far. You've got a pa waiting for you in Santa Fe, and a future husband waiting up North." She wiped at her eyes again and he put out his hand. "Come on, Bonnie girl. Time to ride."

She took his hand and stood up, turning toward him, still keeping her head down. "It . . . has nothing to do . . . with you being a half-breed, or a heathen," she tried to explain. "I . . . I'd never have been ashamed of that."

"I know that," he answered softly. He took her chin and forced her to look up at him. "Don't think this alters your goodness and worth, Bonnie. Nobody but you and I needs to know." He smiled for her. "You do disturb a man, Miss Beaker. Rodney will be pleased with his wife." She sniffed and closed her eyes, blushing at the compliment and the realization that this wild man had been the first to see her and touch her. It was all so strange and unreal. "Don't ever be ashamed, Bonnie," he was telling her. "After a while this thing here will just be a memory, and you'll just shake your head about it and wonder what ever possessed you to care about this heathen. You'll see. You'll look back on all this as just something to tell your and Rodney's grandchildren about." She sniffed and tried to smile, and he took her hands and held them tightly. "Make me a promise, Bonnie, if you truly care about me."

She opened her eyes to meet his dark ones. "Anything," she whispered.

"Promise me that wherever you go to do your teaching, that you'll also listen to what the People have to say, whether they're Sioux or Apache or Shoshoni or Cheyenne, whatever they are, wherever you are. Keep your mind open. Don't be so ready to think that your way is the only way. If you want to honor your feelings for me, then honor my People, Bonnie. You can maybe teach them, but you can learn from them, too. Don't treat them like most whites treat them. Be understanding."

She studied him lovingly. "I will. I promise. And if . . . if

137

you and your wife ever come North of Fort Laramie, please come and see us. I would like very much to meet her. I consider her a very lucky woman.''

He grinned and stroked some of her hair back from her face. "Maybe she isn't so lucky. I can be a pretty hard man to live with sometimes."

A tear slipped down her cheek. "I have a feeling she doesn't even mind the bad times."

His eyes showed their appreciation for her remark. "Well, there have been plenty of bad times for both of us. I guess that's why we're so well made for each other. We both understand a little bit about what hell is like, Bonnie."

She nodded. "I've only begun to learn about it."

Their eyes held and he bent close and kissed her cheek. "You're a fine woman, Bonnie Beaker. I hope Rodney appreciates you." He squeezed her hands, then let go of them, turning and swinging himself up onto the back of the Apache horse, then looked down at her. "You'd like my Abbie," he added. "And she'd like you. We've been intending to get up to Fort Laramie. Maybe we'll make the trip after she's had her baby so you and she can meet." He reached out a hand and she slowly reached up and grasped it. She felt his hard strength as he swung her up behind him as though she were a child. "I have a full-blooded white brother at Fort Laramie, a lieutenant in the army," he told her, apparently trying to lighten the conversation. "His name is Danny Monroe."

Her eyebrows arched in surprise. "You didn't tell me you had a white brother!"

"Well, I do. Three of them, in fact. The other two are still in Tennessee, far as I know. Haven't seen them in years."

She adjusted her skirt and settled in behind him, hesitantly putting her arms around his waist and hoping he couldn't feel her breasts against his back. "I shall look up your brother Danny and tell him hello for you," she told him. "I'll tell him about this crazy experience out here, except I won't tell him—" She leaned back a little, and wished there was some other way to ride besides having to sit so brazenly close. She felt awkward about it now.

He reached back and grasped her hands, putting them back around him. "It's all right, Bonnie. We'll get to Santa Fe and go our separate ways, and when you're all rested, you'll feel better about all this," he told her. Then he took a necklace from around his neck and handed it back to her. "A gift of friendship from me," he told her.

She took the necklace, studying the rows of small bone hairpipes, interspersed with copper trade beads and held together with rawhide. A shell decorated the center of the necklace and each piece of bone was polished smooth and intricately painted with flowers. "Zeke, this must be special to you—"

"Keep it. A gift has no meaning if it isn't something special, something treasured. My Cheyenne mother made that for me years ago. Keep it and tell your grandchildren about the time you were captured by outlaws and saved by a crazy half-breed."

"Zeke, I can't—"

"You must. It's important to me that you keep it. To turn down a gift from an Indian is an insult, Bonnie. Please take it. I want to give you something."

She swallowed back more tears. "Thank you. I'll . . . treasure it forever, Zeke. I mean that. And if you or your wife or children ever need help . . . of any kind . . . if there is anything my father or husband or I can do for you, please come to us. Promise me, Zeke."

He kicked at the horse and got it into motion. "It's a promise." They headed toward the sun, leaving the three dead Apaches behind them. "The necklace was a gift from my mother for my honorable participation in the sacrifice of flesh at the Sun Dance," he continued. "It was there I proved I have little awareness of the white blood in my veins. I proved I was Cheyenne."

She studied the small scars on his back and thought of those he bore on his chest, envisioning the Sun Dance as he had explained it to her. And she knew that here was a man she could probably never fully understand, no matter how she felt about him. Somehow the one called Abigail understood him.

139

"Zeke, tell me something," she spoke up, clutching the necklace tightly as he got the horse moving faster. "The outlaws spoke of this Lady Z for whom you search. They said she had the letter Z carved on her cheeks. Your name is Zeke, and you seem to carry much hatred for her. Was it you who scarred her?"

He rode on for several seconds without replying. "Lady Z is not a woman, Bonnie. She's an animal. I've never harmed a woman, before or since."

Her blood chilled. So, it was true. And yet she was not afraid of him, nor was she as shocked as she had thought she would be. But she knew this man could never have belonged to one such as she, even if he had been free. He was simply too much man, too wild and untamed. Yet what must it be like to be the woman of such a man? To bear his children? Only the mysterious Abigail would know that.

Eight

The tavern at Gila was filled with choking smoke and reeked of cheap whiskey and the body odor of men who cared little for bathing. Inside sat a grand mixture of men of questionable character, some white, some Mexican, most well armed. Talk of raids and women and gun-running for Comanches could be heard above the voices of men betting on card games, but the room quieted when Zeke entered the establishment. Most turned to look at the stranger who had never graced their doorway, for every stranger was someone to beware of, and this one dressed and walked like an Indian, and wore a blade bigger than any they had ever seen.

Zeke's eyes darted around the room quickly, surmising the odds if there should be trouble, which he did not doubt. Indians were not usually welcome in such places. No one made a move to stop him as he strode up to the bar, where a man with a three-day growth of beard turned his eyes to look at the tall, buckskin-clad intruder.

The white man's smell stung Zeke's nostrils, and he could not understand how anyone could bear to live within such a filthy body. His own horse smelled better than most of the men in the tavern, and he suddenly longed for the sweet smell of Abbie's hair, and the way her skin smelled when she just finished bathing.

"Give me a shot of whiskey," he told the bartender, unable to keep his lips from curling at the stench in the room. He turned his head to glare directly back at the smelly man beside him, whose paunchy stomach hung out over his belt and whose cotton shirt was faded and stained so that its

141

color could no longer be recognized. The man spat some tobacco at Zeke's feet.

"Your talk is awful white, mister," the man sneered. "More like a breed. Indians don't get served in here, and half-breed bastards don't even get through the door." He reached out and grasped the bartender's wrist as the man started to pour a shot for Zeke. "You'd best leave while you're still able to walk."

Zeke looked at the dirty hand that held the bartender's wrist. The creases of the knuckles were permanently stained. He slowly moved his eyes back to the man's leering face, his own dark eyes menacing. "Appears to me you have a lot of guts when you're bunched up together with your friends," he answered, surprising them all with the hint of Tennessee accent in his speech.

"You callin' me a coward?" the man at the bar asked, his pale blue eyes cold and vacant. Zeke noticed with revulsion that sleep was matted in the man's eyes.

"I am," he answered. "Most men talk big when they have others behind them ready to do their fighting for them." He looked at the bartender. "Pour that drink. I came here to do business and to get some whiskey."

The bartender looked at the other fellow hesitantly, and the man backed up, facing Zeke. "I ain't shot an Indian in the last couple of days or so," he said haughtily. "Last one I shot was the husband of the squaw I took my pleasure with. She was a right good piece. How many squaws you got runnin' around naked in your tipi, Indian?"

Zeke kept his eyes steady on the man, aware his hand was coming near a gun he wore at his side. "Just one," he answered. Then he grinned broadly. "She's white."

The man's face turned beet-red and he went for his gun without thinking, he was so enraged. But the red face quickly paled to a ghostly white when Zeke's huge blade appeared. Its tip was pushed against the man's adam's apple before he could get his gun out of its holster.

"You just throw that gun aside, dog face, and I'll drink my whiskey!" Zeke growled. "You have an itch to kill an Indian, and I have an itch to show your insides to the sunlight. Right now it's my wish that appears to be ready to be granted, so I suggest you don't provoke me any further. I have a real hunger to run this blade from your throat right down to your balls!"

The man swallowed, shivering as he removed his gun and threw it aside. Zeke kept the knife at the man's throat while he glanced around the room. "You might say I have kind of a reputation with this blade," he told them warningly. "One man makes a move toward me and he'll feel steel sinking real deep into his gut. It will happen so fast he'll never realize what hit him." He reached out with his left hand across the bar. "Pour that drink," he ordered the bartender.

"Yes, sir," the man said quietly. The whiskey bottle clinked against the edge of the shot glass and the man slid the glass into Zeke's hand. Zeke took it and swallowed it, still keeping his eyes on the man who had challenged him and still holding the knife to his throat.

"Now," he spoke up when he finished the whiskey. "I'm here to find out how to contact Lady Z," he told all of them. "Who is going to tell me how to find her?"

The room remained silent. Zeke pressed the knife closer to the throat of the man at the bar.

"How do I find her?" he growled. The tip of his blade nicked the man's skin and drew blood, as sweat beaded on the man's forehead.

"Why—why do you want to find Lady Z?" the man asked in a shaking voice.

"That's my business!"

The man swallowed and tried to smile. "Most men know the Lady," he told Zeke, trying to change his attacker's mood. He laughed lightly, hoping to get a grin out of the smoldering Indian. "She comes around once in a while when she dares to come out of hidin'. Quite an entertaining woman, you might say."

The others laughed, and Zeke knew from what Dancing Moon had been years earlier that she had probably slept with nearly all of them at one time or another. He did not join in the laughter. He pulled the knife away from the fat man's skin, but he still held it out threateningly. "You know how to find her?" he asked the man.

The man shrugged. "Me and these men here have dealt with her a time or two, but we don't run with her gang. None of them is here right now. All me or any of these others here can do is take you to a place where her men have led us when we need to make a delivery of stolen guns—or women. Then they take the goods on up into the mountains to Lady Z."

Zeke's dark eyes darted around the room. "I have gold with me. If someone will take me as far as the meeting site, I'll find her from there. I have something to sell her, and I might even join up with her."

"Hope you got lots of energy in bed!" one man remarked. Laughter filled the room, and Zeke lowered his knife a little more, to the fat man's relief.

"I can take you, mister," the man volunteered, "but you couldn't track a herd of buffalo through them rocks and caverns. Nobody finds Lady Z unless she wants to be found."

Zeke just smiled. "You get me that far and I'll find her."

The man eyed him up and down. "You know the Lady?"

Zeke slowly shoved the knife into its sheath. "Never met her. I've only heard about her, and I know where I can steal some mighty fine horses—women, too. But I don't intend to deal with anybody but Lady Z. If you can't take me, then I'll find somebody else." He looked around the room. "I go with only one man. I don't trust any of you in numbers."

"How much gold you got?" the fat man asked.

Zeke untwisted the ties to a small leather pouch he wore on his belt and plunked it on the bar, turning it upside down and shaking out two hundred dollars in gold coins, his own badly needed money. He had got it from the sale of several of his Appaloosas at Bent's Fort. The fat man and the others stared at the coins, money Cheyenne Zeke did not intend to pay to anyone if he could help it. But for now, if it meant finding Lady Z and possibly poor Yellow Moon and Laughing Boy, he would let the men think they could earn it by helping him.

"Well?" he asked.

The fat man rubbed his lips. "I don't like dealin' with half-breeds," he grumbled.

Zeke scooped up the coins in his hand. "Fine. Maybe one of the others—"

"Wait!" the man interrupted, staring at Zeke's hand that held the coins. "I . . . uh . . . I reckon your gold is worth same as any." He licked his lips. "I need the money. I'll take you." He straightened and pretended to lose his fear of the half-breed. "But you got to pay it to me now."

Zeke shook his head. "No way. Not till we get there."

The man scowled and looked around at the others. "I wouldn't argue with the breed, Smitty," one of them spoke up. "I get the feelin' he don't go no way but his own." The others chuckled at the sight of their short, fat friend challenging the tall, dark half-breed whose meanness radiated from his body.

Smitty sighed. "All right," he muttered. "Have it your way. But you'd best keep your word, mister!"

"I'd be careful leadin' the stranger to the Lady Z," one of the others told Smitty. "What if he ain't what he says he is? Maybe he's some kind of spy. The Lady will string you high if you bring her trouble."

Smitty studied Zeke a moment, seeing only dark meanness about his face. "He don't look to me like a man who'd be on the side of the law," he drawled. "Looks more like the kind of man the law would be after." He turned to the others. "Besides, how much harm can one man do against that gang that runs with the Lady?" He put out his hand to Zeke. "We got off on a bad start, mister, but if you're payin' gold, I got no objection to leadin' the way. It's your skin if you're up to tricks. Lady Z will have you hangin' by the toes with your back whipped open and your privates cookin' over a fire. She's a vicious one."

Zeke's eyes flickered with a thirst for vengeance he found difficult to hide. "So I've heard," he answered. "That's my problem, mister. Yours is to give me a lead to her hideout. You're called Smitty?" He did not extend his hand, and Smitty nodded, reddening with indignation as he pulled back his offer to shake hands and rubbed the hand nervously against the side of his leg.

"You?" he asked.

"Just call me 'Indian.' Most folks do."

"O.K., Indian. When you want to leave?"

"How about right now?"

Smitty's eyebrows arched. "Now? But . . . it's pretty near dark!"

"There's an hour or two of riding time left. I have supplies."

Smitty shrugged. "You're payin'."

"That's right. And you're leading. So let's go."

Smitty looked nervously at the others. Some watched Zeke suspiciously and others just chuckled. Smitty straightened and walked casually out of the saloon, Zeke right behind him. "If you're lucky," Smitty spoke up as they headed for their horses, "Lady Z will spread for a big buck like you, Indian. I'll tell you one thing. You haven't been with a woman till you've been with that one. A man can easily forget them scars on her cheeks when she's got those long legs wrapped around his body."

Zeke wondered how she looked now. It had been a long time since he had seen her, and the last time he saw the scars on her cheeks they were still fresh and bloody, for he'd put them there himself. His heart pounded with anticipation and great joy at the thought of getting his hands on her again, but getting her alone would not be easy, and it was a sure bet she kept herself surrounded with good fighting men, the same kind of men who had thrown him in the snakepit.

He mounted a roan mare he had purchased in Santa Fe, when he'd traded in the tired Apache mount. He thought about Bonnie for a moment. She was probably already on her way North again. He hoped she would be happy. The thought of her again stirred thoughts of Abbie, and his body tingled with a need that could not be fulfilled until he finished his mission here. How he longed to invade her again, to hear Abbie cry out his name! He had not been this lonely for many years. He hoped that when he got back this time, he would never have to leave her again.

Abbie pounded the meat for pemmican, spreading it out on a clean piece of rawhide and pulverizing it with a stone, after which she would pack it into rawhide sacks with heated fat and add nuts and berries. Protected from moisture inside the well-sealed rawhide bag, the pemmican would remain a food staple for months, to be eaten bit by bit, carried by Zeke when he had to be gone for long periods and some saved for the days when the hunt was not good. It was a tasty treat, an ingenious invention of the Indians, a staple that remained good even for periods of years rather than months.

It felt good to be living the Cheyenne way again. It had been years since she'd lived in the tipi in the fashion she had dwelled when she had first come to this land where Cheyenne Zeke lived. She knew how to skin out a buffalo and sew the hides together and how to derive everything from the big, shaggy animal of the Plains, from shields and buckets and snowshoes, to soups, bowstrings, pillows, thread, and glue. Swift Arrow was right. There were a hundred things derived from this one animal, all things that were vital to the survival of the Indian. The Indian didn't know the meaning of waste.

Swift Arrow and Deer Slayer had found a very small herd not far from the fort. To sight a herd in that area was becoming all too unusual of late. The men had hurried back to get some of the other warriors who were still camped at the fort and had managed to take a small kill. Women had been sent for from one of the villages at Hinta Nagi, and had now come to make camp near the fort to do the skinning and preserving. It was like the old days again, when Zeke and Abbie had dwelled with the People, and Abbie had borne her first two children within the tipi. It was a sweet time of freedom, a freedom fast fading.

Little Rock was off now with Swift Arrow, taking lessons with the lance while he waited for his father to return.

There was no taming Little Rock, and now with Swift Arrow returned, the boy was wilder than ever, for Swift Arrow was even worse than Zeke at filling the boy with stories of the hunt and of battles. Little Rock already knew practically everything he needed to know about the Cheyenne tongue, the Cheyenne religion, the Cheyenne ways. Swift Arrow was overwhelmed at how well the boy could ride and proud that Zeke had made the boy all Cheyenne, secretly loving Abbie even more for allowing her son such freedom and for wanting him to learn the Cheyenne way. She did not dote on him and spoil him as so many white women did with their sons.

Blue Sky, always bashful and for some reason frightened of everyone, stayed right beside her mother, and little Young Girl crawled in the grass nearby, chasing a butterfly. Black Elk had ridden off for one more hunt, and his young wife, Blue Bird Woman, sat near Abbie, stuffing buffalo hair into a rawhide pouch for a saddle. She had been strangely quiet all day, and when Abbie glanced over at her there were tears in the girl's eyes.

"Blue Bird Woman, what is wrong?" Abbie asked in the Cheyenne tongue.

The girl swallowed and blinked. "I still am without life in my belly," she answered. "I feel the cramps again, and I know that soon I will bleed and another moon will be gone with no baby to grow inside of me."

Abbie sighed and sat up straighter. "Blue Bird Woman, you have only been married a little while."

She shook her head. "Black Elk beds me almost every night. I know he is anxious for a son. Before he went on the Pawnee raids he also bedded me often. How can a man be with his woman so much and still she has no life in her belly? I fear that I am barren." She covered her eyes and wept, and Abbie's heart pained for her. "You are a blessed woman," the girl went on. "Already you have three children and another grows in your belly. You are fertile and make your man proud."

Abbie wiped her hands on a cloth and moved over beside Blue Bird Woman, putting her hand on the girl's shoulder.

"You just have to be patient."

The girl sniffed. "But if I do not bear a child soon, Black Elk will be looking for a second wife—one who can give him children. I know he wants only me, but a man must do what he must do to preserve the People. A man must have sons. I do not want him to take another wife."

"I don't think he would do that so soon, Blue Bird Woman. Black Elk doesn't want anyone else in his bed but you. He loves you. I see it in his eyes."

"Such things are not important. Sons are important."

Abbie squeezed her shoulder. It was not common, but it was an accepted practice for a Cheyenne man to take more than one wife, if he had a widowed sister-in-law or if his wife was barren and he wanted sons. Sometimes the widows were taken in only as helpmates for the chosen wife, because the man had a responsibility to care for his brother's wife. Often he would only provide for her and teach her sons the ways of the Cheyenne men. But he had the privilege of bedding her if he chose to do so. It was not so much a matter of sexual pleasure as it was a means of accumulating more sons of his own. The practice remained important now, since disease had wiped out over half the Cheyenne nation. If they were to survive and grow again, sons and daughters must be born. It was a matter of survival, a practical means of caring for those left without a husband and without a father; and a way for a man to have many sons, for it was dangerous for one woman to have too many babies, and also very hard on her, for Cheyenne women worked from dawn to dusk, and too many children only made the work harder. The women aged quickly and died young.

It was not uncommon for a Cheyenne man to go through more than one wife, but wives were not usually taken without great affection and loyalty, and the men were always ready to fight and die for the women and the children, for they were the only promise of a future for the People.

Still, the thought of a second wife was difficult for one so young as Blue Bird Woman to accept. Her young heart felt a fierce loyalty to her man, and it would have been difficult for her to humbly accept a second woman in her tipi and let her husband lie with someone else so that he might have sons. Abbie knew she could not herself accept that particular Cheyenne practice. Her white blood could not abide a second woman. But she understood the way of the People, and how it was with a Cheyenne man. A man must have sons, and Blue Bird Woman was anxious now that she would be unable to give any to Black Elk.

"Has Black Elk said anything about it?" Abbie asked her.

The girl shook her head. "No. But I see the disappointment in his eyes every time I flow again. When he came back from raiding with the Pawnee, I knew that he was hoping I would have good news for him. When I told him I still did not carry any life, I saw the disappointment in his eyes, even though he smiled and told me we would just have to keep trying."

"You're terribly young, Blue Bird Woman. That's probably all that's wrong. And perhaps you're trying too hard. Sometimes that can be a problem."

The girl looked at her. "But surely you were as anxious as I, and it did not bring you bad luck. Did Zeke bed you every night?"

Abbie reddened at the forward question, and her loins ached for her husband at the sweet thoughts the girl's question brought to mind. How she ached to hold him, to taste his lips again and feel his manliness inside of her! She was terrified that he would not return—that he would never see his fourth child. How she needed his strength and the sweet comfort of his arms. She smiled and sighed. "Almost every night," she replied. She patted Blue Bird Woman's shoulder. "You shouldn't worry, Blue Bird Woman. It will happen for you. And right now you are Black Elk's only wife. He wants no other. Be happy with that and let things happen as the spirits will."

The girl nodded. "I will try," she replied, wiping at her eyes.

It was then that Black Elk and Swift Arrow both came thundering up to the camp with Little Rock close behind his uncles. The child was laughing and holding a lance in the air

150

like the best of warriors.

"Mother, I am learning to throw the lance!" the boy said excitedly. "Wait until my father comes home and sees what I can do!" He let out a war cry and Abbie gasped as he threw the weapon with amazing strength for his little arm, landing it squarely in a nearby tree. "You see?"

Abbie stood up and put her hands on her hips. "I will thank you to show your father that trick when your sisters are not so close by that they might get hurt!" she scolded.

Swift Arrow watched her with a smile and Little Rock's lips puckered. "You are not pleased?"

"I am pleased. Just do it someplace safer," she replied. She folded her arms. "Your father will be very proud when he gets back, Little Rock," she added. Her smile faded and she looked at Swift Arrow. "If he gets back."

He slid down from his horse. "He will come, just like before," he told her. "Cheyenne Zeke takes care of himself." He glanced over at Black Elk, who was bent over talking quietly to his young wife. Swift Arrow thought Blue Bird Woman exceedingly beautiful. His brother had chosen well, but Swift Arrow already knew that Black Elk was concerned that the girl was too worried about not yet being pregnant. They had talked about it on the hunt. Black Elk was anxious to have sons, but more anxious over the fact that Blue Bird Woman became too upset that she was not yet giving him any.

"Her body is still too young," he had told Swift Arrow. "I can wait. But she thinks I cannot."

"Then you have chosen a good woman," Swift Arrow had replied. "The good ones want to give their man sons right away. She has a good heart."

"And what about you?" Black Elk had replied. "You should marry again and have sons, Swift Arrow. You are a man who needs sons."

Swift Arrow had denied that he wanted another wife, and now he looked down at Abbie's own swollen belly, thinking how pleasant it would be if it was his seed she carried. But no man except Zeke would plant his seed in this white woman. And now he saw the fear in her eyes that her husband would

151

not come back.

"If he does not return, Swift Arrow will see that you do not go hungry, Abigail, and that you are always protected. I will provide for you and teach your son—" he glanced down at her belly, "or sons—the Cheyenne way. Unless you would go back to that place called Tennessee."

She shook her head. "I could never go back there. I would go back to our cabin and live out my days there on the Arkansas River. I would live with my memories and want no more than that."

Black Elk was walking with Blue Bird Woman toward their tipi, and Swift Arrow knew what would take place when he got her inside. He watched them for a moment, then looked back at Abbie, who also watched them, with a strange longing in her eyes. Swift Arrow knew that her thoughts lay with Cheyenne Zeke.

"I will take Little Rock away for more practice with the lance," he told her. He grasped her arm. "Are you all right?"

She nodded, then looked to the south. "It's been almost six weeks, Swift Arrow."

"These things take time. He will come." Again he wanted to hold her but dared not. He, too, hoped Zeke would come soon, for he needed to get away from her—to ride back North, where he would stay for a good long time to come, probably for the rest of his life.

Zeke and Smitty rode for two days through canyons and ridges, through crevices barely wide enough for horse and man to fit. It was no wonder that Lady Z was difficult to find, for not many men would be able to track anyone in such country. Zeke was wearying of Smitty's constant talk about raping women and what it was like to lie with Lady Z—about the many fights he'd been in and won. Zeke had no doubts the man was a braggart and a liar, as well as a coward, and he would have liked nothing better than to sink his blade into the man's soft gut, if not for the fact that he was the only one who could lead him close to the Lady Z.

"Got to tell you, though," the man babbled on the second day of their journey, "that Nick Trapper, he's meaner than you and me put together, Indian. Got no feelin's, you know? Me, I'll rape a woman, even kill one; but I got a soft spot for kids. Would you believe it? But that Nick, he ain't got no soft spot for nobody. Last time he was down to Gila, he was laughin' about how he'd killed an Indian boy, some kid of a woman they'd captured. Joked about how his name was Laughin' Boy, but that the boy wasn't laughin' when he got done with him." He turned to look at Zeke, whose face was strangely immobile, as though the man were struggling not to show any emotion. Zeke stared straight ahead and said nothing. "You ever kill a kid, Indian?"

Zeke did not reply right away, but trotted his horse forward so that Smitty could not see the pain in his eyes. "Once, but it was a mercy killing," he finally answered back, thinking of Abbie's little brother. He wondered if his nights would forever be haunted by what he'd done out of love. Now the pain in his heart was more piercing at the sudden, unexpected news that little Laughing Boy was dead. He had wanted more than anything to bring his little nephew back home.

"Well, what Nick Trapper did wasn't no mercy killin'," Smitty told him. "That black-hearted bastard bellowed it out big as you please while he was buyin' drinks for all of us. Said as how they'd captured some Arapaho woman and her kid. The kid kept tryin' to run off, and they kept herdin' him back like a calf, you know? Laughed about how they had the kid runnin' in circles and cryin' while his ma kept screamin' and beggin' them to stop. Trapper, he kept after the kid the most, till the little bugger got plumb dizzy and walked right into the man's horse and got trampled. Then Trapper, he said he just kept ridin' back and forth over the kid a few more times. Said he was 'tenderizin' the meat' for the wolves. Can you imagine that? Even I wouldn't do somethin' like that. I'd just shoot him in the head and get it over with."

Zeke closed his eyes, struggling against a rage mightier than any he had ever suffered. "They left the boy to the

153

wolves then?" he asked.

"Reckon so. Like I say, Trapper's the one to look out for. Got no soul, that one. And Lady Z ain't much better. Stood and watched with pleasure while Trapper and the other took that Arapaho woman. Lady Z likes to watch, they say. She even lays with some of the women captives herself, they say. Likes women as much as men. She's a hellion, that one. You'd best be careful ridin' into that woman's den of iniquity. She'll have her legs around you one minute, and a knife in your back the next."

Zeke reached deep into his spiritual powers to find the strength to shut off his emotions, for the vision of poor Laughing Boy tore at his heart, making him want to cry out and let blood. "Sounds like my kind of woman," he told Smitty. "I've heard she's also Arapaho."

"Yup. She's a damned pretty piece, too, except for them letters carved in her cheeks. She hates her people, though, 'cause they cast her out for messin' with the men all the time." He chuckled. "I can just imagine!"

Zeke breathed deeply and took on a casual air. "Trapper ever say what happened to the captive woman, the mother of the boy?"

"Oh, yeah. I forgot that part. He said as how she tried to stab herself, but they caught her and kept her from doin' it. Then she just started actin' kind of loony—just sat and stared all the time—wouldn't talk, didn't respond to pain or a man takin' her—nothin'. Last I heard, Lady Z was gonna try to sell her to some whorehouse. Don't know if she ever did. Trapper ain't been back to Gila since then. I reckon he's at the hideout with Lady Z now. Hope you got a real good offer for them, mister, or Lady Z will use you for entertainment. She'll bed you and then have you tortured. She's the devil's woman, that one. And Nick Trapper is the devil's brother."

Zeke rode ahead silently, his mind reeling now with an intense need to deal one on one with Mr. Nick Trapper. "What does Trapper look like?" he asked Smitty. "So I know which one to keep my eye on?"

Smitty grunted. "No mistakin' that one. For one thing,

154

Lady Z always hangs on him. For another, he's a real big man, and everything about him is black—his hair, his eyes, and all his clothes. He don't like colors. Says black is the color of evil and he likes evil things. Believe me, you'll know him when you see him."

Zeke's back was to Smitty, and Smitty did not see the hideous grin on Zeke's face. Cheyenne Zeke was indeed anxious to meet Nick Trapper, for the man would pay for what he'd done to little Laughing Boy. Now he was glad Red Eagle had shot himself, because Zeke knew he would kill his brother himself for selling his wife and son to such men. What a terrible price to pay for a bottle of whiskey!

Danny strapped shut his duffel bag and turned to face Emily, who stood at the doorway dabbing at tears.

"There would be no need for tears if you would come with me, Emily," he told her. "My God, surely you know I can take care of you."

"I know," she whimpered. "Please understand, Danny. Mama always waited here in St. Louis, in . . . in civilization. She always told me I should do the same if I ever married an army man."

He came closer and touched her shoulder. "Your mother is dead now, Emily. And I love you. We've had little enough time to get to know each other, and here we are husband and wife and I have to leave you for God knows how long."

She began to cry harder. "I know. But—I've heard so many stories—about how terrible life is out there. Everything is so . . . so barren and hot. There are no cities . . . no schools and churches . . . no clubs or socializing. And . . . and what about the Indians? Surely you wouldn't want to risk my getting stolen by Indians!"

He sighed as she put her head against his chest and wept, her heart torn with confusion. How he wished she were stronger, more mature. Perhaps in a way it was best she stayed in St. Louis for now, for her constitution was probably not capable of bearing the hardships of the Plains, even though he would make life as easy as possible for her at the fort. He had been swept up so swiftly by her beauty and charm that he had married her without thinking of such things, for all he could think of was being the first man to make a woman of her, and the only legal way to do that was to marry her, which he had done after only a two-week courtship, with her father's blessing, for Major Epcott would forever hold a high opinion of Lieutenant Daniel Monroe.

But his primary goal of getting Emily Epcott into his bed had not brought the excitement he had anticipated, for she was a child in every way, including the ways of sex, and her fear and apprehension and frigidity needed considerable work on his part to wipe them out and replace them with an ability to make love freely and openly. It would take much patience and teaching on his part to make her understand that it was not wrong for a wife to enjoy sexual pleasures with her husband, but there had not been enough time, and now he had to leave her. There were too many things left unfinished, and his blood burned for her, for he felt consumed with a need to bed her over and over until she would take him willingly and gladly and cry out his name in ecstasy instead of pain and fear. He had not realized until after making her his wife, after finally invading her and getting the stars out of his eyes, just how young and spoiled and ignorant she truly was. But the fact remained that she was his wife now, and he did love her, just as he was sure she loved him. He had to make the best of it. But being fifteen hundred miles apart would certainly not be of any help in building their marriage.

"Emily," he said quietly, patting her back, "I've told you about Abbie, my half-blood brother's wife. She was only fifteen when she went West, and she hasn't been back since. She lives out on the Plains along the Arkansas, her only friends the Cheyenne, her only source of supplies Bent's Fort. She has only Zeke, and their children, and she's borne those children alone, with only Zeke to help her. But she's happy, Emily. Happy because she's with the man she loves." He kissed her hair. "I would make life for you much easier than it is for Abbie. You'd be fine, Emily. You'd most

156

certainly be protected at the fort, and there are some other women there. It's not nearly as uncivilized as you have it pictured."

She sniffed and looked up at him. "Please, Danny, not yet," she sobbed. "I . . . I'm just not ready to leave St. Louis yet—to go away to such a far place. I've lived in this house all my life. All of Mama's things are here. I have friends here." She rested her head against his chest. "I'll be true to you, Danny. Surely you know that. I am your wife, and I love you. I . . . I know I haven't been . . . what you expected in bed. But I'll think about it a lot while you're gone, Danny. And perhaps after being apart—"

He struggled to control his temper as he grasped her arms and pulled back from her. "Damn it, Emily! Come with me! This is no way to work on a marriage!"

She studied the handsome blue eyes and wished she could be the mature woman such a man needed. But he made her feel small and childlike as he stood there towering over her. She had no idea what to say to him—what he expected her to say.

"I . . . I will come, Danny. I promise," she said in her tiny voice.

"When?" he pressed.

"I don't know. Soon."

He was tempted to take her and tie her over a horse and force her to go. He had the right. But she would hate him forever if he treated her that way. He had to tread lightly with this delicate creature whose beauty made him lose all his senses. She was not ready for life out West. He should have waited to marry her in the first place, but his physical need for her had made him rush into a marriage that was going to prove to be a shaky one if he did not use his own maturity and common sense now to keep from destroying her love for him. He closed his eyes and bent forward to kiss her forehead.

"I'll be so lonely, Emily. I just wish—I wish you could meet Abbie. If you talked to her, you'd see how happy she is. You'd feel better about it all."

"I'm sorry you'll be lonely," she whimpered. "I'll be

157

lonely, too. But I promise to think hard about it all, Danny. And I will write you every week. And just as soon as I feel ready, I'll come out, and I can meet your sister-in-law and that strange, half-blood brother of yours."

He studied the green eyes that at the moment were swollen with tears. "I love you, Emily. Don't take too long to decide. The nights will be so long and lonely."

She blushed and felt the strange sickness and fear she always felt when it was time to sleep with him and let him put his large manly part inside of her. It had all been so shocking and surprising, for she had no idea such things were expected of a wife. It was not that he was unkind or forceful. He was as gentle as a man his size could be, more apologetic than passionate, and she had tried to respond as he had explained a woman should respond. But somehow it seemed sinful to lie naked with a man and to enjoy it. She wished there were someone she could talk to about it. But there was no one. Her mother was dead, and her girlfriends knew no more about it than she did. Perhaps as she grew older and was more of a woman she would understand.

"Be very careful, Danny," she told him. "Don't let some Indian kill you before I come out to you."

He put on a smile for her. "I won't let that happen." He bent down and met her lips, pressing her close and groaning as he kissed her hungrily. She put her arms around his neck, feeling for one magic moment a fleeting stir in her groin she had not felt before. It was pleasurable and unexpected. Perhaps it was only because her handsome new husband was going away and she would miss him, in spite of the shaky beginning to their marriage. But then she stiffened in his arms, for she was afraid of the hint of naughty desire she had felt. He left her lips and moved his mouth to her neck.

"Come to me soon, Emily," he whispered. "Don't torture me this way."

"I will. I promise," she told him. "I truly do love you, Danny. Tell me you won't stop loving me."

"You now I won't." He pulled away again. "I'll build a little house near my office. I'll have a nice little place all ready for you. I'll make it as much like home as I can, Emily."

She nodded and stepped back. "Good-bye, Danny," she told him. "I'll wait faithfully for you, just as my mother always did for my father. If I don't come out there to live, perhaps I will at least come out to visit. Mother used to do that sometimes—visit my father where he was stationed and then come back home to St. Louis."

His eyes changed from loving to slightly angry. "Emily, we are not your mother and father. We are Emily and Danny. We'll make our own decisions and build our own life on what *we* want, not on what someone else had."

She looked down at the floor, now afraid of him again, for this man had rule of her life now, and it was a strange, new feeling, a frightening feeling, for she hardly knew him. He sighed and picked up his duffel bag.

"I have to go pick up the new recruits and get going, Emily," he told her. "I love you. Think about all this. Come out to me, Emily; not just for a visit. Come out there and be my wife. I don't want a sometimes lover. I want a wife and children—a woman at my side all the time, not just a month or two every year." He bent down and kissed her hair. "Good-bye, Emily."

He walked through the door, every part of him screaming to drag her along with him. But he could not do that to such a delicate creature. She watched him go, a part of her telling her to run after him and go with him. But life was safer and easier in St. Louis, and even though he was her husband, he was still almost a stranger to her, a handsome lieutenant who had walked into her life and swept her off her feet. She had not faced the reality of marriage and sex and belonging to a man before they married. It had all been a sweet little fantasy. Now it was real and frightening. She could not go with him. Not yet. She must think about it. He would be fine. He was a big, strong man. He understood.

He walked down the winding staircase and stopped at the bottom to look up at her. "Good-bye," she said quietly. "God bless."

He only sighed in reply, then turned and walked through the front door. He closed it behind him, and the house was dark and quiet. She went down the stairs to the parlor and sat down to some embroidery. She would not think about her problems right now. It was too much to think about. It was safe and cool and pleasant here in the big house, where everything was familiar and comforting. There was plenty of time for making decisions.

Nine

"This is the spot," Smitty said quietly, reining his horse to a halt. They were deep in the Sangre de Cristo Mountains. "You'll have to find your own way from here, Indian."

Zeke looked up at towering castles of rock, the pine trees at the top of the ridge looking like tiny shrubs because of their distance.

"There's some kind of path hidden around here that leads to the other side of that ridge without havin' to climb up and over it," Smitty added. "The way they talk, there's a real deep canyon on the other side. That's the hideout."

Zeke urged his horse forward slightly, scanning the maze of rocks and crevices with the eyes of a hawk. If there was a secret entrance, he'd find it. But his attention was drawn from the search when he heard the click of a gun hammer behind him.

"Take out that big knife and remove your other weapons," Smitty's voice sneered. "And hand over that gold you promised me."

Zeke sat still and did not turn around. "I'd give you the gold without force," he answered. "What's the gun for?"

Smitty chuckled. "Mister, everybody knows Lady Z is lookin' for a tall Indian with a scar on his face. Maybe the others didn't realize it, but I know who you are. Oh, at first, I didn't even think of it. But the more I looked at you, the more it came to me. You don't want to find the Lady so's you can make a deal. You got other things in mind. You're the one they call Cheyenne Zeke, ain't you?"

Zeke sat staring at the rocks in front of him, and Smitty

161

did not see the smile on his face. "I am," he replied.

"That's just what I thought." The man chuckled again. "Now toss over that gold and remove them weapons. I'm gonna fire a shot and before long somebody from the other side of that ridge is gonna be comin' over here to see what the commotion's about. And when I deliver you to Lady Z, she's gonna pay me one heap of gold for your hide."

Zeke slowly turned his horse, hearing the click of the trigger of Smitty's gun as he tried to fire the warning shot into the air. When Zeke met the man's eyes they were wide with surprise and fast filling with terror, for the rifle had failed to report.

"Now which one is the fool?" Zeke asked him with a wicked smile. "I removed the firing pin from both your guns two nights ago. You white men sleep too hard," he sneered. He watched the man's incredulous stare with pleasant humor. "I knew we were close to our destination; and I can read your ugly, pale blue eyes, my fat friend," Zeke told him casually. "I knew what you had in mind. I am not unfamiliar with your kind."

Sweat broke out on Smitty's face, and he tried to fire the gun again, but still to no avail. His face reddened with rage. "You! You goddamned, half-breed son-of-a-bitch!" He threw the rifle to the ground and pulled out his sidearm while Zeke just sat there grinning. He pointed the gun at Zeke and fired, and again there was only a click.

Then Zeke pulled out his big blade. "Now it is my turn, fat-belly!" he sneered. "I have listened to your talk enough to know that it is better you do not remain on this earth to rob and rape again. I am finished with my need of you!"

The man backed up his horse. "I . . . I kept my end of the bargain, breed! I led you here like I promised!"

"Only because you figured to get more out of the deal than my gold. If that gun had worked, Lady Z's men would be coming for me. We both know what they'd probably do to me. And you'd have sat and watched, counting your gold. I have no feelings for you, fat-belly! No feelings at all."

Smitty swallowed and backed his horse, then suddenly jerked on the reins. The horse reared and whirled, and the

162

man made an effort to ride off. But in the next moment a horrid, black pain seared his back, and in the one fleeting moment of life left in him he knew Cheyenne Zeke's knife had met its mark. His last thought was to wonder why he had considered crossing the notorious half-breed. But there was no time left to consider the answer. He slumped from his horse and the animal galloped on without its rider.

Zeke slowly rode up to the body and dismounted, yanking out the knife and wiping the blood on the man's faded calico shirt. He grabbed Smitty's ankles and dragged the body to the edge of the towering cliff, where he proceeded to cover it with rocks. He stepped back and looked up at the cliffs again. His eagle eyes did not find any lookouts. Perhaps Lady Z's men had only wanted those with whom they did business to think the hideout was just on the other side of the cliff. Perhaps it was not there at all, for if it was, there would surely be lookouts on this side and he would have already been spotted. But his keen ears and eyes detected no human sound or movement. This high perch deep in the Sangre de Cristos was dead silent, except for a soft, moaning wind.

He left the grave and walked around on foot, studying every rock and every shadow and nook. Nothing looked undisturbed at first glance, but he continued to study every inch with trained eyes until he realized that what appeared to be a flat wall of rock in one spot was really two layers of rock, one slightly ahead of the other. The way the sun hit the spot, it was extremely difficult to tell one section was actually behind the other, but the more he looked at it, the more sure he was that there was an opening between the two wall-like slabs.

His heart quickened, and he ran up to the spot, almost letting out a whoop of joy at his discovery. He peered into a hall-like crevice, on the other end of which he could see a shaft of light. Surely if Lady Z and her men used a secret passage this was it. It was barely big enough for man and horse, but they would fit. He walked back to his horse and grabbed the reins.

"Let's go, girl," he said quietly. He entered the hidden

pathway, leaving behind the one called Smitty with no regrets whatsoever. Cheyenne Zeke was not a man to regret killing someone who needed it. Man and horse disappeared into the rocks.

Lady Z felt strangely uneasy, but she shrugged off the feeling, preferring to enjoy the moment at hand. She danced naked around the firelight to the Spanish music one of her men played on his guitar, and her eyes feasted hungrily on the new woman friend Nick Trapper had found for her, a Mexican beauty who would do anything for gold, including satisfying the strange sexual desires of the one called Lady Z. The men watched the two women dancing provocatively, laughing and joking about what an interesting evening it was going to be, eagerly anticipating an exciting and ludicrous demonstration that would take place once the women's bodies touched. They whirled and eyed one another, moving rhythmically and always a little closer, swaying their bodies with precision and evil passion.

Above them an intruder moved with the stealth of a preying wolf and the silence of a snake. He had waited for the cover of total darkness, and his eyes had not missed anything. He had been watching their camp for a long time, counting the men, detecting every lookout, and determining to his relief that at the moment there were no innocent captives below. That was good. He would not have to worry about harming someone who did not belong to the crowd of filth he intended to destroy.

The difficult job would be to get the others without harming Lady Z, for he wanted very much to save her for last. It had taken him another full day to find the hideaway, a hidden canyon a half day's ride beyond the secret tunnel. The tunnel had merely led to a wide, barren pass between the cliff where he'd left Smitty's body and another cliff on the other side of it, which had been hidden by the first towering rocks. He had left his mount there and gone on by foot, aware that from there on a lookout might be anywhere. He followed traces of travel few trackers could have

164

deciphered, walking on silent, moccasined feet, ducking and hiding, always watching the surrounding cliffs, until finally he saw one man on a huge, round rock a good half mile in the distance.

He knew then he was close and he must stay hidden. He ducked down through crevices so small he had to pull in his stomach to get through them, until finally he was looking down into a well-hidden canyon surrounded by yet more cliffs. A crude cabin had been built there from logs they had managed to carry into the canyon, and from his hidden perch, Zeke sat watching for hours, determining his odds, and watching Lady Z with growing hatred.

Even from the distance he could tell she had only grown more beautiful, yet from her actions and laughter he also knew she had grown more evil. The very few good memories he had of lying with her were overwhelmed by the many bad memories of what this woman was capable of doing, and now, as she danced naked with another woman, he felt only revulsion for her.

He also watched the big man who wore only black, knowing he had to be the one called Nick Trapper, the one who had killed little Laughing Boy. Zeke's heart burned with an eagerness to sink his blade into the man, and, if possible, Nick Trapper was another one he would save for last.

Now it was dark, and the Lady Z was engrossed with her new lover, and lost in ecstasy over the thought of performing with the woman in front of the men. They would all be heavily occupied, which was good. Zeke moved almost freely above them without being spotted, as he proceeded to remove his first obstacles, the lookouts. He well knew their positions now. It was not really difficult. It was a simple matter of one strong hand across a mouth from behind, so that the man could not call out, and then a swift slit across the throat. Each of the four men's lives was ended quickly and soundlessly.

He crept closer to study some crates stacked to the side of the canyon, noticing they bore the word "dynamite." He grinned with pleasure. This would come in handy. And while the others danced and sang and laughed and drank, he snuck down to the back side of the crates and pried the top off of one with his knife. He removed several pieces of dynamite and scurried back up through the cover of the shadows of the rocks, returning to his original lookout perch. Now the real fun would begin. He had them trapped, for he sat in their only pathway out of the canyon.

There were ten of them left below, in addition to the two women. The four lookouts were dead. From his vantage point he knew he could get at least five of them before they knew what was happening. He grinned and removed an arrow from his quiver, taking the bow from his shoulder and placing the arrow into it. He pulled back the rawhide string and took careful aim. The instrument of death sang through the air and landed with a thud, square in the middle of the guitar player's back.

The music suddenly stopped when the guitar player grunted, and his eyes bulged with surprise before he slumped over to the ground, the arrow sticking out of his spine.

"What the hell—" Nick Trapper muttered. At first no one reacted, and Lady Z did not even see what had happened until she turned to order the man to continue playing. Her blood froze at the sight, just as another arrow sang through the air and landed in another man's neck. The man screamed and fell backward, and Lady Z's eyes darted over to look at him.

"It is him!" she whispered. "It is him!" she screamed louder then. "It is Cheyenne Zeke!" She ran toward the cabin, and another arrow punctured a man's chest, while the others came out of their surprised stupor and also ran for the cabin, but two more went down on the way as a rifle reported twice from the rocks above. "Get inside! Get inside!" Lady Z was screaming. Her heart pounded with wild fear and her legs suddenly felt like stone, unable to run fast enough to get out of range.

"Where in hell are the lookouts!" Trapper growled, shoving her inside the cabin.

"Dead!" Lady Z screamed. "Surely they are dead!"

"They can't be. There were *four* of them up there!"

"You do not know what he is like! But I thought . . . I thought we would know . . . there would be some kind of warning! I thought we would know when he was coming!"

She screamed the words almost hysterically, her own mind reeling with the memory of Cheyenne Zeke's knife cutting into her face. Trapper grabbed her and slammed a hand hard across her face.

"Shut up, you stupid bitch!" he roared. "How can I think with you acting like this? What the hell are you afraid of? There's five of us left and now we know he's out there. We'll wait him out till daylight, that's all."

She slunk back into a corner like a trapped she-cat, cowering down and eyeing them all. The room was suddenly silent and the air hung heavy. "It is Cheyenne Zeke," she said dully. "He has come. You were supposed to protect me. *All* of you!" she snarled. "Pigs! You are all useless pigs! Now he will come for me and I will die!"

"Not a man in this room is going to die!" Trapper snarled. "Now shut up!" He turned on the men. "Get to the windows and keep a lookout. He's only one man. We'll get him. And try to just wound him. I'll cut his privates off myself and shove them right down his throat, the half-breed bastard!" He threw a chair across the room and took a position at a window, staring out at the campfire, which now danced alone and cast an eerie orange light over the bodies of his dead companions. It had all happened so quickly he felt stunned, and more afraid than he cared to let on. This Cheyenne Zeke was a clever man and a skilled one, for to have found them at all took tremendous ability. Now nine of them were already dead. If not for the fact that the man intended to kill him, Trapper would have liked to meet this Cheyenne Zeke on other terms and get to know the murdering half-breed who had carved his initials into the Lady's cheeks.

He watched the shadows but saw no movement. The total silence was somehow deafening, and his own blood chilled when he heard a piercing war whoop somewhere in the rocks above. Lady Z whimpered and crouched down, covering her face, never having dreamt his coming could happen so quickly and be executed with such surprise. She had been sure the four lookouts and their well-hidden camp would be a trap for Cheyenne Zeke, not a trap for themselves.

The Mexican woman's dark eyes darted around the room in confusion. Who was this Cheyenne Zeke? Why was he after them? She was only in innocent bystander in this strange fight, and she did not intend to be a part of it. She suddenly darted through the door and began running.

"Come back here, slut!" Trapper yelled out. He took aim with his rifle. "Damned bitch!" he muttered. He fired, and she screamed out as a red hole opened in her naked back. She staggered and fell forward, her body falling near one of the dead men. Trapper pulled his rifle inside and reloaded, seemingly unaffected by the fact that he had just killed a woman. "She'd have been useless anyway," he grumbled to the others. "It's best to have her out of the way."

"What do we do now, Nick?" one of the others asked.

"We wait."

"I don't like it. I think we should go out after him," one of the others spoke up.

"He'll be watching this place like a hawk," Trapper growled. "You make one move to exit and he'll shoot your head off. Right now he's got the upper hand. But if we wait long enough, he'll come out of hiding and come down after us. We'll get him, don't worry about that."

"No," Lady Z spoke up, suddenly calm. "If you intend to wait, we will all rot here. You do not know him. If he must wait for a month, he will wait. He is clever and patient, and he is a man of unmatched vengeance. He has his mind set on finding me and now he has found me. He will wait forever if he must. But he will wait."

Trapper studied her a moment, and he suddenly knew the answer to his own escape. Cheyenne Zeke was after the woman, and he most likely wanted to know about his sister-in-law who had been captured by Nick and his men. Perhaps if he gave the breed an answer to both problems, he and his men could go free. Lady Z watched his evil eyes, and she

168

could read his thoughts. Her own eyes blazed and she straightened.

"You coward!" she hissed. "*I* am the leader, remember? I know what you are thinking, my black friend; and if we live through this, I will see that you suffer as you have never suffered before!"

The man only grinned. "Appears to me like we're the ones holding the cards, bitch!" he snarled. He pointed the gun at her. "How long did you think you could control all these men? We've used you just as much as you have used us, my Arapaho whore. And we're all tired of your body." Her eyes widened and he smiled more. "You gave away too much of yourself, Lady. You have nothing left to offer to keep any of us under your control, and right now it appears to me you're our only hope of getting out of here alive."

She spat at him and he swung the rifle, whacking her across the side of the face with the butt of the gun. She grunted and fell over sideways, unconscious. Trapper looked at the other men, who watched in surprise.

"It makes sense," he told them. "We don't need her anymore. We have the gold. We'll deliver her to the breed and tell him where Yellow Moon is. Then we'll get the hell out of here and do business someplace else. What do you say?"

One of them shrugged. "Why not? It's worth a try. Besides, now there's fewer of us to split up the gold. More for each of us."

Trapper nodded and returned to his window. He cupped his hands around his mouth. "Cheyenne Zeke!" he called out. He waited, and his yell echoed through the canyon, calling the name "Zeke . . . Zeke" several times over in an eerie mock. Then there was only silence. "We know it's you!" Trapper hollered out. "We want to make a deal with you."

Again there was only the echo of his voice, but when it died down there came a reply from the shadows above. "Let's hear it!" came the deep, calm voice.

Trapper smiled. "You can have the woman. She's still alive," he called back. He waited for the echoing to stop so

169

his words would be clear. "You can do whatever you want with her. She's all yours." He waited again. "We know it's the Lady Z you're after. And Yellow Moon." He waited yet again for the echoing to stop. "I'll tell you where you can find her."

There were several long seconds of total silence. "It's a deal," came the reply finally. "Show yourselves and bring out the woman!"

"How do we know you won't kill us!" Trapper shouted back.

"You have no choice. Come out in five minutes, or you will find yourselves in a hundred pieces. I will dynamite the cabin! You had better take your chances out in the open, wouldn't you say?"

Trapper's teeth gritted. "That bastard! He's got hold of some of the goddamned dynamite!"

"Now what do we do?" another asked, panic rising in his voice.

Nick breathed deeply, coming away from the window and leaning against the wall. He sat there quietly a moment, then kicked savagely at a chair, sending it flying to the other side of the room. "Damn!" he swore. "How did he do it? He's only one man!"

"I'd like to have that one strung up by the wrists with his back laid open," another one hissed.

"I say we throw the woman out ahead of us and make a run for our horses," one of the others spoke up. "Maybe he'll keep his word once we tell him where Yellow Moon is, and let us go."

"Like hell!" another mocked. "I don't trust no breed! I'm not going out there!"

"But what about the dynamite, Jess?" the other answered. "We've got no choice. I don't aim to get blowed up. At least if we go out there we'll flush him down and maybe we can get a shot at him. It's better than sweatin' it out in here and then eatin' flames and smoke."

"Maybe he's just bluffin' about the dynamite," the one called Jess answered.

"I doubt it," Nick spoke up. "If he's clever enough to get

this far he was clever enough to sneak down here and steal some from our supply. But we have one hope."

"What's that, Nick?" Jess asked.

"The woman—and what we know. Long as the Lady Z is inside and he still don't know about Yellow Moon, he won't use the dynamite. He blows us up, he don't get his information. He needs at least one of us alive, and you can bet he's hankerin' to get the Lady to himself. If he's the one that carved them Zs on her cheeks, he's mean as a snake and has a yen to do more than that now that she's dealt with Yellow Moon."

"Well, then, what the hell do we do? Sit here and rot?"

Nick turned to look out the window again. "We wait till daylight—then decide."

"I don't like it," one of the others grumbled. "You can't be sure he won't use—"

Just then a deafening explosion shook the cabin, and rocks and dirt could be heard tumbling down over the back of it.

"Jesus Christ, he's gonna' blow us up!" one of the men yelled, ducking. He headed for the door.

"Wait!" Nick growled. "He's just trying to scare us out! He won't blow the cabin, I tell you!"

The man whirled and pointed a gun at Nick. "You can sit here like a goddamned beaver in a trap, but I ain't! I'm takin' my chances and runnin' for my horse before the dust settles!" He charged through the door, and Jess followed, just as another explosion went off on the other side of the cabin. A rifle fired twice, its reports shrouded by the deafening explosion, and the two men did not reach their mounts.

The explosions startled Lady Z out of her dazed stupor from Nick's blow to her head, and she looked around in confusion as one beam from the roof of the cabin fell to the floor. "What . . . what is happening?" she moaned, holding the side of her head.

"You goddamned bitch!" Nick grumbled, going over and grabbing her by the arm. "You got us into this. If I'd half believed the bull you told me about that breed, I'd never have stayed with you. I'd have delivered you to him

171

myself!" He pulled her toward the door.

"What are you doing?" she whimpered, beginning to fight him.

He wrenched her arm behind her. "You are going to meet your old lover, bitch!" he told her, shoving her to the doorway.

"No!" she screamed. "Nick, do not take me out there! Please, Nick! You were my favorite! We are friends! We can take the gold and go away!"

"With the breed on our asses all the time? No thanks, sweet Lady. There's plenty more where you came from."

He pushed her out the door, keeping her in front of him for protection and forcing her along with him as he walked well away from the cabin while the remaining two men ducked down to wait inside, sure now that they would be safe once Nick Trapper told the breed where Yellow Moon was and handed over Lady Z. Trapper's eyes darted everywhere, trying to see where Zeke might be but seeing nothing in the dark.

The dust settled and the canyon quieted, until there was no sound but the moaning wind and Lady Z's quiet crying, bodies and debris glowing in the light of the campfire. Trapper inched toward a large boulder at the center of the canyon, backing up to it and keeping Lady Z in front of him. He waited several minutes in silence, hoping that perhaps Cheyenne Zeke had himself been wounded by one of the explosions. Sweat poured down the man's face as he watched all the shadows, and he gripped his rifle tightly.

"Here she is, breed!" he finally shouted out nervously. "You want to know about Yellow Moon?"

"No, do not tell him!" the Lady whined.

"Shut up!" he growled, jerking her arm again. He searched the shadows again. "I'll tell you where she is, breed. And you can have the Lady here. Just let the rest of us go!"

His reply was another explosion. This time it was the cabin itself. They could hear horrified cries from the inside, the last to be heard from the remaining two men. Nick ducked over Lady Z as debris flew in every direction, and when he slowly rose again the cabin was a ball of flames.

"The gold!" he mumbled. "He blew up all the damned gold!" He swallowed and scanned the canyon wall again, realizing that now the half-breed had accomplished exactly what he wanted. All were dead, and Nick Trapper and the Lady Z were left in the open with no protection. His blood chilled, and he kept the Lady tight against him, his back against the large rock.

"Breed!" he shouted. "I've still got the Lady. Promise to let me go or I'll shoot her, I swear! And then if you kill me you'll never know what happened to Yellow Moon!"

He waited in agony and torment, for there came no reply. The roaring flames lit up the canyon like a giant torch, and Nick could feel the heat from them. But then to his horror he felt cold steel against the back of his skull.

"Let go of the woman and drop your weapon," came the low, threatening voice.

"Oh, my God!" the Lady wept, hanging her head.

"Your tears are like music to my ears," Zeke sneered, shoving his rifle hard against Nick's skull. "I said to let go of her and throw aside your weapons!" he barked again.

The man swallowed and let go of the Lady. She turned and looked up at Zeke as Nick threw his rifle aside and began unbuckling his gunbelt. For a brief moment their eyes held, and she saw that the years had not taken anything away from his handsomeness or his strength. He towered over them, standing on the very boulder beside which Trapper had been hiding himself. He wore the familiar buckskins, and his long black hair hung loose. His face was painted with warpaint, for he had been prepared to do battle.

"Zeke," she said softly. She searched for some kind of softness in his eyes, some kind of forgiveness. But there was none. His night in the snakepit and the fact that she had tried to kill his Abbie were not things a man like Cheyenne Zeke forgave. His eyes told her there was no place now in his heart for memories. She was wicked and wanton and had tortured and killed innocent people. She dropped her eyes.

"Turn around and back up," Zeke ordered Trapper. He glanced once more at the Lady Z, noticing that in spite of the

173

rough, wicked life she had led, she was still amazingly beautiful and well preserved. Every curve of her naked body was still perfect, her breasts still full and firm, her long legs dark and smooth. Even the letters he had carved into her cheeks did not really seem to take away from her beautifully etched face. But he had seen with revulsion what she had become and he knew what she was capable of doing to others. He turned to Trapper again. "Tie her up," he told the man, pulling some rope from his belt and tossing it at the man.

Trapper frowned and slowly bent down to pick up the rope. "Why?" he asked.

"Tie her up!" Zeke repeated. "She can watch while you and I fight over her."

Trapper slowly approached the Lady, jerking her arms behind her and wrapping the rope around her wrists. "What are you talking about?" he asked Zeke, beginning to sum the man up now. Their sizes were nearly identical, and Nick thought himself just as mean and skilled as Cheyenne Zeke.

"I'm going to give you a chance to live, Trapper," Zeke growled. "First I want to know where Yellow Moon is."

Trapper shoved Lady Z to the ground and began wrapping more rope around her ankles. "She's in Santa Fe. A place called Anna's Place—a whorehouse owned by a woman named Anna Gale. She bought her from us."

Zeke felt a chill. He had been in Santa Fe. He had been close and had not even known it.

"What kind of hell did you put her through first?" Zeke asked coldly, "Besides killing her son, I mean."

Trapper froze in his movements and slowly raised his eyes to meet Zeke's. "Who told you that?" he asked.

"Never mind. I can tell by looking at you that it's true. I ought to carve your guts out while you're still alive, but I thought it would be more fun to fight it out—you and me, Trapper—just the two of us—with knives. That gives you a fair chance, doesn't it?"

"No!" the Lady shouted. "The knife is his favorite weapon, Nick! You cannot win such a fight!"

Trapper's eyes lit up with the realization that he would at

least be given a chance to live. He'd fought with knives before. Perhaps there was a chance.

"Tell me about Yellow Moon," Zeke said, raising the rifle and pointing it at the man's face.

"She, she went kind of crazy after the boy died," the man replied, swallowing again. "She just sits and stares. But we didn't do her any physical harm."

"Other than all of you taking turns with her, destroying her dignity and pride, taking away everything that was important to her!" Zeke growled through gritted teeth. "And what about the Lady Z? Did she have her fun with Yellow Moon, too?"

The Lady closed her eyes and turned her head away.

"The Lady has strange desires," Trapper replied.

Zeke's lip curled. "I've heard," he sneered. He walked over and kicked Trapper's guns farther away, then threw his own rifle and sidearm over beside them. He removed his big knife and threw it at Trapper's feet. "I'll even let you have the biggest one," he told the man, removing a much smaller knife. "That gives you the advantage, Trapper. I can carve you up just as good with this small one once I get it through your skin. You'll regret the day you killed that little boy! If not for that I might have let you go."

Trapper reached down and picked up the knife. "And you'll regret you ever was stupid enough to fight me this way, breed!" he snarled. He lunged at Zeke, but Zeke quickly darted out of the way, while Lady Z watched with terrified eyes. The two men danced in a circle, the fringes of Zeke's jacket swaying in the eerie firelight, his painted face making him look like a spirit of the devil. Trapper lunged again and again, taking aimless swipes with vicious energy, but to no avail. Zeke seemed to sense every move, and his speed at ducking and dodging was frustrating to the now frightened and sweating Nick Trapper. He knew by instinct that Cheyenne Zeke was only playing games with him, stretching out the inevitable. He'd been in many fights, but he had never fought one quite like this, and his fear made him plunge and strike wildly and blindly until he felt the first piercing pain in his side.

175

He grunted and stood still and terrified as Zeke yanked the knife out and stepped back. "That was only the beginning, Trapper. You made my little nephew suffer, and now *you* shall suffer!" he growled.

Trapper stumbled forward and lunged again at Zeke, but Zeke grasped the man's wrist and held it with a mighty strength brought on by his rage at the thought of this big man hunching over poor Yellow Moon, and the thought of his riding over and over little Laughing Boy's body and then leaving it for the wolves. He squeezed on the wrist of the weakening man until the big knife fell to the ground, and then Zeke plunged the smaller knife into the man's privates. Lady Z's scream at the sight was mingled with Trapper's own screams.

The man went to his knees and Zeke quickly picked up the bigger knife. Lady Z turned away. She knew the things Cheyenne Zeke was capable of doing with the knife. If he wanted a man to die slowly, he died slowly, and Nick Trapper's screams of agony filled the canyon. Lady Z curled up and felt ill, not caring to look and see what Zeke was doing, but at the same time wishing she could be doing the same thing to Zeke if the tables could have been turned.

But then Trapper's cries were drowned out by a mighty, unexpected explosion, as burning debris from the cabin had set surrounding short grass on fire and the flames had crept to the remaining stored dynamite. The force of the explosion sent Zeke flying, and he landed a few feet from Lady Z, stunned for a moment. The Lady lay screaming and curled up, and Zeke threw himself over her as more explosions ripped through the dynamite. She clung to the buckskin shirt, drinking in the familiar smell of him, and wondering if perhaps this man could be enticed into letting her go. After all, in that one brief moment he had thrown himself over her protectively, but when he raised up to look at her face, she could see by his eyes he had only saved her so that he could end her life the way he chose, rather than to let the dynamite kill her.

Their eyes held for a moment, and in the bright orange light she was beautiful indeed. Beautiful but evil. Her

176

breasts heaved with her heavy breathing, and her lips parted slightly. Then another explosion shook the canyon, and for a brief moment he could see Abbie and remembered her bruised and bleeding body after this woman had attacked her. He remembered the hissing snakes and the night of horror he had spent with the spirits of the underworld. He remained on top of Lady Z until the explosions appeared to be ended, then moved down and quickly slit the ropes at her ankles. He jerked her up by the hair. Slabs of rock were beginning to slide down from the canyon walls.

"Let's go!" he ordered. "This whole place is ready to cave in!"

He hurried over and grabbed his own rifle and sidearm, sliding both his knives back into their sheaths, and Lady Z gasped and felt ill when she glanced at Nick Trapper's mutilated body. The man opened his eyes and looked at her but he could not speak. Zeke gave the woman a shove. "Get moving before we're buried here!" he ordered. "He'll be dead soon."

The sound of crashing boulders roared through the canyon then, as Zeke hurried her forward toward the only exit. It was easy to see their way, for the whole canyon was lit like daylight. Lady Z's feet were quickly bruised and bleeding from running over the gravel and rock, but Zeke kept shoving her ahead of him, urging her up the pathway out before it became lost in the debris of rocks.

Twice they fell and he shielded her from falling rock, then jerked her up again. "Keep climbing!" he yelled. But she fell again. The entire canyon shook as though a great earthquake had hit it, but luckily it was the other side from which most of the rock was tumbling. But Zeke knew they had only minutes before their own side would completely give way. He climbed ahead of Lady Z and pulled her along by the wrists until they were finally at the top. He ran with her, half dragging her as they climbed through the maze of rocks above where he had located and killed the lookouts. They reached the broad, flat rock that he had found after exiting the hidden entrance and they ran across it, leaving the fast crumbling canyon behind, the dead bodies of the Mexican

177

woman and all of Lady Z's men being buried by the falling rock, where they would lie forever in their accidental grave.

Lady Z was sobbing now. All were gone! Her dreams of running the biggest and richest gang of outlaws were gone. The gold was gone. There was nothing left now but this man who hated her and who had already scarred her once. What would he do to her now? They stumbled down the other side of the boulder, and the noise of the crumbling canyon walls became more dim. The air was cooler and it was dark now. She heard a horse whinney and he pushed her down. He went to the horse and took something from it, then threw it at her.

"Put that on and cover yourself!" he growled, coming over and slitting the rope at her wrists to free her hands.

She looked down at one of his own buckskin shirts. She felt of its softness, then put it over her head, again smelling his unique, manly scent. "I think you want me to wear this because to see me naked makes you desire me," she sneered, wiping at her eyes. "You still want me, Cheyenne Zeke!"

Her jerked her up again, pressing her tightly against him. "About as much as I'd want to lie with a rattler!" he hissed. "We're alone now, Dancing Moon," he growled, using the name he knew her best by, and speaking in the Cheyenne tongue. "We'll have a good time together—you and me— and my *knife*!" He squeezed her so hard that her breath left her for a moment, and she saw by the wildness in his eyes that to try to entice him was fruitless, at least at the moment. Horror enveloped her, for his hatred for her was great, and she knew how vicious he could be. She had had many nightmares of the knife cutting into her face, of lying still for hours until the rattler finally crawled off her belly. She had baked in the sun then until she was finally found, nearly dead of exposure and thirst, by Apache Indians, who had taken her and healed her, then fought over her. She had had a good time with the Apache men before she'd finally managed to escape them.

But there would be no escaping Cheyenne Zeke. The worst part was that he knew how to bring death slowly, and choking tears of fear welled up in her throat. But her tears

178

did not touch him.

"I'm going to Santa Fe, slut!" he growled, pulling back from her and tying her wrists again, this time in front of her. Then he tied another piece of rope to the one around her wrists. "And you are going with me—at least most of the way. I won't make it easy for you by ending your life here and now. I want you to think about it for a while. Once we get through the entrance, I'm going to mount up and ride easy, and you, my Arapaho lover, are going to walk—all the way to Santa Fe! You're going to feel pain and thirst and hunger! Your feet will bleed and blister and your lips will crack. You're going to suffer the way you've made your captives suffer, and you'll regret the day you attacked my Abbie and all the other vile things you've done to innocent people because of your animal desires and your greed! When I'm through with you, you'll wish I'd have cut your heart out the day I left you in the desert instead of just carving up your face!"

He took the bridle of his horse and walked ahead of it, leading it through the hidden entrance to the canyon. She groaned as she felt herself being jerked forward.

"Zeke, don't do this! Please!" she begged. "I am sorry . . . for all of it! All of it! Truly I am! Do not do this to me!"

He only smiled and stared straight ahead, concentrating on Abbie's sweet face and the feel of her body close to his. Soon he would complete his mission and could go back home—to his little girls and to the son that he loved with such passion and pride. And to Abbie. Every bone in his body ached for her. And the woman he was half dragging behind his horse had tried to kill her. It was good to hear her tears and begging.

Ten

Rain poured down steadily, pattering rhythmically against the skins of the tipi. Inside the spacious dwelling a fire kept out the dampness, and Little Rock sat to the side with his stepgrandfather, Deer Slayer, playing a game with stones. Blue Bird Woman had gone back to the village with Black Elk and some of the others, but Swift Arrow had stayed on. Now he sat nearby also, telling stories to Little Blue Sky to help keep her occupied while the children had to be inside.

Abbie sat with her back to them, while Young Girl quietly fed at her breast. Occasionally Swift Arrow would glance at her, studying the whiteness of her shoulder where the tunic fell away, untied in order to feed her daughter. She had never been able to overcome her white-woman's embarrassment at letting anyone see her feed her child. An Indian woman would have readily dropped her tunic in anyone's presence to nurse her baby, for it was the natural thing to do. But not Abbie. She would always cover herself or turn away. Swift Arrow smiled and returned to his stories to Blue Sky, forcing back his thoughts of Abbie. She was Zeke's woman, and he honored both of them.

Abbie's heart was heavy. It had been almost two months since Zeke had left. Not only was she worried for his life, but she also missed the ranch and worried about Dooley, who was left alone there to guard things. The ranch was home now, the most home she had had since leaving Tennessee eight years ago. She longed to be back there, with Zeke at her side; to know that everything was all right and they were

180

a family again. She could feel movement in her belly now, and wondered if Zeke would ever see this child.

Someone rattled the buffalo hooves that hung at the entrance flap to the tipi, announcing their presence. Swift Arrow looked at the doorway, and Abbie quickly laid Young Girl aside and tied her tunic at the shoulder. The child seemed contentedly full, for her eyes quickly dropped to sleep. Abbie covered her and rose to draw aside the entrance flap, while Swift Arrow sat ready with his hand on his tomahawk in case the visitor was an enemy.

"Hello there, Miss Abbie," he heard a gruff voice greet her. "You may not remember me. I'm Zeb Crawley. I met you once before when you was visitin' the old fort a few years back with your husband. Me and Zeke go back a long ways—hunted and trapped together. I know your husband well."

"Yes, I remember you, Mr. Crawley," she answered with a frown. Her heart began to tighten. "Is there something wrong? Have you seen my husband?"

He removed his battered leather hat. "Oh, no, ma'am. I've not seen Zeke in years. I've come from your ranch. A man there told us Zeke was off huntin' up some Arapaho woman that got captured and that he'd sent you here to the fort for safety. I'm . . . uh . . . I'm here on a different matter." He saw the disappointment in her eyes. "I'm sorry I don't know nothin' about Zeke. He been gone long time?"

She nodded. "Too long." She stood aside. "Come in, Mr. Crawley."

"Please, call me Zeb, ma'am," he answered, stepping aside. He hesitated when he saw Swift Arrow sitting there looking at him distrustfully.

"It's all right, Swift Arrow," Abbie told him. "Mr. Crawley—I mean, Zeb—is a friend of Zeke's." She looked at Crawley. "Zeb, this is Swift Arrow, one of Zeke's Cheyenne brothers." She nodded toward Zeke's stepfather. "This is Deer Slayer, Zeke's Cheyenne father. And these are our children, Little Rock, Blue Sky, and the baby over there, Young Girl."

Zeb scanned the little family and Abbie, noticing her

181

swollen belly. She blushed a little and put her hand to her waist. "Number four is still unnamed," she told him.

Zeb grinned. "Appears things are going fine for you and Zeke," he told her.

She smiled lightly. "They are. I just hope he's safe."

"I wouldn't worry too much about that. Sometimes it takes time to find a person in this country. He'll be back." He stood there fumbling with his hat and glanced around the tipi again.

"What is your business here, Zeb?" Abbie asked him. "You said you came for a purpose, and you've been to the ranch. You mentioned 'us' when you spoke of being at the ranch. Is someone else with you?"

He sighed. "Yes, ma'am. I'm scoutin' for a railroad man by the name of Henry Page. He's at the fort now—wants to meet you. I've told him a lot about you and Zeke, and he's curious to meet you."

She frowned in confusion. "I don't understand. A railroad man? Out here? Why would he be way out here?"

Zeb shifted uncomfortably, glancing from Abbie to Swift Arrow and back to Abbie. "Well, ma'am, you'd best come over to the fort and talk to him yourself. It might be best that way."

Abbie looked at Swift Arrow, who glowered at Zeb Crawley distrustfully. "Will you go with me?" she asked him.

"*Ai*," he answered. "I do not want you to go alone."

Abbie looked at Zeb Crawley. "Is it all right if Swift Arrow comes?"

Zeb rubbed his jaw. "I have a feelin' Henry Page won't like it. But then I ain't real crazy about Henry Page either. Just doin' a job, Miss Abbie. Need the money, don't you see? I got no interest one way or the other."

"Interest in what?"

He swallowed. "Just come on over with me, will you?"

She shrugged. "Let me brush my hair first. And I'd like to put on my white tunic. It's much prettier."

The man nodded. "I'll meet you in the supply store. Mr. Page is set up in a room at the back of it. I'll go tell him you'll be along soon." He nodded to Swift Arrow and ducked out of the tipi. Abbie turned her eyes to Swift Arrow.

"Turn around while I change," she said quietly. "We will go and meet this Henry Page. But I don't like the sound of it."

"Nor do I!" he replied heatedly. "Why is a railroad man here on our land? We need no iron horses here! I have heard of these things called trains, but I have never seen one. I only know they bring white people and scare away the buffalo!"

She stepped closer to him. "Swift Arrow, when we go there, please try to stay calm. I have a feeling it would be best not to anger this man. Promise me. He's a white man. Let me do the talking."

He folded his arms. "I make no promises—except to protect you." He turned around. "Change your tunic. We shall go and see this Henry Page."

"Keep your temper," Deer Slayer warned his son. He also turned his eyes from Abbie as she slipped off her plain tunic, totally trusting both of them. "The man is white. Abbie is white. Let her do the talking, Swift Arrow."

Abbie slipped on the white tunic that was decorated beautifully with paintings and colored beads, a gift from her good friend Tall Grass Woman. Her heart pounded with worry over what Henry Page might want, but whatever it was, she would be as presentable as possible. She was Cheyenne Zeke's woman and her own heart was Cheyenne. This Henry Page would know that.

The trip to Santa Fe was a nightmare of agony for Lady Z, for Cheyenne Zeke kept his promise that she would walk all the way. After five days with little rest, they found themselves three miles from the city, and Lady Z could go no further. She staggered and fell, this time unable to rise again.

Zeke grudgingly dismounted and walked back to her, cutting the rope at her wrists and dragging her to a nearby stream. He threw her into the water to revive her, and she coughed and choked, then gasped at the feel of the cold water on her raw feet and dusty, cracked skin.

Zeke stood there watching her. This was much better than killing her would have been. He took great pleasure in seeing the scars he had put on her cheeks and the pain written in her eyes. He could have killed her back at the canyon and probably should have, but seeing her suffer was much more enjoyable. He pulled her out of the water and she grasped his wrists with weak fingers.

"Please, kill me or let me go!" she whimpered through swollen lips. "How much more . . . must I pay?" She met his eyes. "I . . . loved you . . . Zeke," she said in a near whisper. "You . . . never knew that . . . did you?"

He grinned. "You always were a good liar!" he sneered. "What kind of a fool do you take me for?"

It was the first time he had spoken to her at all in those five days. He had refused to speak to her or touch her, tossing her bits of food and allowing her one drink of water a day. She had offered all the information she could, hoping it would soften him. She had begged his forgiveness for hurting his white wife, pleaded with him that she hadn't wanted to throw him in the snakepit but that she couldn't stop her men and had had to go along with them. She cried and pleaded, screamed and begged, but could find not a trace of mercy. He looked at her only when necessary, gave her no bedroll at night and remained silent. She tried to explain that after the People had banished her she had had to turn to whatever she could do to survive, that she had been forced by circumstances into the life she led. But nothing worked. And now he no longer needed her. She knew it was only a matter of time before he ended her life, and she knew it would be by the blade. The worst part was that she truly had feelings for him, deeper feelings than for any of the other men. If only he hadn't brought his white wife to the village! Her soul still raged with jealousy over that first day Abigail Monroe had come to live with the Cheyenne! For she had known that the white woman would keep Zeke from ever returning to her own bed.

Now he pulled out his knife again, his left hand grasping

184

her hair so tightly that it pained her. She tried to pull away, waiting for the horror of the blade, but instead there was a quick jerk at her head, and the next thing she knew he stood there grinning before her, holding most of her long, thick mane of hair in his hand.

She gasped and put her hands to her hair, feeling the short, stubby uneven clumps that were left, and her blood felt cold. She could not think of a more humiliating thing he could have done than to cut off her hair. She looked at him, wide-eyed with shock and horror.

"Bastard!" she finally screamed. "You . . . filthy bastard! You half-blood skunk! Why do you not kill me and get it over with?" She went to her knees and cried with rage and despair.

He tossed her hair into the wind, then knelt down in front of her and jerked her hands from her face.

"I haven't killed you because you aren't *worth* killing, slut! You have brought shame and a bad reputation to all Arapaho women! You aren't a woman, Dancing Moon, or Lady Z, or whatever you choose to call yourself! In my whole life I have never hurt or killed a woman, nor have I wanted to, until you! I sometimes have wondered why— how I could do these things to a woman. And the same answer always comes to me. You're an animal and *not* human. And you're a disgrace to the Arapaho nation! If you had let poor Yellow Moon go, seen that she got back to her People, I never would have done this to you. I would have called us even! But you knew it was Yellow Moon, one of your own kind. And you abused her, touched her with your slimy hands and enjoyed her with your twisted mind! Then you sold her to a whorehouse!"

Her eyes blazed and she spat at him. "She deserved it! They all deserve it! They cast me out! They banished me!" she hissed.

"You brought it upon yourself because of your animal desires!"

"I would have stopped if you would have made me your woman!" she spat back at him. "It was always only you I wanted. Why could you not see that?" Her body jerked in hysteria, the shirt he had given her untied at the breast and revealing most of her large bosom. "I still want you, even after what you have done to me. Even though I hate you, I want you!" Their eyes held, and she brought her face closer. "And you still want me, Cheyenne Zeke. Your body burns for me. I can tell. All this time we have traveled together, in the night I could feel your thoughts. You were wondering how it would feel to be inside of Dancing Moon again, to feel the way only Dancing Moon can make a man feel." Her voice quieted. "Deny it, my half-breed lover. Deny that you need to know just once more what it is like to lie with Dancing Moon!"

She could not read his eyes. Had she won? He stared at her for a long moment, half smiling, a faint hint of desire in his dark eyes. He laid her back and moved on top of her, pinning her arms over her head by pushing on her wrists with one hand, the knife still in his other hand. Then he kissed her savagely, the way he knew she liked to be kissed, allowing the animal in him to bring on the hardness she would expect and pushing himself against her belly until she was sure she had brought Cheyenne Zeke under her spell.

She returned the kiss hungrily, groaning in sudden desire for this man she hated so vehemently for preferring a white woman over her. At last she would claim him again! At last she would prove she still had power over him! His tongue searched her mouth while his body forced her legs apart, and he felt her relax and knew she truly thought he would make love to her. Then in an instant his left hand moved down and grasped her jaw and he raised up slightly, and in the fraction of a second it took the sharp blade of his knife sliced off the end of her nose.

He held her jaw so tightly for a moment that she could not scream, but he saw the horror in her eyes with great pleasure.

"What you don't understand is that my Abbie gives me more pleasure in one night than you could give me in a life-time!" he hissed at her. "It was never just me and you, Dancing Moon," he went on, again using the old name most familiar to him. "It was you and a hundred others. Now you

186

have been properly branded, the way you should have been years ago. I told you you were not worth killing. I would feel dishonored killing the likes of you. It is much better this way. All your men are dead—and I have made you ugly. See how far you get now, my Arapaho whore! See how many men will want to share your stinking bed. See how many men will crawl after you with your hair a stub and your nose half gone—and my initials in your cheeks!"

He got off her and abruptly left, while waves of nausea swept over her. She screamed obsenities at him as she rolled to her knees, trying to stop the blood that poured from her nose. He did not look back. He would leave her there to fend for herself. Her screams mingled with weeping were very pleasant to his ears as he urged the roan mare into motion, heading for Santa Fe. It seemed he rode a very long way before her screams finally became distant and then faded completely. He grinned and began riding faster until the horse was at a gallop. He liked to feel the wind in his face, and he longed to have Little Rock racing beside him. He would hurry to Santa Fe and find Yellow Moon—and then go home—to Abbie.

Abbie followed Zeb Crawley into the fort and to the supply store, followed by a suspicious Swift Arrow, whose eyes darted about as though he feared someone intended to grab Abigail and haul her away. They went into a back room, where a neatly attired man with rings on his fingers sat at a table amid shelves of flour and dried beans and other supplies. Maps were spread out on the table. Abbie stood on the other side of the table, with Swift Arrow so close behind her she could feel his breath on her hair.

"Mr. Page, this here is Abigail Monroe," Crawley was telling the man in the three-piece suit. "The lady I told you about. The man with her is her brother-in-law, Swift Arrow, a Cheyenne."

Page rose slowly, his eyes scanning Abbie as though she were naked, and showing a hint of surprise. He glanced at the defiant Swift Arrow, whose hair hung long and straight,

187

adorned with beads and feathers, his powerful arms folded and making Abbie look like a small girl as she stood there in front of him. He looked at Crawley.

"Why is the Indian here?" he asked.

"Swift Arrow goes where I go," Abbie answered for Crawley. "My husband is away. Swift Arrow is watching out for me until he returns. Anything you have to say to me can be said in front of Swift Arrow."

Page watched her with obvious annoyance, but he decided he'd best keep the conversation on a friendly basis. He put on a smile. "All right, Mrs. Monroe," he replied. He put out his hand. "I'm just not as accustomed to Indians as you are. Can't blame a greenhorn like me for being worried at first. I'm Henry Page, and I'm very honored to meet you. I have heard a lot about you."

Abbie shook his hand reluctantly. "What is it you want with me, Mr. Page? I have to get back to my children."

His eyes dropped to her swelling waist, then moved back to meet her defiant look.

"You needn't be so defensive, Mrs. Monroe," he told her. "I must say, you are much more beautiful than I expected. And you speak very well."

"Why should you expect otherwise? Because I am married to a half-breed Cheyenne?" she answered, her temper rising. "Perhaps you thought I had some physical affliction, or that I was ignorant and illiterate! I can read and write, Mr. Page, very well. I am a Christian woman of morals. And I happen to love a man named Zeke Monroe— enough to live here among his People and be a part of them. It is people like you who made us decide to live as remotely from most whites as possible. We knew what their attitude would be, and I can see in your own eyes that Zeke was right."

He put on a bigger smile. "Now, now, Mrs. Monroe, you're misunderstanding me. I meant no insult, truly. I was only complimenting you. Most women who live the hard life you live—well, they age quickly, you know. You have remained a very beautiful woman," his eyes scanned the beautiful Indian garment she wore, "even in that tunic. Do

188

you always dress this way?"

"Most of the time. It's much more comfortable and practical. Would you please explain your business, sir? I really want to get back."

He sighed and motioned to a chair. "Please sit down, Mrs. Monroe. Please. I mean you no harm. Would you like some coffee? A drink of some kind?"

"No, thank you." She moved to the chair and sat down, and Swift Arrow remained standing, planting himself right beside her. She sat waiting for Henry Page to get to the point. He lit a cigar before doing so, hesitating before he put the match to the end of the smoke.

"Do you mind?" he asked. "Some ladies don't care for cigar smoke."

"Be my guest," she replied. "My husband sometimes smokes. I don't mind."

He leaned back in his chair and studied her a moment longer. "Your husband is a very lucky man, finding a woman who will give up the comforts of a white woman's life just for him."

He was trying to be complimentary and friendly, but she could feel the vibrations of curiosity, the unspoken insults, the disdain for a white woman who would sleep with a half-breed. She sat up straighter.

"Mr. Page, you have no idea what the circumstances are around my marriage to Zeke Monroe. You have no conception of what I went through when first I came West. My husband and I have been through things that go above and beyond social opinions. Our love is not based on the animal desires that you are insinuating." He reddened as she continued. "We have much more than that together. We have saved each other's lives. He has risked his life for me more than once. I dug a bullet out of his side, and he dug an arrow out of my chest. He helped me bury my whole family, and I have helped him forget a horrible memory he left behind in Tennessee when he was young. We both have deep emotional wounds that only each of us understands. Zeke is everything I want and need in a man, and I in turn give him the love and support he needs from a woman. Half his blood

189

is white, Mr. Page, and both of us are from Tennessee. Why should it be so unusual that we could love each other and want to marry? There was a time in my life when if not for Zeke I would have wanted to die. He has given me love and a family and something to live for, and I will not sit here with the guilty shamed look on my face you are expecting from me. I have no guilt or shame. I am proud to be Mrs. Zeke Monroe. And if you will please get to the point, I can get back to my children."

The man puffed his cigar quietly, moving his eyes from Abbie to Swift Arrow, who stood there with half a grin on his face. Then he looked back at Abbie.

"I honor your position, Mrs. Monroe. You just have to understand mine. To find a white woman living out here like an Indian is not exactly a common sight." He leaned forward. "However, as to my business here, Mrs. Monroe, I work for the railroad. And I'm here to tell you—perhaps I should say, warn you—that there is a great possibility we will be running tracks across your property."

She watched him steadily, trying to think and not panic. "You . . . can't do that. Not without our permission," she answered. "Zeke would never allow it, and I certainly do not intend to sit here and tell you it's all right. You should be speaking to my husband."

He grinned as though he'd won a battle. "Mrs. Monroe, what you don't understand is that I'm trying to be nice about this, to give you a chance to move on to other places. I don't have to talk to either one of you. I'm only doing so because I think it's the only right thing to do. That land you are squatting on is government property. We can do what we please with it."

She rose from her chair, her eyes blazing. "What do you mean—squatting! We've *claimed* that land! Zeke has worked night and day for years to get it in shape and build our cabin. He raises Appaloosas on that land. And it's *ours*."

The man puffed on the cigar again. "Perhaps you have papers, Mrs. Monroe. I'm aware William Bent outlined what you supposedly own and that he signed the papers and

190

both of you signed also. And it's true that it was in unorganized territory at the time, there for the taking. But that land has since been reorganized. It is part of the Indian Territory awarded under the Treaty of 1851. As such, it belongs to the government. If we need a railroad through there, we'll put one through."

Abbie looked helplessly at Zeb Crawley, who dropped his eyes, apparently feeling guilty for being a part of Henry Page's railroad plan. She looked back at Page. "Indian land is *Indian* land!" she spat back at him. "How can you award land to the Indians and then say it belongs to the government?"

"Because technically it does. All a treaty does, Mrs. Monroe, is set aside land that whites cannot enter and settle on. But it doesn't give ownership of that land to the Indians. It belongs to the United States government. If we need roads or railroads or anything else put through that land, we'll do it. It's that simple."

"*E-have-se-va!*" Swift Arrow sneered. He grabbed the maps from the table and jerked them off, wrinkling them slightly before tossing them to the floor. Page paled, but he rose and stood his ground. "The land belongs to the Cheyenne!" Swift Arrow growled. "And Zeke's land belongs to *Zeke!*"

"He *can't* own land." Page answered. "He's part Indian."

Swift Arrow's eyes blazed, realizing more fully than ever what the government's attitude was going to be toward the Indian.

"Then why do we have a treaty at all?" Swift Arrow hissed. "You say the land is ours, but it is *not* ours! You say whites cannot settle there, but they can put roads and iron horses through it, destroying more forests, dumping more garbage on the land, chasing away the game. You talk with a double tongue, white man. It is Indians like myself who will stop you from invading our sacred lands!"

Page's eyes sparked. "You'll never win such a fight!" he sneered. The two of them stood there, Page more than a little worried that Swift Arrow would draw out a knife or a tomahawk and feed the vengeance in his eyes. Abbie stepped

191

in front of Swift Arrow, turning to face him.

"Stay out of it, Swift Arrow," she warned. "Please. You made me a promise."

His nostrils flared with his quick breathing and his eyes blazed. He looked down at her. "It is as I told you!" he glowered. "The treaty means nothing! The sooner the Southern Cheyenne know this, the better off they will be!" Their eyes held in understanding and he stepped back a little while Abbie turned around, remaining between Swift Arrow and Henry Page.

"The land is in my name, Mr. Page," she told the man. "I am all white."

"Are you?" he sneered, scanning the tunic again. He grinned. "Even so, your children have Indian blood. They can never inherit the land. And the fact remains that it isn't yours to own in the first place. You're living on borrowed land and borrowed time, Mrs. Monroe."

She blinked rapidly, refusing to cry in front of him but feeling helpless and alone. She stepped back closer to Swift Arrow.

"Zeke and I will stay on that land, Mr. Page," she told him. "And if you try to come through there with a railroad, you'll have a fight on your hands, not just from us but from the whole Southern Cheyenne nation. You'll get no go-ahead from any of us."

He grinned and shook his head. "I don't need your go-ahead. I was just trying to be nice about this, Mrs. Monroe. I had hoped you, being white, would understand the situation and would try to talk some sense into your husband so that no one gets hurt. We aren't asking you to leave the ranch. We are simply telling you that if we choose to put a railroad through there, we will do it. If it happens to go right through your cabin, you'll have to rebuild someplace else. It's that simple. Believe me, I didn't call you over here to upset you or cause a commotion."

Their eyes held. "Didn't you?" she asked. "I think you did. I think you and others like you will do everything in your power to anger the Cheyenne and any other Indian nation that gets in your way, so that you will be able to talk about the 'savage' Indians and then have free license to come through this land and wipe out whatever red men get in your way and be able to boast that it was necessary. I am ashamed to say we are of the same blood, Mr. Page!" She whirled to leave and he called out her name. She hesitated at the door.

"Do you have a marriage license, Mrs. Monroe?" he asked with a sly smile.

She turned to meet his icy eyes. "I have a paper," she replied. "Signed by Mr. Jim Bridger himself, and the man who married us, Mr. Page. Out here in the wilderness one must make do. We were in love and there was not a minister to be found where we were. I had nearly died from an arrow wound and was still recovering. Zeke had to leave me at Fort Bridger, but he refused to leave without making me his wife first. We were married before God and several witnesses, Mr. Page, by a Mr. Winston Harrell, who was on our wagon train, a church deacon and brother to a minister. We spoke our vows with our hands on a bible and Christian words spoken over us."

"A deacon is not an ordained minister," Page sneered, his eyes laughing at her. "I'd say you're married the Cheyenne way, ma'am, but that doesn't count for much in the white world. A Cheyenne man simply takes a woman to his tipi and she's his wife, I'm told." His eyes drifted over her body again. "Is that how it was for you?"

She began to redden with helpless rage.

"Now wait a minute—" Zeb Crawley growled at Page.

"It's all right, Zeb," Abbie interrupted, her voice shaky but strong. She kept her eyes steadily on Henry Page. "Zeke Monroe and I were married before God and man, Mr. Page," she told him calmly. "If you choose to make it something cheap and ugly, that is your affair. But I know what is in my heart, and my God knows what is in my heart. I am Zeke Monroe's wife and the mother of his children. In the wilderness God understands we must sometimes substitute. But the love and the intent is the same, the vows are just as sacred because they're sworn before God, not to a piece of paper."

"But is Zeke Monroe a practicing Christian?" Page pressed.

Abbie refused to fold in front of him. She wanted to scream and lash out at him, and she knew now how painfully right Zeke had been about the way whites would treat her, at least those fresh from the East who did not understand this land.

"Zeke Monroe is Cheyenne," she answered bluntly. "He worships Maheo, and sometimes I, too, worship the Cheyenne spirits. I am not so certain that the Cheyenne's Great Spirit and my God are not one and the same. But for my sake, Zeke swore his vows to my God, with his hand on a Christian bible."

"I'd say it wouldn't be too hard for me to prove you can't legally hold that land under the name of Abigail Monroe, ma'am," Page answered coldly. "Perhaps, until you find an ordained minister to legally marry you, the title should be to whatever your maiden name is."

"You got no right talkin' to this fine woman like that!" Crawley put in, stepping closer to Abbie. Swift Arrow had watched curiously, unsure of just what the implications were of Henry Page's accusations, but aware he was deeply upsetting Abbie.

"I need a fresh scalp!" he hissed through gritted teeth. He started past Abbie, but she grabbed his arm.

"No!" she yelled. "Let it be, Swift Arrow! He wants you to make trouble!"

Swift Arrow hesitated, and Page stood there grinning, eyeing her again. "You're a clever woman, Mrs. Monroe; or should I say, Miss . . . uh . . . what is your maiden name, by the way?"

She stepped in front of Swift Arrow. "My name is Abigail Monroe, Mrs. Ezekiel Monroe!" she told him in a cold, calm voice. "I own a piece of land on the Arkansas, and no one is going to take it from me or put a railroad through it. Zeke doesn't really care about owning land, Mr. Page, because he's mostly Cheyenne, and the Cheyenne don't understand owning land. He claimed that property for me, because he loves me and wanted me settled; because he wanted to make life a little easier for me. And now that I have it, I love it. And if I ask Cheyenne Zeke to kill every man who steps onto it to try to take it away, he'll do it—for me! So I suggest you stay off my land, Mr. Henry Page!"

The man tried to remain cool and casual, but behind the fake smile his hard, icy eyes told her he wanted very much to hurt her. "Believe me, Mrs. Monroe," he answered coolly. "I have your best interests in mind. You should understand what you could be up against in the future. I suggest you get a legal marriage license. I only warn you because we *are* of the same blood. And if your children do not have white names, I suggest you have them baptized and give them white names. I further suggest you educate them and dress them as whites. Otherwise, the day may come when you will find them living on reservation lands with their Cheyenne relatives, while you live with whites. You wouldn't want to be separated from your children, Mrs. Monroe, would you?"

She met his eyes coldly, holding her chin proudly. "*Sesenovotse!*" she spat out at him. She whirled and left, followed by Swift Arrow. Page turned to Crawley.

"What did she say?" he asked angrily.

"She called you a snake!" Crawley answered. "And I'm inclined to agree. If I'd knowed you was gonna upset her like that I'd not have brought her here!" He removed a compass from his belt that Page had given him and threw it on the table. "Get yourself another guide, Page," he added. "I'll earn my money some other way!" He stormed out of the room.

"Wait!" Page called out. "What will I do for a guide?"

Crawley did not answer. He walked outside, mounted his horse and rode out.

Abbie marched to the tipi, and Deer Slayer looked up in surprise as she began shoving things into parfleches angrily, while tears streamed down her face, mingled with her rain-drenched hair.

"What are you doing?" he asked as Swift Arrow entered.

"I'm going home, grandfather!" she declared. "I'm going to the ranch!"

"You are not to go there!" Swift Arrow told her, grabbing her arms. Their eyes held and then she burst into tears, resting her face against his chest. He put his arms around her, sensing she needed to feel his strength, knowing she would much prefer it was Zeke. He glanced at Deer Slayer, who gave him a dark, scowling look of warning.

"Take me home, Swift Arrow!" she sobbed. "I'd be safe with you and Deer Slayer and Dooley there. I need to go home! Please!" She looked up at him pleadingly, her body jerking in sobs. "Please take me home! I'd feel closer to Zeke! And I'm afraid. I should be there to protect our land. Please take me home!"

He could not say no to her. He nodded. "I will take you. I will wait there until Zeke returns."

Eleven

Zeke approached the back door of the plush saloon, called simply Anna's Place. He knew from the fancy stained glass windows, the velvety red wallpaper and tinkling chandeliers he could see through the swinging doors at the front that an Indian would be less than welcome in such an establishment. Perhaps he would get his information from Anna Gale more easily if he spoke to her quietly behind closed doors.

He had washed and shaved, wanting to rid himself of the filth of Lady Z. He felt as though the smell of her was on his clothes and skin, and he had rinsed his mouth with tooth powder to get rid of the taste of her heated lips—lips that had touched a hundred men and God only knew how many women. Now his hair gleamed clean and soft and was brushed out long, with one small braid decorating one side, set off by a colorful, beaded ornament of a circular design, with otter fur twisted through the braid. He wore the white beaded buckskin shirt that Abbie liked, with a bone hair pipe necklace adorning his throat and an eagle feather twisted into another tuft of hair behind his left ear.

He had decided he was better off showing as much of his Indian side as possible. Anna Gale must not doubt that he was related to Yellow Moon, or she might not believe his story. His best hope was that she would turn the woman over to him with no trouble, and believing that he was a relative might help, if there was a human side to this Anna Gale, which he considered doubtful.

He walked around to the back door of the establishment and pounded on it. After a few moments a man with an apron tied around his middle opened the door, looking startled to see an Indian standing there.

"What the hell do you want, redskin? If you figure on taking my scalp, you'd best think twice. Santa Fe is a settled town now. You'd be in a heap of trouble."

"I want to speak with Anna Gale," Zeke answered, surprising the man with his good English.

The man eyed him up and down. "What would you want with Anna? She doesn't do business with Indians!"

Zeke quelled his anger. "I am looking for someone. Miss Gale supposedly knows about her. She might even be here in this place."

The man frowned. "Wait a minute." He slammed the door in Zeke's face and Zeke waited outside, finding it difficult to keep from breaking down the door and charging inside to ransack every room until he found Yellow Moon. The minutes seemed like hours until the man finally opened the door again and motioned for him to come inside. Zeke stepped in cautiously as the door was closed.

A woman of exceeding beauty stood across the room, her eyes drinking in his masculinity. Her skin was milky smooth, her breasts billowing over the low-cut bodice of her deep pink satin dress. She was not as heavily painted as most whores painted themselves, and he could smell a very light, pleasant perfume as she stepped closer. He looked straight back challengingly into her intense blue eyes. Her thick black tresses hung fetchingly over white shoulders, and her form was exquisite.

"My, my," she finally spoke up, smiling a beautiful, provocative smile. "I don't believe a more handsome or finer specimen of man has ever graced my establishment, Indian or not," she added, coming even closer. She reached up and traced a delicate finger over the designs on the front of the white buckskin shirt, feeling an intense need in her loins at the scent of man and leather and the sight of the broad, powerful shoulders and dark, fiery eyes that looked down at her. "What is it you want, mister?"

"I am Cheyenne Zeke," he answered curtly. "You are Anna Gale?"

198

She grinned more, stepping back and eyeing him up and down again. "I am. You speak good English for an Indian."

He did not give her an explanation. "You bought my brother's wife from a woman called Lady Z. She was taken against her will. I am here to take her home."

She raised her eyebrows and put her hands on her hips. "Is that so?"

"It is. She is called Yellow Moon. Bring her to me and I will take her home."

"Just like that?"

He put his hand on the handle of his knife. "Just like that."

The man who was still in the room reached for a rifle, but in a flash Zeke whirled, waving the knife. "I would not touch that gun, unless you like the feel of steel in your belly!" he growled.

The man froze, and Anna just stood quietly studying Zeke. His grand stature and his obvious ability to use the knife ripped at her insides. She wanted this man.

"Leave the room, Stuart," she said quietly.

"But, Anna—"

"Leave!" she commanded. "I trust him."

The man scowled. "You're nuts! If he gives you any trouble, you give a holler!" He stalked out of the room, which appeared to be a storeroom for food and whiskey. Zeke, still holding the knife, shifted his eyes back to Anna.

"Put that thing away," she told him gently. "This town has law now, mister. If you want to get your sister-in-law and take her home instead of her staying in Santa Fe and you hanging by the neck, you'd best put the knife away. I'm willing to bargain with you."

He cautiously slid the knife back into its sheath. "Bargain? I make no bargains."

She stepped closer again, her eyes glittering with desire. "I paid good money for Yellow Moon. She's a beautiful girl," she told him. "I'll not give her up without getting something back for it. If you want this Yellow Moon, then you must do two things for me."

He watched her carefully, seeing the hunger in her eyes.

This woman was not unlike Lady Z, except that she was more civilized and sophisticated, cleaner and more clever. She was obviously a wealthy woman, and there was no doubt as to how she had become wealthy. "What do you wish me to do?" he asked.

"Dancing Moon is with a friend of mine. If you go there, you must not tell him who gave you the information. We have a certain—relationship—that is secret. He's a very wealthy man, and owns half of Santa Fe. He's married to a very proper woman and it is not well known that he and I are . . . business partners, you might say. If he knew I told you about us, he would be very angry. Besides, he won't want to give up Yellow Moon, who his wife doesn't even know he uses for sexual purposes. She's simply their maid, as far as his wife knows. He would be very angry if he knew I was the one who led you to him. I need his power and his money. Do you understand what I am saying?"

He nodded. "I understand. He will not know. You have my word."

She smiled provocatively. "I've always heard the word of an Indian is true."

"It is. What else is it you want from me?"

She studied him for a long moment. "How badly do you want this sister-in-law?"

"Very badly. She is—or was—a sweet and lovely woman. She should go home—to her people. It is important. I have been through much danger and hardship trying to find her. I want it over. I want to take her home."

She traced her fingers over the fine outline of his lips. "I've never been bedded by an Indian before," she said softly. "That's the other half of the bargain."

He stood there rigid for a moment. It would be an easy debt to pay with such a beautiful woman, but he had no true desire for her.

"I have a woman," he answered coolly.

She laughed lightly. "Any squaw would understand. Some Indian men even have more than one wife, I'm told."

He held her eyes. "White women do not understand such things. My woman would not understand."

Her smile faded and she stepped back slightly. "Your woman is white?"

He nodded. "We have three children and a fourth on the way. I have no wish to be disloyal to her." His eyes scanned her body. "I have no doubt that what you offer me is worth more than what you paid for Yellow Moon. You are probably priced high. But I cannot accept that part of your bargain. Ask something else of me. I have money."

Her eyes hardened. "No! I want *you*! Surely it isn't a difficult thing I ask of you. You're a man, and I'm good at what I do! Most men would gladly accept such a bargain. Come to my room and we can have it over with and you can have your precious Yellow Moon! It's the only way you'll get the information you need from me!"

She whirled. "Wait!" he called out, his blood boiling with anger and confusion. She turned and their eyes held as though doing silent battle. "How do you know I won't slit your throat when we're alone?"

She grinned slyly. "I'm the only one who knows what happened to Yellow Moon," she answered. "You can't harm me before you bed me, because you need some answers. And afterward you and I will go down the stairs and into the gambling hall, where there are plenty of witnesses. Then I'll tell you where she is. You won't dare harm me there, Mr. Cheyenne Zeke, or you'd be shot or hung. And that white woman you're married to and are so bent on being loyal to would never see you again. Now, you wouldn't want that to happen, would you?"

He stepped closer, putting his hands to the sides of her face and pressing tightly so that it hurt. "You are a clever woman. Don't you know I could crush your skull right here and now—that it wouldn't bother me in the least?"

She stared right back at him defiantly. "Then you'll never find Yellow Moon!"

His grip lightened.

"Besides," she added. "I know my men. You are a violent man. I am sure you've killed many men in your time, out of necessity, defense, most surely some out of revenge. Perhaps you have even killed women. But there is a gentle

201

side to you, my Cheyenne friend. There is compassion behind those angry eyes. If it were not so you wouldn't be here looking for your sister-in-law, and you wouldn't be so concerned about being disloyal to your wife. You have nothing personal against me. I mean you no harm, and you have no need of revenge against me. You won't kill me. You won't even harm me. Because more than any other reason, you want to get safely home to that wife of yours."

He held her gaze for several long seconds. He suddenly felt in more danger here in the middle of civilization and in the hands of this one woman, than he had felt in the wilderness against all of Lady Z's men. Everything she said made sense. If he tried to beat the information out of her, a posse of men would be on him in no time, for even now he sensed that the one called Stuart was listening just outside the door, perhaps peeking through a secret vantage point. This woman was too clever to let herself be truly alone with a savage. Civilization was Cheyenne Zeke's greatest danger, for laws meant arrest and jail, and for an Indian, and especially a half-breed, that meant an unfair trial and certain death. But his sweet Abbie and his children were waiting for him.

Anna watched him tremble with indecision, one side of her feeling excited and victorious, another side of her feeling sorry for his almost pleading eyes. She was amazed that to lie with her should be such a difficult duty to perform, for he was, after all, just a man. All men cheated on their wives at one time or another. To do it with a prostitute was certainly not uncommon. She took his hands.

"Come now. Am I that obnoxious?" she purred, bringing a sweetness to her vivid blue eyes.

"You are beautiful," he replied. "But I do not want you, Anna Gale, not in the way a man should truly want a woman. Not in the way I want my woman."

She shrugged. "It isn't necessary that you want me that way. The point is I want you. I've never been with an Indian. Consider it stud service, my tall, dark savage. It doesn't matter to me. I have something you want, and you have something I want. It's that simple. A business deal."

202

A strange weariness suddenly overwhelmed him. It had been a long, tired journey from the day he had left his family at Bent's fort. The wound in his shoulder still ached and kept him awake at night. He was tired and lonely, and to cause trouble in this town would only prolong his absence from home—perhaps forever. And more than anything now he wanted to go home to Abbie. Apparently to lie with this woman was the only way he was going to get there. If he hurt or killed her, he would not only be a wanted man in Tennessee, but also in this territory, and that would be no life for Abbie.

His dark eyes remained fixed on her blue ones, each challenging the other, trying to read each other's thoughts. "If you do not tell me afterward, or if you lie to me, woman, I will kill you, no matter what the consequences!" he hissed.

His frightening appearance only made her want him more. "I won't steer you wrong," she replied firmly, her blood on fire for his raw savageness.

He grasped her hair tightly, making her wince slightly. "Then I shall serve the bitch in heat, like the great bull buffalo serves the cows!" he growled. "You may have my body, my lovely whore, but be sure you know my heart and my soul belong to someone else, and what you ask of me means great sacrifice for me. But one like you would not understand, for you have no heart and no soul!" He bent down and met her lips angrily, violently, for he had promised her his body, but he did not promise that he would be gentle with her.

She returned the kiss with passion, in spite of his own bruising kiss, for he brought out a savageness in her own being she did not even know was there. His forcefulness only made her want him more, for no man had ever dealt with her this way. She was always the master, the men usually shy, most of them not even coming close to the things they bragged about themselves. But this man would be every bit the man she expected to find beneath the buckskin leggings. She had no doubt.

He released the kiss, and his dark eyes were bright and watery with a mixture of anger and passion. He had been long without a woman. He would use this one and then discard her to return to the woman he truly wanted, the one who made him desire her in so many more ways than this, the one who was quiet and gentle and patient, the one whose sweet, soft belly carried his life and who had brought him that kind of precious love the half-breed had found so little of in his life.

"Follow me up the back stairs," Anna was telling him, her voice husky with passion. She walked ahead of him and he hesitated. But again he thought of poor Yellow Moon—and of going home. She turned to look at him. "Have you changed your mind?" she asked softly, unbuttoning the front of her dress.

"No," he replied curtly. She turned and proceeded up the stairs, and he followed. Anna licked at her sore lips and did not care that they hurt. For once in her life she would be lying with a real man.

Bonnie walked hesitantly from the bedroom of her new cabin into the kitchen, where Rodney Lewis sat removing his shoes. Their marriage ceremony had been a simple one, performed by her own father, who had decided to leave Santa Fe and accompany his daughter North this time to be sure nothing happened to her. He had intended to come to the small settlement anyway at a future date, but after her kidnapping and her salvation at the hands of the half-breed man who had brought her back to Santa Fe, Conrad Beaker was afraid to let her leave again without him.

Rodney had been panicky with worry by the time they finally arrived, and there was great "rejoicing to the Lord" at their first small church service, held out of doors.

But Bonnie had found Rodney's embrace strangely cold now. Was it because her heart burned silently for Cheyenne Zeke? Of course. But she must forget him. There was nothing else she could do. She must live the proper life and marry the proper man. That man was Rodney.

Now it was their wedding night, and she was determined to take her man willingly. Perhaps once their bodies became one together, it would help her forget and bring her warmer feelings for him. Rodney looked up at her. He seemed thinner than when she'd known him back East, his shoulders not so broad, his hands too white, his mannerisms too meek. Why did he seem so different?

She blushed as his eyes moved over her standing there in her nightgown and robe. "You look lovely," he told her, his voice sounding strained.

"Thank you," she said with a smile. "I—brushed my hair out." She fingered the long blond tresses that graced her shoulders. "You've . . . never seen my hair down." She blushed more. But to her surprise he also blushed. He rose and came to stand before her, putting his hands on her shoulders.

"Bonnie, I . . . I thought perhaps . . . since you must be a little nervous and . . . afraid, I—I want to be a good husband, Bonnie. I don't want to . . . offend you on our wedding night."

She frowned. "Offend me?"

He kissed her forehead. "Yes. I know it's supposed to be . . . difficult for a woman who's never . . . never been with a man. I wouldn't want you to hate me, Bonnie. So I thought for tonight we'd . . . we'd sleep apart—get to know each other better, feel more at ease with each other. We've been apart such a long time, and we got married so quickly."

Her body felt icy with disappointment, but she didn't know how to tell him she wanted him—wanted to make love and be a woman. If she told him, perhaps he would think her less than proper. She nodded. Yes, she was afraid; but the man was supposed to know how to help the woman, how to break down her inhibitions. She suddenly saw with acute disappointment that it was not her fear that bothered him, but his own. He was afraid! She could see it in his eyes.

"I . . . appreciate your concern," she told him softly, not wanting to embarrass him by screaming out that it was he who was afraid, by asking what kind of man he was that he would be afraid to bed his own wife on his wedding night.

"It's difficult . . . for us both, Bonnie. I have . . . prayed . . . that God will help me be a good husband. I think

205

I should start by . . . by giving you time . . . to adjust. After what you went through being captured and all, it must be difficult for you . . . to come up here and marry right away."

She hung her head, realizing now that he had probably never been with a woman before himself. How was she to learn about these things from a man of no experience? She should have understood that before, but it had not occurred to her. She patted his arm.

"Good night, Rodney," she said quietly, turning away to hide her disappointment.

"Good night, Bonnie. I'm . . . so proud and happy that you are my wife. I'll sleep out here on a bedroll. I'll be fine. I want you to rest easy tonight—relax and get plenty of sleep, my darling."

"I will," she replied almost inaudibly. She forced her legs to walk back into the bedroom of the tiny cabin. She went to the dresser and pulled open the small top drawer to look at the bone hairpipe necklace, the gift from Cheyenne Zeke that she would treasure forever. She touched it with her fingers and a tear spilled onto the back of her hand. Zeke would have known what to do. Zeke would have made her forget her fears and inhibitions. But she was not married to Cheyenne Zeke. She was married to Rodney Lewis, and perhaps in time. . . .

She picked up the necklace and kissed it, then softly closed the drawer and went to the bed, burying her face in the pillow and stifling her tears so that Rodney would not hear.

Anna Gale carefully rose from the bed, gently pulling a satin sheet over Zeke. The man was apparently totally worn out from whatever he had been through searching for Yellow Moon. He had told her Lady Z's men were all dead, and she did not doubt it was by his own hands. If so, this man had apparently gone up against the Lady's entire gang, no easy accomplishment. Now he slept hard, probably in a decent bed with a roof over his head for the first time in

206

weeks, if a bed and a roof meant anything to such a man.

She watched him as she pulled on a robe, her body surging with renewed desire at the sight of the broad, dark shoulders and the scars on his chest. He was a man who had suffered much in his lifetime, yet had remained strong and sure. He was a man of violence and passion, and apparently capable of great love, for serving her had been very difficult for him. It was not that he had any trouble being a man for her. He had pleased her more than any man she had ever slept with. But she could almost feel his hatred of the act the whole time, an inner pain that seemed to move into her own body as he invaded her physically. He was a man of mystery, who spoke little and demanded much.

She stretched, feeling sore all over, as though he had beat her, which in a sense he had, for he had been as hard and violent as he could be in his anger. Yet it had been thrilling, and she suddenly realized she had a certain feeling for him she had never had for a man. She did not want to see him go, but there would be no keeping such a man. He was hell-bent on finding his sister-in-law and getting back to the mysterious white woman he loved. There would be no stopping him, and no denying her promise to tell him where Yellow Moon had gone.

She walked over to her dresser and splashed cold water on her face. She glanced at his gear, which she had ordered brought up from his horse so it would not be stolen. She wiped off her face, then peeked over to be sure he was still asleep before quietly walking over to his large parfleche, hoping to find some clue to who his wife might be, what she looked like. She pulled open the parfleche and glanced inside, where two little straw dolls lay, and she was suddenly touched. They still had price tags on them. He had apparently bought them for his children. She spotted a little black velvet box and quickly reached inside to see its contents before he awakened. She opened it and was greeted by a gold ring with four tiny diamonds in it. It appeared to be some kind of wedding ring. She quickly put it back inside and glanced at a brand new rifle, also still carrying a price tag, stashed in the corner beside his own rifle.

"For the son," she thought to herself. She rose, suddenly feeling empty and lonely. He stirred then and stretched, then suddenly bolted upright, as though ready to do battle, apparently having forgotten for a moment just where he was. But then his eyes met hers. They were not so angry now, but they did show a certain hatred. He rose, still naked, and she felt an urgency in her groin at the sight of him. He did not look at her as he walked over to the parfleche, rummaging around inside it until he found a clean loincloth. He tied it on.

"Where is she?" he asked bluntly, walking over to his leggings and pulling them on.

"About two miles north of Santa Fe, on the main road. You'll see quite a grand estate, a mansion of a house. The signpost reads Mr. Winston Garvey. He's a very wealthy man. I knew him back in Washington, years ago, when he was a senator. He owns a considerable amount of real estate out here now, as well as several businesses and a good share of my saloon, although I'm trying to get out from under my debt to him. He backed me financially when I first came out here."

He pulled on his buckskin shirt, covering the muscular arms and shoulders she would have preferred to continue looking at. "What's the man like?"

"Ruthless—like most men in power. Be careful, Zeke."

He glanced at her, detecting a sincerity in the remark. He seemed to soften slightly. "I'm always careful," he replied, coming back to the parfleche. He took out a homemade brush and started brushing out his long mane.

"I . . . I'd like to brush your hair," she told him, seeming suddenly subdued and more like a real woman than an unfeeling prostitute. "May I?" she asked hesitantly.

Their eyes held and then he handed her the brush. He went to the bed and sat down on it, and she climbed onto the bed behind him and began brushing his hair, noticing how clean and soft it was, not at all the way she had pictured an Indian man's hair.

"Garvey's first wife was killed by Comanches on her way West," she told him. "She was very young. Her little boy

208

was with her. He saw his mother die—never forgot it. It left the boy a little touched in the head. He thinks Cheyenne did it, because the Indians told him they were Cheyenne. But it was Comanche arrows they found in the bodies. They left the boy alive."

"Cheyenne don't do those things," he told her. "You can bet it was Comanches. But the Cheyenne are getting angry and restless. It won't be long before they'll join the others against the damned, lying whites."

She ran her hand gently over his hair. "Zeke, I . . . I'm not as terrible as you think," she told him, changing the conversation. She suddenly didn't care about Garvey or the Indians. It was suddenly important that this man not go away hating her. She continued brushing his hair. "I'm sure being a half-breed, you suffered much in growing up— torture, humiliation, insults. I was an orphan, Zeke. It was much the same for me. Orphans back East are treated like something not quite as important as a dog. They're outcasts, Zeke, unloved and unwanted, as though they carry some kind of disease. You either grow up working the alleys, stealing to stay alive, selling your body for pin money; or you live in an orphanage where they beat you and loan you out to factories where you work sixteen to eighteen hours a day for a pittance. I was one who worked in a factory. And then one day my foreman ordered me into his office, where he closed the door and proceeded to show me how he could make life easier for me. He 'adopted' me and took me home with him, supposedly to care for his ailing wife. But he came to my bed every night and forced himself on me until I quit resisting. I was twelve years old."

She stopped brushing and sighed. He turned to face her, the hatred finally gone from his eyes, and it was the first time she cared what a man thought of her.

"I, too, had a hard life when I was growing up. I am wanted in Tennessee for killing the men who raped and murdered my first wife and our little son," he told her. "But I did not use my hardship as an excuse to harm innocent people."

She searched his eyes pleadingly. "I do not harm

209

innocent people. People come to me willingly. All my girls are what they are for their own personal reasons. You must believe me. The only reason I took Yellow Moon was because they told me she was retarded, a mute. She never resisted anyone. She just . . . sat there." She looked away. "Or laid there. I felt kind of sorry for her, and I didn't know what else to do with her. If I hadn't bought her, Lady Z would have killed her. But then she became a burden here. The way she acted frightened the men off rather than attracting them. Then Senator Garvey said he'd take her." She looked back at him. "Oh, I knew what he'd do with her. But at least she would be comfortable and safe." Her eyes teared. "I don't know why, but it's important that you believe me, Zeke. I'm not like Lady Z—truly I'm not. She was an animal. I seldom did business with her."

He held her eyes, and his handsome face made her heart ache with the wish that she could keep him. "Did you ever sleep with her?" he asked bluntly.

She reddened with indignation and straightened. "No!" she answered coldly. He could see the truth in her eyes. "I'm not that kind, and neither are any of my girls!"

He looked almost relieved. He rose from the bed. "Thank you for the information," he told her, walking over and beginning to strap on his weapons.

She rose from the bed. "That's it?"

He nodded. "That's it. I've done my service, and you've done yours. A business deal, remember? I have a family to get back to, soon as I can get there."

She came closer, hanging her head. "I hate to see you go." She met his eyes and put on a smile. "You're some man, Cheyenne Zeke. Too bad you're taken."

His eyes dropped to her breasts that swelled beneath the thin robe.

"I am sure there are many men who are glad you are not taken," he replied. "They will keep you company." He slung the parfleche over his shoulder and picked up his rifles and gear, heading for the door.

"Zeke!" she called out. He turned to face her once more. "Tell me you don't hate me. Tell me you understand—just a little. I . . . I was playing games last night, I admit. But once you . . . once we were . . . together . . . I didn't want to play games anymore. I just . . . wanted you . . . as a woman wants a man she . . . cares for."

A hint of compassion flickered in his eyes. "You are too much woman to be so wasted," he replied. "But you are very good at what you do, Anna Gale. I can understand why you are so wealthy. I suppose I understand . . . a little. I understand the tortures of childhood. It made you a woman of prostitution. It made me a man of vengeance."

She reached toward him. "There is coffee downstairs. Won't you stay and have some before you leave?"

He shook his head. "I must go. I am anxious to get home."

Her eyes saddened. "Of course you are. Good-bye, Cheyenne Zeke."

He studied her a moment longer. "Good-bye, Anna." He left quickly, and she listened for his footsteps, but his moccasined feet made no noise. He had simply vanished, and she suddenly wondered if he had been there at all. She walked over to the bed, touching the side where he had slept. It was still slightly warm. She closed her eyes and a tear slipped down her cheek. Never had any man made her heart feel so heavy. Never had she regretted seeing one walk out her door. And she had known this one for only one night.

Zeke headed his horse north to find the estate of Winston Garvey. But his anticipation at finding Yellow Moon was momentarily overwhelmed by what he had sacrificed to find out where she was. His unfaithfulness to Abbie weighed heavily on his mind, for even though he had not wanted to do what he did, the fact remained that he had done it, and he felt as though someone had cut out a piece of his heart.

A payment had to be made—a sacrifice for being untrue physically to the woman he loved. He was not a man to keep secrets from his wife. He would tell her because that was the kind of man he was, and if he tried to keep it a secret she

211

would see it in his eyes, and it would be cause for constant friction between them. He did not want that. Not with his Abbie.

His heart ached so that he groaned aloud, his eyes tearing. Abbie! How he wished it was Abbie who had lain beneath him. Sweet Abbie! She was home waiting patiently and loyally for him. But his body had been with another woman, and he must atone for it. For his heart, his very blood, pulsed only for his Abbie, and he'd broken a vow. It was not his nature to break a vow, especially one that had been made to the woman he loved more than his own life. There was something he must do before he went for Yellow Moon.

He found a stream of icy water that ran down clear and bright from a mountain. He dismounted and tied his horse, then stripped off his shirt and threw back his head, facing the sun.

"Maheo give me strength for what I must do!" he groaned. It would not be easy, but it was the only answer. He removed his hatchet from his mount and went to kneel beside the stream, placing his left hand on a flat rock. He stared at the hand for a long time, again praying for strength. He had betrayed his woman, whether it was for good reason or not. It was done. He breathed deeply, his chest aching for her, his body crying out, his mind praying that she would not hold it against him. For sometimes white women did not understand such things, and their love had never been tested in that way. There was only one way that might make her understand how difficult it had been for him.

He blinked back tears and his right hand shook with apprehension as he raised the hatchet. He felt weak with a great temptation to refrain from doing what he must do, but he was Cheyenne. He was a man. He had suffered the tortures of the Sun Dance. He could suffer this. In the next moment the hatchet came down hard, and the end of his little finger disappeared.

At first there was no pain. He threw the hatchet aside and quickly dipped his hand in the icy waters, holding it there and letting the blood flow to clean the stub. He loosened a rawhide strip from his shirt and quickly tied it around the end of the finger, using his teeth to pull it tight to stop the bleeding. He sat down then, his back against a rock. Soon he would drink some whiskey for the pain. In a day or two he would go and get Yellow Moon and it would be over. He could go home—to Abbie. His mission would be finished. He would not leave Abbie again. It hurt too much to be away from her. But then perhaps she would not want him now.

Twelve

Zeke approached the massive arched stone gateway to the sprawling Garvey estate, deeply disturbed at the idea of wealthy whites coming West to claim land. He well knew it could mean the same kind of doom for the Plains Indians as had befallen the Cherokee, the Creeks, the Choctaws, the Seminole and the many other Eastern tribes, some of them totally extinct now. The invasion had begun into Unorganized Territory, and he envisioned it as an earthen dam, beginning to bulge with the weight of flooding waters behind it. Soon the dam would break, and the waters would cascade over everything below it. The water represented the invading whites. The dam represented the flimsy treaties, the futile efforts of the army and the Indians themselves to keep the whites out of Indian territory. The dam would break, and when it did, the Indian would drown. His heart felt heavy with the sureness of his vision.

He trotted his horse through the archway, studying the huge, two-story stone mansion that loomed in the distance, looking wavy from the rays of the desert heat. To Zeke the house was like a giant tombstone, for it was beneath the homes of such people as Winston Garvey that the Indian would someday lie. He moved ahead slowly, spotting a cloud of dust in the distance. He had expected a greeting party, and apparently he was getting one. A man like Winston Garvey would not leave himself unprotected. He halted his mount and waited as the horses drew closer, five men, all carrying rifles. He sat quietly waiting, making no move for his own weapons. He had no quarrel with these men and did not care to challenge them unnecessarily. They galloped up close to him, bringing their hard-breathing mounts to dusty halts. Zeke's horse whinnied and tossed its head.

"What are you doing here, Indian?" one of the men asked. He was clean-cut and shaven, a hard-looking man who Zeke could see knew how to use his rifle but was also the kind of man who knew how to take orders.

"I am called Cheyenne Zeke," he replied. "I am here to see Mr. Winston Garvey."

"About what? Garvey doesn't want to see any Indian. What kind of business would you have with Garvey?"

Zeke eyed them all warily, his dark eyes coming back to the apparent spokesman, his hand resting casually on his knife in case he should need it. "Garvey has an Indian woman here—a maid, I believe," he answered, watching the man's eyes. He could see the man knew or at least suspected Yellow Moon was more than just a maid. "The woman is called Yellow Moon," he went on. "And she is my sister-in-law. She was stolen by slave traders. I am here to take her back home."

The man laughed lightly. "Is that so? Well, maybe Mr. Garvey isn't wanting to let her go."

Zeke held the man's eyes steadily. "Maybe you should ask him," he answered. "Maybe you should tell him I'm here, and that I know a few things about him that perhaps he wouldn't want others to know. And you might add that I have some Comanche and some Apache friends who are ready to ride down on this place and make a bonfire out of it if he refuses to talk to me—or if he chooses to try to kill me."

It was a lie, but Zeke knew that for the right price, he could find Comanches or Apaches who would do just that, and for now he needed a bluff. He glared at the spokesman, the look in his eyes making the man believe him. He saw a flicker of doubt and hesitation, and the man even glanced out at the surrounding hills.

"You're lying," he declared.

Zeke shrugged. "If that's what you want to believe. But I don't think Garvey would like the kind of trouble my friends

215

can bring down, mister. I think he'd like to at least know the choices and decide for himself. You want to be responsible for this place being raided?"

The man's lips were tightly set in confused anger. "Follow me!" he growled.

Zeke suppressed a grin and followed behind the man, while the other four men stayed behind him. The mansion seemed a mile away, and Zeke figured it probably was at least three-quarters of a mile before they reached the house. He remained on his horse while the leader dismounted and went to the great double doorway. He opened one side, and Zeke noticed the doors were made of a fine, heavy oak, probably shipped out from the hardwood forests of the East.

Several minutes later the leader emerged, motioning for Zeke to come inside. Zeke dismounted and tied his mount, walking silently up the cement steps past white pillars and through the grand entrance. He stepped inside, amazed at how cool it was. The entranceway was dark, and everything was marble. He felt like a thorn among roses, standing on an oriental rug in his moccasins and buckskin clothing, adorned with enough weapons to face an army, his hair long and straight and decorated with beads and bonepipes.

The man who had motioned him inside disappeared down the hallway, and Zeke waited. He glanced at the walls, which held paintings of obvious worth. A maze of little tables holding plants and painted vases adorned the entranceway, and the thought of the wealth some whites were capable of obtaining gave him a chill, for the ones like Winston Garvey cared not how they obtained their money, as long as they got it.

"Let's get this over with!" he heard someone grumble farther down the hall. The two men emerged from a doorway and headed toward Zeke, the second man a short, very fat man, wearing an expensive pair of silk pants and a white silk shirt, with a vest to match the pants. A big cigar hung from the man's puffy lips. He was aged and balding, and at the moment he was huffing and puffing and grumbling like a steam engine. Zeke wondered how many layers of fat he would have to cut through to get to the man's vital organs if he should decide to use his knife on the fat Mr. Winston Garvey, for he had no doubt that was who was approaching.

The man glared at Zeke as he came closer, his eyes running up and down Zeke's fine physique and quickly summing up the fact that this Cheyenne Zeke was not a man to argue with or try to cast out lightly. This man was trouble, and most certainly the type who probably really did have any number of Comanche or Apache brothers who would raid the ranch at his bidding.

Garvey and his hired hand stopped in front of Zeke. "Get on outside," Garvey told his man, his eyes still on Zeke.

"But, sir, he might try to harm you."

Garvey squinted, studying Zeke. He did not want his hired hand to know all about Yellow Moon—or some of the other things this Cheyenne Zeke might know. "How about it, mister? You got a yen to take my scalp?"

"I am not here to harm you. I am only here to take my sister-in-law home. It's that simple. There are alternatives, but I don't think you would like them, Mr. Garvey. Unless, of course, you think Yellow Moon is worth all the heartache and loss I can bring to you."

Their eyes held challengingly. Cheyenne Zeke meant business. Winston Garvey was shrewd enough to know that. There were not enough soldiers yet in this territory to protect one ranch, and it was a fact that other ranches just as big had suffered great losses from raids. Winston Garvey did not intend to literally invite such trouble. He looked at his man.

"Go on. I'll talk to him in my study."

"But, sir—"

"Go on!" the man barked. He turned and opened another thick oak door and ushered Zeke into a plush, cool room, while the hired hand left reluctantly, grumbling on his way out the door. Garvey closed the door and motioned Zeke to take a seat in one of the heavy red leather chairs near the man's desk. Red curtains hung at the windows, blocking out the torrid sun, and a surprisingly pleasant breeze flowed through the room between facing screened windows.

Zeke sank gratefully into the chair, more tired than he cared to admit, after having spent a second sleepless night of pain because of his severed finger. It still throbbed annoyingly, but the pain was duller now, more of a nagging nuisance than the unbearable agony it had been the past forty-eight hours. It was wrapped tightly with gauze that showed fresh bloodstains. The bleeding had been difficult to stop, and it still recurred at the least little movement or bump.

"You're a half-breed?" Garvey asked, moving around behind his desk and sitting down himself. "You speak good English."

"My father was white, from Tennessee," Zeke replied.

"But you say you are related to Yellow Moon?" The man tamped out his cigar and leaned back in a high-backed leather chair that groaned from his weight.

"I have three half-brothers who are full-blood Cheyenne. I live with the Cheyenne most of the time. Yellow Moon was married to one of my brothers, who is now dead. She was stolen by slave traders and then sold to a house of prostitution. I traced her here and I have come for her. I have been searching for many weeks, Mr. Garvey. I have killed people to get here, and I will kill again if necessary. It is that simple."

Their eyes held, both men powerful but in different ways. Winston Garvey's power lay in his money and his ability to order people around. Cheyenne Zeke's power lay in himself, his raw courage and open daring. Garvey frowned.

"Who led you here? Did that scheming, deceiving Anna Gale set me up like this?"

Zeke thought for a moment about Anna, tempted to tell the truth and let her and this Winston Garvey fight it out. But he was a powerful man, capable of hurting her or perhaps even killing her. He had made her a promise. It was part of the bargain.

"No," he lied. "I found out through the Lady Z. She sold Yellow Moon to Anna Gale, and she heard later that Anna Gale had in turn given the woman to you because she was too much of a burden." He watched the suspicion and

218

apprehension in the ex-senator's eyes. "You needn't worry about your secret relationship with Anna Gale, Mr. Garvey. I know all about that, too, through Lady Z. But the Lady is no longer in business, and the men she rode with are all dead. She is no longer in a position to tell anyone of your secret, for I guarantee she has greater problems of her own. I will tell no one about Anna Gale either, unless you give me trouble. Your longtime relationship with the notorious prostitute would make a juicy newspaper story, here as well as in the East, would it not?"

Garvey glowered at him, his fat cheeks turning red. "You think you're pretty clever, don't you?" he grumbled.

"No, Mr. Garvey. I just try to think of all the angles."

Garvey squinted. "What did you mean about Lady Z being out of business? I've always heard stories about her ruthlessness. The law was never able to find her. How can she be out of business? She rode with a tough bunch of men."

Zeke grinned wickedly. "Perhaps the law could not find them, Mr. Garvey. But I found them."

There was a long moment of silence, while Winston Garvey absorbed the statement. He paled slightly as he took in the meaning of the words.

"You? You killed them all?"

"It isn't difficult when a man has the advantage of surprise, Mr. Garvey," Zeke replied. "But before I cut off the Lady Z's nose, I got what information I needed from her. I intended to kill her, but I decided she would suffer more by having to be alive and ugly. So I let her go. But her men are all dead and she is in no position to scare up another gang. That's all over with now. I came directly here after getting my information. I do wish, though, that I would have needed to talk to this Anna Gale. I have heard she is quite beautiful. But then I guess you would know better than anyone how she looks—from head to toe and in between— would you not?"

Garvey leaned forward and removed a handkerchief, patting his damp forehead. He was stunned to think that this man could single-handedly have destroyed the Lady Z's

219

band of men, and that he was ruthless enough to cut off a woman's nose. It was obvious the man would also gladly tell the whole world about Anna Gale and Winston Garvey if necessary, or bring down a whole nation of Comanches on the ranch. The man sighed deeply and tried to retain a calm appearance. He leaned back in his chair again. "Do you have a white name, Cheyenne Zeke?"

"Monroe. Zeke Monroe."

Garvey folded his arms across his fat belly. "Well, Zeke Monroe, you seem to have thought of everything. Personally, I don't consider Yellow Moon something important enough to cause a lot of trouble over. I am remarried to a very nice woman, Mr. Monroe, a woman of means, I might add. She's a pillar of high society—the frail sort, I might add. Living out here has not been easy for her. Your presence would alarm her, to say the least. But luckily she's upstairs lying down and doesn't even know you're here." Their eyes held. "I obviously don't want my wife to know or even suspect the real reason why I have Yellow Moon, which I am sure you do know. And I am equally sure you would see to it that my wife knew about it, for you are obviously a man without feeling."

Zeke's eyes flashed with anger. "I would say you are the one without feeling, Garvey," he said coolly. "Taking advantage of a poor, beaten, lost woman. I know your kind, Garvey, so don't play games with me. You don't give a damn about that wife of yours except that she's rich. And you don't give a damn about Yellow Moon, either. You don't give a damn about anything but yourself. You're a fat, greedy slob of a man who uses people to his advantage. But you won't use me, Garvey, and after today you won't use poor Yellow Moon anymore, either!"

Garvey's eyes narrowed and he leaned forward. "Don't you threaten me, you bastard half-breed! How dare you bring your stinking presence into this house and make demands!" He spoke up too quickly out of anger, accustomed to others cowering before his wealth and power. But such things did not impress Cheyenne Zeke. It seemed only an instant before Zeke had leaped out of his chair and was leaning over the desk, his menacing, dark presence making Garvey lean back again and break into a sweat, wishing he had kept the conversation calm.

"And how dare you keep an innocent woman behind closed doors for your devious sexual needs!" Zeke growled. "I've come for Yellow Moon and I don't intend to leave without her, Garvey, unless you want to lose this house and your wife and son and your own life to the Comanches and find out what pleasure they take in torturing people! Or perhaps you'd like the whole world to know about you and Anna Gale, as well as the fact that you sleep with an Indian woman on the side!"

Garvey's face reddened more. "I could have you killed, right now!" he threatened. "I have a lot of men."

In the next instant Zeke's knife was out and deftly flicked a button off the man's shirt, then rested against Garvey's fat neck. Sweat trickled down the man's face and he looked down cross-eyed for a moment at the knife, then back into Cheyenne Zeke's eyes. In all his comforts and grand living, he had forgotten that in this land some men still lived by raw violence. He had figured Zeke would say his piece and leave. But this man was turning out to be much more dangerous than he had anticipated.

"You call one man into this room, Garvey," Zeke was growling, "and you will be the first to die! And before they can kill me, enough of them will know about you and Anna Gale and Yellow Moon to spread the rumor. Your wife will know and your friends will know. You won't die with much dignity and honor, will you, Garvey? I don't think you want to die in that kind of disgrace. Not a big-time businessman like yourself. So why don't you do this the easy way like we talked about. Swallow your pride and just hand Yellow Moon over to me so I can take her back to her people."

Garvey swallowed and remained rigid. "Why in hell do you care, Monroe?" he asked. "Why did you go risking your neck with the Lady Z and then come here and risk it again just for one used-up Arapaho woman?"

Zeke's heart tightened at the way he had described poor Yellow Moon, still so young and once so pretty. "Because I care about my People," Zeke answered. "And I care about anyone related to me, especially when they are as innocent and good as Yellow Moon was. God only knows what she's like now!"

Garvey was paling, worried now about how Zeke would react when he saw her. "Look, Monroe, whatever shape she's in now is the way she was when I got her. You have to believe that. She . . . doesn't speak. She just obeys orders without protest. I . . . I haven't hurt her, understand? If she's hurt, it's the others who did it. Not me." He swallowed again. "She does menial work about the house."

"And sometimes you visit her in the night and use her body," Zeke added for him.

Garvey closed his eyes for a moment to keep his composure, the steel blade of Zeke's knife still tingling the skin of his neck. "I don't deny that," he answered. He opened his eyes again and glared at Zeke. "But it was Indians that killed my first wife, Monroe, so don't expect me to have fond feelings for them!"

Zeke moved the knife against the man's cheek. "And it was *white* men who killed *my* first wife, Garvey," he snarled. "And she was a white woman." He straightened then, pulling the knife away but keeping it out threateningly. "There's good and bad of all colors, Garvey! And I'm no damned fool when it comes to your kind. I've seen all the others like you." His lip curled in a sneering grin. "It isn't your first wife's death that makes you hate Indians, Garvey. You're not the type. You hate the Indians because you're greedy for wealth and power. You hate them because they stand in the way of your ability to get more land under your belt. They're a nuisance to men like you—no better than bugs to be stepped on and swept out the door! You've come out here to suck up every piece of land you can consume— every bit of trade, every business—everything! You're building yourself an empire, and your wife was just one of the necessary sacrifices for coming out here! Now your second wife will continue to provide needed money."

"Now wait a minute—"

"I know what goes on in Washington, Senator! I know all

about the plotting and scheming, the greed and the attitude toward the Indian. I walked the Trail of Tears, Garvey. So don't sit there and tell me about Indians killing your wife! You have a much grander plan in mind than revenge, and it started long before your wife was killed. Yellow Moon isn't a matter of revenge. She's the object of your own filthy white man's lust and your attitude that all Indian women are good for only one thing! Now hand her over before I let my hatred of men like you get the better of me! I have little patience left for your fat, greedy hide!"

Garvey glared back at him. He was a smart man—smart enough to know that at the moment it would be wise to give this half-breed what he wanted and avoid any further commotion. He had thought a challenge might back the man off, but nothing had worked. He was a busy man with much better things to worry about than one mute, used-up Arapaho woman.

"All right, Mr. Zeke Monroe," the man replied, slowly rising and secretly shaking. "I'll give her over. But I'd better never see your stinking half-breed face in my house or on my property again."

"Glad to oblige," Zeke growled. "I feel soiled standing here." He gripped the knife tightly, suddenly longing to get out of the massive tomb of a house. He felt the walls closing in on him, smothering him. He watched Garvey carefully as the man walked to the door and opened it, calling out to a maid who came scurrying.

"Is my wife still napping?" Zeke heard him ask.

"Yes, sir. She's lying down upstairs."

"Good. Go get the Indian woman from her room in the attic—quickly!" he ordered.

"Yes, sir."

Zeke's anger rose at the thought of Yellow Moon being kept in a hot attic room. He waited restlessly, while Garvey stood near the door as though ready to run if need be. He turned once to study Zeke again, still astonished that the man had apparently single-handedly taken care of Lady Z's men. He was a man of tremendous skill that Garvey did not care to challenge any further.

Zeke finally heard footsteps and the maid entered hesitantly, leading Yellow Moon by the arm. "Here she is, sir," the woman said, looking frightened and hurrying out of the room right away.

Zeke's heart tightened at the sight of his once-happy and beautiful sister-in-law. In the few weeks she had been missing, she had turned to hardly more than a skeleton. Her hair did not have its former sheen, and she wore a white woman's dress that bagged on her, a simple, faded calico that looked out of place on the dark-skinned young woman who should be wearing a tunic. She stood with her head hanging, staring at the floor, as though waiting for a beating. Zeke's eyes teared at the thought of her witnessing Laughing Boy being killed before her eyes beneath the hooves of Nick Trapper's horse.

"Yellow Moon?" he spoke up gently. She did not reply. He looked at Garvey. "What the hell have you done with her?"

"I told you, damn it! She was like this when I got her! The only difference was she had more meat on her bones. I didn't pay for her because I took her as a favor. The girl was a problem after Anna bought her. She wouldn't eat and the men complained that she . . . she didn't respond to them. Anna didn't quite know how to get rid of her, so I took her."

"To use until she finally dies of hunger!" Zeke hissed, coming closer. "I should kill you! You should have got a doctor for her!"

The man sneered. "For an Indian? Be serious, man! Even if I had tried I wouldn't have found one to help her. Actually I did her a favor. I got her away from that whorehouse and all those men—gave her a room in a nice quiet house. I tried to make her eat. I swear it!"

Zeke glowered at the man. "If I wasn't so concerned about getting Yellow Moon back to her people, I'd slit you from ear to ear, you fat-assed hypocrite!" he declared. "But I don't care to have men chasing me all the way back home. You're lucky this time, Garvey, but if we ever meet again your luck just might run out!" His hand moved restlessly on his knife. He sorely wanted to use it on the man, but it was

224

then he noticed the boy.

A young, dark-haired youngster of perhaps six or seven years old stood staring at him, his eyes on fire with hatred. He walked up to Zeke and glared at him a moment, then spat at him.

"Indian!" he hissed. "Dirty Indian! G-g-gooo away!" he stuttered. "K-k-k-kill m-my m-m-mother!" He began beating on Zeke, and Yellow Moon looked at the boy with frightened eyes and backed away from him. Zeke grasped the boy's arms firmly while tears began to stream down the boy's face.

"That's not true, son," he tried to explain. "It was not me or my people who killed—"

Garvey was there then, jerking the boy back. "Get your hands off my son and get the woman out of here. You wanted her. Now leave!"

Zeke wanted to hit the man, but not in front of the boy. "Why don't you explain to him—tell him the truth!" he growled. "It's only through the children there can be any peace out here with all the Indian unrest. Tell him the whole story, Garvey, about the good and the bad on both sides— about the Trail of Tears and—"

"Never!" Garvey replied, realizing he had the upper hand because of the presence of the boy. "It's through boys like mine, whose minds are disturbed because of some barbaric Indian attack, that we will find the men of tomorrow who will be ready and willing to ride against your kind and wipe them off the map! You see what the death of his mother did to him. I'm helping him all I can. And some day this fine boy is going to ride in uniform and help rid this fine land of its lice-infected scavenger savages! That's the only truth he needs to hear!"

The boy kicked at Zeke and Garvey jerked him back. Their eyes held challengingly and Zeke nodded. "Yes. Raise an Indian hater, Garvey," Zeke said quietly, many things suddenly even more clear to him. "Teach him right, just as I will be teaching my son right. Perhaps one day they'll meet!" He moved back toward Yellow Moon and took her arm and she did not protest. "You've laid your plan well, Garvey. It's too bad your son doesn't realize he's just a part

225

of your plan, like your wife was, like poor Yellow Moon was. Men like you have it all figured out, don't you? You do everything you can to make my people look bad, even to using your own son to do it. May the Gods forgive you for what you're doing to him!"

He led Yellow Moon past the boy toward the door and she cowered from the child again. He gently urged her through the door and outside, and all the while she followed him docilely and obediently, protesting nothing but seemingly unaware of who he was. Zeke lifted her onto his horse, then mounted up behind her, putting his arms around her to take the reins, afraid to let her ride behind for fear she wouldn't even have the sense to hold on to him. He left with the boy standing on the veranda shouting obscenities at him.

For three days of riding Yellow Moon said nothing. Zeke explained who he was, but she only stared vacantly. She sat motionless while he tried to make her eat, lay down wherever he told her to lie for the night and let him cover her, remaining almost unmoving through the night. She would put out a fire or make one, saddle or unsaddle the horse as he instructed, obeying all commands like a trained animal.

His heart bled for her. She could not go much longer without eating more, and he pondered just what he could do to bring her out of her stupor. It was not until he found her staring one morning at a dead prairie dog that the idea came to him. He had not mentioned Laughing Boy at all, afraid of what the memory would do to her. But Indians, the women even more than the men, needed to bleed and suffer when a child died. Yellow Moon had not been allowed that sacrifice. She was not at peace about her son's death.

He removed a knife from his belt, not the big one, but the smaller one. He walked over to her and sat down beside her, pointing to the dead prairie dog.

"Does the prairie dog remind you of Laughing Boy?" he asked gently.

She seemed to flinch at the mention of the name and her eyes blinked. Her mouth opened as though to say something, then closed again.

"Laughing Boy is dead, Yellow Moon. He's dead, and he needs to be sent along Ekutsihimmiyo, where his spirit can ride free and his heart can sing forever, where he will wait for his beautiful mother who loves him and whose blood runs in his veins." He moved in front of her. "Look at me, Yellow Moon. Look at me!"

Her eyes gradually moved from the prairie dog to Zeke. He saw terror and remorse behind them now, the first hint of feeling and recognition he had seen in her eyes since he had taken her from the Garvey mansion.

"It's over, Yellow Moon. But there is something you need to do isn't there? You know very well who I am. You aren't crazy—except that you're crazy with grief." He held up the knife before her eyes. "Here, Yellow Moon. Do what must be done so that you can think and feel again, and so that your soul can rest and Laughing Boy can also rest. Grieve the way you have a right to grieve!"

Her body began to tremble, and she slowly reached for the knife with a shaking hand. Tears began to well in her eyes as he allowed her to take the knife, and he folded both his hands around hers.

"Cry, Yellow Moon. Cry and chant and bleed for your son. It's all right now. You're safe, and I'm taking you home with me, to Abbie. You can stay with us."

She searched his eyes. "Zeke?" she spoke aloud.

He reached out and pushed some of the tangled, dry hair behind one ear. "Zeke," he replied. "I'm taking you back to the People, Yellow Moon."

He let go of her hand and she held the knife, staring at it a moment. "Laughing . . . Boy," she said quietly, meeting his eyes again, the tears now making their way down her cheeks. "He is . . . dead."

Zeke nodded.

"My . . . husband?"

He stroked her hair again. "Red Eagle is dead also," he told her gently. "He loved you, Yellow Moon. But the whiskey destroyed his mind—his ability to think—to choose right from wrong. He was ashamed when he realized

227

what he'd done. He shot himself, Yellow Moon."

She trembled more and closed her eyes against the pain, nodding that she understood. "Go . . . away from me!" she whispered. "You . . . should not touch me. I am . . . soiled."

"No, Yellow Moon. You are my sister-in-law. You are the People. And you did not ask for what happened to you. You aren't soiled, Yellow Moon."

A strange choking sound came from her throat. She opened her eyes to meet his steadily. "Take your knife, and cut off my hair," she asked him, holding her chin higher. "Then prepare a sweat lodge for me, so that I might purify myself before you touch me again—before I see the People again. I will make my blood sacrifice while you do these things for me."

He sighed and frowned. "Yellow Moon, I can't—"

"It must be done!" she interrupted. "You understand this."

Their eyes held and he nodded. He took out his big blade and moved behind her, grasping her hair in one hand and sliding the knife through it with ease, thinking how different he felt cutting off Yellow Moon's hair than he had doing the same to Lady Z. It was quickly done. She unbuttoned the white woman's dress she wore and pulled it down to her waist, and he turned away to hunt some rocks and build a sweat lodge of skins and blankets. She raised the knife to her chest and touched the tip of it to her skin.

"Laughing Boy!" she groaned. "My Little Laughing Boy! The spirits will hear your laughter and be glad you are with them, my little smiling son!" She drew the knife across her chest. It felt good to bleed. She wanted to bleed.

Lady Z approached the small group of white men with caution. She was dirty, and her nose still had a scab on it, and she knew it would not be easy seducing anything out of them. But she needed food and a little money. She had started out this way, by seducing men and putting them under her power. But she had little left to work with since

Cheyenne Zeke had scarred her and cut off her hair. Still, she had a body. That was all most men needed.

These men were well dressed. They were engrossed in a card game when she approached, puffing fine cigars and drinking what looked like expensive liquor. Their tents were well made, and some kind of strange instruments lay nearby. One finally noticed her as she came closer and he made a face as though disgusted.

"Hey, boys, looky there," he commented. "Looks like an Indian woman that's been unfaithful. Look at her nose."

She put her hand to her nose and stood silent.

"What you want, squaw?" another asked.

"Not one of us, I hope," a third one laughed. "I don't mind squaw women, but going down with that one is a little too much to ask!"

They all laughed and she straightened with anger. "I . . . need food," she told them. "And . . . just a little money."

"Oh, do you now?" They all laughed again. "Hey, boss!" the first man hollered. "Come out here and see what strayed in looking for vittles."

Henry Page came out of his tent shirtless. He, too, was somewhat repulsed by what he saw, but Lady Z walked boldly up to the man.

"I ask only a little food," she told him. "And a little money. That is all. Will you help me?"

He studied the dark, provocative eyes. "Who are you? Why are you here?" he asked her suspiciously. "We're a team of surveyors, not do-gooders. We need our supplies."

"Sur—Surveyors? What is that? Surveyors?"

He grinned haughtily, enjoying her ignorance. "We survey the land—you know . . . measure it and so forth. Figure out the best places to build railroads, that kind of thing."

She nodded. "I see." She unlaced her tunic, exposing part of her breasts. "I can pay—with my body. I do not mind. I need food."

His eyes quickly scanned her dark, dusty skin and the scars on her face. "No, thank you, squaw. But we can give

229

you some food. And I suppose a couple of bucks. Might be proof back East that we're trying to help the Indians, not harm them."

"I am grateful."

He looked over at his men. "Give her something to eat." He started to turn, then looked her over again. "You're a far cry from the squaw I met back at Bent's Fort. She was clean and educated." He grinned haughtily. "Of course she was also white, which explains part of it." He shook his head. "I sure am seeing some strange sights out here, that's for damned sure. A white squaw and an Indian woman with half her nose cut off and Zs on her cheeks. What will happen next? Maybe a purple buffalo!"

He turned to leave but she grabbed his arm. He looked down at her hand in disgust, as though some horrible disease had leaped onto his skin. He jerked the arm away.

"Please," she spoke up. "You saw a white squaw?"

He frowned. "I did. What's it to you?"

Her heart pounded with excitement. "At Bent's Fort?"

"Yes. Do you know this white woman?"

"Was she called . . . Abigail? Abigail Monroe?"

He grinned a little and shook his head. "I'll be damned. How can such a big country be such a small world? Yes. That was her name."

Lady Z put on a smile. "She is . . . a friend," she lied. "I have not seen her for many years. Tell me, does she live at the fort?"

Page's eyes darkened with the memory of Abbie's haughty attitude. "No," he replied. "She lives on the Arkansas River, about three days' ride from the fort. In fact, she lives on some land we may use for a railroad. Bent's Fort is a few days north of here, if you're wanting to see her."

Lady Z's eyes burned suddenly black with the fires of revenge. "Yes," she said, moving her eyes to the horizon. "I would like very much to see her!"

"Well, you won't get far in that condition. Go on over there and eat something. And for God's sake clean yourself up. But leave by morning, mind you. I don't want any trouble in my camp, and you smell of trouble."

She smiled. "Do not worry. I shall leave early in the morning. I am anxious to get to Bent's Fort now. I thank you for your help, white man. What are you called?"

"I'm Henry Page, from Washington, D.C."

She held her head high, in spite of her ugly nose and short hair. "And I am called Lady Z," she replied with a smile.

Thirteen

Abbie hung a heavy black kettle over the hot coals in the stone fireplace, then leaned over to stir the vegetables inside it. She had insisted on a garden, in spite of the difficulty of growing anything in the dry, rocky soil of their land. But the river was nearby, and after Zeke had purchased seeds for her from traders at Bent's Fort, she had planted them and faithfully watered them. When she returned to the ranch, she was glad to see that Dooley had kept up the job of watering and hoeing for her, and now a few tomatoes and peppers and some squash had ripened. Mixed with spices and buffalo meat, potatoes and turnips, she had concocted a tasty stew. She only wished Zeke were there to try it.

She straightened and watched the stew begin to heat. It was good to be home. She felt better now, happier, in spite of the fact that Zeke had still not returned. Here she could feel close to him, just by being around familiar things, touching his clothes, walking outside and watching the Appaloosas prance in the corral.

This small piece of land in the vast plains that stretched north and south of the Arkansas was home, the perfect place for them. Three days to the east lay Bent's Fort; and to the west it was just a week's journey into the Rocky Mountains. Throughout this territory roamed their only family, the Cheyenne. Here they could be close to Zeke's relatives, and to the sweet people who had become such good friends to Abbie. Here they were remote from most whites, at least those like Henry Page, the railroad man. She shivered at the thought of him. Now she saw more than ever what Zeke meant by the way some whites would treat her. Henry Page had made it all too real, and now that she was home again she was more determined than ever that she would fight any efforts by the railroad to come storming through their quiet, peaceful little ranch. This was their land—Cheyenne country—where Zeke could find relative peace from his own haunting memories of the horror of Tennessee. Here the sky was wide and there was no sound but the softly flowing waters of the Arkansas, the whinny of a horse and the singing of birds. Here they could walk along the banks of the river in the shade of the cottonwoods; or walk several yards behind the cabin to a little secret place they kept for themselves, where the grass was amazingly soft and purple iris grew, and a clear stream rushed from a hidden spring to meander out to the Arkansas. Here was home for a white woman who loved and dwelled with a half-breed Cheyenne.

The thought of the little hidden place by the stream pained her heart. It was their favorite place to sit and talk, and sometimes they made love there. She wondered if that would ever happen again. She reached up to the fireplace mantel and touched the fine mohogany mantel clock Zeke had bought for her early in their marriage, his humble attempt to bring her a little piece of her former life. She kept the clock polished constantly, for it was a fine timepiece. Now she blinked back tears as she brushed a little dust from it, tears at the awareness of the love the clock represented, for the purchase of the clock was just another of Zeke's attempts to insure against his secret fear that she would one day regret marrying a half-breed and long to live among her own kind, with all the comforts that come with such a life. Many times she had detected the almost little-boy look in his eyes, when he would worry that she would leave him for the white world; for a city, or for a settled farmer who could give her a fancy house and fine clothes and the social life most other white women led. Perhaps a handsome soldier would come along, sporting a fine blue uniform, and offer her the grand life of a soldier's wife, attending military balls and dancing in lovely, full gowns.

She smiled and shook her head, hardly able to picture

233

herself leading such a life even if she had wanted to. But she didn't want to. She wanted only to live in this peaceful little place along the Arkansas, in her simple cabin, wearing Indian tunics . . . and sleeping in the arms of Cheyenne Zeke. How could any man, whether a wealthy merchant, a successful farmer, an army officer, whatever he might be, offer her more than Zeke offered—a fierce, protective love that few women got from a man; a sweet, open honesty that betrayed all his feelings; a body hard and strong but a touch and manner that was always gentle for his woman. He was never demanding or forceful. He simply had a way of making her want to do his bidding, by his teasing words and touches; and she in turn could rule him with a smile or a tear. Making love was always joyful and exciting, made that way by the most vital ingredient to their marriage—an enduring, warm friendship, a oneness few people shared, each able to feel the other's pain or joy, each totally unselfish in his or her attitude toward the other.

Yet now she wondered, after his absence of two months, if Cheyenne Zeke would make it back to share that friendship again . . . to share bodies again. He had been gone too long. She fought an urge to scream in her terror that he would not come back this time. He had gone on a dangerous mission, yet it had been as natural for him to go as to breathe. So often she had thought of him as invincible, but the fact remained that he was a man, flesh and blood, capable of hurting, bleeding—dying. If he did not return soon, she would lose her mind from worry, she was sure. The only thing that kept her going was the children, her precious babies whose lives had been fertilized in her womb by Cheyenne Zeke, that same life growing once more even now inside of her. It was all she had left to cling to.

She bent to stir the stew once more, the cabin quiet except for the ticking of the clock and now the gentle steaming and bubbling of the stew. She would let it cook while she prepared venison and eggs in a griddle that sat on a grate below the boiling pot. It was time for breakfast. The stew would cook all day and serve as supper. Little Rock was out for his habitual morning ride, only this time he was with

234

Swift Arrow, who had remained faithfully camped outside the cabin since they returned from the fort. Deer Slayer had stayed also, sleeping quite comfortably inside on the hard floor of the main room.

Four other Cheyenne men had remained with Swift Arrow and Deer Slayer as well, to help guard Abbie until Zeke could return, and she loved them all for their loyalty. Black Elk and Blue Bird Woman had joined the bigger village two days to the east, but the fact remained that there were six Cheyenne men plus Dooley and her own children to feed. It was not easy cooking for so many, but still it was enjoyable, for she never minded working hard when it was for those she loved, and their company was sorely needed by her during her lonely wait for Zeke.

At the moment Blue Sky was with her Cheyenne grandfather at the corral, as were the rest of the men, all watching the new foals recently birthed by Zeke's fine Appaloosa mares. The Cheyenne were great horse lovers and good breeders, who took great pleasure in watching a healthy foal's comical, gangly-legged antics. Abbie was alone in the cabin, except for Young Girl, who slept quietly in the loft.

She walked to the table and a large ball of bread dough she'd left there to rise. She had been up at four o'clock that morning to beat and roll the dough for a second rising. Now she would separate it into bread pans for baking, sprinkling cinnamon and sugar into two of the loaves for Swift Arrow's sweet tooth. The sweetened bread would be good with the venison for breakfast. She hummed a nameless tune quietly as she scattered the sugar and cinnamon over the dough, rolling each flattened piece into a cylinder shape and then squishing it into a bread pan. Again she longed for Zeke, for he dearly loved her cinnamon bread. She blinked back tears and kept humming as she opened the hinged wrought iron door to the stone oven built into the side of the fireplace, beneath which hot coals warmed the stones to a perfect baking temperature. She slid the pans inside and closed the door, turning to mold the rest of the dough. It was then she heard the curious sound.

It came from the bedroom. She'd left the wooden shutters

235

open that morning to let in the sweet, summer morning air through windows that still had no glass in them. She put her hands on her hips.

"Little Rock is that you? Are you playing your Indian tricks on your mother again, seeing how quiet you can be?" She smiled, but there was no reply. She was certain she'd heard movement in the bedroom and was equally certain her son was playing games with her. She marched through the curtained doorway, ready to scold him, but she gasped when a powerful hand grasped her arm and whirled her around.

"At last we meet again, white bitch!" came the hissed words.

In Abbie's surprise and horror, she could not seem to move or even scream. Dancing Moon! She stood there like a horrid evil monster, her stubby hair sticking out in all directions, puckered, white Zs on her cheeks, and an ugly red flat place where her nose had once been, making her look more frightening and vicious than Abbie's memory of the dark, animallike woman. The worst part was that if this woman was here and alive, then where was Zeke?

Her senses suddenly came alive, and she tried to pull away, but Dancing Moon was bigger and much more powerful than she. Abbie felt a stinging blow to the side of her face that sent her reeling to the floor. She tried to think quickly, tried to rise. But already Dancing Moon was slapping her again, then gripping her hair tightly and yanking her over to throw her down on the bed of robes. Abbie made an effort to scream, but Dancing Moon's strong hand was at her throat, pressing the air away just enough so that Abbie could make no sound and holding back enough with her long arm so that Abbie could not reach her to scratch at her face and eyes.

"You will *die* today, white bitch!" the woman hissed through gritted teeth. "Your bastard husband put these marks on me, and you are part of the reason! For that you shall die, but before you do, you should know that Cheyenne Zeke is also dead! Dead!" she growled. "My men killed him—slowly and painfully," she lied, wanting Abbie to suffer with the thought of it. She grinned with pleasure at

236

the look of terror and pitiful disbelief on Abbie's face. "Yes, white bitch! Your stud Cheyenne has gone to the Happy Hunting Grounds, and you will soon join him; and I, Lady Z, will have the pleasure of knowing I killed you right under the very noses of the brave Cheyenne men who are supposed to be guarding you!"

Abbie struggled but could barely move now for lack of air. Zeke! Zeke! He could not be dead! Surely it was not true! But if Dancing Moon was here to tell her so, then it must be true! The thought of it ripped through her insides with over-whelming agony, and suddenly it did not matter if Dancing Moon did kill her.

Dancing Moon could see that Abbie was weak enough from the strangling to let go of her for the moment, for she could barely move by then and could utter no words through her purple lips. The Arapaho woman remained straddled over her on the bed of robes, her own heart surging with jealousy at the thought that this was where Cheyenne Zeke made love to his white woman. She looked down with rage at Abbie's swollen belly, then ran her hand over it and up over Abbie's breasts, squeezing them pain-fully.

"It is too bad there is not time to take my pleasure with you, white woman!" she sneered. "But at least Zeke will never do the same again. After you are dead, your stinking half-breed children will be next! I will steal your daughters and sell them to the Mexicans or the Apaches!" She threw back her head and laughed, fondling Abbie's breasts more while Abbie coughed and struggled to get her air back. "I will keep your son and see how much torture the little Cheyenne brave can take!" the woman added. Then she yanked a knife from a belt at her waist and raised it.

Where Abbie found her strength then she could not know, except that perhaps it came from a mother's love and unparalleled need to defend her children. She did not want to live without Zeke, but she could not let this evil woman live to harm her children, and it was for them that she grabbed Dancing Moon's knife hand and managed to find the strength to hold it back, even though the blade of the knife began cutting into her hand and blood was fast streaming down her arm.

Both women pushed hard, one pitting her superior muscle and hatred against the other's simple determination to defend her children, and, from somewhere deep inside her spirit soul, Abbie found the strength to finally roll over, shoving Dancing Moon to the floor. She still was having trouble getting her throat to work, and the scream she tried to utter would not come. Her vision was blurry from Dancing Moon's vicious blows, and for a fleeting moment she wondered if she would lose the fetus in her belly from the attack. The thought made her fiercely angry at this woman and more determined to fend her off, for if Zeke was dead, she wanted to give birth to the life in her belly more than ever. It would be Cheyenne Zeke's last gift to her.

Now Dancing Moon's blurry form was coming toward her again, and Abbie struggled desperately to get to her feet. But then there was someone standing at the bedroom doorway.

"Mother!" she heard her son's voice.

Dancing Moon whirled.

"Run, Little Rock!" Abbie grunted. "Run!"

The boy turned away for a moment, and Dancing Moon crouched, knife in hand, stealthily walking one step closer to the doorway. Abbie's eyes widened with fear for her little son, and with what strength she had left she groped for the sewing box she always kept on the floor near the bed. She still could not get a voice loud enough to scream, and pain ripped through her left hand and arm from the severe cut she had suffered from Dancing Moon's knife. The hand hung limply as she felt with her right hand for the fine new pair of scissors she had bought at Bent's Fort before returning, never dreaming they might be used to defend her child's life.

Everything happened in only seconds, yet it seemed to occur in slow motion for Abbie. Her hand found the scissors, just as Little Rock hurried back into the room carrying his lance, which he always kept standing in the corner of the main room. Somehow Abbie had known her little son would not run away, but would rather try to defend his mother, and that was why her sixth sense had told her to get the scissors.

"You hurt my mother!" Little Rock was growling at Dancing Moon, looking every bit just then like a grown Cheyenne warrior bent on revenge. There was the look of Cheyenne Zeke in his dark eyes then, and he thrust the lance at the evil Arapaho woman. Dancing Moon jumped back, then smiled.

"It will be a pleasure killing you, the son of the white bitch!" she sneered. She lunged at the boy, but Little Rock thrust the lance again, piercing her side and surprising her with a strength she had not thought the child would have. Dancing Moon's eyes widened in surprise as the boy jerked out the lance, and she quickly grabbed the weapon from the boy with her own fierce strength, whacking it across the side of the boy's head as soon as she got it away. His little brown body flew into the wall, and Dancing Moon made ready to plunge the lance into his small, round belly.

The sight of her little boy lying helpless gave Abbie that last little ounce of strength necessary to do what she must do. She had finally managed to get to her feet, and she half fell into Dancing Moon as she plunged the scissors hard and deep into the woman's spine. Both of them fell across a trunk, and Abbie, horrified and repulsed by what she had been forced to do, groaned and moved off the woman. Dancing Moon clung to the trunk, her body jerking strangely, strange bubbling and choking sounds coming from her mouth. She turned, the scissors still sticking out of her back. She stared at Abbie with wide, surprised eyes, her hideous, scarred face a vision that would haunt Abbie for the rest of her life. Blood began to trickle from the woman's mouth and Abbie backed away more.

"Bitch!" Dancing Moon sighed with her last breath before slumping down beside the trunk. Abbie stared at her, her head reeling, her stomach nauseous over what she had just done, blood pouring from her severely cut hand in dangerous quantity. She tried to get to Little Rock, who was getting up then, rubbing at the side of his head, but she suddenly felt nothing, and the room swirled around her.

Zeke picked a shallow spot to cross the river, while Yellow Moon hung on tightly as the water swirled around her thighs. Zeke talked softly to the roan mare, urging it forward and up the bank on the other side. Then he drew the horse to a halt, and Yellow Moon felt his body tighten. He sat still, as though listening for something.

"What is it, Zeke?" she asked him quietly. "We are close to the fort now, are we not?"

"It's a couple of days' ride to the north and east," he replied.

"Then we should hurry. Abbie will be waiting anxiously."

He turned his horse in the opposite direction. "Something is wrong. I feel it," he replied.

She frowned. "What do you feel, my brother?"

He kept his head high, as though sniffing the air. "I can't explain it, Yellow Moon. I only know I feel an urgency to go to the ranch first, rather than the fort."

"But Abbie is at the fort."

He urged the horse forward, then stopped it again, looking to the east and then to the west. "That's where I left her. But she's a single-minded woman sometimes, Yellow Moon. She might have gone back for some reason. I only know I have this strong feeling, and when it comes to me and Abbie, these feelings usually prove to be right. I don't care where I left her. I'm going to the ranch."

"You have strong spirit, Zeke. Your soul is as one with hers. Perhaps she calls you."

Zeke's heart began to pound with a nameless fear. The fact that he had not killed Dancing Moon earlier had nagged at him for several days. He had thought Abbie safe at the fort, and had left Dancing Moon in such a sorry state he did not think she could find her strength and wits for some time to come. But what if she had, and what if Abbie had gone home for some unknown reason? He shook off the thought. It was all too impossible. And yet he felt something pulling him to the west, toward his ranch, rather than toward the fort. Whether it was Dancing Moon or something else, something was wrong. He felt it in his bones. He kicked at the horse and Yellow Moon clung tightly as he urged the animal into a faster gait.

They crested a ridge toward dusk, the very ridge on which Zeke and his son had sat to have their talk before Zeke left to seek out Yellow Moon. Now Zeke looked below at a small circle of tipis. Smoke drifted lazily from the chimney of the cabin and he could see his horses grazing peacefully. All appeared well, except that no one was supposed to even be there but Dooley. He could not understand the presence of the tipis.

A fat Indian woman exited one of them, and even from the distance he knew it was Abbie's good friend, Tall Grass Woman. It was Tall Grass Woman's daughter Abbie had saved from drowning years before, an act that had helped Abbie earn her place in the hearts of the People. But death from cholera had later claimed the little girl. In her sorrow, Tall Grass Woman had taken a liking to little Blue Sky and was one of the few people Blue Sky would allow herself to be alone with besides her own mother and father.

Normally, Zeke would have been glad to see that Abbie had so much company. But he felt a heaviness now, for Tall Grass Woman walked toward the cabin with her head hanging. A little girl stayed close behind, and he recognized little Blue Sky. But why was Blue Sky not with her mother? The child was always close by her mother when her mother was present, not even going to Tall Grass Woman unless Abbie should be gone. His heart tightened and he began carefully guiding his horse down the steep embankment.

Someone shouted from below, and three Cheyenne men were quickly mounted, riding up the bank to meet him, jerking their mounts to halt when they recognized him.

"Zeke!" one of them exclaimed. It was Swift Arrow, and both men faced each other with equal surprise, for Zeke had not expected to see his brother anywhere in the south, let

241

alone here at the ranch. A hundred thoughts passed through both their minds, for Zeke was well aware of Swift Arrow's special feelings for Abbie, although he never worried that the man would do anything to betray those feelings or to bring dishonor to Abigail. "We thought . . . you were dead!" Swift Arrow exclaimed.

Their eyes held. "What's happened? Why are you here? And where is Abbie?" Zeke asked quickly.

Swift Arrow's eyes filled with pain and sorrow. He held out his bare arm to his brother. "It is your right to draw blood from me," he said, his voice husky with regret. "I have failed you, my brother. I was here to protect your wife and family, and I failed. If you wish to use your blade on Swift Arrow, I will not protest or run away."

A sharp pain rose in Zeke's chest. "Explain yourself!" he growled, his body tensing.

Swift Arrow held his head high. "I came South with Black Elk to see our father. I did not intend to even come here—to the ranch. But Abigail was at the fort. I did not expect this. She asked me to stay. She wanted the company and the protection." He pulled back his arm. "But a man came there, a railroad man. He threatened her and threatened to take away your land. She started crying and begged me to bring her home, to the ranch." Their eyes held. "You know what she is like when she cries. It is difficult to tell her no. So I brought her, and brought four other braves to help protect her and the ranch. But we thought—we thought if there was danger, it would come in the form of many men, riding down on the ranch. This we could have handled. But we were surprised. And while all of us were close, standing down at the pen of horses, she came."

Zeke's horse whinnied and strutted sideways, feeling Zeke's tension. "Who came?" Zeke hissed.

"Dancing Moon."

Zeke's eyes widened as his whole body tingled with horror. Yellow Moon gasped and pressed her hands tightly against Zeke's sides for support.

"She sneaked into the house when Abbie was alone inside," Swift Arrow went on, sorrow evident in his voice

242

and eyes.

Zeke struggled with his own fierce anger, not at Swift Arrow but at himself, for not killing Dancing Moon as he should have done. He closed his eyes, trembling with black fear. "Is Abbie dead?" he managed to groan.

"No. Dancing Moon is dead. Abbie killed her."

He opened his eyes again, and waters of relief flooded through him as his eyes teared with a mixture of joy that Abbie was apparently alive, and sorrow at the horror the experience must have been for her. "I'll go to her," he said brokenly. But Swift Arrow reached out and grabbed his horse's bridle.

"There are things you should know first," he told the man. "So that you are prepared to help her. She is badly injured, but she will heal. It is the injuries on the inside that you must help. Violence is not an easy thing for a white woman. I do not know what to say to her, but you will know. She thinks you are dead. Dancing Moon said you were. Seeing you alive is the best medicine she can receive." He grasped Zeke's shoulder. "My heart sings with joy at the sight of you, my brother; and with sorrow because I did not protect her. I am ashamed. Her pain brings me pain. You know this. If I could change what happened by giving my life, I would do it."

Their eyes held and Zeke reached up and grasped his brother's wrist tightly. "It is I who am ashamed, Swift Arrow. I had the chance to kill Dancing Moon. But my thirst for vengeance was so great that I wanted her to suffer. To live ugly and scarred for life would mean more suffering than to kill her. So I cut her and let her go. I was so blind with hatred that I did not act wisely, and it almost cost me my wife. You bear no part in this, Swift Arrow. I am grateful you stayed here to protect her. You could not have known it would happen this way. The fault is mine, not yours."

Yellow Moon slid quietly from the horse, stepping aside and hanging her head. The other two warriors glanced at her, noticing her shorn hair.

"It almost cost your son also," Swift Arrow told him, turning his hand and grasping Zeke's wrist as well in a handshake of friendship. He held Zeke's wrist supportively, watching the fear in his brother's eyes. "The boy is fine. But he came in and saw Dancing Moon attacking his mother. He tried to kill Dancing Moon himself, with the lance. But he was not quite strong enough, although he did injure her. Dancing Moon hit him and tried to kill him, but Abigail found strength to stab Dancing Moon with scissors. She did it to protect her son."

Zeke closed his eyes and swallowed, not sure if he should laugh with joy at the thought of Abbie's being alive and Dancing Moon dead, or if he should weep for the terrible thing that had happened to his Abbie because of his own blind hatred for the Arapaho outlaw woman. Yellow Moon reached up and touched his leg.

"It is over now," she said quietly. "Finished. Neither you nor Swift Arrow should blame yourselves. You can only go to her now, Zeke, and hold her. She will need your strength. She will be fine when she sees you."

Swift Arrow released Zeke's hand and looked at Yellow Moon, truly noticing her for the first time. His heart ached at her terribly thin condition and her shorn hair. He knew the Indian way. He knew why her hair was cut off. It was part of the purification. Apparently many men had touched her, and it angered his already burdened heart. She met his eyes, then looked away. "Where is Laughing Boy?" he asked.

"He is dead," she answered quietly.

Swift Arrow jerked as though someone had hit him. "*Katum!*" he swore, feeling grief and anger at the loss of his little nephew.

Zeke reached out and touched Yellow Moon gently, turning to look at Swift Arrow. "It's a long story, Swift Arrow. Yellow Moon has suffered greatly, but she's come home to the People. She will need their love and support."

"She shall have it," he replied, raging on the inside at the fact that his now dead brother had brought on all this sorrow because of his thirst for whiskey.

"There are many things to talk about," Zeke was saying. "But first I must go to Abbie. Take Yellow Moon down with you."

Swift Arrow nodded.

"How bad are her injuries?" Zeke asked.

"She has many bruises, especially about the throat where Dancing Moon tried to strangle her," Swift Arrow replied remorsefully. "She has a bruise and swelling on the left side of her face where Dancing Moon hit her with her fist. But the worst injury is her left hand. It was cut badly. We cleaned the wound and your friend Dooley stitched it. But she wept so badly, saying only you could sew up cuts the right way. She lost much blood, and her hand is swollen and painful. It will heal, but it will take much time."

"When did it happen?"

"It has been five days. She is sick and thin, unable to eat. She thinks you are dead, and because of that she has no life in her. She has not even had milk for Young Girl. Tall Grass Woman came here to be with her, and Big Bear's wife has come to feed your youngest. She has just had a child and her breasts are full."

"What about the baby Abbie was carrying?" Zeke asked, fear in his eyes.

"She has not lost it. It is a miracle. She says her God will not let her lose it because it is your last gift to her."

Zeke could see the love and longing in his brother's eyes. Swift Arrow would not have minded the life in Abbie's belly being his own.

"I only stayed because she asked me to stay," he told Zeke, as though reading Zeke's thoughts. "And I brought her here because she begged me to bring her. The railroad man frightened her. Deer Slayer and the others and I stayed on to protect her until you should return."

Zeke nodded. He had never been able to hate Swift Arrow just because of the man's feelings for his wife. Swift Arrow was a proud and honorable man. To care for Abigail was in turn a sign of the highest respect, for few Cheyenne men had any respect or liking for any white woman. But Abbie was counted as a sister, and for Swift Arrow to have deep feelings for her only proved just how honored she had become among the Cheyenne.

"I will leave soon now that you are here," Swift Arrow told him. "I only came to see our father," he reiterated, as though having to explain. "I will go North again and not return." He sat straight and proud.

Zeke sighed. "Do what you must do, Swift Arrow. For now I'm glad you're here—glad you were with her. This could even have happened at the fort. All Dancing Moon needed was to catch her alone—anywhere, any time. I failed her miserably." He thought of Anna Gale and his severed finger. "In more ways than one," he added. "I hope she will forgive me."

Swift Arrow grinned then with a sudden quickness. "Abigail not forgive you?" he asked. "Does the sun not rise every morning? Do the birds not sing? If you would beat her every night, she would forgive you just as often."

Zeke's heart swelled with an aching love. "Is she in the cabin?" he asked.

"No. We made her get outside and walk today! Dooley took her to the stream—a place where she said you and she used to go. You know the place?"

An urge to cry caught in Zeke's throat, and he had to look away. "I know it," he said huskily.

"Another brave has taken your son out riding. Go to her first. There will be time for the children. I know you are anxious to see your son and daughters, but they do not know yet that you are here. Go to Abigail first. It is best."

Zeke nodded and started forward. "Zeke," Swift Arrow stopped him. Zeke turned to look at him, and his brother's eyes were red and watery. "I rejoice that you are alive," he told him sincerely. "And I offer my flesh to you. If you wish to take out your anger on me for failing her, I will not stop you. It would be proper vengeance."

Their eyes held and Zeke swallowed against tears. He felt suddenly weary and broken. "I have no anger left in my heart, Swift Arrow. While I was gone I reaped much vengeance. I killed many men, and my body was on fire with hatred. Now I just feel tired. And my only anger is at myself. If I had to leave Abbie in someone's care again, I can think of no better man than you, my brother."

He turned his horse and headed around the other side of the ridge, staying out of sight of the cabin and the tipis so that his children would not spot him. It was as Swift Arrow had said. Abbie must come first. But one corner of his heart raced with eagerness to see his son, who had bravely tried to defend his mother with the lance. He smiled at the thought of it. Little Rock would be a fine warrior some day.

Fourteen

Abbie sat on the bank of the stream, wishing there were a way she could die and yet remain behind to tend her children. She must live for them, but life without Zeke would be like walking in a vacuum. She felt as though she were falling through a black hole that had no bottom, reaching out into emptiness for light and warmth but finding none. She had cried until she was weary, and her stomach would hold no food. There was a constant, painful knot in her middle, and she was almost glad for the added pain in her hand, for it seemed right to feel pain. It seemed to help.

She put a hand to her belly and closed her eyes. How was she going to do it? How would she continue a life without Zeke? Where would she get her strength, her wisdom, her courage? Zeke gave her all those things. He had been friend and lover since she was fifteen years old. She could not survive without his arms, without resting her head against his broad chest and feeling his power. She could not sleep again without breathing in his raw, manly scent of leather and fresh air.

Everything around her spoke of him—the Appaloosas, the Indian tunic she wore, her little warrior son. Their bed of robes carried his scent, and his clothes still hung in the corner, mostly buckskins and furs. She could feel his presence everywhere, sometimes see him standing beside her, hear his voice. Waves of black despair kept rippling through her, reminding her over and over with relentless cruelty that he was dead. He was not coming back to her. Once before she had only suspected he might be dead, years earlier when he had had to go away. But this was different. This was real. Dancing Moon had declared it and Abbie did not doubt it. For if Dancing Moon was alive, it was certain Zeke was dead.

The word echoed in her ears. Dead. It had such a finality to it. Was she to die, too, then? Yes. At twenty-three she was dead, in spirit. Her body would trudge on, but only for the children. There would be no other man, because none could match Cheyenne Zeke. He had been the first and the only man to invade her body, and she would never desire another.

The wave of utter despair pulsed through her again, constantly reawakening the pain, as though someone wanted to torture her. Zeke! She felt as though someone had drained the blood from her body, and her stomach tightened again. She tried to find consolation in this pretty place where they used to come, thinking that here she could feel close to him. But there were no colors in the grass and sky, and there was no music to the rippling water. She could not hear the birds singing, and in spite of the hot sun, her body felt cold. Never had she known such utter desolation and loneliness, not even when first she lost her family on the wagon train and was alone in a strange land. For then Zeke was there. Zeke was always there, strong and sure and wise and protective.

She dabbed at new tears, wondering where on earth they had come from, for her body should be dried up from so much crying. It was then she saw them, purple iris, dozens of them broken off and floating in the stream.

Her heart quickened and she studied them curiously, afraid to allow herself to think what they could mean. Only Zeke knew of her love of the purple iris. He often picked them for her, especially here in their favorite place where they grew abundantly. She leaned forward and reached into the water to grasp two stalks, then lifted them to her lips, feeling their wetness and smelling them. But where did they come from? Dooley didn't know about the iris, and even if he did, he wouldn't do this. It would be a cruel trick.

There could be only one answer, and yet it didn't seem

possible. Her heart pounded so hard she had trouble getting her breath, and then she heard a light splashing in the water near a thick clump of yucca bushes. She raised her eyes from the iris and first saw only the moccasins and leggings. She was literally terrified of looking further for fear she was dreaming, or that perhaps some other Indian would be standing there. He came closer and reached down to gently touch her hair.

"*Ne-mehotatse*," he said softly, speaking the Cheyenne words for "I love you."

She trembled and let out a groaning sob that tore at his heart as she reached out and grasped him around the leg without even looking up, breaking into choking tears that seemed to come from some deep pit in her soul, her body jerking and shaking uncontrollably.

"It's all right, Abbie girl," came the beautiful, wonderful voice as he knelt down and pulled her arms from around his leg.

"Oh, God! God!" she wept, moving her arms to around his neck and half strangling him with her amazingly strong hold. She wept so hard she had difficulty breathing in again after each choking sob. He enveloped her in the strong, sure arms and stood up, holding her there with her feet off the ground. Her bandaged hand hung limply at his back, and his heart ached at how thin and bony she felt in his arms in spite of her pregnant condition.

"Settle down now, Abbie," he told her gently. "You'll lose the baby if you keep this up. Please, Abbie."

He kissed her hair and she struggled to stop crying, but for the next several minutes it was impossible. There was so much to be said, but it all would have to wait. For now he was here. He was alive! Already she felt a magic strength begin to surge through her veins, life flowing, muscles getting stronger.

"She . . . said you . . . were dead!" she sobbed.

"God, Abbie!" he whispered. "What have I done?" He kissed her hair again and gently urged her down onto the grass, but she would not let go of him. He laid her back and held her, letting her cry until she was able to control herself, his own silent tears wetting her hair. She nestled into the crook of his arm and he smoothed back her hair, finally pulling away slightly and feeling acute pain at the sight of her drawn, tired face and the circles under her eyes. He took hold of her left arm and pulled it away to study the bandages on her hand.

Her body continued to jerk in deep sighs then as her tears subsided. It seemed impossible that he could be here beside her. He raised up on one elbow to wipe the tears from her cheeks with his fingers, and she studied him, the face and its fine scar still the same, the dark eyes still full of love for her, the shoulders broad and powerful. She reached up with her good hand and touched the firm chin, closely scrutinizing him to make sure Lady Z had not done something horrible to him. But he was all Zeke and all there, except that she noticed part of the fresh scar near his left shoulder, which was not all hidden by the vest he wore. He wore only the vest, for it was a hot day. She pulled it aside and touched the new skin, and her eyes flashed with fear.

"You've been hurt!" she whimpered.

He grasped her hand. "I'm all right. It's such a long story, Abbie girl. The important thing now is you." He gently picked up her bandaged hand and lightly kissed the heavy gauze wrappings. "Forgive me, Abbie," he said softly. "I could have killed her, but I let her go."

She frowned and touched his hair, taking great joy in every movement, every touch, every inflection of his voice.

"You did what you thought was best at the time," she replied.

He stiffened and met her eyes. "I did a stupid thing!" he said hoarsely. "I hated her so much that all I could think of was to make her suffer. I wanted her to suffer for a good, long time! Killing her made it too easy for her."

She watched the pain in his eyes, then raised up and kissed his cheek. "How can you think I would blame you, when you've just come back from the dead?" she asked softly. "Do you think any of it matters now, Zeke? A moment ago I was wondering how I could continue in this life without my husband. And now you're here! Nothing

251

else matters. Nothing!" She ran her fingers over the straight, handsome nose and the finely chiseled lips, while his dark, pain-filled eyes studied her intently, glittering with unspeakable love. "Zeke!" she whispered. "Kiss me so that I know you're real. I'm too ill for anything else, but if you would just . . . kiss me—"

In the next moment his lips burned into her own, and a groan of remorse combined with long-denied desires left his soul as he laid her back again and moved partially on top of her. He gently ran a hand over her side, aching at the fact that he could feel each and every rib. He moved it up over one breast and she whimpered, returning his kiss with her own long-buried hunger. She wanted so much to do more, but she felt so weak and spent, and she sensed that he, too, was weary. He had been through some bad times, of that she was certain. Both of them had been. Both bore wounds, inside and outside. The healing would take time. But now they had time. He would not leave her again. Not ever, if he could help it.

His lips moved to her cheek and throat. "There is so much to tell you, Abbie girl," he groaned, his heart exploding with the pain of having been untrue to her. How would he tell her? How could she forgive him?

"I know," she whispered. "And I have much to tell you." His lips moved down and he pulled her tunic aside to gently kiss the white of her breast.

"Abbie! Abbie!" he moaned.

She stroked the long, loose hair and smiled, looking up at white, puffy clouds.

"Thank you, Jesus," she whispered.

He moved back up to her throat, then lay down beside her again, pulling her close. "We'll go back and see the children," he told her. "Then we'll come back here. I want to be alone with you for a day or two. I sent Dooley back to the cabin to dig up some supplies—blankets and whatever. We'll set up the tipi here, Abbie girl, just you and me. Tonight we'll just sleep together. It will be so good to sleep with you beside me again."

She turned her face up to look into his eyes. "Don't stop

touching me," she whispered. "At least for the next twenty-four hours. I'm so afraid I'm just dreaming."

He smiled sadly. "I won't stop touching you. I feel like I'm dreaming myself." He kissed her again. How hungry he was for her! How he longed to take her here and now. But she looked so weak and tired. He must treat her gently, carefully, like a china doll. She had been through so much, and there was the baby to think about. He would not rush her or sap her of the little strength she had left. He lightly tasted her sweet lips, his groin aching for her, his blood on fire for her. But he would wait. He moved a big hand gently over her back, and she was lost in him, suddenly no longer feeling the pain in her bandaged hand, which rested lightly then against the buffalo jawbone handle of the big knife that now rested quietly in its sheath. Its job was finished—for a while. There was no room for violence when he was with his woman.

Swift Arrow stood a short distance from the cabin, staring out toward the hill beyond which Zeke and Abbie had raised the tipi to be alone. He could not see the tipi, but he knew where they were, and he thought about how nice it would be to be the one holding Abbie through the night. He had wanted so much to comfort her after the terrible ordeal of Dancing Moon. But he dared not touch her, not just because she was forbidden, but because he had shamed himself by not protecting her. He would never forget this failure. He was a mighty and respected dog soldier and had been in many battles against enemy Indians. Yet when his dear sister-in-law had needed him most, he had not been there, after promising to protect her.

"She will be all right now," came a soft voice behind him. He whirled to see Yellow Moon. Their eyes held.

"You would make a good warrior, woman," he told her. "You walk lightly."

She looked down at the ground. "In the days when Red Eagle was a respected dog soldier, he used to talk about the things a good warrior had to do."

253

He studied her a moment, seeing that she was still a fine-looking woman, except that she was much too thin.

"I am sorry about Red Eagle—and I am most sorry about Laughing Boy," he told her. "My brother threw away the most important things in his life. I lost my wife and son to the spotted disease many winters ago. But I never would have done what Red Eagle did. You were a good wife to him, Yellow Moon. You are a fine woman, and I am glad Zeke was able to help you."

She remained standing there with her head hanging, appearing nervous. "My . . . mother and father are dead now," she told him. "And my husband. I . . . have no one. I will be a burden." She swallowed, clenching and unclenching her fingers in her nervousness. "I come to you, Swift Arrow . . . to humbly explain that it is the custom . . . for a woman to go to a brother of her dead husband."

He folded his arms and waited, aware of what she would say. He had already given it much consideration. But it had to be as much her choice as his.

"Black Elk has . . . a new, young wife," she went on. "She would not like to have a second woman around right now. And Zeke . . . is married to a white woman. She would not understand these things, and besides, he is already burdened with a large family. I . . . have no one . . . to turn to," she raised her eyes to meet his boldly then, "except you. I must know . . . what you intend to do . . . so that I can find another man who can provide for me."

He saw the fear in her eyes at the thought of going to just any man. His eyes dropped over her body again. She was pleasing to the eye, and he already knew her to be a loyal and devoted wife. He stepped closer and reached out to touch the side of her face with the back of his hand.

"I know the custom," he told her. "I did not intend to ever again take a wife, but I am the most logical one." He touched her shorn hair. "You have been through much pain and torture," he said quietly. "I do not . . . love you . . . as a young man pants after his first woman. But neither can I let you go to just any man, for I do not trust another to leave you alone in the night as you should be left alone. You will

254

come North with Swift Arrow. I will provide for you and protect you, and you will build my tipis and carry my wood and cook my food like any wife. But Swift Arrow will not come to you as a husband until you tell him you are ready again for such things."

She closed her eyes and hung her head again. "I am grateful," she said quietly. "I will not be a burden to you. I will tend your horses and mend your shields and make warm moccasins for you in the winters. I will—"

"Ho-shuh," he spoke up softly. "Do not make so many promises. There will be time for these things. For now your heart must heal. I make no demands of you, Yellow Moon." He stepped closer and encircled her in his arms. To think of Abbie was to be a foolish man. It was time to forget such things and go back North where he would stay. Perhaps his foolish thoughts were merely brought on by his own aching loneliness, a loneliness he always denied to others. But Abbie had told him once he was too young to live out his life alone. She had seen the loneliness behind the proud eyes. She was a woman of wisdom and insight. He would take Yellow Moon and go North. Perhaps in time Yellow Moon would give him sons and daughters. He pressed his arms more tightly around her in a sign of reassurance, and she finally began to relax against him.

"We shall leave at the second sunrise," he told her. "We can be with the Sioux in time for the Sun Dance."

Abbie snuggled in closer under the buffalo robe, for the morning was cool, as it always was. She pushed her back against Zeke's front, and he automatically pulled her tightly against him, both of them only partially awake. The movement brought them more fully awake, and he was suddenly kissing her hair and pressing himself against her bottom, his hand gently moving over her breasts, her stomach, her groin and hips. She took his hand and brought it up to her lips, kissing the palm, her heart full of renewed joy at the realization that he was here, and they had slept close beside each other all night. Her husband was alive and was beside her, and already she was feeling stronger.

"Good morning, my husband," she said softly.

He leaned over and kissed her cheek. "Good morning, my wife."

"Are you hungry?"

He kissed the back of her neck. "Not for food."

She smiled. "I see you haven't changed."

He chuckled. "Do such things ever change?"

She kissed his palm again. "I suppose not." She turned to look into his face. "That was a fine rifle you gave Little Rock yesterday. There was such pride and happiness in his eyes."

"He deserved it."

They kissed lightly. "His greatest happiness was seeing you again. He missed you so much, Zeke. His whole world revolves around his father. He was so afraid you wouldn't come back."

Their eyes held, and he marveled at how pretty she could be in the morning when she hadn't even combed her hair yet.

"I hope he understands I'm proud of how he tried to help you," he told her. "He seemed to think I would be angry, because I had told him he was to watch out for you and then you got hurt."

"I think he knows you understand he tried his best." Her face clouded. "It was so terrible, Zeke. I think the worst part was seeing my little boy standing there with that lance in his hand. For a moment he looked . . ." she blinked back tears and turned to her side again. "He looked like a man . . . in his eyes. I've seen the look he had right then—in you. It's the same look you get in your eyes when you have vengeance on your mind. He'll be just like you."

He petted her hair. "Is that bad?"

She sighed. "No. It's just . . . different . . . when it's your child. I can already tell he's going to lead a dangerous life, and I don't want him to get hurt, Zeke. I get so afraid sometimes thinking about the future."

"And you think I don't?"

She turned to face him again.

"I don't want him to get hurt either, Abbie. He is my son,

256

you know. But I also want him to be a man. And because of the troubles that lie in the future, he's got to know how to take care of himself."

"I know," she whispered sadly, running her finger over the hard muscle of his arm. "Violence is so natural to you. But not to me, Zeke, in spite of the violence I've seen myself. I don't know how . . . how you can take your knife . . . and feel it going into someone's . . . flesh." She closed her eyes and gasped, pushing her face against his chest. "Oh, Zeke, I'll never forget! I'll never forget how it felt . . . pushing those scissors into that horrible woman's back! In spite of what she was, I didn't like doing it! It was so . . . gruesome!"

He pulled her naked body close to his own, running a big hand over her soft, white back. "You can't let it eat at you, Abbie girl. I've told you so many times that we often have to do things we don't want to do—things that may be totally against our basic character—out here in this land. It's being practical that matters—doing what must be done." He kissed her hair. How he wanted and needed to make love to her! He had told her everything about how he'd found Yellow Moon, except the one thing he was most afraid to tell her. He knew he did not have the right to be a husband to her again until she knew, for she must make the decision then whether or not she still wanted him.

"It was . . . different than when I shot those Crow Indians," she was telling him quietly. "Somehow they were more . . . distant. It was more like . . . like being in a war. I didn't have to touch them, feel their breath on me, see their eyes." She· shuddered. "But with Dancing Moon it was a desperate fight for my very life, and for my son. I had to . . . touch her . . . watch her die." She groaned and he held her tight against him.

"We've got to go on from here and start over, Abbie. That's all we can do. We'll get our lives back together and I won't leave you again. I'll help you forget all of this." He kissed her hair and pulled back slightly, moving his lips down over her cheek and throat, gently squeezing one breast with his hand. "Don't think about it, Abbie girl," he

257

said softly. "You did what you had to do. She would have killed our son. Your God understands that."

"Do you truly think He does? It will haunt me forever, Zeke."

He kissed her neck and raised up on one elbow to meet her eyes. "He understands. Why do you think He helped you find those scissors in the first place? You told me you could barely move or see." His heart pained at the sight of the bruise on the side of her face, and the ones that still remained at her throat where Dancing Moon had tried to strangle her. He bent down to kiss them again.

"I never thought of it that way," she told him.

He kissed her eyes. "That sounds like something Bonnie Beaker would have said," he replied. "Sometimes I don't think you Christians understand your God at all. Surely He would not have expected you to lie there and watch Dancing Moon stab your son to death. He made you a mother. He would expect you to protect your child."

She lightly touched the scar on his chest. "I'm glad you were able to help that woman, and that she knew how to take out a bullet," she said quietly. She studied his eyes. She had seen a strange kind of guilt there, an unnamed "something" that was standing between them, for although he wanted her, he had not tried to take her; and after his long absence, she had thought he would have tried by now, in spite of her condition. She knew the feeling of being lost and alone, how easy it was to turn to a man who was one's only refuge and protection.

"What was she like—Bonnie Beaker, I mean," she asked.

The worried look came back to his eyes. He pulled away and covered her, rising to put a little wood on the fire. Her blood surged at his striking physique, his most intimate parts covered by only a loincloth.

"I told you she was a little older than you—blond—quite pretty," he replied. He met her eyes. "But she was a very proper lady. She was simply a woman in bad trouble and I helped her. She's probably up North and married by now. Those were her plans."

She watched him quietly for a moment as he stirred the

coals of the fire. He was strangely defensive. Was it because of Bonnie Beaker? Surely not. Perhaps he had been compelled to hold and comfort the woman a time or two; perhaps they had even become fine friends. That would be natural. His return alive was too wonderful for them to have words over a poor, helpless woman he had saved and befriended. Yet there was this strange wall between them, and it frightened her. He was not truly himself, and she felt something had been left out. Yet no matter what it was, she was sure of one thing. Zeke Monroe loved her more than his own life. She had never once doubted it and did not doubt it now.

He met her eyes again and could read her thoughts. His own eyes filled with pain, and he rose and came to kneel beside her. "I love you, Abbie," he told her. "If someone told me to hold out my arm and let them saw it off so that you might live, I would let them do it. You believe that, don't you?"

She searched his eyes, her heart pounding. There was something terribly wrong, and she was not certain she wanted to know what it was.

"I believe it," she replied. "We've been through too much together, Zeke. There is no room for doubting such things."

He swallowed. "Abbie—" He closed his eyes and sighed, rising and turning around. "Damn! Damn!" he groaned.

She sat up, keeping the robe around her. "Zeke, what is it? There is something you aren't telling me. Is it . . . is it about Bonnie?"

He let out a long, deep breath and shook his head. "No," he answered. "Bonnie was . . . a fine lady. You'd like her. Perhaps one day you can meet her. I would like very much for her to meet you." He did not intend to bother telling her of Bonnie's feelings for him. For those feelings were surely brought on by the woman's helpless condition, and by now she was herself a married woman. That was not what bothered him at the moment. He secretly prayed for courage, then turned to face his wife, holding out his left hand.

259

"You asked me yesterday about this," he told her.

She glanced at the little finger, half of it gone now. The stub was still pink with fresh skin. She nodded. "You . . . you said it was a sacrifice, and that you didn't want to talk about it. I thought . . . I thought you had done it for little Laughing Boy. It's the Cheyenne custom—"

"It wasn't for Laughing Boy!" he interrupted, seeming almost angry. Her heart pounded harder and her mind rushed with confusion. "It was for you, Abbie! For *you*!"

She blinked back startled tears. "I . . . I don't understand. It . . . must have been so painful . . . so horrible."

"Do you think it is easy to lay your own hand out on a rock and raise a hatchet and chop off your own finger?" he asked.

She choked in a sob. "Zeke, you aren't being fair. I . . . what did I do . . . to make you do such a thing?"

He came close and knelt in front of her again, taking her face between his hands as she choked in a sob. He bent forward and kissed her forehead. "You did nothing, my sweet Abbie. You are the best wife a man could want. And that is why I did it, as a token of my love for you, my sorrow for having been untrue to you."

A sickening chill crept under her skin as she opened her eyes to meet his. She blinked away tears, but by then there were tears in his own eyes. "What do you mean?" she whispered.

"You know what I mean," he replied bluntly. It had to be said. He may as well get it over with. The pain in her eyes tore at his heart. "It was not Bonnie," he explained. "She was a fine woman, like you." He held her face tightly between his hands, feeling her tremble with a jealousy she had never before felt. Would this white woman ever forgive him? Could he make her understand? "I . . . did not want her," he whispered, his head held straight and proud, a tear tracing down his cheek near the scar.

She opened her mouth to ask why, but only a little whimper came out, as she struggled with a mixture of desires, wanting to scratch out at him, yet wanting to hold him and scream that he belonged to her.

"Let me explain, Abbie," he asked, in an almost begging tone. How weak she could make him feel sometimes! He could take on many men at once, murder them ruthlessly, vent his anger with amazing courage and cruelty. Yet this tiny young woman had a way of bringing him to his knees. "Tell me true, Abbie," he continued, still holding her face, afraid to let her look away from him. "If I, or our son or daughters, were in grave danger; and their only rescue, their only help, your only hope of finding them, depended on your letting a strange man lie with you—would you sleep with him?"

She studied his eyes as she thought about the strange question. How full of love and remorse his eyes were! She pondered the question and the agony of such a decision.

"Yes," she finally answered flatly. "I would do anything to help you or the children, even if it meant that."

He nodded, moving his hands to entangle them in her long, lustrous hair. "Sometimes we are left with no choices. Lady Z sold Yellow Moon . . . to a woman called Anna Gale, who ran a house of prostitution." He watched the pain and jealousy in her eyes with terror. He would lose her now! "Anna Gale was the only one who could tell me what had happened to Yellow Moon," he went on, needing to get it over with now, no matter what the consequences. "Her price for the information was me. I was in Santa Fe. She had many men, all ready to take me and hang me should I try to hurt her. I am already a wanted man in Tennessee, Abigail. I do not care to become one out here. I have a wife and three children, with a fourth on the way. I just wanted to get home to them. I was tired and wounded and surrounded by the law. She wanted me. So I gave her what she wanted. It was that simple."

She studied the dark eyes with jealousy burning at her heart. How handsome he was! Of course a prostitute would want this man in her bed! Any woman would want him. But he did not belong to just any woman! He belonged to Abigail Monroe!

A strange whimper ripped through her throat as she jerked back from him. "Let go of me, please!" she whispered. "Just let go of me for a moment!"

His chest hurt so badly that he thought perhaps he might be sick. He released her and she moved back a little. She sat there breathing deeply, her eyes closed, for several long seconds.

"God, Abbie, I love you," he groaned. "Don't go away from me."

She turned her face away. "A man . . . can't do such a thing . . . unless he wants the woman . . . unless he . . . enjoys it," she choked out. "How else can he . . . perform? She must have been . . . beautiful . . . desirous. How else could you—"

He startled her by grabbing her arms tightly, shaking her slightly. "She was a whore!" he hissed. "A whore! I *made* myself want her because it was the only way I would get to Yellow Moon!" he went on, his voice a low growl of desperateness. "Look at me, Abigail! Look at me!" She raised her eyes to meet his, and the hurt there tore at his guts. "How can you think I would want such a woman in the way I want my *wife*? How can you think I would have wanted her at *all*! Yes, I performed for her, if that is what you wish to call it. I was stud service to her, and that is all her kind understands. I gave her what she wanted, but I did not make love to her. There is a difference. If there were any other way, I would have taken it. You are my woman. You are all I want in this life—ever!" He shook her slightly again at the words. "You I do not want just physically. I want you in *all* ways, Abigail. You are my woman, my wife, the mother of my children. She was as nothing to me. Nothing! An animal has more feelings for its mate than I had for that woman. I gave her only my body and nothing more. I made my payment, like a damned stud horse mates for its owner's profits. I got what I came for and I left and it was over!"

She shook her head and in the next moment his lips were on hers, savagely devouring her mouth as he forced her back onto the blanket. She wanted to fight him, to push him away, but she could not, and she sensed he was determined to have her even if she had objected. There was only one way to settle the matter, and she returned the kiss with equal savageness, for this was her man, and she would reclaim him and make sure he remembered whom he belonged to.

She cried out in her torturous desire for him as his lips left her mouth and moved to her neck and he groaned her name, moving down to her breasts, rubbing his cheek against them and tasting their sweet nipples as she arched up to him against her own will. He had cut off part of his finger for her. How could she hate him or refuse to forgive him? Who else would have gone after Yellow Moon? Who else would have cared that much?

His lips traced their way over her body, tasting, devouring, whispering words of apology and love, his huge, dark frame moving over her, commanding her, breaking down all resistance. Somehow his loincloth was gone and they were naked and on fire, and even with her swollen stomach she had never looked more beautiful to him.

She could find no words as he moved over her. She could only weep and whimper, as she moved her good hand over the hard muscle of his arms and shoulders and through his hair. His lips were on her mouth again and she wrapped her arms around his neck as he moved between her legs. It must be done quickly. They had been too long apart, and there was too much to prove now, too much to make up for, too much to reclaim.

He tore into her body like a man possessed and she cried out his name and pushed up to him, consumed with a raging jealousy at the thought of some woman she had never seen enjoying this man, this husband of hers who could give a woman so much. She grasped him with her good hand, digging her nails into his arm and drawing blood, in a combination of terrible jealousy and hatred, and terrible desire and lust. She would make sure he never wanted another woman. But she knew deep inside that he never truly had; that he had simply performed a necessary duty. But the fact remained he had given some other woman this pleasure, and her mind seemed to be exploding with the pain of it.

He surged inside of her, bringing on the glorious explosion in her loins that no other man had experienced

263

with her. This was the only man who had ever touched Abigail Monroe this way, and the only man who ever would, and she cried out his name, bursting into tears as he came down and wrapped his arms around her, pushing himself deep and releasing his life into her already blossoming womb. He groaned out her name and relaxed, remaining on top of her, holding her as she wept.

They lay there for several minutes, and he kissed her over and over, whispering sweet Cheyenne words, seemingly unable to get enough of her sweet lips; and suddenly she felt his hardness growing inside of her again. They had been a long time apart. There was a great hunger to be fed, and much forgiving to be done.

A bird sang sweetly in the nearby yucca bushes, and Abbie wrapped the towel around her shoulders and waited. He had helped her bathe in the stream and was returning from bathing himself. Both were still naked as he sat down behind her and took the towel from her shoulders. He slipped a tunic over her head and told her quietly to put it on so she wouldn't get chilled. She put her arms through the sleeves and let it fall to her lap while he gently rubbed at her wet hair with the towel.

"Was she . . . beautiful?" she asked quietly, her back still to him.

He did not answer right away and she waited patiently. Then he kissed the back of her neck. "She was beautiful— physically," he finally replied.

Her heart burned hot again and she stared at the painted flowers on her tunic. He kissed her hair.

"What difference does it make?" he added. "She did not have the kind of beauty that makes a man want a woman— want to give a woman his heart and his soul, his whole life. Not many women have that kind of beauty, Abbie girl. You are one who does." He ran his hand over the dark, wavy locks of her hair. "You aren't just beautiful to look at, Abbie. You have the kind of beauty that makes a man hungry for you at the end of the day, even though your hair might be a little messed up and maybe your dress dirty because you've been working hard all day for your family; even though your belly is swollen with your man's life; even though you don't wear an ounce of paint or a fancy dress. A woman like you attracts a man more than all the painted, flowery, lily-white ladies of the night he's ever known. I will never think of that woman again. Never want her. Never miss her. But you, even when I am with you every day, I ache for you. I always want you, whether your belly is flat or big with child, whether you wear a ruffled dress or a plain tunic, no matter what. I love you, Abigail, and I will never love another. If I lose you, there can be no life for me at all. I cannot imagine life without you."

He rose and went inside the tipi, emerging with the little velvet box. He sat down in front of her and handed it to her. "I got this for you. If you still love me—still want me as a husband, then take it, and we shall never speak of this again."

She took the box hesitantly, again noticing the pink stub of the little finger he had severed. She knew his constant fear of losing her. What he had done had brought him much pain and remorse. To sacrifice part of a finger was a sign of tremendous devotion and sorrow, a Cheyenne sacrifice for a atonement, for he had feared her white woman's heart would be unable to forgive him.

She opened the box, her breath catching in her throat at the sight of the tiny gold ring with the diamond settings.

"I never got you a proper wedding ring," he told her. "Now you have one. It is the white woman's signature of marriage."

She looked at her bandaged left hand. "Oh, Zeke, I can't even put it on!" she wailed, bursting into tears.

He patted her hair and pulled her against his shoulder. "It is all right. When your hand is healed you can put it on."

She cried harder and he frowned, sensing another reason for her tears. He kissed her hair. "Do you have doubts now about wanting to stay with me? How else can I explain my sorrow, Abigail?"

She shook her head and pulled away from him, covering her face with her hand. "It isn't that," she sobbed. She looked at her lap. "The . . . railroad man. He said . . . he said if we weren't married by a real preacher . . . we weren't married at all." She met his eyes with her own beautiful, sad, dark eyes. "He made it look . . . so ugly," she whimpered. "He said we aren't legally married, and then he said if I don't get a legal marriage, and give my children Christian names, the . . . government might take them away from me . . . some day . . . and make me live apart from them!"

His dark eyes flashed with anger and he pulled her close. "I would like to meet this man some day!" he hissed, holding her tightly. "Let him try to take my land or my children or my woman from me!" He grasped her shoulders and pulled back, meeting her eyes. "You have been in my bed at night for almost eight years, Abigail Monroe. And even before we spoke our vows before Jim Bridger and a host of witnesses, we had already sealed our love before the spirits and before your God and with each other! No man can tell me I am not your husband and you are not my wife and our children were not born out of love and devotion. Let him say what he wants! You are my woman—my wife! And I will kill any man who tries to insult you and say otherwise!"

"Zeke, he scared me. That was why I came back here. I wanted to be close to my home, feel closer to you. I felt like . . . like if I was here . . . no one could take me away from here, or take my babies away from me."

His eyes raged with anger. "Let any man come here and try to take your babies from you. They would have to go through Cheyenne Zeke first! I think they would regret the day they stepped on this land!"

She searched his dark eyes. How good it was to have him here! She could feel safe now, protected, braver herself. But she knew the white man's world—knew its regulations and social attitudes.

"Zeke, we must have a license—a legal marriage license. I . . . I fear it may be important some day, just as I should have the children baptized and given Christian names. I know such things mean little to you, but you know yourself how the government can be. The surge has started, Zeke.

You walked the Trail of Tears. Papers and proof of things might become important."

He studied her lovingly, reminding himself how white she was. And being white, she also understood her kind even better than he did, for he had been long away from the totally white world. He stroked her hair gently.

"You are my wife, Abigail. Just as surely as if you had been married in a grand cathedral in a flowing wedding gown. No man and no God would deny otherwise. That man was only trying to frighten you, and I see he succeeded." He bent forward and kissed her forehead. "You have suffered much, and I will do whatever it takes to make your heart lighter. I will find a way to get us a marriage license— somehow. And when next we find a preacher you may have the children baptized in your Christian way and give them white names. But I never want them to forget or deny that Cheyenne blood runs in their veins."

"I would never allow that and you know it. I am proud of their Cheyenne blood. And I am proud of my Cheyenne husband."

He searched her eyes. "Then you still want me as a husband? I am forgiven?"

She picked up the little box and held it out to him. "You told me that if I put this on it would mean I still love you and want you for my husband—and that we would never speak again of another woman. Take out the ring and put it on my right hand. I will wear it there until my other hand is healed. It's too beautiful to leave in the box. I want to wear it."

He removed the ring and slid it carefully onto her right hand, then bent down and kissed the back of her hand gently. "You are a good woman," he whispered. "*Nemehotatse*. You are my beloved."

She looked down at the ring and watched the little diamonds glitter. Surely it had taken nearly all the money he had made from the sale of his horses.

"It's so beautiful, Zeke. It means so much to me." Their eyes held. It was over. They would not speak again of the woman called Anna Gale. It was time to forgive and forget many things, time to pick up their lives again. "We must get

267

back to the children soon, and then there will be little privacy," she told him, beginning to smile teasingly. "They will want all of your attention for a while once we get back."

He grinned slyly and nodded, aware of the meaning of her words. "You are a wise woman." He picked her up and the towel fell away from her breasts. He lifted her higher and nuzzled their soft whiteness before taking her back inside the tipi. He closed the flap.

Outside the birds continued to sing, the little stream splashed in greeting to the morning sun, and purple iris fluttered from a gentle mountain breeze.

Fifteen

A big man rode into the parade ground area of Fort Laramie, his buffalo skin coat wrapped tightly around his neck against a biting wind on the unusually cold November morning. He dragged a travois behind his mount, and soldiers and citizens who went busily about their duties at the sprawling, unwalled fort paid little heed to what looked like simple gear and supplies packed onto the travois. The man dismounted in front of officers' quarters and untied the travois from his horse. He took a few things from it, tying them onto his animal, then simply rode off.

For a few minutes the travois just lay there, until a soldier noticed something move beneath the robes that lay on the apparatus. He frowned and approached it, then heard a light groan. He knelt down and pulled back the robes, revealing a very young, very pretty, but obviously very sick Indian woman. He covered her and ran to the officers' quarters, almost forgetting to salute when he entered.

"Lieutenant Monroe, sir!" he exclaimed as he barged through the door.

Danny looked up with a frown, and the young man quickly saluted. Danny returned the salute. "Shut the door, Private!" he grumbled, the cold air quickly filling the room and chasing out the heat provided by a pot-bellied stove. "A knock is preferred before entering, I might add."

The private swallowed. Lieutenant Daniel Monroe had not been quite as easy to serve under ever since he had returned the past spring from St. Louis, a married man with no wife on his arm. He was short-tempered and irritable

269

much of the time, and a man could find himself in the guard-house for the most minor offense.

"I'm sorry, sir, but . . . a man just rode in and left off a travois, sir, right out front."

"So?" Danny replied, bent over a form he was filling out. He was tired of forms, and tired of excitable new recruits.

"Sir, there's, there's a woman on it, an Indian woman. She looks mighty sick, sir."

Danny looked up then, putting down the quill pen. "Did the man leave?"

"Yes, sir. I don't know who it was, sir. I seen him come in and stop. Then he just untied the travois and left. My guess is it was his squaw, sir, and she got sick on him so he dumped her. What should we do?"

Danny sighed and rose, grabbing his wool cape and throwing it around his shoulders. "I'll check it out." He walked outside ahead of the private. Some of the troops were marching in formation in the parade ground, shouting out a cadence, and a supply wagon rumbled past the travois on the partially frozen ground, no one else aware of the package on the travois. Danny walked down the wooden steps of the building and approached the travois, kneeling down and pulling back the robes.

He was surprised at the loveliness of the woman beneath the robes. She was young and pretty, but her face was drawn and thin. Her dark eyes widened with a mixture of fear at being among white army men, and with a gentle pleading for someone to help her.

"She's Sioux, and she's in a bad way," Danny spoke up, strangely touched by her helpless state. He bent down and lifted her up in his arms. She was light and easy to carry. "Open the door," he told the private.

"Yes, sir." The young man scurried to accommodate his commanding officer and Danny carried the woman inside and into a back room where he kept a cot. The tiny white frame house he had ordered built nearby for himself and Emily had yet to be occupied. So he kept residency in the small room behind his office. It was too lonely living in a house built for a wife who was not there.

He laid the Indian woman on the cot. There were beads of sweat on her face in spite of the cold air she had been in. "Go get the doctor," he ordered the private.

The young man left, and Danny took the robes away from the woman. Her doeskin tunic was soiled, and she watched him with big eyes as he started to remove it, then tried to scratch at him. He jerked back, grabbing her wrists firmly.

"I don't want to hurt you," he told her in the Sioux tongue, a language he had been compelled to learn in his duties. "I just want to clean you up. I want to help you. Help you," he repeated. He smiled for her and she studied the fascinating blue eyes and the blond, curly hair and strange mustache. His eyes were kind. They were not like the eyes of most white men who looked at her, not like the eyes of the man who had bought her off her Pawnee abductor and beaten and raped her.

"You . . . will not hurt me?" she gasped in her own tongue, her breath becoming harder and harder to find.

He shook his head. "I want to help you—make you feel better—give you good medicine to make you feel better. What is your name? You are Sioux, are you not?"

She nodded, still watching his eyes carefully. *"Ci'kala Mahpi'ya,"* she spoke up in a tiny voice.

Danny grinned more. "Small Cloud. That is a pretty name." He moved to take her hands and he squeezed them. "Let me help you, Small Cloud. You are sick. I have a big, flannel shirt you can wear, instead of this old tunic. Wouldn't you feel better if you were washed and wore something clean?"

Her eyes teared. "It is not . . . my fault," she whimpered. "He . . . would not let me . . . wash myself." She put a hand to her face. "I am ashamed," she whispered.

He patted her hair, unable to understand why this particular woman touched him. He had been around many Sioux women, some quite pretty. But he had found no particular attraction in any of them, for soldiers were not to allow themselves any emotional or physical involvement with Indian women, for obvious reasons. Danny Monroe was well aware of how easily the men could get out of control if

271

not strictly disciplined in the area of squaws, and most of them had the attitude that Indian women were free for the taking, which they most certainly were not. A tight hold on the men's actions was just another method of keeping the peace with the restless Sioux and the Northern Cheyenne. He had personally never found it particularly difficult to keep his thoughts from the Indian maidens, for he was a soldier above all things; and since marrying Emily, his mind and heart and physical needs had been full of her, tortured by her absence. Perhaps that was why this young girl stirred him, for he longed for Emily with a fierce ache in his heart and body. This girl was about the same age, and she looked like an abused little puppy dog. Her present shame tore at him, for the Sioux and Cheyenne women prized cleanliness.

"It's all right," he reassured her, quickly slipping the tunic over her head while she seemed more subdued. She was naked beneath it, and he struggled not to notice her dark, provocative beauty, the slender thighs and velvety skin. She curled up against his eyes, and he frowned at bruises seemingly everywhere on her body, obvious even through her dark skin. "Who did this to you?" he asked, pulling the robes back over her and going to a dresser. He pulled out a flannel shirt.

"White man . . . bought me," she replied weakly. "Pawnee stole me . . . sold me to white man. My first man. Hurts. Everything hurts," she groaned. "I . . . cannot breathe!"

She gasped and arched, and he rushed back to her, bending over and patting her hair again as she struggled for her breath.

"The doctor will come any minute, Small Cloud. You'll be all right. I promise." He considered sending someone after the man who had left her off at his doorstep. But it would do no good. There were no laws against buying and selling Indian women, nor against abusing an Indian, whether it be man, woman, or child. In fact, it seemed that more and more of late the behavior of whites toward Indians was governed by no rules but those of the "free for all." Too often Indians caught alone were shot for no good reason. Things would only get worse for the red man, and it worried

272

him, for his half-brother, Cheyenne Zeke, and his white wife, Abbie, lived to the south among the Cheyenne. Here in the North Zeke's Cheyenne half-brother, Swift Arrow, rode with the Sioux, his attitude becoming more and more rebellious. Danny's life was deeply involved with both worlds now, and he knew that decisions in the future would not be easy for him. There would be times when he would simply have to put duty above personal feelings, for he was an army man first, and he was, after all, white.

Small Cloud seemed to relax a little again, and the doctor finally arrived, grumbling all the way into the back room. "What's this about a damned Indian woman!" he barked. "I don't doctor Indians!"

Danny's eyes clouded and he rose to turn and face the man. "I'd like you to doctor this one," he replied. "I know you're a civilian, Montrose, and I can't give you orders. But the woman is very sick. I think she has pneumonia. I'd like to help her."

The doctor glanced at the young face. "You would, would you? It wouldn't by any chance be because she's young and pretty, and you're getting a yen for a woman, would it, Lieutenant?"

Danny's eyes flashed. "Watch your tongue, Montrose," he threatened, his big frame towering over the doctor's. "The Sioux are getting damned restless, and perhaps if we show a little compassion once in a while and help one of them, it would help keep them quiet! Now I intend to help this woman, with or without you, Montrose. And then I intend to ride out of this fort with a troop of men and take her back to her people. She was stolen from them by the Pawnee. Perhaps that one little act on my part will help stabilize the very fragile friendship we have with the Sioux. It doesn't hurt to try peace instead of war, doctor."

The man sighed and glowered at Danny. "I shall see what I can do—just this once," he told Danny. "I'll give you a diagnosis and some medicine. After that she's yours. And I'd just as soon no one knows I treated her. If the whites in these parts find out I've helped an Indian woman, they won't want me treating them."

Danny's look chilled him. He moved past the lieutenant and grudgingly yanked the robes from the frightened, whimpering girl, bending over to put a stethoscope to her chest. Danny felt an urge to let his eyes rest on her full, young breasts. But he kept his back turned and started to leave the room.

"Stay!" came the frightened voice in Sioux. She liked his kind eyes, but she did not like the doctor's eyes. She had no friends here among these leering, white soldiers, about whom she had heard terrifying stories. But the tall man with the blue eyes seemed sincere in wanting to help her. Somehow she knew he might protect her.

Danny stopped at the doorway and turned to meet her pleading eyes. He smiled for her again. "I will stay," he said quietly.

It was that same November that Abigail Monroe lay in childbirth. Actually it was an easy birth. Too easy. And too fast. This time Zeke Monroe got the second son he wanted, but his joy was quickly shrouded by abnormal bleeding. Abbie had not produced this child in the healthy manner she had birthed the first three. He was born so fast that it left her in shock. Her bleeding was alarmingly heavy, and Zeke worked frantically with towels and cold snow on her belly, doing everything he could think of while his eldest son, himself only six, was left to clean up his new baby brother with his clumsy little hands, and to wrap and hold the squalling, red baby, whose eyes were blue.

All the children and Dooley sat in the main room of the cabin waiting for orders from Zeke, whose face was desperate and drawn every time he came out of the bedroom to give more orders. Dooley was up and down, in and out, fetching some cow's milk for Little Rock to squeeze into the baby's mouth to stop its crying, for Abigail was bleeding and weak and unable to feed the child. He continued bringing in what little snow there was, for there had been a light sprinkling of it the night before, and Zeke hoped that packing the snow on Abbie's belly would help. But it was not working.

"Dooley!" Zeke called out again, his voice strained. "Come in here, will you?"

The longtime friend and faithful ranch hand obeyed. He had known Zeke in the old days of trapping in the Rockies, the days when Zeke was free of the burden of wife and children. But he knew Zeke didn't mind the burden, and he knew how much the man loved Abigail Monroe. Now as he entered the bedroom, the woman looked very much as though she was dying, and he tried to hide his shock at her hideous, almost gray complexion and the deep circles under her eyes. She lay motionless and quiet, and Zeke turned to him with terror in his eyes.

"I don't know what else to do!" he moaned. "I called you in here because I didn't want to frighten the children." He stepped closer, his eyes filled with desperate pain. "Dooley, she's bleeding to death!" he hissed. "I don't know what else to do!"

Dooley sighed and took hold of Zeke's arm squeezing it, wishing there were a doctor or a midwife present. He left Zeke and walked closer to her, bending over and studying her face, then looking back up at Zeke.

"I got an idea," he told the man. "But it might kill her just the same as bleedin' will."

Zeke's eyes lit up with the tiny ray of hope. "What does it matter? This way she'll die for sure. I have to try something, Dooley—anything that might help her!"

Dooley rubbed his chin and looked back down at poor Abbie. "Well, Zeke, there just ain't enough snow out there to keep her packed up in it, and it melts down too fast. What she needs is to be packed up good and cold from the waist down for a long time, not just a few minutes. Why not take her outside to that little creek and plunk her right down in it, make her sit in it to the waist for a while."

Zeke's eyes flickered with horror at such a thought and the pain it would bring her, yet it made sense.

"I know it sounds cruel, Zeke," Dooley was saying. "But what the hell else can you do? That creek's cold as ice right now. I know it's dangerous as hell. She might take pneumonia—might go into worse shock. Hard to say. But it's

275

better than this, friend. Sure as I'm standin' here, she's dyin', Zeke. And believe me, I don't want to see that happen to this woman any more than you. She's a hell of a woman."

Zeke rested his eyes on her stony, gray face. He blinked back tears. What on earth would he do without his Abbie? She was his whole reason for existing now. There were his children, yet what would a man like Cheyenne Zeke do with four little children and no wife? His wife was as important to him as breathing and eating. Abbie, sweet Abbie! She was still the fifteen-year-old woman-child he had claimed one night in the foothills of the Wind River Range of the Rockies. He met Dooley's eyes. Dooley was the only man who had ever been allowed to see tears in Cheyenne Zeke's eyes, other than Zeke's own brothers. And almost always the tears had been over Abbie.

"I'll try it," he told Dooley. "I'll need your help. She'll fight me, and I've got to try like hell to keep her out of the water from the waist up. If she slips all the way in it will kill her for sure. Maybe if I can keep her clothes and some robes around her from the waist up she'll be all right."

"You know I'll help." Their eyes held. "I got too much respect for her to be lookin' at anything I shouldn't be," he added with sincerity. "I just want to help if I can."

There was nothing more to be said. Zeke bent down and lifted her from the bed and she groaned, hanging limply in his arms. "Let's go!" he muttered to Dooley. Both men hurried out the door, Zeke ordering the children to stay inside and keep the baby warm. All three older ones watched quietly with frightened eyes, for they sensed their mother was deathly ill.

Abbie was only vaguely aware of being carried in her husband's arms. She felt no pain, only darkness and an odd weakness, so intense that to speak was too much effort. She wasn't even certain if she'd had a boy or a girl, or if the child was even alive, and yet she could not find the strength to ask. But then there was the sudden, shocking cold, a stinging agony at her lower half that made her cry out in spite of her weakness.

"Hang on to me, Abbie girl!" came the gentle voice. She

had no idea what was happening to her. Only that he was there, shrouding her close to his chest beneath a heavy buffalo robe. Perhaps she was dying. If so, at least she would die in Cheyenne Zeke's arms. She could think of no more comforting place to meet her Maker.

It was three weeks before Abbie was able to get out of bed, another four before she was strong enough to travel to the village for the celebration for Cheyenne Zeke's second son. She wanted very much to have the customary celebration, but by then winter had set into the Rockies and had spread across the plains, and Zeke would not let her out of the house. And so they named the child themselves, calling him Ohkumhkakit, Little Wolf. Zeke prayed and chanted before the hearth, offering the pipe to the spirits of the four directions, and to the spirits of sky and earth, praying for his son's health, as well as Abbie's.

The boy was not dark like his older brother, but neither was he as fair as Young Girl. He was a blending of both, with sandy hair and blue eyes and reddish skin that looked as though it would easily pick up the sun yet never be as naturally dark as Little Rock's and his father's skin. His hair had some wave to it, rather than being stick straight, and he was not as robust as Little Rock had been as a baby.

Abbie was happy with having another son, for she had wanted the boy dearly for Zeke. She was equally happy with the way her figure reverted to its young, trim form, for surely Zeke would be pleased when they made love again. And yet he seemed strangely distant since the birth, almost cold. She sometimes wondered if he was angry with her for something, yet there was no possible reason that he could be. She had given him another son. Surely he was greatly pleased. She could see it in his eyes every time he held the boy in his arms. He worked faithfully with Blue Sky and Young Girl, and most especially with Little Rock, to include them in the care of the new arrival, for he had seen the hint of jealousy in Little Rock's eyes. Until now Little Rock had been the only son, and therefore a favored child, the apple of his father's eye. Now there was another boy invading the

Monroe family, and Zeke could see that Little Rock felt challenged. But the animosity quickly faded when Zeke faithfully took Little Rock on the morning rides, even in the winter cold, continuing to teach the boy the ways of survival, continuing their long, private talks, and continuing to praise him for his accomplishments, telling him it would be his honored responsibility to help train his little brother in the same ways.

Abbie ignored Zeke's odd coldness toward her, deciding it was only because she had been weak and ill and unable to be a wife to him in the night. But when she was healed and stronger, there was still no effort on Zeke's part to renew their sexual relationship. And on the very night that she had planned to cajole him into making love and getting that part of their lives back in order, he made the unexpected and cold announcement. He came into the bedroom and saw that her shoulders were bare. He felt a surge of intense desire for his woman again, knowing she was naked beneath the robes; but he had lived for weeks with the nightmare of the horrible, nearly uncontrollable bleeding; lived with the memory of what it was like to think she was going to die. Anything was better than losing his Abbie.

"I will sleep in a bedroll in the main room in front of the hearth from now on, Abbie," he told her matter-of-factly, walking to the corner of the room to pick up some extra robes and blankets.

Her blood chilled and she lost her smile. She sat up, holding a robe in front of her. "What are you talking about?"

He turned to meet her eyes, deliberately keeping his cold and determined. "You know what I'm talking about. Other husbands and wives do it when it's dangerous for the woman to have any more children. I'll not let you go through that again. Something went wrong this time and might go wrong again. There will be no more children in this house. Little Wolf is the last one."

He headed toward the curtained doorway.

"Zeke!" she gasped. He hesitated. "You might have consulted me!" she said angrily. "I don't care how

278

dangerous it might me. I'll not live out my life without my husband in my bed. How dare you make such a decision without even talking about it!" Her voice choked. How could he even consider never touching, never holding, never needing her? Or that she could live without the strength she derived from his life surging within her? He turned to meet her eyes, his own red with tears, his jaw flexing with stubborn determination.

"What was there to talk about?" he replied. "You've never been closer to death—not when you took that Crow arrow and not when Dancing Moon tried to kill you two different times. You nearly died bearing the life that I put inside of you! I touch your lips and you're pregnant! Your body needs a long rest, and even at that it could happen again. Other couples abstain for the very same reasons."

"We are not other couples!" She blinked back tears.

"We love each other and we have our children. That's all we need. Indian men often do this for their wives when it is dangerous or too burdensome to have more children. They have the strength that is needed to do what is practical."

"Practical!" she exclaimed, shaking with a mixture of rage and desperation. "I hate that word! I'm sick of practical! And you're only half Indian, Zeke Monroe!"

"White men have done the same for their wives."

"And most of them get what they need from the prostitutes!" she wailed. "Is that what you intend to do?" She had never yelled at him before, but never had she felt so desperate. She needed him, now more than ever. But the stubborn Cheyenne blood was running full force, and she saw the determination in his eyes.

"Don't talk foolishly," he answered quietly. "It's decided and there is nothing more to say about it. Anything is better than losing you to death, Abbie. When you think about it, you will understand that I am right."

He turned and went through the curtained door, and she sat there watching the curtains move until they were finally still. She lay back down, then rolled over and wept into the robes. Surely time was all they needed. Surely after a while he would find it impossible to abstain. But how long would

279

that take? It was like a death sentence, to think of living without her man until her childbearing years were over.

Danny Monroe made Small Cloud his personal project, obsessed with making her well and taking her back to her people, torn by the pitiful way she had been abused just because she was an Indian. He nursed her, bathed her, fed her, kept her warm, more like a father and a friend to her than a man who would want her physically, although he could not help but be attracted to her. He cared little about any gossip that might arise out of his efforts, for he felt it necessary to prove to her there could be kindness offered from white men, and through her other Sioux would learn the same. Frequent visits by a widowed middle-aged woman who was one of the cooks in the staff kitchen helped quell the gossip. The woman was the only other person Danny had found who would help him willingly with the Indian girl. He got no other aid unless he himself ordered it. But the men did appreciate the presence of the Indian woman for one very important reason. Lieutenant Daniel Monroe's attitude had been greatly changed since her arrival. His heart was somehow lighter, his walk had more life in it, his personality was easier to live with, and there were fewer stays in the guardhouse. Lieutenant Monroe had a personal project going, and it had helped take his mind from the fact that the wife he loved and needed was not there with him.

Small Cloud mended, and during the mending she and Daniel Monroe shared many talks, teaching each other about one another's world and lifestyle. Danny saw in her a certain openness and gentleness that few white woman possessed, except perhaps Abigail Monroe. When she was well enough that it looked suspicious to keep her in his own cot, she went to stay with the female cook who had helped nurse her. The woman took Small Cloud under her wing like a mother. But Danny had warned Small Cloud that soon she must go back to her people. He knew he should take her back right away, but he could not bring himself to take her, always bringing up as an excuse for not taking her that he was too busy with "army matters." Actually he did not want to lose her friendship and their conversations. His loneliness for Emily and for true companionship was intense. He had never had a problem with loneliness before he'd met Emily, but ever since his return without her he'd been fighting it. Small Cloud seemed to alleviate the pain.

Her arrival in November turned into what looked like permanent residency by January. By then the bitter prairie winds and deep snows gave Danny a very natural excuse for not returning her. She had been long recovering from pneumonia. It would be dangerous to expose her to the cold for an extended period while they searched out her own particular tribe. It would be better to wait until spring.

Sixteen

There was no strength left in Abigail Monroe, no life and no laughter. The collapse had come in early May of 1854, after an especially hard day of noisy children inside the small cabin, a physically hard day of trying to wash clothes and hang them around inside the house, as well as baking a week's supply of bread. Others had seen Abbie steadily losing her vitality over the past several weeks, but Zeke had tried to ignore it, having slowly shut out all feelings for her so that he would not desire her. Since his announcement that he would no longer share her bed, she had grown thinner and more quiet, short-tempered and listless. She seemed especially irritated with Little Wolf whenever the child let out the tiniest whimper. Conversations between herself and Zeke, which had once been vital and had always come easy, had almost ceased. And then came the fatal day when she literally fell to the floor. Zeke carried her to the bed, and thus began the strange affliction that seemed untreatable. She simply had no strength whatsoever, and, most strange of all, she didn't seem to care. It was as though she wanted to give up her life.

Zeke had never felt more helpless about what to do for her. Tall Grass Woman was sent for. Hopefully her happy countenance and strong friendship with Abbie would help Abbie recover from the strange ailment, and in the meantime she could help keep the children fed and cared for. Zeke tried to avoid his worry by absorbing himself in working even harder on the ranch, but a black fear that she might be dying gripped at his insides. If only there were a

282

good doctor who could look at her. Perhaps she had some strange disease. He felt desolate and alone, and himself strangely weak and uncaring. Something had gone out of his life. Something had gone out of both their lives. The love was still there, but it seemed buried by something. Perhaps it was just the strain of the long years in the wilderness. Perhaps Abbie had simply had all she could stand. Perhaps she should go back to Tennessee after all, and live where there was civilization. Perhaps to think she could live this hard life among the Cheyenne had been a foolish dream, after all. She had always seemed so strong, so determined, so happy, in spite of the hardships and dangers. She had survived a serious arrow wound when only fifteen, survived the loss of her entire family on the wagon train. She had survived an outlaw attack and two life-threatening attacks by Dancing Moon. She had survived that rugged first year with the Cheyenne, moving North with them on the buffalo hunt, living in a tipi. She had borne her first two children in a tipi. And once she had taken a bullet out of his own side. She was a woman of strength and great courage, highly respected even among the strict and demanding Cheyenne. The Abbie who lay listless and seemingly dying now in the cabin was not the Abbie he knew, and his heart lay heavy in his chest. Before he could help her he needed to find his own strength again, and he could get that no other place than from his People. He finally decided to have Dooley watch after the ranch while he went to speak with his father, Deer Slayer. He needed some advice and a renewal of his spiritual strength. Tall Grass Woman could stay with Abbie. He did not want to leave her as she was, yet he seemed to be no good to her in his own weak condition. He was losing his woman.

Danny sat down to compose the long-overdue letter to his half-brother. He had no idea just exactly where Zeke and Abbie were living, except he was certain it was among the Southern Cheyenne. He should have sent a runner the summer before to find Zeke and tell him the news about his no longer being a wanted man in Tennessee. But then he had got involved with Emily, and had been so wrapped up in his personal problem of returning to Fort Laramie without a wife that he had put off getting the news to Zeke. All too quickly winter had set in, and it was not practical for either Indian or soldier to make the journey south in the midst of ravaging winter winds and snows. But now it was May. He would get word to Swift Arrow somehow, and Swift Arrow would send runners south to find Cheyenne Zeke and tell him he was a free man.

If Danny had thought it mattered enough to Zeke, he would have tried harder to tell him sooner. The news would be more important to Abbie, who always feared bounty hunters, and in that respect he felt guilty about not letting her know sooner. But Zeke feared no man, and he most certainly had no plans to ever return to Tennessee, especially not to see their father. Zeke had never forgiven his white father for dragging him from his Cheyenne mother at the tender age of four and selling the woman, taking Zeke to a land of whites where he was cruelly treated.

Danny dipped the quill into the ink. He must get the news to his brother and not put it off any longer. With the spring thaw, troops would be moving out to keep an eye on the restless Sioux. This was a good time for returning Small Cloud to her People, and at the same time he could find Swift Arrow and give him the letter for Zeke. But the thought made him put down the pen again. He did not like the idea of returning Small Cloud. He would miss her dearly. But to keep her at the fort any longer might force him to face feelings for her he would rather ignore. She was a Sioux, and he was a married man—two facts that made her forbidden to him. But he felt a lovely warmth whenever she was near, and he had begun to detect a dangerous attachment in her eyes. She must go back, no matter how painful the parting might be.

He started writing again when the door opened and Small Cloud herself timidly peeked inside. Danny glanced up and immediately smiled. "You are busy, with your soldier work?" she asked him.

He leaned back in his chair. "Never too busy for you, Small Cloud."

She smiled and came inside, her hair brushed long and full, a yellow scarf tied about her head. She wore a yellow checkered dress, a hand-me-down from one of the very few wives who lived at the fort. The dress fit her nicely, and Danny's eyes took in the pleasant curves of her body as she came to stand in front of his desk.

"It is not true, is it?" she asked in her own tongue. "That you will take me back tomorrow?"

He watched the hope in her eyes and his heart pained. "It is true, Small Cloud. You simply can't stay here any longer. It isn't right for you . . . or for me. You belong with your own kind. Don't you want to go back, to your family, your friends?"

Her smile faded. "I want very much to go back. I miss Old Grandmother. And I have my small sister. But . . . it is only that I do not want to leave you. You are a good man to me . . . a good friend. I would miss you too much."

Their eyes held, and he forced himself to remember Emily. In spite of, or perhaps because of, his wife's frequent "empty" letters, it was becoming difficult to remember his feelings for her, for they had been long apart, and he was beginning to wonder if she would ever make the promised visit.

"I will miss you, too, Small Cloud. But it is best all around that you go, and go soon."

She swallowed and blinked back tears. "It is not right that your woman is not here with you. I do not wish for you to be lonely. I could be your wife, too. Indian men often have more than one wife."

His heart quickened with the pleasantness of such a thought, and with a desire not to hurt her. It was the first time she had blatantly revealed feelings he had suspected were building, and he was angry with himself for not returning her to her people much sooner. His own loneliness had compelled him to want to cling to her friendship, but now there were other feelings to deal with. He sighed and leaned forward, resting his arms on the desk.

"I would be honored to call you my wife, Small Cloud," he replied gently, "if I were free to claim you as one. But white men have only one wife. Our customs are different, and I have to cling to mine. I am not free to take another wife. That is what I mean when I say you belong with your own kind—and I with mine."

A tear slipped down her cheek. "I . . . could learn your ways . . . be your friend—"

"No." He shook his head. He wanted to rise and hold her, console her. But if he touched her he would be unable to release her. "I could never just be your friend, Small Cloud. Not forever. And even if I were a free man, there is the fact that I am a lieutenant in the United States Army, and you are a Sioux Indian. Our worlds couldn't be further apart. The army is my life. And you . . ." his eyes roved her body once more. "You belong out there free on the prairie, the woman of some handsome, brave Sioux warrior. You should marry a Sioux man, Small Cloud. You could never be happy in this place, among people who don't treat you kindly. Tomorrow we go. I'll not put it off any longer."

She hung her head. "Good-bye, then, my lieutenant friend. I say it now, while we are alone." She raised her head again to meet the blue eyes that made her heart race. "You are good and kind. I owe you my life. I shall never forget you. There is a special place in my heart for you." Her voice broke on the last words, and she whirled and ran out before he could reply.

Danny stared at the door. He wanted to run after her, yet knew it would be foolish. He returned to his letter, wondering if he should tell Zeke about Small Cloud, and about Emily. He dipped the pen again and held it over the paper.

No. How could he explain such things in a letter? He suddenly wished Zeke were there to talk to. Anyone, for that matter. He threw the pen across the room, and ink spattered against the wall.

*   *   *

The night came all too quickly and would probably go much too fast. Danny lay with his eyes wide open. Tomorrow she would go. His problems with the restless Indians and with his absent and childish wife seemed suddenly overwhelming. Why did things always seem magnified in the night? Why did the heart weigh so heavy?

He rolled onto his side. He would write Emily again— soon. He made himself that promise. Again he would implore her to come to Fort Laramie to be with her husband. He knew what her answer would be, but he must try or go AWOL to return to St. Louis and see her. It seemed urgent now that he see his wife; that he remind himself of how much he loved her in spite of her refusal to leave St. Louis. Even if she didn't enjoy making love, he had to feel her nakedness and to take his pleasure in his wife. How many times had he dreamed of being one with her again; of awakening to her lovely body and sweet face in the morning? But always it was just that—a dream.

He turned back over, then sat bolt upright, startled to see a shadowy figure standing next to the cot. He reached for his revolver, but then came the sweet voice.

"It is I, Small Cloud," she said quietly.

"Small Cloud! But what on earth—how on earth did you get in here?"

He could feel her smile in the darkness, even though he could not see her face. "Do you know how quiet an Indian can be?" she replied. Then he heard a light giggle. "You soldiers should learn to be so quiet!"

He had to smile, his mind reeling with the fact she was there in the darkness. A distant voice screamed at him to make her get out right away. But he said nothing.

"I am here to thank you, my lieutenant friend," she told him. He heard the rustle of her clothes as she removed them. "Your woman does not come to you, so I come to you. Tomorrow we must part. I understand this. But tonight I am still here, and I desire you, just as I know you desire me. And a man without his wife has many needs. Tonight will be our secret."

287

He stared at her almost dumbfounded, wanting her to do what she was doing but also angry with her, and with himself for not objecting. His needs were too great, his loneliness too unbearable, her body too soft when she brazenly pulled back the covers and moved in beside him, touching him delicately with her fingertips and rubbing her cheek lovingly against his chest.

"The other white man was cruel to me," she told him. "But I know you will not be. I know it will be good. We are good friends saying good-bye."

She turned her face to his, and his lips met her mouth tenderly as he pulled her beneath his body.

Zeke sat staring at the flames of the little fire. His eyes were hollow and his face drawn, and he felt closer to the Spirits and his inner power, for he had fasted for five days and had prayed constantly, asking for a return of his vitality and for a return of his wife's health and vigor. His Cheyenne stepfather, Deer Slayer, had stayed faithfully at his side, watchful that no one should come to the cave along the river where Zeke had gone to fast and pray for Abbie, quietly guarding his son and sometimes speaking to him to advise him in the Cheyenne way, sharing the religious peace pipe with Zeke in offerings to the Spirits of the Four Directions, the Earth and the Sky. He had seen Zeke's strength slowly return as the man himself returned to the Cheyenne Spirits through sacrifice and prayer. But still there was something wrong. Still his son was deeply troubled, and Deer Slayer worried, for it would be dangerous for Zeke to fast any longer. He refused to eat, insisting that until his prayers were answered, he would continue to suffer.

Now in the very early morning of the sixth day, before the sun had even risen, Zeke was awake and watching the flames of the fire his stepfather had made for him. He sat staring vacantly, frowning slightly, as though perusing a puzzle, then turned weary eyes to his father.

"I had a dream last night, Deer Slayer," he told the man. "I think perhaps it was a vision sent by the Spirits, to tell me something. Perhaps it was supposed to be an answer to my prayers, but I am not sure."

Deer Slayer nodded. "Tell me the dream, my son, and let me see if it makes sense to me." He stirred the fire. "Unless you do not want to share it."

Zeke reached out and touched the man's hand. "I do not hesitate to share anything with you, Deer Slayer. You know that."

The old man smiled. "You are a good son—as good to me as my blood sons. Better in some ways, for Red Eagle turned into a drunkard, and Swift Arrow has left me to ride in the North. Your mother is dead. All I have is you and Black Elk." He patted Zeke's hand. "Tell me your dream, Lone Eagle," he urged, using Zeke's Cheyenne name.

Zeke withdrew his hand and picked up a stick, tracing it in the dirt. He thought quietly for several seconds before finally divulging the very personal vision. "There were two eagles, circling a canyon," he finally spoke up. "One kept deliberately flying close to the other, trying to touch their wing tips. But the second eagle would always move aside, staying inches away from the first and never letting the first touch it. The first eagle was crying out that one of its wings was broken, and that it could not fly much longer without the help of the second eagle, but the second eagle scoffed at the first and told it that it must fly on its own, that it must draw on its inner powers to stay aloft. But then the first eagle began to fall. When it fell, something pulled on the second eagle, as though a rock had been tied to its leg. And in spite of its health and strength, it, too, began falling. It struggled to stay aloft, unable to understand what was pulling at it. It descended so quickly that it soon caught up with the first eagle, and by accident their wings touched." Zeke took his eyes from the tracings in the earth and met Deer Slayer's eyes. "When their wings touched, the burden was lifted from the second eagle, and the first eagle's wing was suddenly mended. They were light again, and they soared into the clouds." He frowned. "What do you think is the meaning of the dream, Deer Slayer? I don't understand it."

Deer Slayer actually smiled again. "You just don't want

289

to understand it . . . because you are afraid."

Zeke looked back at the fire. "I don't know what you mean."

"I think you do. All of these days I have been waiting for you to tell me something you have been leaving out. You forget that Tall Grass Woman is a good friend to your Abbie, and Abbie confides in her. Tall Grass Woman in turn confides in her husband, who has spoken to me a time or two on quiet nights." Zeke looked down at the tracings again, refusing to meet his father's eyes. Deer Slayer only smiled more. "I think I know the whole answer to your problem, Lone Eagle, and even to Abbie's. The vision has also told you the answer. The first eagle was Abbie, reaching out to you, asking her man to hold her, to be one with her, for it is in this way the woman finds her strength. She draws it from the man. You are the second eagle, telling her she must draw on her own strength alone, for you will never touch her again. Now her wing is broken, Lone Eagle. She is falling. She needs your touch, your strength. You also began to lose your strength. You are falling with her, like the second eagle. You need to touch your woman to be strong."

Zeke closed his eyes and shook his head. "I almost lost her," he groaned. "You . . . weren't there. You didn't see all the blood! Her horrible, gray face! I'll not do that again to her. There must be no more children!"

"Do not be such a fool, Lone Eagle. Only the Spirits can make these decisions. All childbirth is different, and the next one may be no trouble at all. Tell me which is worse, my son: to have her die this way, cold and lonely and tired, without ever having held her again; or to die giving birth to the life you have planted in her belly out of your good love, to die knowing she gave everything to her man and he gave her everything in return?"

A strange choking sound came from Zeke's throat and he dropped the stick, putting his head down with his arms over it, his shoulders shaking. Deer Slayer reached over and touched his shoulder gently.

"How strange it is that a man such as you can go out and

kill men with no feeling, take on many men at one time and send them all to their grave, fight Apaches and crawl out of snakepits and know no fear. And yet one tiny woman can bring you to weeping because of your terrible fear of losing her." He squeezed Zeke's shoulder, his heart torn at the pitiful memories that scourged his half-breed stepson's heart and made this brave, strong and often violent man weep for the love he secretly needed. "You must touch wings with her," he told Zeke quietly. "When you touch, you will both be healed. I am sure of this, Lone Eagle. Neither of you will be strong until you are one again."

"I can't . . . live without her!" Zeke groaned.

Deer Slayer patted his back. "Then you have the answer to your sorrow," he replied. "You have been too blind to see it, my son. For in what you have done, you are already living without her. She is as much as dead to you, and you are dead to her. Think on this, and you will see that I am right."

Dooley carried Abbie outside to an old wooden rocker that had been set up near the corral. She wanted to feel the sun and watch the horses, but she could not walk. She was certain she didn't have much longer to live. She wanted to feel the sun once more, to hear the birds singing and to hear her children playing in the distance, suddenly sure it would be the last time she heard the songs and laughter. There was no laughter left in her own heart, no sun and no singing.

Dooley set her gently in the chair and folded the blankets around her. "You sure you want to be out here, ma'am?" he asked.

"I'm sure," she nodded weakly. "Where . . . is he, Dooley? Why doesn't he . . . come?"

"He's gone to pray and fast for you, Abigail. He's out there someplace with Deer Slayer, I think."

"He's not coming back," she said quietly. "We've grown apart, Dooley."

The man just smiled. "That man would walk over burnin' coals to be with you, ma'am. You're talkin' plum foolish

291

now." He patted her head and walked off to draw some water for the horses.

Abbie closed her eyes and listened to the children. Blue Sky was carrying poor Little Wolf everywhere with her, pretending to be the baby's mother, while Little Rock strutted beside her carrying his lance, pretending to be the protective father. The two older children conducted themselves in a manner far beyond their years, caring for the new baby that their mother was barely even able to feed. The faithful Tall Grass Woman did her best to take care of the "white woman's" house and feed the big family, and little Young Girl seemed always off in a world of her own, playing quietly alone with her straw doll.

Abbie's heart tightened with sorrow for her new baby, whom she had not held very often, except to feed him. Lately she had not even had enough milk for him and cow's milk had to be used. She loved him, yet she had been unable to keep from blaming him for the terrible coldness between herself and Zeke. If not for Little Wolf . . . she put a hand to her breast and wanted to scream in anger at herself. How could she blame her tiny baby for her own troubles? She would leave this world never having been a good mother to her second son. She laid her head back against the rocker and wanted to weep, but she was too weak to do even that. The tears had all been wrung out of her long ago.

She opened her eyes again at the sound of a horse, and in the distance she could see someone coming down the hill toward the corral. It was Zeke. There was no mistaking the physique and the grand Appaloosa he rode. But even from the distance he looked thinner. Her heart quickened at the sight of him, for he had been gone nearly a week and she had actually doubted he would return. That might actually have been easier, for his presence only made the distance between them more painful, and she suddenly wondered if she was to die without ever having been held in his arms again.

He came closer, and her chest tightened at the sight of the drawn and thin look of his handsome face. His dark eyes were hollow and his stomach almost too flat, but the broad, bronze shoulders were the same and there seemed to be something different about him as he drew the horse up close to her, sitting nearly naked astride the animal, wearing only the loincloth. Their eyes met quietly. She wanted to look away but could not, for his own eyes were warmer than they had been for months. How strange that their love could have been so strong and yet they could have grown so far apart; that the talking could cease; the warmth for one another could go out of them. If only he would touch her, love her in the old ways, tease her and laugh with her. If only he would do those things again, she might want to live, might be able to fight this strange affliction. How many times had she tried to explain that, only to have him turn coldly from her. How she wanted to tell him now. But she had given up trying to talk to him. Yet now his eyes were different, looking more like they used to before Little Wolf was born.

He slid from the horse and stood before her, bending over and planting his hands on the arms of the rocker so that his face was close to hers, his long, shining hair loose and falling over his shoulders. All the time their eyes continued to be locked, and to her surprise he bent closer and lightly kissed her cool lips. Her heart swelled with guarded hope, and a tingling of new life seemed quietly to trace its way through her veins. He pulled back and studied the surprise in her eyes, and he knew Deer Slayer was right. She was dying of starvation, hungry simply for affection and the strength only he could give her. And Zeke was shriveling from the same hunger.

"It seems I'm always asking you to forgive me," he told her quietly. "I've done a terrible thing to you, Abbie girl. But it's been because I love you so much, and I get so scared I'll lose you."

He had called her "Abbie girl!" How long had it been since he'd used that affectionate name? How long since his warm lips had touched hers, and the sweet love had been evident in his eyes? Did she have the old Zeke back again,

293

the one who used to make love to her with spontaneous surges of desire? The one who often took her riding to their secret place by the stream? The man who had so gently and tenderly made a woman of her those many years ago when she was lost and alone, wanting to die as she had been wanting to die now?

"Zeke," she whispered, searching the provocative dark eyes, wanting to be certain the man she had fallen in love with at first sight was still there, that he had truly returned. "I have . . . no strength . . . without you. I feel like . . . like you died and I've had to . . . struggle alone without you." A tear slipped down her cheek. "Help me!" she whimpered. "I need you . . . to hold me. Just to hold me . . . if nothing more."

He flashed the smile that she had not seen in months, the special, warm smile that was meant only for his Abbie. He took his fingers and gently brushed the tear from her face.

"I have in mind a lot more than just holding you, Abbie girl, once you're stronger," he answered. "We have a hell of a lot of time to make up for, so you'd best start eating and get yourself stronger, woman. You can just imagine what a bad way I'm in. You just might regret wanting your man back in your bed."

He reached down and scooped her out of the rocker. She put her arms around his neck and breathed in his manly scent, too weak even to cry as she needed to cry. Her tears came in pitiful little whimpers and he squeezed her close. He looked over at the little cabin, and the children playing near it.

"Let's go home, Abbie girl, and see what Tall Grass Woman has cooked up for us. I'm suddenly the hungriest man that ever walked on two feet."

She smiled through her tears and kissed his neck, then his cheek. He turned his face and their lips met tenderly, hungrily, and every part of her body seemed to be reawakening from a long sleep.

Dooley came up from the bank of the river, carrying two buckets, and saw them in the distance. He set the buckets down and watched them for a moment, as Zeke headed toward the cabin with his wife in his arms. The children were running then to meet their father. Dooley grinned widely.

"Well, I'll be damned," he muttered.

It was early in June that summer of 1854 when the Cheyenne runners came down from the North with the news. They told of strangely dressed people from a land across the sea, who traveled in great numbers with fancy wagons and were well armed. These people had invaded the Northern country, following the Platte River, the Tongue and the Powder Rivers, killing buffalo for sport, sometimes keeping the heads, sometimes not even that much. The animal was being killed off by the hundreds, even by the thousands. The Sioux and Northern Cheyenne were up in arms over the slaughter of their prime food staple, and to Zeke and Abbie's surprise, one of the scouts for the foreign invaders was Jim Bridger himself, a man who had always been a friend to the Indian. It was difficult to believe, but obvious now that as more whites invaded the land, other whites who had formerly been friends to the Indian would turn to their own kind.

The news lay heavily on Zeke's and Abbie's hearts, and the burden was made worse when the runners told them of a son born to Yellow Moon—a half-breed son fathered by the fat white man from whom Zeke had rescued her the summer before. The boy was deformed, his left leg crooked and the foot twisted nearly to the back side of the leg. The People considered it a weakness, a curse brought on by the fact that the boy's father was an evil white man. He was called Crooked Foot, but in spite of his affliction and the circumstances surrounding the child's conception, Yellow Moon had chosen to keep him, for he was a part of her, and he helped replace the emptiness left in her heart over the death of little Laughing Boy.

Zeke stewed for days after hearing the news, fuming over the foreigners who were making sport of killing buffalo; and even more over the ex-senator, Winston Garvey, who had brought so much heartache to poor Yellow Moon. Hardly a day passed that he did not threaten to go to the senator's estate and kill the man, and Abbie was worried about the trouble such a thing would bring them. She considered how she could calm him down, and her answer came when they received the letter from Danny. Their hearts were lighter when they learned that Zeke had been cleared of murder charges in Tennessee. The news left Zeke feeling a strong indebtedness to his younger white brother, and a concern for him as well. For he sensed from the letter that there was more Danny had wanted to tell him. Everything seemed to be leading to one conclusion. This was the summer they would migrate North with Black Elk and the others.

After much cajoling from Abbie, Zeke was convinced it was the only logical thing to do, in spite of the fact that she still was not quite as strong as she should have been. But they had discussed for years going along again on a hunt, and going back to Fort Laramie to see Danny. Now there was the deformed child to think about. Abbie was concerned that Swift Arrow and Yellow Moon might need some kind of help with the infant, and because the baby was a half-breed like Zeke, she felt a special love for him and wanted very much to see the child.

"Zeke, we have every reason to go," she pleaded with him in the night, using his weakest moment to talk him into the journey. "We should see both Swift Arrow and Danny, and find out what's going on up there. We could see that poor baby, and the trip would be fun for the children, especially Little Rock. You know how he loves to ride. If you tell him we're going North to see Swift Arrow he'll be ecstatic. And for once I'm not pregnant. We can do it, Zeke. We could even take some of the Appaloosas with us and sell them at Fort Laramie—maybe trade some to the Sioux for new robes. We need new robes, Zeke. There are more buffalo in the north. It will be easier to find fresh robes there."

He sighed and ran his hand over her ribs and hip bones. "Abbie, you're still so thin—"

"I feel good, Zeke." She kissed his chest, sweet desire pulsing at her loins for him. It had only been two weeks

296

since she had been strong enough to be a wife to him again, and now their lovemaking seemed sweeter and more passionate and pleasing than ever, for they had been apart and then had rediscovered one another. Now when they touched and were one, there was always the desire to make up for all the pain they had suffered when they had grown apart. His movements over her were full of hungry intimacy, and she gloried in the joy of having her man back in her bed. "It would be good for us to spend a summer living the way we did when we were first married," she purred, moving her lips to his neck. "And don't deny you would love to ride North again, be with Black Elk and the others, ride free on the plains again and help with the hunt."

Her hand traced its way lightly over his flat belly and to places she always touched bashfully, but touched just the same because she knew how it pleased him.

"You don't play fair, Abbie girl," he told her softly, bending down to lightly kiss a firm nipple.

She laughed lightly, and it was music to his heart to hear her laughing again. Never would he leave her bed again, or let himself grow away from her. He kissed her lips hungrily, running his hand to the inside of her thighs.

"All right, we'll do it," he told her. "But you ride, understand? No walking. If you get too tired to ride, you'll lie on the travois. I'll not do anything to risk your health."

"Whatever you say," she whispered, lightly touching the finely carved lips. Her breath caught in her throat and she closed her eyes as his hand caressed secret places that were the property of one Cheyenne Zeke. "Now you aren't playing fair," she said with a gentle smile.

His powerful frame moved on top of her, and she was again small and helpless beneath his compelling masculinity. "That makes us even, Mrs. Monroe," he told her.

"We'll never be even," she teased, running her hands over the hard muscle of his arms. "You put your brand on me when I was a lonely, ignorant little girl, Cheyenne Zeke. After that I belonged to you, you savage."

"I don't recall any objections at the time," he answered, moving his hands under her hips.

She traced a finger over the scar on his cheek. "And you won't get any objections now," she replied.

She breathed deeply as he pushed his life inside of her, feeding her the strength that kept her going, and taking from her his own emotional nourishment. How good it was to have him back this way again. There was time now only for this. The discussion about going North was ended. They would go.

Seventeen

Abbie's theory that the trip would be good for them was proven correct. Zeke and Little Rock were both where they belonged, migrating across the plains with the People. Both father and son wore only loincloths, their long, black hair blowing loose around their shoulders, their Appaloosas painted with suns and moons and eagles, feathers tied in the manes of their mounts. There was more laughter among the Monroe family than there had been in months, and Zeke's own strength and vigor seemed to grow with every mile of riding the wind.

Little Wolf's cradleboard hung at the side of Abbie's horse, where the child spent most of the trip sleeping snugly, while Abbie kept Young Girl on her mount in front of her. Blue Sky took turns riding either with her father or behind Little Rock, but Little Rock was so prone to trying to do tricks with his horse that Abbie was afraid to let his sister ride with him. There seemed to be a constant but light-hearted battle between herself and Zeke over allowing Little Rock's trick riding, Abbie always worried he would get hurt and Zeke always telling her to let him go. Abbie knew it was a losing battle, especially the day when Little Rock came charging in circles around them standing on his horse's back and yelling war whoops.

Abbie's breath caught in her throat at the sight, but Zeke only grinned and some of the other men in the tribe cheered him on, yipping and howling and joining him, turning the entire affair into nothing short of a circus.

"Look at me, Father!" Little Rock yelled, dashing by and

leaning to the side of his mount, pretending someone was shooting at him and he was ducking aside and using his horse for protection. "No enemy will ever get me!"

"Oh, Zeke, stop him!" Abbie protested, putting a hand to her breast. Little Rock rode in a circle around them, clinging to his horse's neck, and other warriors followed, some hanging nearly all the way under their horses. There was no arguing that the Cheyenne were unmatched in their supreme horsemanship, and Abbie had seen them practice their almost militarylike maneuvers many times. But these kinds of antics were their favorite, and it would have been entertaining if her own son were not part of the show. The next thing she knew, Zeke was handing Blue Sky to old Deer Slayer, while he kicked his horse's sides and moved into the action himself, charging ahead and offering a race to his son. Man and boy galloped forward, so far that they disappeared for several minutes, while Abbie watched helplessly.

"Do not worry so, Abigail," Deer Slayer told her, bringing his horse close beside hers. "Such things are as important to Zeke and his son as eating."

She stared into the distance for several seconds before she replied. "I'm losing my son to the wildness in his veins, Grandfather," she told the old man.

He reached over and patted her arm. "All mothers lose their sons to manhood, child. But he is yet a small boy. You will have him for a while. And on the inside, they are always small boys. Do you not sometimes see the boy in Zeke's eyes, especially when he is hurt?"

She turned to the old man and smiled. "Yes. I do," she replied affectionately.

He smiled and squeezed her arm before taking hold of his own reins again, keeping protective arms around his little granddaughter. "And how is it with you and Zeke now?" he asked. "From the look in his eyes and the joy in your own, it seems you have found one another again."

Abbie blushed and kept watching the horizon for her husband and son's return. "We have. The last baby—"

"I know how my son felt, Abigail. I was with him in those

300

days of fasting. You have a powerful hold on him. You can keep him strong, or you can make him weak. Only you can do this, Abigail."

She thought of their tender nights in the tipi, when they quietly made love while the children slept. "It is the same for me, Grandfather," she answered wistfully. "Zeke has been my friend and my strength ever since I lost my family on the wagon train. I can't imagine being without him."

Now they were returning, Little Rock standing up on his horse again. Abbie shook her head. She would do no more protesting. What was the use?

It was late August when they crested a ridge in the Black Hills, Paha-Sapa to the Sioux, the Sacred Hills. Below lay a vast Indian camp, hundreds of tipis in circles of clans and greater circles of tribes, many of the tipis recognizable as Cheyenne. Smoke curled up from fires built to smoke some of the fresh hides, and women could be seen fleshing out more hides. Strips of meat hung out to dry or be smoked, and more brewed quietly in great black pots over hot coals.

"They have had a good hunt," Black Elk told Zeke as they looked below. "We will go down and see if they know of Swift Arrow, share with them some of our own meat, trade with them." He turned to face his brother. "These Sioux may be important to us one day, my brother. They are good friends to the Cheyenne, and good warriors. One day we shall do battle together. I see it in my dreams."

The wind moaned ominously, and everything seemed to become quiet. It was like the calm before the storm. Abbie's heart tightened at the thought that what she was looking at now could one day all too soon vanish. At the center of the village she recognized the tipi being prepared for the Sun Dance ritual, for it was of massive size.

"Perhaps the sacrifice of the flesh at the Sun Dance will bring us luck," old Deer Slayer spoke up.

"I will sacrifice some day!" Little Rock spoke up boldly and without hesitation. "My father has told me what is done. I am not afraid. I will be a man."

Abbie closed her eyes against the thought of it. She had watched the ritual once, determined to know everything there was to know about these people and to show them her own strength and courage. But it had not been easy to see the priests force the skewers through the flesh of the participants' breasts and tie them with rawhide to a pole, hoisting them up so that only the skin held them. Red Eagle had been a part of the Sun Dance the summer she had watched, a proud man then, a brave warrior, before the white man's whiskey destroyed him. She remembered how Yellow Moon had watched with pride and love in her eyes. They were not even married yet, then. How quickly time went by! And how quickly things could change.

"You have a few years to wait, son," Zeke was telling Little Rock. And Abbie knew that if Little Rock wanted to participate, Cheyenne Zeke would not stop him.

A few men gathered below, having spotted the band of Cheyenne. They mounted up and rode up the hill, yipping and yelping. The Cheyenne waited and the Sioux men surrounded those in front.

"You come to join in the Sun Dance celebration?" one of them asked in his own tongue. "In one week it will take place."

Old Deer Slayer nodded. "We bring meat and hides. We have been hunting also, but we saw few buffalo."

"It is the same everywhere!" one of the Sioux replied angrily. "Come into our village. You are welcome. The Cheyenne are our friend." They started forward, but then the man spotted Abbie and charged in front of her mount, his eyes glowering at her and the blond-haired child behind her.

"Whites are not welcome!" he growled. It was the first time Abbie had felt true animosity. In that first year when she had ridden with the Cheyenne and had dwelled with them among the Sioux, she had been readily accepted. But this young man had an obvious hatred for anyone with white skin. "Who claims this white woman? Who dares to bring her here?"

"I do!" Zeke answered quickly, forcing his mount

forward and confronting the man. "She is my wife, and an honored woman among the Cheyenne. She is loyal to the People and they are loyal to her."

The Sioux man spat at Abbie and she gasped, seeing for the first time just how dangerous the Indian hatred was becoming for the whites. *"Voxpas!"* the Sioux man sneered at Zeke. "I can see you are a half-blood by the way you speak. A white belly!"

Zeke was off his horse in the blink of an eye, blasting into the Sioux man and knocking him from his horse. Abbie screamed his name as the two went tumbling, and the wrestling match was on. Abbie backed her horse and watched in fear, but Little Rock only grinned with excitement.

"Show him who is the greater warrior, Father!" the boy yelled. "Yeee! Yeee!" He put his little fists in the air and gritted his teeth, his face taking on the look of a wild warrior. Black Elk also watched in good humor, aware of Zeke's skill, always enjoying a good fight.

Dirt flew and the two bodies tangled viciously, while those closest gathered in a circle to watch, picking sides and shouting them on. Zeke was on his back with the Sioux warrior straddled over him, a hatchet in his right hand. Zeke held the hand away from his face with his left arm, but Abbie's heart froze, for his left arm had been weaker ever since taking the bullet in his left shoulder when he had gone to rescue Yellow Moon.

Zeke's knee came up between the Sioux's legs and he shoved hard, flipping the man head over heels onto his back. Zeke was instantly on his feet, and the big blade was out then, as the two of them circled, teeth gritted, arms out in defense, fringes of the buckskin leggings dancing, broad, bronze chests bare and now caked with dirt.

Zeke waved the huge blade, then made a quick swipe with it, deftly slicing through the straps that held the Sioux's quiver of arrows. They fell to the ground and a red line of blood appeared on the man's chest where the tip of Zeke's blade had slit the skin. There was a moment of hesitation on behalf of the Sioux man, who was startled at the sudden, accurate movement. This Cheyenne half-blood was a good fighter. He slashed through the air at Zeke, but Zeke arched back and Little Rock laughed with glee. His father had drawn blood and the Sioux man had not. Little Blue Sky hid her face in fear and Young Girl giggled, thinking it all a game, while Deer Slayer took in the excitement with a calm sureness that his son would not be hurt.

The men circled again and a horse thundered up. "Stop this!" someone shouted. Abbie looked over to see Swift Arrow, and she breathed a sigh of great relief. Swift Arrow stalked angrily up to the Sioux man and kicked at his ankle, landing him on his face. The man quickly got up and turned on Swift Arrow.

"What do you think you are doing?" he roared.

"You fool!" Swift Arrow growled back. "Do you wish to die today for nothing? We need our good warriors for battles that are important!"

"Who says I shall be the one to die!" the man spat back, turning to get Zeke back into his sight.

"I do! This man is my half-blood brother, Cheyenne Zeke—called Lone Eagle by the Cheyenne. No man walks who is better with the blade! Do you wish to show your gizzard to the sun today?"

The Sioux man straightened slightly and blinked, looking from Swift Arrow to Zeke. "I . . . have heard of this Cheyenne Zeke," he said, suddenly humbled. "He is an honored warrior among the Cheyenne." He looked up at Abbie. "But he brings a white woman to our camp! We need no whites here!"

Swift Arrow looked over at Abbie, surprised to see her there. He saw the worried look in her eyes. How wonderful she looked, sitting there proudly on her mount, wearing a tunic, just as she had in that first year she had come to the People and he had taught her many things. He looked back at the Sioux.

"This woman is as honorable as any Sioux or Cheyenne squaw," he told the man. "If you choose to insult her or tell her she is not welcome, then finish your fight with her husband! You deserve to die!"

Their eyes held challengingly and the Sioux's jaw flexed in anger and indecision. Then he shoved his hatchet into the waist of his leggings. He turned to walk away.

"Wait!" Zeke shouted. "You will not leave this fight unless you apologize to my wife! If you do not, we finish what we started!"

The Sioux man whirled and glared at him. Zeke's eyes blazed and he still held the menacing blade. The Sioux looked down at his chest, where blood now trickled down over his stomach. He had heard many stories about this Cheyenne Zeke. It might be wise to give him the benefit of the doubt. He turned and walked up to Abbie, removing a necklace of quills painted bright colors. He held it up to her.

"You are welcome here," he told her.

She did not understand the Sioux tongue as well as that of the Cheyenne, but she understood the gesture. She took the necklace and nodded, and he saw in her eyes a certain pride and a lovely gentleness he'd never seen in other white women.

"Ha-ho," she replied, thanking him in Cheyenne.

The Sioux man turned and pushed his way through the circle of people, mounting up and riding back to the village. Zeke shoved his blade back into its sheath and Swift Arrow walked over to grasp his wrist in welcome.

"This is a surprise!" the man told him. "How is it you come all the way up here, my brothers?" He turned to greet Black Elk in the same manner, eyeing young Blue Bird Woman but noticing she carried no papoose and her belly was still flat. Black Elk's wife had still apparently been unable to get pregnant.

Zeke wiped his brow and began brushing dirt from his arms and chest. "Mostly Abbie's idea," he replied. "We've been through some bad times. Thought it would be good to get out and go on the hunt with the People again. And we were concerned about stories of a buffalo kill. We came to see for ourselves. Abbie has always wanted to come back North, but with the ranch and a baby coming practically every year, some things just don't get done."

Swift Arrow hurried over to his father as the man slid

from his horse. They embraced warmly. "It is good to see you, Deer Slayer!" Swift Arrow told the old man. "Good to see that you are yet strong enough to come North with the others."

"I was worried, my son, about these people killing the buffalo, and about the news that Yellow Moon has given birth to a crippled child, a half-blood."

Swift Arrow's eyes saddened, and he stepped back. "*Ai*, the boy is badly crippled, but he has brought a little joy to Yellow Moon's empty heart." He turned to help Abbie down from her mount, noticing with concern how thin her waist felt. She hurried to Zeke while Swift Arrow lifted the golden-haired Young Girl to the ground also. Her little hands were lily-white against his dark skin, and he could not get over the fact that Cheyenne Zeke could have fathered so fair a child.

He turned to Zeke. Abbie was fussing over him, helping brush him off and making sure herself that he was unhurt. "I enjoyed every minute of it," he was telling her. "I haven't been in a good scrap in a long time, Abbie girl."

She put her hands on her hips. "Zeke Monroe, you get in enough trouble without looking for it out of pure enjoyment," she chided him.

Swift Arrow grinned. Always there would be certain things about her that were purely white. No Indian squaw would ever be upset that her man was in a fight. Fighting was as natural as breathing. But Abigail had a way about her that was amusing, for even when she scolded she was pretty and pleasing, and it was understood that she was not truly angry, but only worried. He walked up to them both, putting a hand on each of them and looking at Deer Slayer, then up at Black Elk, who still sat perched on his horse.

"You will all stay for the Sun Dance?" he asked them. "There will be much celebrating all week, for we have had a better hunt than usual, and we are preparing for the Sun Dance in five days. Many will come, for we need our power and strength now as never before."

"We will stay," Black Elk replied. "It is true then, about these people who come and kill the buffalo?"

306

Swift Arrow's smile faded. "*Ai*, my brother. It is true." He turned his eyes to Zeke. "I do not wish to talk about sad things this day. Today we celebrate that you are here. There will be war games soon. You should take part in them Zeke. Show the Sioux what my half-blood brother can do, huh?"

Zeke glanced at Abbie and winked. "My woman will fuss the whole time, but you know how I love the war games, Swift Arrow."

Swift Arrow laughed, but there was an odd sadness in his eyes. Abbie felt an urgency about him, as though he were trying to cling to happy moments and treasure them forever.

"How is Yellow Moon, Swift Arrow?" she asked the man. "And the boy?"

The man frowned and lost his smile again. "Yellow Moon is well." He looked at Zeke. "We are man and wife now." He reached for the reins of his own mount. "I did not come to her as a husband for many moons, for her heart and mind were broken. At first it was bad when she knew she was with child by that white man. She did not want it. But when he was born with his crooked foot, she felt sorry for him, and her mother's love broke through her loneliness. The child helped heal her heart, but he will forever be a burden, and because of his white blood some of the others turn away from Yellow Moon. There is much hatred in the air now for the whites." He glanced at Abbie again. "I will make sure no harm comes to you, but you must be careful, Abigail, and follow the Indian ways while you are here. You are greatly honored, but there is much bad feeling."

"Is it really that bad, Swift Arrow?" Zeke asked with grave concern.

"As bad as it can be," the man replied with blazing eyes. "Thousands and thousands of whites came through this country last summer and this one, destroying the game, the forests, the water. There has been more disease. Sometimes it seems more die than are born. It will not be long before these warriors will fight back as never before. The whites show us no mercy, and now we shall do the same to them. We give them a little and they want it all. But they shall not

307

have it. All we ask is that they stop taking our game. Our lives depend on it. Look down there." He waved his arm toward the village, where the hides were staked out for drying. "That is the center of existence, the symbol of our people, our life-blood. The sacred buffalo. From him we get clothing, utensils, bedding, tipis, weapons, medicine, fuel for our fires. And most important of all, food. Everything. Everything! We are kin to the beast. We die without him. And yet these whites come and kill them off like flies, for the sport of it, calling themselves great marksmen and brave hunters!" He spat again. "I would like to skin them out like the buffalo!"

"It is worse in the South also," Black Elk spoke up. "We came North to hunt, Swift Arrow, in spite of the fact that we have been told to remain south of the Platte. For in the South there are barely any buffalo left. We no longer heed the treaty, for still it has not been signed."

"And it never will be!" Swift Arrow snapped. "The Southern chiefs were fools to sign that worthless paper! The Great White Father keeps changing his promises."

He turned fiery eyes back to Zeke and Abbie, then softened when Abbie's eyes teared and she looked away, walking to her horse to take Little Wolf from his cradleboard. Swift Arrow sighed, glancing at Zeke, who he knew was concerned over all the talk about whites in front of Abigail. Swift Arrow turned and went to her side.

"I cannot help the way I feel, Abigail," he told her almost apologetically.

"I know that." She looked up at him and smiled. "You will always be my good friend, the man who taught me many things about the People," she answered. "And you haven't seen our fourth child, Swift Arrow. Zeke has a second son." She held the boy up for him and he grinned and grabbed the infant.

"Ah! This is good! Good!" He smiled at Zeke, who had not missed the way Swift Arrow still looked at Abbie. "Another son! You are a blessed man, my brother, to have this woman who gives you many children and is so loyal to you!" He handed the baby to Abbie. "But you are thin, Abigail. You have not been well?"

"The baby's birth was not a good one this time, Swift Arrow. But I am healing now."

Swift Arrow looked back at Zeke. "This is so? She is all right?"

"It's a long story, Swift Arrow."

"Then let us go down to the village where you can see Yellow Moon and her son, and we can talk about the many things we must know about one another. We have been too long apart. Come!"

They followed him down the hillside. There was much Abbie wanted to ask Swift Arrow, but her presence was apparently a delicate situation, and she knew it would be wise to follow Indian customs carefully, or her welcome might not last. She stayed behind Zeke and Swift Arrow and kept her mouth closed. Once they were inside the privacy of Swift Arrow's tipi, she could have her say, where other braves would not see her and chide her for her "loose tongue."

Wild dancing and chanting and singing went on half the night. It would have been a frightening sound to any white who did not understand the People. But Abbie watched unafraid. Zeke joined in the celebrating, his eyes alive with the joy of venting his wildness again in the old ways. He had been unsurpassed in the knife-throwing contests and beaten by only one man in the wrestling, and that only after he had wrestled so many that he had grown tired and old wounds had begun to ache. Little Rock was ecstatic at his father's successes, and he joined in the dancing and celebrating. Abbie watched her son with a mixture of pride and worry. He was more Indian all the time, and some day his wildness would take him from her. It was becoming more and more difficult to make him sit still for his lessons, yet she could not help but be proud of the courage and skill he was already showing at his young age.

Abbie turned to Yellow Moon, who sat beside her holding her little crippled baby. The child was quiet, and according

309

to Yellow Moon he almost never cried. He smiled easily but seldom moved the crooked leg, and Abbie suspected he surely felt pain whenever he did move it. Her heart ached for the child, yet she was glad that at least Yellow Moon seemed to accept him and love him. She wondered what the senator would do or say if he knew he had a half-breed son living among the Sioux. Fate seemed to deal strangely with some people, and it was odd that a man who hated the Indians should have a son who was half Indian. But Abbie had no doubt that Mr. Winston Garvey would have no affection for such a son, and would probably try to have him killed if he knew.

The women laughed and shouted provocative words to their dancing warrior husbands, who strutted proudly in their finest regalia, brandishing weapons and parading their colorfully painted bodies. Some of the young ones would soon undergo the terrible ordeal of the Sun Dance sacrifice, hanging by the flesh of their breasts and arms until the skewers in their skin would break away, and that sacrifice would take place after three days without food or water. Zeke and all three of his Cheyenne brothers had participated in the Sun Dance, and Abbie had witnessed it once. It was not something she relished witnessing again, but she would do it out of stubbornness, to show these Sioux and Northern Cheyenne that the white woman Cheyenne Zeke had married was not weak in the knees. She noticed with happiness how Yellow Moon watched Swift Arrow now. The two of them had apparently found happiness in their "logical" relationship that was absent of the kind of passionate love that comes to those who marry out of choice. Swift Arrow had provided Yellow Moon with food and shelter and protection, taking the responsibility for his brother's wife; and Yellow Moon had in turn dutifully taken on those things expected of a wife, including a sexual relationship, for she was determined to give Swift Arrow a son of his own to repay him for caring for her. Abbie had always worried about Swift Arrow's being alone after the death of his first wife and son. Now he had someone to care for him again, and she was glad for him and for Yellow Moon, who

310

had found a little happiness after losing Red Eagle and Laughing Boy.

Soon the men moved back into a large circle behind the women, and the Cheyenne blanket dance began. Wives and lovers began circling the campfire inside the circle of men, opening blankets they wore about their shoulders and moving provocatively for their men. The drums beat rhythmically, and the men smiled and made remarks. Abbie remembered another time, the first year of their marriage, when she had joined in a blanket dance for Zeke. But Dancing Moon had been there then. She had joined also, and had stripped herself in front of Zeke, throwing her blanket over him as a sign of wanting to mate. The memory of the jealousy she had felt then combined with the heady, provocative feelings the blanket dance brought on to make Abbie rise and pick up her own blanket. She joined the circle, determined to prove to these people in the North that she knew and often practiced their ways. They watched with surprise as she moved with the other women, and Swift Arrow felt his blood warm at the sight of the beautiful white woman who could be so Cheyenne.

But there was no doubt for whom she was dancing, and it was not long before she moved toward Zeke, who stood watching her with desire in his eyes, his body healthy now, alive for his woman, excited by the day's events. She threw her blanket over his shoulders.

"Are you tired, my husband?" she asked him.

He picked her up in his arms and she laughed. "Not that tired," he replied. "The young ones sleep in Yellow Moon's tipi, where Blue Sky and Little Rock will soon go for the night. Tonight we shall be alone in our tipi for the first time since we left the ranch. You will not hide yourself under a blanket tonight Abigail Monroe."

He carried her off, amid gentle laughter and teasing remarks from the Indian men. Swift Arrow watched after them until a blanket was thrown over his own shoulders. He turned to face Yellow Moon, who traced her fingers over his thighs. "You want a son of your own," she told him. "Come with me and I will try to give you one." She picked up Crooked Foot's cradleboard and walked into the shelter of the woods beyond the fire. Swift Arrow watched her slim hips move rhythmically beneath her tunic. Red Eagle had chosen well. Yellow Moon was a good woman, and very pleasant to lie with. But her heart would never truly be happy again. He would do what he could to bring her what little happiness she might be able to find in his arms.

For Abbie the problem of Crooked Foot and that of the slaughtered buffalo were set aside for the night. Cheyenne Zeke was on fire, drunk with the joy of being Cheyenne again and of being unmatched at the knife and greatly honored among the Sioux and Northern Cheyenne. As a half-breed, to be so accepted was vital for him. The scars he bore on his chest and arms were a sign of how far he had once gone to prove himself. Now he stood before her, his dark skin glowing in the light of the small fire inside the tipi, his breathing heavy and urgent. Abbie bashfully but gently untied his loincloth and cast it aside, and he in turn untied her tunic, slipping it down to her ankles, kissing and tasting her body on the way down, lingering at her slim thighs and the softness between them.

Since their reunion and reawakened sexual relationship, it seemed their lovemaking was more exciting and heated than ever. His lips moved back up over her flat belly and full breasts to her neck, and then he suddenly moved a foot behind her ankles and pushed, knocking her off her feet and holding her as she went down to the blanket he had already spread out behind her. There were no words this time. He would take her the Cheyenne way, with little talk and little foreplay. It mattered little to her how he took her, as long as she at least had him back this way again, as long as she could take him inside of herself and draw strength from him.

She closed her eyes and gasped as he took liberties with her she could never have allowed any other man, his warm, gentle lips exploring, ravaging his woman in ways he had a right to take her, for he was the man and a woman should please her man in whatever ways he needed. And in pleasing Cheyenne Zeke she found her own pleasures. He moved between her legs, on his knees then and looking down at her almost victoriously, as though she were some captive prize. He ran a hand gently over her groin and thighs, then grasped her from beneath and pulled her up to him, literally holding her up to himself with powerful arms while he invaded her, moving rhythmically then with the drums that beat outside.

She cried out at the invasion, the sweet smoky smell inside the tipi making her heady with passion, his dark, provocative body a blur before her, the designs inside their tipi seeming to dance around her. She was sixteen again, living that first year with the People, migrating with them, the wife of Lone Eagle.

Their stay turned into a pleasant one, and Abbie made many friends among the women and gained some grudging acceptance among the men. Their suspicion of her was understandable, and she had no bad feelings toward them because of it. She only worked harder to prove to them that not all whites were their enemy, as well as to prove that she was as good as any Cheyenne or Sioux squaw. She fleshed hides, pegged them out to dry, hung meat, and even made a shield for the Sioux man who had insulted her when first she arrived. The man was taken by her gesture and amazed at her skill at making the shield. The gift humbled him, and the next day he came to Zeke's camp with a fine pair of knee-high moccasins, lined with the hair of the buffalo.

"Warm feet make a happy heart," he told Abbie. "I have seen few white women," he went on. "Those I have seen look at me as though I were a crawling snake. You look at me with honor in your eyes. You are good person."

Zeke interpreted as he stood defensively at Abbie's side, and she reached out and accepted the gift, thanking him. There was some giggling among the women present, and the Sioux man whirled on them, shutting them up with his look. It was comical to see, but Abbie knew better than to smile.

Others also brought gifts for the white woman with the little warrior son, blankets and jewelry, toys for her "many" children, even some food, which she knew they could not afford to give. But they would be insulted if she refused it,

313

so she accepted the gifts graciously, her heart tightening at the round, friendly faces of these once-happy, trusting people. They did not want war. They wanted only their freedom, to roam and hunt as they had always done. The answer to peace was so very simple, but the white man had a strange way of taking the hard road, sure that these people were just savages bent on murder and plunder. They were really quite the opposite, but who was going to convince those strangers back in Washington of that—people who had never even been west of the Mississippi, had never even met an Indian. They tried to keep to themselves, to leave the white man alone. But it was the white man who would not leave them alone, and the day was soon coming when they would no longer be able to accept their pride and intelligence's being constantly poked at and ridiculed and ignored. The day was coming when they would break loose and show the white man he'd best keep his word.

Abbie attended the Sun Dance ritual, surprising the others with her understanding of the Sioux and Cheyenne religious event and by the way in which she watched it without flinching. But her heart ached at the thought of Zeke's experiencing such a thing in his determined effort to prove his Indian blood. Little Rock watched with great interest, but Blue Sky started to cry with fright at the sight of the blood, and Abbie held the child close to her breast, instructing her that she must not make a sound and must not shame her warrior father by leaving.

The visit created hope in Abbie's heart that there still would be peace for Swift Arrow and the others, but the morning of their intended departure for Fort Laramie to see Danny brought an ominous warning that things were most certainly as bad as Swift Arrow had predicted. They awoke to a great commotion, as horses thundered through the village and war cries pierced the morning air. Zeke and Abbie both arose and quickly dressed, and Zeke grabbed his rifle and tomahawk before exiting the tipi, warning Abbie to stay inside with the children. A moment later she recognized Swift Arrow's voice outside the tipi.

"We break camp—quickly!" Swift Arrow was telling

314

Zeke. "We go to Little Thunder's camp to the east to avoid the soldiers, my brother. There is trouble!"

"What kind of trouble?" Zeke asked anxiously.

"Miniconjou Sioux. One of them has killed a white man's cow by mistake. The runners have told us. The Sioux man's family was hungry, and the animal strayed into their village. The white people were called Mormons. They complained to the soldiers and the soldiers sent men against the Sioux."

"Just for killing one cow?"

"This is what you should understand, my brother!" Swift Arrow replied sneeringly. "The whites can come to our land and kill thousands of our buffalo. But if one Indian shoots just one cow, the soldiers send many men after all of us! Now do you see?"

"Why do you run, Swift Arrow? Your village wasn't involved."

"The soldiers will come for all of us—any tribe. Yesterday the bluecoats went after the Sioux who had stolen the cow, but they attacked the wrong village. They attacked a clan of Brulé Sioux instead of Miniconjous. The Brulés were very angry. They killed them all!"

There was an odd silence as more horses thundered through the camp. "What are you saying?" she heard Zeke say hoarsely. "That the Indians killed every soldier?"

"*Ai*, my brother. All were massacred. Their leader was called Grattan. We are splitting up now, to confuse the soldiers, for they are sure to send out more after what has happened. We will go in all directions. Yellow Moon and I will go to Little Thunder's village. Black Elk is going also, and our father. It is not wise just now for them and the rest of the Southern Cheyenne to head out for a hunt, or even to head back south. The soldiers will attack and kill every Indian they find! They will be thirsty for blood. We must scatter until they have had time to cool their anger!"

"We'll go with you, Swift Arrow. I'll not leave you until I know this thing is settled. I'd never rest easy."

"But what about Abigail? She should not be in the middle of this. There will be more fighting, and she walks among the enemy now, for her white skin makes us her enemy."

Abbie came outside then, facing Swift Arrow with uplifted chin. "We will go with you, Swift Arrow. Don't ever say that the Sioux or the Cheyenne are my enemy! You are family! And we shall not leave old Deer Slayer. He is like a father to me. We will follow you to Little Thunder's camp." She turned to face Zeke, and he could see by her eyes that there would be no arguing. No matter what the danger, they would go. Somehow when the worst blew over, they would get to Fort Laramie and Danny.

Eighteen

The journey to Little Thunder's camp was silent. No baby cried, no horse whinnied, speaking came in whispers. To stay hidden from the enemy meant keeping still.

An ominous pall hung over their fleeing band. After much arguing and persuasion on behalf of Zeke and Swift Arrow, Black Elk was convinced he should head directly north and then west to the land of the yellow stone and hot waters, where buffalo could be found. He was to take Deer Slayer with him, away from danger. Black Elk wanted to stay and fight if the soldiers should come, but an all-night family session convinced him that Deer Slayer should be allowed to live out his days in whatever peace could be found. It was obvious that, for a while, there would be no peace in the North. Even in the South things were worsening, but at least there was no imminent danger of conflict as there now was in the North.

Black Elk pointed out that Zeke and Abbie should also go, that a white woman should not be involved in the impending conflict. But Abbie would not hear of it. They still had not seen Danny, and now it was more important than ever to see him. And as long as they had to stay North long enough to go to Fort Laramie, they would first see Swift Arrow and Yellow Moon and her little crippled baby to Little Thunder's camp. Abbie felt an urgency now, as though every last moment must be treasured. For she knew it might be a long, long time before they would ever meet again, and she would worry about little Crooked Foot. Zeke urged her to go with Black Elk to the North, and he would meet her at the land of the yellow stone after seeing Danny, but she would not hear of it. More than anything else, she would not allow them to be apart again. The thought frightened her. She would rather stay and risk her life at his side than to be separated again, and after a torrent of tears that Zeke could never seem to argue against, he agreed to let her go all the way to Little Thunder's camp.

The parting was not easy. Over half the Southern Cheyenne who had migrated North left those heading to Little Thunder's camp, led by Black Elk. Tall Grass Woman and her husband and son were among those who would not stay, and the hefty woman, who was Abbie's good friend, hugged Abbie so fiercely that it hurt Abbie's ribs.

"You should come with us," the woman lamented, tears in her eyes.

"It's all right, Tall Grass Woman," Abbie replied, patting the woman's shoulder. "We'll meet you at the Big Timbers in the Drying Grass Moon."

"No good. You are white. This is not your trouble, good friend. What would Tall Grass Woman do if you did not come back to us? You come now. Be safe."

Abbie pulled back, her hands on the woman's shoulders. "As long as I'm with Zeke, I'm always safe," she replied. "It will be all right. You'll see. This will all blow over."

Their eyes held, and Tall Grass Woman's usually happy, innocent face was sober and full of despair, much the way she had been for many months after her precious daughter had died of white man's disease. She shook her head, patting Abbie's cheek. "No, good friend. These winds of hatred will blow hard and strong for many moons, perhaps many winters. It will blow us all away until these plains no longer hold a buffalo—or an Indian." A tear slipped down her round cheek. "But no matter what these whites who hate us do to us, Tall Grass Woman will forever be your friend. We share hearts, you and I. You are the white woman who risked the deep waters to save my little Magpie, but the disease of the bad whites killed her after all. I do not forget what you have done, and your daughters are my daughters, your sons my sons. I will pray for you, Abigail Monroe, for the white woman who calls the Cheyenne her family."

Abbie blinked back tears. "And I shall pray for you, Tall Grass Woman." She stepped back. "Go now. We will meet at Hinta-Nagi."

She turned to Zeke, burying her face in his chest while those leaving proceeded north. She had said her good-byes to old Deer Slayer and could not bear to watch the old man now as he receded into the horizon with Black Elk and Blue Bird Woman and her good friend, Tall Grass Woman.

"You should be with them, Abbie girl," Zeke told her.

"No. I'll not be away from you, Zeke," she replied through tears, hugging him tightly. "But I'm scared!" she whispered.

He kissed her hair, and Swift Arrow watched from a ridge. He let out a bloodcurdling war cry and raised his lance, ordering those remaining to follow him on to Little Thunder's camp.

There were several days of relative peace, during which the women managed to reorganize and decide how to divide up the hides and meat they had managed to bring along. The good hunt the Sioux and Northern Cheyenne had experienced was spoiled by their rapid flight, for there had not been time to pack everything properly, and some freshly stretched hides and fresh cuts of meat were left behind, along with the great lodge that had been built for the Sun Dance ritual. It seemed unreal to Abbie now that there had ever been the happy visit and joyful celebrating. Now everyone was quiet and sober. Abbie worked hard helping divide up the supplies and helping turn meat and berries into a plentiful supply of pemmican. In times when flight might be necessary, pemmican could be a lifesaver, for it was easy to pack and carry and could be kept for months without spoiling. Things were so peaceful at Little Thunder's camp that Abbie and some of the others began to think that perhaps the soldiers would not come after all. No more runners had come with any bad news. Things were settled. It was decided that she and Zeke could safely leave in the

319

sixth morning of their stay, say their good-byes to Swift Arrow and Yellow Moon and little Crooked Foot and head for Fort Laramie.

Abbie jumped awake at the earth-shaking boom, her sleepy mind thinking at first it had been a terrific clap of thunder. Zeke sat bolt upright, and another explosion, seemingly right behind their tipi, tore at Abbie's eardrums. The tipi shook and swayed, and then they could hear screaming outside, as well as men shouting orders and horses whinnying.

"Zeke, what is it?"

He bolted to the tipi entrance, rifle in hand, wearing only his leggings. Another boom sent a piece of wood through the top of their own tipi, and Abbie could not help screaming.

"Howitzers!" Zeke yelled. "Cannon! The goddamned soldiers are blowing the village to hell!" He grabbed his weapons and scooped up Young Girl. All the children were awake by then, wide-eyed and frightened by the terrible noise. "Get out!" Zeke was yelling at Abbie, who was quickly pulling on her moccasins. "Get out of the tipi!"

Her heart pounded with the worst fear she had ever experienced. Zeke grabbed a parfleche and flung it over his shoulder, then grabbed up Blue Sky in his other arm, ducking outside loaded down with the two children, the parfleche and his weapons.

Abbie grabbed up Little Wolf in his cradleboard and hastened Little Rock out ahead of her, where Zeke waited impatiently.

"Run, damn it! Run, Abbie!" he ordered. "That way!" he pointed to her right. "There's a gully over there, and a place where the earth goes under a big rock. It's a dried-up creek bed! Run, Abbie!"

She had hesitated only a moment, finding it difficult to beleive what was happening. Several tipis were on fire, and all around them lay dead Indians, including women and children. Could all this be necessary? Was all of this just over a stolen cow? Her heart raced and her soul wanted to scream and lament all the dead bodies, but there was no time for that. She ran blindly, Zeke behind her with the two girls. More explosions sent dirt, bodies, and tipis flying, and now there was also the sound of gunshots and women screaming, babies crying. She wondered desperately where Yellow Moon could be, and Swift Arrow.

She glanced at a ridge to the left, to see several Indian men already mounted and shouting war cries, heading up the ridge toward blue-coated soldiers. Surely Swift Arrow would be among them.

Gunshots were fired close behind them, and Abbie whirled to see two soldiers bearing down on them. Little Rock was running toward them, carrying his lance and shouting Cheyenne obsenities at them, thinking they intended to hurt his mother and sisters.

"Little Rock, no!" Abbie screamed. Zeke's eyes widened, and he released his hold on Blue Sky and Young Girl and the parfleche.

"Take the girls and get going, Abbie! Get to that gully!" he ordered, before turning and going after Little Rock.

"Zeke!" she screamed. To her horror one of the soldiers turned and shot down an Indian woman, then deliberately aimed his gun at the woman's baby, pulling the trigger again. Then he turned on Little Rock, who was close by then and running with his lance held straight, aiming for the soldier's leg.

The soldier took aim again, while the second soldier raised a sword. But a gun went off, and a hole exploded in the first soldier's shoulder. The man fell from his mount and the second soldier hesitated, having been so absorbed in beheading the little Indian boy running toward them that he had not noticed the father, one Cheyenne Zeke, whose smoking rifle was still in his hand when he yanked out his knife and threw it, landing it in the second man's ribs. The man screamed out and fell forward, then slid from his horse, while Zeke grabbed Little Rock and shoved him in the other direction.

"Get back there with your mother! Now!" he ordered.

"I want to fight the soldiers!" the boy shouted, tears on

321

his cheeks.

"You go and protect your mother! Hurry, Little Rock. Do as I tell you!"

Their eyes held for one brief second. There was no time for arguing with his commanding father. He turned and ran toward his mother, who had been unable to bring herself to keep running until she knew her son was all right.

"Zeke!" she screamed, as another soldier came galloping up behind him. Zeke whirled, swinging his rifle and landing the butt with a smashing crack across the oncoming soldier's face. The man landed hard and lay still. Zeke yanked his big blade from the second soldier's ribs. He considered carving open all three of their trunks, for they had killed women and children and would have killed Little Rock. But it flashed through his mind that any soldier murdered and mutilated would be one more tool against the Indians. They would take the brunt of the blame for any deaths, and it would be especially hard on them if soldiers' bodies were deliberately desecrated. He left the wounded but still living men and ran after Abbie, as two more explosions ripped through the now burning and destroyed village. Bodies were strewn everywhere, and other women could be seen fleeing with old ones and children. The circling, yipping Indians were keeping most of the rest of the soldiers busy for the moment, allowing their women and children time to flee. Zeke shoved Abbie along again, pushing her and the children down into the gully as quickly as possible.

"Get down under the rock and stay there until I get back!" he roared at Abbie.

"Zeke, no!" she screamed. "Where are you going? Don't leave me!"

"I've got to see if I can help any others!" he shouted. "Now stay put! That's an order! If soldiers come and find you, don't give them any trouble. Do as they say and tell them who you are! Tell them to get a message to Danny! He'll help you!"

He disappeared. She screamed his name again, but her only reply was the thunder of hooves and more gunfire. She huddled into the gully, struggling against screaming tears. She did not want to frighten the children any more than they had already been frightened. Blue Sky sat with her hands over her ears, her dark eyes wide with terror, while Young Girl cried quietly. Little Wolf squirmed, but was oblivious to his danger. Little Rock was silent and stony, his little-boy face showing a fiery hatred and stubbornness not unlike the look Abbie had seen in Zeke's eyes many times. He clung tightly to his lance. He would not forget this day, the sight of the bluecoat soldiers shooting down women and little babies. He had had no idea such things were done. But now he knew and he would remember.

The gunfire finally began to dwindle, but then horses and squeaking saddles and clanking swords could be heard in the distance.

"Round up those squaws and their brats!" she heard a man shout. She huddled closer under the rock, holding all the children close and praying they would not be found. She whispered to Little Rock not to try to chase a soldier, or the soldiers would find his mother and sisters. It tore at her heart that she should have to be so afraid of her own kind, finding it ironic that she should be in such a situation. But she knew instinctively how she would be treated, a white woman with Indian children.

It seemed hours that they crouched there hidden. She could hear more commands to take the "captives" to Fort Kearny, orders to pick up wounded soldiers and round up stray horses. A man asked about the wounded or dead Indians and was told to leave them where they lay. "Let the wolves have them," came the cold reply. "The scum will pay for massacring Grattan and his men."

She wanted to run out and shout that these people had done nothing, that they had no part in stealing anyone's cow and no part in the fight with Grattan and his men. But she could not reveal herself, and it would have done no good anyway. For it was obvious that for every act committed by one Indian, all Indians would suffer. There would be no such thing as an investigation, a trial, any form of justice. The Indians were in the way of important matters, and any excuse that could be used to annihilate the red man was welcome. The Grattan massacre was the best excuse possible to ride down on all Sioux and Northern Cheyenne.

Not until sunset did the sound of soldiers' voices fade away. Abbie remembered Zeke's orders and stayed put, wondering frantically if it was safe to go out and if Zeke was all right. Then she heard the pounding of a galloping horse. It drew to a halt beside her hiding place.

"Abbie!" came the welcome, shouted voice. "Abbie, are you all right?"

She broke into sobs of relief, crawling out from under the rock, immediately swept up into his arms. She cried against his chest, clinging to him in a mixture of relief and terrible sorrow.

"We chased some of them off," he told her in a strained voice, patting her hair. "But more came and captured women and children. They must have taken at least sixty or seventy off with them!" His body jerked and he hugged her more tightly, and she knew he was crying. He said nothing for several seconds until he found his voice again. "My God, Abbie, I was so afraid they'd found you! I thought I was going to lose my family today!"

He kissed her hair, then pulled away from her, sweeping up Little Rock and Blue Sky into his arms while Young Girl clung to his leggings. The terror in both the little girls' eyes worried him, but there was no fear in Little Rock's eyes— only an obvious relief that his father had not been hurt.

The boy hugged his father, then put a finger to a cut on Zeke's head.

"You're hurt!" Abbie said, noticing the cut then herself.

"I'm all right," he replied, setting the children down and wiping at his eyes with the back of his hand. "You're the one I'm worried about. You don't even have all your strength back yet. You should have gone with Black Elk and the others."

She put her arms around him again. "I'll not be separated from you again, Zeke. And I'm all right, really I am. I'm just so glad Deer Slayer went with them." She looked up at him and he kissed her lightly.

"Swift Arrow is searching for Yellow Moon, but she might have been one of those captured," he told her.

She closed her eyes and rested her head against him again. "Oh, Zeke, what is happening? This is so terrible! And what on earth do they want the women and children for?"

"To bring the warriors to their knees," he replied coldly. She could feel him tensing as he said it. "They'll hold them until the men promise to remain peaceful and to leave the whites alone. Perhaps they'll try to talk them into another treaty."

"But they *were* being peaceful," she replied. "They weren't doing anything wrong."

"They don't have to, Abbie girl. They just have to be Indians."

The statement seemed more like a prediction.

It was then that she felt his body tense even more. "My God!" he groaned. Abbie turned to see Swift Arrow coming toward them, carrying Yellow Moon's body. Her heart tightened as he came closer, his eyes hard and cold, determined to show no feeling but the terrible desire for vengeance that was flooding his soul. Behind him lay the smoldering village and the strewn bodies, where other men searched out their families, some falling to their knees and crying out, slashing at their chests.

"She is dead!" Swift Arrow said coldly and flatly. He bent down and gently laid Yellow Moon on the ground while Abbie covered her mouth in a groan and kneeled down beside her. She bent over the young woman and wept over poor Yellow Moon's short and tragic life. Swift Arrow held Zeke's eyes. There was nothing to say. Zeke knew the pain of losing a wife, especially to such a violent death. Yellow Moon had been the only happiness Swift Arrow had found since losing his first wife. He had taken her out of duty, but they were close, and there had been the promise of sons for Swift Arrow. "The crippled boy is still alive," Swift Arrow told Zeke. "I left him in the shelter of tall grass." His eyes

325

were pleading. "I . . . cannot take the child. He is not mine. I wish only to be the greatest dog soldier who ever rode a horse and made war. For I will surely make war against every bluecoat who comes to this land! You tell your lieutenant brother this, Lone Eagle. You tell him that after this day the soldiers will regret they have done this just because of one stolen cow! No soldier in this land will rest in peace, no treaty will be signed! Their blood will run, for the Sioux and Cheyenne are great warriors and they do not forgive men who would shoot down little children!" His voice broke and he stopped to regain control of himself. "I . . . know it is a burden, my brother. But I wish . . . I wish that you would take Crooked Foot. Only you understand a half-breed. I will find no one among these people who will take a crippled child who is half white."

"I'll take the child," Zeke told him gently.

Swift Arrow swallowed. "We have found a few of your horses. The soldiers captured the rest. I think perhaps they have taken the horses and women and children to Fort Kearny. That is the direction in which they rode. We will go there in the shelter of darkness and send a spokesman to go and find out what it is the soldiers want of us to get our women and children back. Perhaps you could do this for us? Talk to them? Perhaps then you can also get your horses back."

It was obvious the man was struggling against his pride. He would rather have gone and killed all the soldiers, and so would Zeke. But the time had come for bargaining, at least for the interim, until the women and children were safe again. This was a new kind of war. The Indians must have time to plan their strategy against the bluecoats.

"I will talk to them," Zeke answered. "We'll ride to Fort Kearny together, Swift Arrow. Abbie and I won't leave until the women and children are released."

Swift Arrow nodded, a tear slipping down his cheek. Abbie rose to face him, and he studied her lovingly, this time longing to be held by her rather than to hold her. "I will get Yellow Moon's son," he said in a strained voice. "I can think of no better woman to care for him than the white

326

woman with the Cheyenne heart."

She reached out for him but he stepped back, glancing at Zeke, then back to Abbie. "I am glad you are not hurt, Abigail," he told her. He turned and went to get the baby he had hidden.

They headed for Fort Kearny with heavy hearts. The joy had gone out of their visit. The only thing in which Abbie could take consolation was that they had been with Swift Arrow when it happened and could take little Crooked Foot with them. With Yellow Moon dead and his heart bitter, the man had no feelings or concern for the crippled half-breed who was not of his own blood. The baby had no one now, and Abbie took him in like a she-wolf accepting yet another cub. But she had barely enough milk for both Crooked Foot and her own little son, and Zeke was worried about the effect the tragedy and the extra child would have on her health. He had a lot of time to think as they rode, and one thing he knew was that this was definitely not a good time for his wife to be burdened with yet another baby. Something had to be done quickly before Crooked Foot became too deeply embedded in Abigail's soft heart.

They camped under the stars, surviving on the meager supplies they had managed to salvage. Their tipi was gone—burned. The subject had not been discussed, for Zeke well knew how heavy Abbie's heart was at the loss of the tipi, made by her own hands in the first year of their marriage. Some of the images painted on the dwelling had been done by the hands of his own Cheyenne mother before she died. The tipi had been of great emotional and sentimental importance to Abbie. Now it was gone. Too much was gone, and she was too quiet. He would not talk about the tipi until they were home again in familiar surroundings. Then he would go and search out all the buffalo he could find and bring her the hides so she could busy herself building another tipi and perhaps help heal the wounds of her loss. For now they would take a day at a time, and a problem at a time. For now, Swift Arrow held back from the others, pre-

327

ferring to be alone while the wounds he had inflicted upon himself over the loss of Yellow Moon healed. And for now, there was still the problem of the added burden of Crooked Foot.

"Abbie," he spoke up quietly over the glow of their campfire. "I want to talk to you about Crooked Foot."

The children slept close by, all huddled together for warmth. Abbie was holding her own baby son to her breast, while Crooked Foot slept beside her on a blanket. Zeke watched lovingly as his son fed at his mother's breast, and Abbie looked across the fire at him. In the nearby grasses crickets sang, and the moon was high and full. All was peaceful, as though the terrible disaster at Blue Water Creek had not happened.

"What about him?" she asked.

Zeke met her eyes. "The child is too much for you. I think I know of another way to help him, possibly an even better way because of his affliction."

She swallowed back tears. "He has no one, and I love him. I can take care of him, Zeke."

"I love him, too. I risked my life to save his mother. But I'll not let you take on this burden, Abbie girl. Not now."

"But . . . we promised Swift Arrow—"

"I promised I would take the child. I promised I'd look after him, and I think I know someone who could love him and possibly help his crippled condition."

Abbie frowned, telling herself not to be angry with him. Cheyenne Zeke would never turn away a child. If he had another idea, it must be for the good of Crooked Foot, or he would keep the boy in spite of her health. "I don't understand."

"We aren't that far from Bonnie Beaker's settlement. It's somewhere north of Fort Laramie. I want to take him to Bonnie Beaker. Hopefully she's still there. Her father is a doctor. He might know how to help the child."

Abbie pulled the now sleeping Little Wolf away from her breast and laid him in her lap, then pulled up her tunic and tied it. "How can you be so sure they would want to help him?"

He looked away from her and took out the infamous blade, laying it on a flat rock and picking up another rock to sharpen its already fine edge even more. So much blood had been shed with the blade that Abbie wondered that it was not permanently stained red.

"They're missionaries," he answered. "You know how I feel about the pious attitude of most so-called Christians. And you know I don't call myself one. But there are a few special ones, like yourself, who really do practice all that love and forgiveness and concern. Bonnie Beaker is one of them. She's likely married by now, but her husband is a minister. Her father is a kind man and a physician. I think we should find them and see if they're there and let them look at Crooked Foot. If they think they can help him or maybe know a doctor in the East who could help him, we should leave him with Bonnie." Abbie caught the odd tenderness when he spoke the name. "They could get word to us later as to how the boy is doing and we can make our decisions then. They told me once that if there was ever any way they could help me or my family that I should let them know. I don't like asking for help, but in this case I don't know what else to do."

She watched him quietly a moment, as he raked the rock over the edge of the big blade. She thought about the mysterious Bonnie Beaker, to whom he had given a necklace that was very dear to him. "She would take Crooked Foot for another reason, wouldn't she?" she asked softly.

Zeke stopped honing the knife and met her eyes. "Meaning?"

"Meaning it isn't just because she's Christian and loving that she might take the child. She would take him just because you would ask her to. She would do it for Zeke Monroe, the man who saved her, the man she might even think she loves."

Their eyes held for several long seconds. "She was just a nice lady and a good friend, Abbie," he told her. "For her part—" He shrugged. "A person's thoughts can get all turned around when they're scared and alone." He began scraping the knife again, then looked back over at her when she did not at first reply. A soft smile crossed her lips.

"How can such a mean and vicious man be so easy to love?" she asked.

He smiled himself then, almost bashfully. "Beats me," he replied. "I never reckoned myself as anything anybody would much love." He shoved the knife back into its sheath. "I reckon what it is, Abbie girl, is that most people in their lifetime find only one person who really, really loves them—like the way I love you and you love me. But there might be lots of others who admire them, others who could love them if it wasn't that they already belonged to somebody else. You have your share of admirers, you know. You're a damned pretty woman, and a good wife and mother to boot. Lots of men admire you."

She smiled more. "I don't believe it. I don't even see 'lots of men,'" she teased. "The only men I see are old Deer Slayer and Black Elk—Dooley and Swift Arrow, and once in a while a passer-by or some old friend of yours from your trapping days."

He nodded. "They all admire you, Abbie girl." He picked up a stick and toyed with it in the flames, thinking of Swift Arrow. "And a couple of them love you, from a distance." He met her eyes. "I can't blame them, long as they know who you belong to."

She glanced over at the sleeping Crooked Foot, then met his eyes boldly. "Then it is the same for me. It doesn't matter what woman might think she loves you, as long as she knows who you belong to."

He grinned more then, and his smile looked wonderful. There had been no smiles since Blue Water Creek. His face was drawn and tired, but the smile was as fetching as ever.

"We'll take Crooked Foot to Bonnie Beaker," she told him. "Perhaps you're right. Perhaps they can help him."

He nodded. "It's the best thing for both of you," he told her. "Then we'll go home, Abbie girl. Back to the Arkansas. Long as we have each other we can ride out this storm. But it might get bad, Abbie. Real bad."

*   *   *

330

The land seemed dotted with forts now. A week later found them at Fort Kearny. All the way there Swift Arrow had kept his distance, usually to be seen riding a ridge looking down on the others. At times he would let out an echoing, eerie cry, and some of the warriors would answer, including Zeke. They were long, wailing tones, ended with short, clipped yips, calls of mourning for the dead, calls for vengeance. Goose bumps rose on Abbie's skin every time she heard them. It was as though the very land was crying out in agony. The proud warriors had temporarily lost the battle. Their women and children were either dead or captured.

Zeke ordered Abbie to stay back in the hills while he rode forward with some of the other warriors down to the relatively new fort, which had an unfinished look about it. Young cottonwoods were freshly planted around the perimeter, and the officers' quarters and housing facilities were not totally finished and were still unpainted. Several covered wagons were scattered about and white settlers mingled with soldiers, stopping at the fort to rest and to purchase supplies. Several of them were congregated around a corral, where the Sioux and Cheyenne women and children were penned like horses, with no food and only a little water, which was not fresh. Their dignity had been destroyed when they were forced to squat in front of spectators to relieve themselves when they were no longer able to hold back their bodily functions. They were filthy and tired, and some looked sick.

Zeke's rage knew no bounds, but he knew how futile it would be to cause a ruckus. Several soldiers surrounded him and the others as they rode boldly into the fort, and settlers scattered as though some evil monster had come upon them. Guns were cocked and aimed, and Zeke and the others reined to a halt.

"Who's in charge here?" Zeke asked, surprising the soldiers with his English. A grudging sergeant stepped forward.

"I am at the moment. Colonel Harney is headed farther into Sioux country. You men coming in to give yourselves up?"

"We're here to take the women back," Zeke replied coldly. "And the Appaloosas you have corraled in the other fence over there belong to me. My name is Zeke Monroe. I was with the Cheyenne and Sioux at Blue Water Creek. I have a full-blood Cheyenne brother."

The sergeant grinned. "You do, do you? Well, I'd say that puts you at a disadvantage, mister. You a breed?"

Zeke bristled. "I am a man who has come for his horses, and to help his Cheyenne friends get their women back."

"Well, mister, fact is we was about to turn the squaws and their little worms loose. Figured we've had them long enough to teach the savages a lesson, and they're getting to be kind of a nuisance. You know what I mean. They smell worse than the horses."

There was a round of laughter, while all the Sioux and Cheyenne men struggled violently with their desire to sink their lances into the soldiers. Not all of them understood what had been said, but the sneer on the sergeant's face told them it was not kind.

"Now I don't know about them Appaloosas," the sergeant continued. "They're mighty fine animals, and I don't know as I have the right to just turn them over to some breed who rides in here claiming they belong to him."

"The horses are mine!" Zeke growled, his eyes putting fear in the heart of the sergeant. "I raise them down on the Arkansas. I herded them North to sell to the army, but after what I've seen I think I'll find other buyers. At the moment I'm headed for Fort Laramie to see my brother Lieutenant Daniel Monroe."

The sergeant's smile faded. "Lieutenant Monroe? He's white."

"That's right. We share the same father. I would suggest you turn my horses over to me, Sergeant, or I'll report you to the lieutenant. We're very close. If I ask him to throw you in the guardhouse or have you bullwhipped, he'll order it. You can count on it!"

The sergeant's face reddened. He wasn't sure if he should believe Zeke or not, yet the man had introduced himself with the same last name as the lieutenant's. "How do I know

332

you ain't lying?" the man asked.

"You don't. But I don't think you want to suffer the consequences if I'm not."

The sergeant moved closer, resting the barrel of his rifle against Zeke's middle. "All right, mister. You can have the horses. But you'd best know I'd just as soon blow your guts out, breed. Only reason I don't is because I have orders not to do anything to start any more trouble with the Indians for the moment."

Zeke stared straight back at the man. "And the only reason you are alive this very moment is because I have chosen not to start anything with the soldiers," he replied. "Otherwise you can rest assured your gizzard would already be hanging out of your fat belly and drying in the sun!"

Their eyes held challengingly, and then the sergeant backed up. There were too few men at the fort to hold off an Indian attack. Only a few had been used to herd the women and children, while the rest had ridden on with Colonel Harney deeper into Sioux territory.

The sergeant scanned the small representative group of warriors, perfectly aware that many more probably lurked in the hills around the fort, ready to ride down upon them if the women were not turned loose.

"You tell your red-skinned friends something, breed," the sergeant sneered. "You tell them that at this very moment Colonel William S. Harney is riding deeper into Sioux country to show his force to the rest of the savages. After what they did to Grattan, they'll learn it was a very unwise decision. They've seen our force, seen what we can do with our big guns. It will happen again if they do any raiding, any stealing, any begging, raping or murdering. What happened at Blue Water Creek is only a taste of what will happen next if they don't keep their asses to the land that's allowed them and stop giving the settlers trouble. And if you're riding to Fort Laramie, you ask that brother of yours about it. He'll tell you the same thing. Harney is out to teach the Sioux and Northern Cheyenne a lesson that all Indians can learn from. And any Southern Cheyenne that's up here nosing around where they don't belong had better get the hell back down to the Arkansas where they belong. Your brother will tell you that, too. In the colonel's own words, the Southern Cheyenne and the Arapaho had better stay out of the North, or he'll make war on them and sweep them off the face of the earth."

There was no arguing with such a man. Zeke felt ill having to hold back his rage, but he had to think of the captured women and children. If shooting broke out, there would only be more death, and the women would not be released.

"I will advise my Southern brothers to stay to the South," he replied. "But I advise you, Sergeant, to be wary of the Sioux and Cheyenne. Don't underestimate their fighting skills. You will be surprised some day and find a lance protruding from your back."

The sergeant only grinned nervously. "Go get your horses, breed. And tell your scummy friends to go get their smelly women. In the meantime I intend to send a messenger to Fort Laramie and find out if the lieutenant really has a half-breed brother named Zeke. If he doesn't, I'll have you hunted down sure as you're sitting there now."

Zeke moved his mount closer to the man. "And if any of those women have been manhandled or raped, Sergeant, I'll have *you* hunted down. Lieutenant Monroe will order you strung from the highest tree!" He charged through the soldiers, shouting something in the Cheyenne tongue to the warriors, whose faces lit up as they rode to the corral to release the women. Zeke broke open the gate to where his horses were kept and rode inside the corral, yipping and calling, herding the animals outside to freedom and heading them up a ridge. At the top of the ridge sat Swift Arrow, watching silently. One battle had been fought, with wins and losses on both sides and no true victor. But there would be other battles, battles for which he would be ready.

They parted at the North Platte, the migrating Sioux and Cheyenne giving Zeke and Abbie enough food and blankets to see them to Fort Laramie. The Indians would head further north into the Black Hills to lick their wounds and try to find more game so that they could replenish their heavily destroyed robes and rations.

"Tell my father I may not see him again before he walks Ekutsihimmiyo," Swift Arrow told Zeke. "I cannot come South now, and it would be wise that he stay down on the Arkansas. There will be trouble there also in time to come, but perhaps he will not live long enough to see the sadness."

Their eyes held, and Abbie had to look away, biting her lip to keep from weeping aloud. Swift Arrow moved his mount closer to Zeke, reaching out and touching little Young Girl's cheek, his dark skin a stark contrast to her satiny white complexion.

"It will be easy for this one," he commented, touching her golden curls lovingly. "Those of fair skin have nothing to fear." He met Zeke's eyes again. "But those of us with the dark skin know what is coming. The scars of your own childhood have told you this."

Zeke nodded. "I have always known."

Swift Arrow turned to his left, where Little Rock and Blue Sky sat astride one of their father's Appaloosas. "For these two it will be harder. They are Cheyenne." He tugged at a strand of Blue Sky's long, dark hair. "This one bears the strange beauty that comes to those of mixed blood. Many men will offer you gifts, my brother, for this one's hand. You must ask a high price for her and be sure her man is honorable." Zeke grinned and Blue Sky giggled. Swift Arrow smiled sadly, turning his eyes to Little Rock. He pulled out a fine knife, its handle molded from a large buffalo bone. "A gift to my little warrior nephew. You carry the Cheyenne blood proudly, Little Rock. You will be a fine, strong man. Already you show much courage and skill."

The boy's lips puckered. "Will I see you again, uncle?"

Swift Arrow sighed. "It is hard to say. I will pray that we do, for I wish to see my nephew when he is grown and know the kind of man he becomes."

"I will miss you," Little Rock pouted, struggling to act manly and not cry in front of Swift Arrow. "Thank you for the knife. I will learn to use the knife as my father does." Swift Arrow smiled softly. He reached out and pulled the boy from the horse, giving him a firm hug.

"I shall miss you, too," he told the boy. "And I know you will learn to use the knife with the proud skill of Cheyenne Zeke."

Abbie sniffed and wiped at her eyes. Swift Arrow backed his horse and turned it, trotting the animal over beside Abbie. He glanced at the faces of the two babies who hung in cradleboards at the side of her horse.

"The son of Yellow Moon does not look Indian. Perhaps it is best he stays with those white people who might be able to fix his crooked leg. Life will be easier for him." He reached down and touched the boy's cheek, then touched the cheek of Little Wolf. He raised his eyes to meet Abbie's. "I am grateful that you would take Yellow Moon's son. I know that if the white doctor cannot take him you will take him. Zeke's white woman has a big heart. Yellow Moon's son would be her son."

She sniffed again, then turned away, covering her mouth and crying. It seemed ironic that this man had been the one most against her coming to live with the Cheyenne in that first year of her marriage to Zeke; yet he had become her good friend, teaching her many things about the Cheyenne way, and once risking his life for her when Zeke was gone and white men raided their village and tried to take her away with them. Memories of past years flashed into her mind. Always there had been a loneliness about Swift Arrow that made her sad.

She felt his gentle hand on her arm. "Abbie," he said softly. She felt an odd warmth. She could not recall his ever having called her that. It was always Abigail. The way he said it made her turn to meet his eyes, and it was said in that one moment. She was speechless.

"There are few like you," he told her, his voice strained. "It is no wonder my brother could not free himself from the spell your goodness put upon him. Always you will have an honored place among the Cheyenne . . . and here." He put a fist over his heart.

Abbie glanced over at Zeke, whose eyes were strangely unreadable. She thought of his remark that she was loved by

336

other men. Had he known something that she did not know? Did the two of them share a secret they had kept from her? They were close. It would be logical for Zeke to hold no anger over such a thing, yet the thought was overwhelming. She met Swift Arrow's eyes again.

"I will pray for my husband's brother," she told him. "For he holds a special place in my heart also. He is my friend and brother. I wish you would come South with us, Swift Arrow."

He squeezed her arm lightly and shook his head, releasing her arm and touching her face for just a moment, then moving back from her, circling his painted pony around and over to Zeke.

"I do not need to tell you to take care of your woman. Her blood runs in your veins. If she dies, you die. I know this." He put out his hand, aware that for one brief moment he had allowed feelings to show that might have offended Zeke. But Zeke grasped his wrist firmly.

"May you always be able to ride the winds of freedom, Swift Arrow," he told the man. "Let no arrows pierce your skin, no bullet take your life. Stay close to the Spirits. I will pray for you every day."

"And I for you. These troubles will be hard for you, for you walk on both sides, my brother. It is painful."

Zeke nodded, his eyes watery. "All life is painful." He breathed deeply. "Send messengers at times to let us know you are all right, Swift Arrow."

The man nodded. "I will do this." He hesitated, still gripping Zeke's wrist and holding his eyes. There was nothing more to say. He glanced over at Abbie once more as he released his grip.

"Always remember the old days and hold them close," he told them both. "They are gone forever." He whirled his horse and let out a war cry, then galloped off to catch up with the others.

Zeke looked over at Abbie, then prodded his horse into motion and walked it over close to her. Their eyes held in a new understanding, and he bent over and kissed her cheek.

"Life hurts bad sometimes, Abbie girl. Both of us know

337

that full well, don't we?" She nodded and her body jerked in a quiet sob. He grasped her shoulder and squeezed it. "Let's go see Danny." He picked up Young Girl and placed her in front of Abbie. "Now that the men are all gone, I'll have to herd the horses myself. I can't do that with this little thing sitting in front of me." He started to leave to go and circle his Appaloosas, but stopped and turned. "I love you, Abigail Trent Monroe, more than this land, more than the Cheyenne, more than anything, including my own life. I love you."

She watched him turn and head on out toward the horses. "And I love you . . . more than my own life, more than this land, more than the People," she answered quietly. It was easy to know and to say, for he was her life, he was the land, and he was the People. She glanced back at Swift Arrow, who had already become a small dot on the vast horizon.

Nineteen

They headed down a ridge toward the sprawling Fort
Laramie. It struck Abbie how many more soldiers there
were there now, compared to only three years earlier when
the first great treaty had been signed by the Southern
Cheyenne and the Arapaho. What a grand adventure it had
been to be present at that great gathering of thousands and
thousands of Plains tribesmen. It had been an event of joy
and celebration as well as many serious counsels; a time of
dancing and singing and feasting; a time when the Cheyenne
displayed with great pride their unequaled horsemanship
before the impressed soldiers and government representatives. It was supposed to be the beginning of peace. But the
government still had not signed its half of the treaty, and
peace was beginning to look like no more than a far-off
dream.

Zeke and Little Rock herded the Appaloosas into the fort,
while soldiers and settlers alike stared at the small boy who
handled his big mount with more skill than most men. Zeke
was not anxious to sell his horses to the army, but the fact
remained that he had a large family and game was harder to
come by every year. He had to sell his horses to survive, and
if the army didn't get them from him, they would get them
someplace else. At least here he would be selling them to his
brother.

Abbie came into the fort behind her husband and the
horses. Young Girl and Blue Sky sat on the travois behind
their mother's mount, and the two papooses hung on her
horse. The white woman in an Indian tunic drew stares and

whispers, and she had no doubt that some of the things being said were cruel. She held her head high and looked straight ahead, while Zeke moved his horses into a fenced area where army mounts were kept. By the time Abbie reached him there were bluecoats all around him and her heart tightened with fresh, ugly memories.

"Speak your piece, Indian," one of the men told him. "What the hell do you think you're doing riding in here with those horses? You steal them?" He glanced at Abbie, and the shock on his face was almost humorous as he stepped back further. The shock turned to anger. "What the hell is this? Where did you get this woman? What have you done to her?"

Zeke actually grinned. "I married her . . . about nine years ago." They all looked even more shocked at his good English. "Her name is Abigail Monroe, and I'm Zeke Monroe—Cheyenne Zeke to some—Lone Eagle to the Cheyenne. These are my horses. I raise them. I brought them here to sell to the army, unless the army isn't interested in having the best damned mounts east of the Missouri."

"Cheyenne Zeke?" one of the other soldiers spoke up. He poked at the first man. "Isn't that what the lieutenant calls his half-breed brother when he talks about him?"

The first man looked up at Zeke. "You related to Lieutenant Daniel Monroe?"

"I am. He's my half brother. That's the main reason I'm here. I haven't seen him in two years."

The first man lowered his rifle, looking sheepish. "Sorry, mister, but you sure look all Indian, and we've been having trouble with them."

Zeke's eyes turned colder. "I know. I was at Blue Water Creek."

The small crowd quieted for an uncomfortable moment. Most of the soldiers turned their eyes back to Abbie, all making their own guesses as to why a white woman would marry a half-breed and dress like a squaw. Zeke knew their thoughts and bristled.

"Where can I find my brother?" he asked quickly.

340

The first man tore his eyes from Abbie and pointed to the officers' quarters. "Fourth door of that big building over there. But don't make too much noise when you go in. Rumor has it he hung one on real big last night."

Zeke frowned. "Hung one on? You mean he drank too much?"

There were a few chuckles. "The lieutenant does seem to do that lately."

Zeke looked at Abbie. It was not like Danny at all. He was not a heavy drinker. He was straight and all army.

"If yer brother's wife would come on out here with him, mebby he'd be so busy doin' somethin' else he'd fergit about the booze," one of the men spoke up.

Zeke looked at the first man. "My brother is married?"

The man shrugged. "So he says. But none of us has ever seen the woman. She lives in St. Louis—too scared and too delicate to come out here where she might get a little dirty or get mixed up in an Indian fight. That's the rumor, anyway."

Zeke glanced at Abbie again. "Let's get over there and see what the hell this is all about." He urged his horse into motion and Abbie followed, feeling eyes on her back all the way to the officers' quarters. One troop of men who were practicing marching actually slowed their pace and stopped calling out their step, standing and staring at the white woman in the tunic.

Zeke dismounted and knocked on the door to Danny's office. The door was only a screen because of the heat of summer. He heard heavy footsteps, and a moment later a shadowy figure stopped for a moment inside the door, then quickly opened it. Zeke was surprised at how thin his younger brother had become, how tired-looking. His eyes were red, and for a brief moment Zeke thought of Red Eagle and his drinking. He had to get to the bottom of Danny's problem quickly and keep him from going the same route.

Danny's face brightened with joy and an odd relief, and he literally hugged Zeke like a child, saying his name over and over and slapping the man on the back.

"Goddamn you're a sight for sore eyes!" the man kept saying. He trooped over to Abbie, reaching up for her and

341

hugging her as he pulled her from her horse. "Abbie, sweet, beautiful Abbie!" he exclaimed, clinging to her as though reluctant to let go. Her heart ached for the empty sadness that seemed to hang over him. He pulled back and kissed her cheek. "Damn, you're as pretty as ever. I can't believe you can live down there with the Cheyenne and with that half-breed brother of mine and stay so pretty and young-looking."

There was a round of introductions. He had never seen Young Girl or Little Wolf, and he teased Zeke and Abbie both about producing so many babies. Abbie showed him Crooked Foot. "A half-breed baby we've sort of adopted for a while," she told him. "It's a long story."

He herded them all inside, ordering another soldier to bring some cold, fresh water for them and to draw a bath in the cook's quarters for Abigail. Abbie and Zeke took chairs and the children sat on the floor, staring at their white uncle, Little Rock not sure now if he should trust the man. He liked his dark-skinned uncles, Swift Arrow and Black Elk, much better. But he vaguely remembered how good this man had been three years earlier at the treaty signing, and he knew his father respected Danny wholeheartedly. They were not just brothers. They were good friends.

The conversation went on for over an hour, while Zeke filled his brother in on the events of the past three years, Red Eagle's death, his experience in finding and saving Yellow Moon, and then the tragic ending to her life at Blue Water Creek. Through the telling Danny sobered more and more, and when Zeke mentioned Colonel Harney and Blue Water Creek Danny stared at his desk. He opened the drawer and started to pour a drink with a shaking hand. Zeke reached over and grasped his wrist firmly, almost painfully.

"Enough of the general visiting, brother. What the hell is going on? Do you think I don't recognize a drunk when I see one? What are you trying to do, get demoted?"

Danny jerked his hand away, grabbing the bottle and taking a long swallow. "What the hell would it matter?" he growled. He set the bottle down hard on the desk and the children jumped. Blue Sky started crying, for now the bluecoat looked angry. She had bad memories of angry blue-coats. She crawled up on her mother's lap and Abbie held her close, watching Danny with a heavy heart.

"What do you mean, what does it matter?" Zeke asked him. "You're a damned good soldier, Danny Monroe. You earned a medal for valor in the Mexican War. You're a lieutenant and you earned the rank through bravery and because you have a good head on your shoulders. At the moment I'm not exactly pleased with the United States Army as a whole, but I'm damned proud of you as a brother and as a person." He grabbed the bottle and held it up. "This isn't you!"

A soldier came in sheepishly with more ice water and Danny turned away. Zeke lowered the bottle and set it on the floor and the room was quiet until the soldier left. Danny sighed and remained with his back to them.

"I'm married, Zeke."

"I already heard," Zeke answered, sitting back down and studying Danny's slumped shoulders. "Why isn't she here?"

Danny laughed sarcastically. "That's what I keep asking her!" He turned and walked back to his desk, sitting down wearily. "Her name is Emily. She's the daughter of Major Epcott, the man I saved way back when down in Mexico." He raised his eyes to meet Zeke's. "By the way, and this is just between you and me. No one else is to know. But Epcott is the one who arranged to have you written off in Tennessee. He did it as a favor to me, for saving his life. He knew how important it was to me, and to our two brothers and our father."

Zeke softened. "I owe you one, brother."

Danny shook his head. "You don't owe me anything. You paid me back years and years ago when you saved that little dog's life. Remember how bent Pa was on killing it? But you saved it. I never forgot that."

"I remember," Zeke replied coolly. "I remember your father didn't have much feeling. He treated my Cheyenne mother worse than he treated that dog."

Danny sighed. It was obvious Zeke Monroe was not going

to admit to any feelings for his blood father and even referred to the man as Danny's father, not his own. "Well, anyway, you're a free man now."

"Danny, I can't tell you how happy I was to find out!" Abbie put in. "I'll be forever grateful."

He smiled for her, wishing Emily could be just a little bit like Abigail Monroe. But the thought brought his heart back to reality, and his face clouded again. He sighed deeply. "Emily is beautiful," he said wistfully, staring at a stack of papers on his desk. "She's delicate and refined, with auburn hair and eyes green as the sea. I'm afraid I was infatuated at first sight, and like a fool I practically tripped over my own feet going after her. All I could think about was making her my wife and getting her in my bed."

Abbie reddened and Zeke grinned a little. Danny glanced at both of them. "I'm sorry, Abbie. I just—I was lost in thought." He looked a little embarrassed himself. "I . . . uh . . . I married her. It wasn't until after that that I came back down to reality. She's young and ignorant and spoiled. To Emily being a wife at night is a necessary burden, and coming out to a place like this is out of the question. Her pampered mother always stayed in St. Louis—in 'civilization,' as Emily puts it. She wants to live out my career that way, seeing me once every year, if that much. But I can't live that way. I love her, in spite of her ignorance and frivolous ways. I need her companionship. I'm lonely. I need her here and she won't come. She promises to come, but she never does." He sighed and shook his head. "I was a fool to marry her so quickly. And yet the damned little vixen has me going in circles. I never would have rested easy without making her my wife before returning from St. Louis. And I can't help thinking that if she'd come out here and we could be alone together for a while, away from her empty-headed friends, away from her doting father, she'd grow up a little and we'd do okay."

"She just needs time, Danny," Abbie put in, trying to sound hopeful. "I was scared to death when my pa told me we were going West. I didn't want to go, but he was going and I had no choice. And then I lost my family and I was even more frightened."

He held her eyes. "But you stayed. You didn't go running back. You married my brother and agreed to a life you knew would be difficult at best. But you did it anyway, because you're a good woman, a strong woman. And because you love your husband and you understand what loving a man means." Anger flashed in his eyes and he stood up again, walking to a window. "Emily only loves herself."

"Surely if you loved her so quickly you saw a goodness there that will eventually show itself as she matures, Danny," Abbie offered. "But turning into an alcoholic and perhaps even losing your rank certainly won't make her love you more and want to come out here to be with you."

He stared out the window for a long moment. "It isn't just Emily," he replied carefully. "Last fall a young Sioux girl was left at my doorstep, almost dead from pneumonia. I nursed her back to health. We became . . . good friends." Silence hung in the room as the reality of what he was telling them sank in. "There's something about Indian women," he added. "They have a certain lovely gentleness about them, a way of loving a man so . . . openly . . . so generously . . . no strings attached, no demands. Just a sweet . . . quiet love. You're a lot like that, Abbie."

Zeke sighed and rubbed at his eyes. Danny Monroe had stepped far out of bounds for an army lieutenant. But Zeke did not blame him. Abbie blinked back tears, unable to find the right words.

"Her name was Small Cloud," Danny went on quietly. "And in a few short months she was more of a wife to me than Emily will ever be, because she was a good friend. She cared. She only came to my bed once, but it was the most beautiful experience I've ever had, even though I knew it was wrong. I had already waited too long, but I finally took her back to her own people once she was strong enough, about three months ago, to be exact. I later learned she was killed when some settlers attacked a small band she was traveling with." His voice broke and he swallowed, then breathed deeply for several seconds to regain his control.

"I'm damned sorry, Danny," Zeke told him.

Danny shrugged. "It never should have happened, but it did. It doesn't change how I feel about Emily. If she'd been here, it never would have happened at all. But that's no excuse." He finally turned to face them again. "At any rate, I'm not so sure I want the army anymore, Zeke. Because of you, and because of the friend I made three years ago of Swift Arrow and some of the other Cheyenne and Sioux, I can't bring myself to go out there and slaughter them. And that's exactly what Harney is doing. This is just the beginning. I'm so mixed up that sometimes I just wish I could die. I'm lonely, married but without a wife, in love with a dead Sioux woman, and I have to sit idly by while aristocrats from other countries come through here asking directions to the nearest buffalo herd! It's all a farce, all of it! Army men, civilized men going out and shooting up women and children and calling it a victory." He shook his head. "I can't be a part of something like that."

"Don't be a fool," Zeke snapped. "The army is in your blood. And your knowledge of the Indians and your concern for them is all the more reason to stay out here and do your job, Danny." Danny looked at him in surprise. "The Danny I know has guts and brains," Zeke went on. "Use them, damn it! Quit pining away over things that can't be helped. Stay out here and do what you can to change things. One person may not be able to do much, but he can try. If you're really concerned about the Indians, Danny, then stay out here and make sure their rights are protected! They need army men like you, not a bunch of greenhorns fresh from West Point who don't know an eagle feather from goose down and who think all Indians are just unfeeling savages who go around lifting scalps and panting after white women!" He rose from his chair and faced his brother, both of them tall and commanding, of almost equal stature, having gotten their builds from their father, a man Abbie wondered if she would ever meet. Zeke grasped Danny's arm tightly. "Remember who you are, Danny. You are Lieutenant Daniel Monroe and you have experience with the Indians. You belong out here. There are going to continue

346

to be other wrongdoings, but at least you can do your own part to help keep the peace."

Danny sighed and their eyes held. "You always did know what to say to me, big brother."

Zeke squeezed his arm. "Lay off the whiskey damn it! If you had seen what happened to Red Eagle—hell, you've seen what it's done to a hundred Indians, a thousand. And you've seen what it's done to a hell of a lot of white men. That isn't you, Danny boy. And your wife will come around. You'll see." He released the man's arm. "I can't imagine a woman would let a man like you out of her sight forever. She just has some growing up to do. In the meantime, maybe you can get leave to go back to St. Louis."

Danny sighed. "Yeah. Maybe." He moved back around behind his desk.

"Danny, perhaps I could write to Emily," Abbie spoke up. "Do you think that might help? I could . . . well, perhaps tell her how happy I am out here, in spite of the hardships; explain to her how important it is for a woman to be with her man. It may not do any good, but—"

"Abbie, you're a treasure," Danny interrupted with a grin. "Sure you can write her. It might help. God knows you of all people should know the right things to say." He picked up his quill pen and took out a piece of paper. "I'll give you her address and you can get a trader at Bent's Fort to take her the letter. I wish to hell she could meet you."

He scribbled on the paper, then looked up at her again, moving his eyes from her to Zeke. "Jesus, I'm glad you're here. Damned glad. You'll stay a day or two, won't you? Let Abbie rest up, sit and soak in a tub for a while, stock up on supplies?"

Zeke grinned and nodded. "Just a couple of days. We have to head north to see a doctor I know about Crooked Foot, and then get headed back home. We don't have a lot of time now. The summer is getting late, and with a woman and four kids along a man doesn't move too fast. By the way, I brought along some Appaloosas. You interested in buying?"

"From the best horse breeder in these parts? Hell yes!"

Danny's eyes were brighter, his smile broader. Zeke was glad they had come. Danny had really needed to talk, and Zeke needed to talk as well, to find out more about the buffalo hunters and the government's attitude toward the Indian. This land and the white migration westward were having an effect on soldier and Indian alike. He was glad there were at least a few soldiers in Indian Territory like Danny . . . men who cared. And in spite of the blue uniform, he loved his white brother, even though he hated the man who had fathered them both.

It was not difficult to find the little settlement. Danny had heard of it and told them how to find it. Now Bonnie stood at the doorway of the crude log church her husband and father had built, having come to the doorway at the sound of horses. She watched at first in near shock, her face glowing brighter, as she realized who was dismounting from the grand Appaloosa and walking toward her then.

"Zeke!" she gasped.

"Hello, Bonnie," came the deep voice. His smile was as fetching as she had remembered, his face as handsome, his stature as powerful and commanding. She exited the little log church with haste, coming down the steps and grasping his hands warmly, her eyes watery and full of obvious love. Bonnie Beaker Lewis was unmistakably thrilled to see the man who had saved her from outlaws the year before, and the joyful radiance in her eyes stirred a twinge of jealousy in Abbie's heart, for the woman was lovely, blond and blue-eyed and gentle of countenance.

"I never thought I'd see Zeke Monroe again," she was telling him with a bright smile. "How are you? What brings you here?" She looked as though she wanted to hug him, but she stepped back and looked him over. "You look wonderful!"

Zeke grinned. "So do you, Bonnie," he replied, giving her hands a squeeze. She blushed under his gaze, wondering if she had greeted him with too much enthusiasm. Could he see that she still loved him? That he had been on her mind almost constantly since he left her in Santa Fe? How wonderful his big hands felt around her own, supportive, warm, strong. How strange that she should feel that way about hands that had killed so many men. "I brought my wife, Bonnie. I want you to meet her, and our family, and we need your help."

Her smile faded at the humble pleading in his eyes. "Of course," she answered, eager to do something to repay him for saving her. "And I . . ." She suddenly stepped back from him, all at once flustered that she had greeted him with such enthusiasm in front of his wife. She had been so elated at seeing him she had not even paid attention to who was with him. She turned and looked over at the beautiful young white woman who sat proudly on an Appaloosa, the mysterious woman who had been Cheyenne Zeke's wife since the tender age of sixteen, the woman he had called out for when he was wounded. Here was the woman Bonnie had secretly envied for so many months, especially during the nights, when Rodney groped at her with clumsy, inexperienced hands.

"I'm so happy to meet you, Abigail," she said with sincerity. "Zeke spoke about you so often when he was taking me back to Santa Fe, and he called for you when he was wounded." She stepped closer, smiling warmly now. "I knew the mysterious Abbie had to be someone very special. And you're just as lovely as I had you pictured."

Abbie smiled for her, sensing the woman's genuine gladness at meeting her. "I'm very glad to finally meet you, Bonnie," she replied. "Zeke spoke about you so often." Their eyes held for a moment and Bonnie blushed, then reached up for her. "Please, come inside the chapel where it's cooler. I want to meet your children, and I most certainly am anxious to find out how it is we can help you."

Abbie dismounted and immediately Bonnie's arm was about her waist. "This is wonderful!" she said, looking over at Zeke. "I was so worried, Zeke, knowing you still had to go after that awful woman and those outlaws after you left me in Santa Fe. I'm so glad to know you are all right."

Abbie glanced at Zeke with pain in her eyes, and he knew she would not want these people to know she had killed Dancing Moon with her own hands. He gave her a consoling look and a gentle smile. He would not tell them.

A man was exiting the church, and Bonnie called out to him, leaving Abbie's side for a moment. "Rodney! Rodney, this is Zeke Monroe, the man who rescued me last summer." She walked over to join the man. Rodney Lewis approached Zeke and put out his hand, and Zeke thought to himself how small the hand felt within his own, how weak the handshake.

"I'm Rodney Lewis, Bonnie's husband," the man said with a gentle smile.

"Nice to meet you, Rodney," Zeke told him, shaking his hand firmly in return and towering over him like a bear. "This is my wife, Abigail," he added, reaching his arm out and putting it around her shoulders as Abbie came closer. Bonnie struggled to ignore the wish that it was she he was calling his wife. But the past was the past and could not be changed. Abbie wondered at how pale and waspish Rodney Lewis appeared and was curious at how a man of his frail stature cold survive in the rugged West. She surmised he must be a very dedicated man, for surely he would rather be back East in the comforts of civilization.

"Bonnie's father is at the cabin," Rodney was telling them. "Bring your children there and we can talk."

Zeke turned and walked to the travois, whisking up Blue Sky and Young Girl into each arm, bringing on shock and laughter at the sight of Young Girl's blond curls. The love in the Monroe family was immediately evident, and Bonnie sensed already from their brief meeting that Abigail Monroe was a remarkable woman. Abbie led her horse with the two cradleboards on it toward the cabin not far from the church, and Little Rock brought up the rear of the little procession, stubbornly quiet. He did not care to make good friends with any white people. But his father and mother liked these

350

people, so he would simply quietly accept their hospitality.

Conrad Beaker ran his hands over Crooked Foot's little naked body, while Bonnie watched her father's expert touch. Her heart ached for the poor, unwanted child, who cried occasionally whenever her physician father touched him in certain ways.

"A bad case of club foot," the big, bearded man spoke up. "But it's possible the child can be helped. There are doctors in the East who might be able to fix him up enough that he can walk, at least with a brace of some kind. That's the most I can promise, but that's not to say it isn't possible they can fix him up even better than that."

Zeke sighed. "I was hoping perhaps you could do something with him yourself, Mr. Beaker, perhaps in payment for . . . I mean, you told me if I ever needed help—"

"Oh, I'd most certainly do it myself if I was good at that kind of thing, Zeke. But this takes more skill than I have. This takes a specialist."

Bonnie watched the pain of humble honesty in Zeke's eyes. He was a proud man, not accustomed to going to anyone for help. "Mr. Beaker, I'm afraid I don't have that kind of money. Not for a specialist. I figured maybe you could help him. Otherwise we'll just have to take him home with us and make do, help him all we can, love him and work with him—"

"I didn't say you'd need money, Zeke." The doctor looked up at Zeke. "I told you once to come to me if there was any way I could help. You've come. And I shall help. I have friends back East who will cover this, people in the church who support my work out here."

Abbie's eyes teared and Zeke glanced at Bonnie. "Not all us Christians are like those pious people back in Tennessee who chased you out of school and church, Zeke," she told him. "And not all of us hate Indians."

Their eyes held and he nodded.

"After seeing what happened at Blue Water Creek, it's

351

good to hear someone say that," he told her. "It was a real bad experience, especially for poor Abbie, seeing what her own kind were doing to Indian women and children. But I wasn't too surprised, not after living in Tennessee, and not after what I saw done to the Creeks and Cherokees on the Trail of Tears. I'm not surprised it's beginning to happen out here."

"Well, neither I nor my father nor my husband will ever be a part of such a thing," Bonnie replied. "Leave the child with us. I'll be a mother to him and love him, I promise," she added, while Rodney watched her curiously. "We have a goat we can get milk from." She reddened, almost embarrassed that she had not yet had a child of her own and was not pregnant. Could Zeke see through her and tell that her own husband seldom bedded her and had little of the natural desires most men had?

"Thank you," Zeke told her quietly. "I'll not worry about the boy if he's with you."

"I'll take him East myself, stay with him through whatever it is they have to do with him. And I'll write you. Just tell us where to send word."

Zeke nodded, turning to the preacher. "I hate to ask you for so much, but I'd like one more favor."

"And what is that?" Beaker replied, folding a blanket around little Crooked Foot.

"I'd like you to fix up a legal marriage license—date it August thirtieth, eighteen hundred and forty-five."

The preacher looked at him curiously, as Abbie hung her head, unaware that Zeke had intended to make such a request. Zeke reached over and took her chin gently in his hand, forcing her to look up.

"You hold your head up, woman," he told her firmly as she blinked back tears. "You're my wife, sure as I'm standing here breathing—always have been." He looked back at the preacher. "Mr. Beaker, I love Abbie. I loved her back in forty-five when I met her on the wagon train I scouted for. She's an honorable woman, and I intended to keep it that way. I wanted her to be my wife, and out there

352

on the trail, especially back then, preachers were hard to come by. We had one along on our train, but he got killed. So a schoolteacher married us—before a lot of witnesses. He happened to also be a church deacon, and his brother was a preacher. We figured that was close enough. We were married under the sun in front of your God—spoke the real vows with a bible in our hands. Last year a government man came along talking about putting a railroad through my land. The man threatened Abbie, telling her she wasn't legally married to me—told her she'd best get legally married and have papers to prove it—and told her our kids should be baptized and have Christian names or they could be taken from her. He scared her to death. I don't mind for me. It's for Abbie that I intend to have those things done, so nobody can come and try to shame her." He put his arm around her waist and pulled her closer. "I want you to marry us and date the license like I said. She has a real wedding ring now that I got for her last year in Santa Fe. And I want you to give Christian names to my sons and daughters and baptize them. I don't believe your way, nor do I say it's wrong. Your God doesn't sound much different from mine, so I don't reckon baptizing them is going to do them any harm."

Beaker glanced at his son-in-law, and Rodney just shrugged. "We've had to do a lot of rule-changing out here, sir. They're good people, and if not for Zeke Bonnie might not even be alive. I don't see any harm, and we certainly can't object to baptizing a child."

The preacher nodded, and Bonnie breathed a sigh of relief. "All right," Beaker told Zeke. "All of you be at the church in the morning and we'll do it. In fact, you may sleep in the church tonight, if you wish. You'll need a roof over your heads and this cabin is small."

Zeke reached over and shook the man's hand, while a tear slipped down Abbie's cheek. "Thank you, sir," Zeke told the man. Rodney studied Zeke, trying to picture the savage way in which Bonnie had described his killing the outlaws. This was a strange man indeed, a man of extreme savageness, and

353

obviously a man of surprising gentleness, with a capability to love as deeply as he could hate.

Abbie bent over and picked up Crooked Foot, holding him close and kissing his cheek, wiping her tears on his blanket. She looked at Bonnie. "Thank you," she told the woman, "for saving my husband's life last summer—and for your generous offer to take care of Crooked Foot. I've begun to love him like my own. I'll feel better knowing someone like you will have him."

Bonnie glanced at Abbie's small wedding band, noticing the cruel scar on her left hand and wondering how it got there; wondering how much the woman had suffered to be with Zeke Monroe, and knowing she would suffer the same gladly if she could be Zeke's woman. Their love was obviously sweet and good, strong and enduring.

Bonnie smiled. "I'll enjoy it. When Rodney and my father ride the circuit visiting settlers, I get very lonely. It will be nice to have the baby to tend to—and it will be pleasant being able to go back East for a while with him."

"It will be good practice, for when you have your own children," Abbie told her.

Bonnie blushed and looked down, wondering if she would ever get pregnant. The baby would be more welcome than they realized. She needed the distraction. And indirectly the child was a part of Zeke Monroe. For that reason alone she would take him.

It was done. They had a marriage license with the correct date shown on it. The children were baptized, Little Rock acquiescing grudgingly. Little Wolf was called Jeremy Trent Monroe, after Abbie's dead little brother, and her own maiden name. Young Girl was named LeeAnn Bonita, Lee-Ann after Abbie's dead sister who had also been blond and pretty, and Bonita for Bonnie Beaker. Blue Sky was named Margaret Elaine, after Abbie's dead mother. Little Rock made the stubborn announcement that he did not want a white name. He wanted only to be called Little Rock and later he would change his name to another Indian name

354

after he had his vision.

Abbie's heart ached at his decision, and she thought of scolding him and insisting he accept a white name, for she wanted to name him after her father, Jason Trent. An odd silence hung over their little group as Zeke and Little Rock studied one another while Abbie choked back tears, knowing instinctively that some day her firstborn would surely break her heart. He was a good son, but he would go away from her as surely as she stood there watching him then, his straight black hair covering deep brown shoulders, his mouth rigid as he stared back at his father with eyes too old for a seven-year-old. "Please do not give me a white man's name," he repeated to his father. "I wish to be Cheyenne."

"You're too young to know what you want," Zeke told him. "Anyway it's only a formality, son. A protection against someone coming along and taking you away."

The boy folded his arms firmly. "They would never catch me!" he declared.

Zeke could not suppress a grin, and the others had to smile also.

Abbie fought a desire to cry out in anguish and grab him close to her. She reminded herself that she had known one or more of her children might choose to admit only to their Cheyenne blood; and perhaps some would deny that blood. She would have to strengthen her heart against both, for either decision would be painful for her.

"Let it be, Zeke. I don't want to force him into it," she spoke up to everyone's surprise. "My Little Rock is Cheyenne, and that's what you always wanted him to be. I'm proud of him. We'll have more children, perhaps another son. If we do, we can name him after my father. There's no sense giving him a name he'll never use."

Zeke met her eyes lovingly. "You sure, Abbie?"

"I'm sure." She turned to the others. "And be sure that both their Cheyenne and white names are shown on the baptism papers. They are never to forget that both bloods run in their veins."

Preacher Beaker nodded. "So be it."

355

Abbie turned to look up at Zeke. "Let's go to Hinta-Nagi. I miss home. I want to go home, Zeke. I am suddenly very tired."

His eyes were watery as he stepped closer to her and put a big hand to the side of her face. "Then we'll head for home just as fast as we can get there, Mrs. Monroe." He kissed her forehead lightly and Bonnie turned away so no one would see her tears.

Twenty

Emily read and reread the letter from the sister-in-law she had never met. Its flowing words about the joys of loving a man and giving him children made her think more deeply than she ever had in her young life. Her mother had never mentioned that there should be pleasure in taking a man, joy in serving a man, or fulfillment in bearing children. There had been no mention of "taking your strength from your husband and in turn being the source of his strength." Emily had no idea that she could be that important to Danny's welfare, or that it was not wrong to enjoy her husband sexually.

Abbie's written words were disturbing, yet Emily felt that this mysterious woman who was married to Danny's half brother was speaking the truth when she wrote that sharing a man in body and in heart was beautiful and right. It must be true. Why else would Abigail Monroe stay out there in the wilderness, living among Indians and bearing her children alone? The woman was obviously educated, judging by the neatness and proper spelling in her letter. Emily had somehow had a different impression, but, now as she read the letter, she was impressed by the lovely words and the appearance of the letter.

She put the letter down and glanced across the parlor at her father, who sat reading a newspaper nearby. "Father?"

"Hmmm?" He did not look up.

"All those years when mother lived in St. Louis and you were off in some other part of the country, did you some-times wish she would come out to wherever you were stationed and live with you there?"

Major Epcott glanced up then at his daughter, surprised at the question. Her searching eyes compelled him to tell her the truth. "I wished it night and day," he replied.

Emily frowned. "But you both seemed so content."

He sighed. "Your mother wasn't a strong person, Emily. She always loved St. Louis, so I let her stay. But I would much rather have had her with me. I just never told her so. It would have upset her."

"But weren't you terribly lonely?"

He smiled sadly. "Of course, my darling. I was very lonely." He studied her closely. "Are you considering going to Fort Laramie?"

She folded the letter. "I don't know. It frightens me." She dropped her eyes and reddened a little. "But I don't feel like much of a wife this way. I don't even understand how to be a good wife, but I can't learn when we're so far apart. Danny is such a sweet, patient man, it makes me feel guilty, knowing how lonely he is."

For some strange reason the memory of being in Danny Monroe's bed brought a sudden, unexpected, and very pleasant urgency to her insides, much like his last kiss had done.

"Well, Emily, right now the Indians are in a bit of an uproar out there, and winter is settling in on the plains. Danny will get a two-month leave come spring, and I'm certain he'll head for St. Louis as fast as he can get here. You can talk about it and decide then. At least that way if you go out there, your own husband can escort you for protection."

Her eyes brightened. "You mean you wouldn't mind?"

He smiled. "Why would I mind? A woman belongs with her husband, unless it's too difficult for her, like it would have been for your mother. But you're much stronger than she was, Emily."

"But I thought—I don't want you to be lonely, Father. I hate to leave you."

He rose and came over to take her hands. "Emily, there comes a time when a child must leave the nest. I understand

358

that. Don't ruin your marriage to a very fine young man just because you don't want to leave your father. I'm headed for Washington in the spring anyway, for an unknown length of time. Your future lies with your husband, and he's a good one. I expect he'd be the happiest man in the world if you told him you'd return with him."

She smiled and hugged him briefly. "I must write him right away!" she told him, turning and hurrying off to the study. She did not understand what was happening to her heart, or that a woman's hormones were finally beginning to surge into her childish body. She only knew that she suddenly missed her husband very much and wanted to find out if things really could be the way Abigail Monroe said they could in her letter.

By July of 1857, two more daughters had been born to Abigail Monroe; Ishiomiists, Rising Sun, was born in December of 1855, her Christian name Ellen Lynn, after Zeke's first wife. The next daughter and sixth child was Meane-ese, Summer Moon, born in July of 1857 and given the Christian name of Lillian Rose. Ellen was as dark as a Cheyenne child, but with blue eyes, a promising beauty. Lillian was of medium complexion, with light brown hair and brown eyes. She was a frail baby, but sweet and loving. She was a worry to Abbie, for she was always prone to colds and fever, always too thin, and a child who tired easily.

To everyone's delight, Blue Bird Woman gave birth to a son for Black Elk, just two months before Lillian was born. He was called Hotsehaxe-voha, Bucking Horse, for he kicked his mother mercilessly before he was born, and kicked wildly as soon as he was out of his mother's womb. He was a fine, strong boy, and no one could have been happier than Blue Bird Woman, who had tried for four years to give her husband a child. And to further gladden their hearts, a letter was received from Danny only two days after Lillian was born, telling them of the birth of his own daughter in April of 1857. She was called Jennifer Abigail, her first name that of Emily's dead mother, and her middle

359

name in honor of the sister-in-law so deeply respected by Danny, for he was certain it was Abbie's letter that had helped influence his wife's decision to come to Fort Laramie.

But all of the happiness over the birth of the children was overshadowed by the tragedy that was building for the Cheyenne and the Sioux. Colonel Harney continued his rampage through Sioux country, demanding in writing that all Cheyenne and Arapaho withdraw from the Northern plains and also that they make peace with the Pawnee. Cheyenne runners were sent South by Swift Arrow to warn Black Elk and the others to stay to the South, and a few Northern Cheyenne fled South with them, for Harney was making life very difficult for those in the North. The Indian agent for the Southern Cheyenne, John Whitefield, found himself trying to control several thousand alarmed and confused Indians. To Abbie's sorrow, Zeke struggled fruitlessly to calm his brother and the others, but he was unable to keep them from storming new Bent's Fort in 1856 and threatening to scalp William Bent if Agent Whitfield did not include guns and ammunition as part of their annuity from the government that had betrayed them by making dramatic changes in the Treaty of 1851, changes that were not agreed to by the Indians. The Cheyenne smelled trouble in the air even in the South, and they intended to be ready by demanding the badly needed rifles.

To further alarm and anger all the Cheyenne and Sioux, the government mapped out new routes for wagon trains, taking emigrant wagons through the heart of Cheyenne country rather than around it. One road was gouged out through the Kansas River area, the Solomon River area and the Smoky Hill River region, all prime hunting grounds. The Cheyenne began to fear a total loss of game, and there were frequent skirmishes with soldiers and settlers alike, as the Indians harassed wagon trains, trying to dissuade them from coming into their territory. The great Cheyenne leader Dull Knife strove for peace, but his angry followers were not ready for it. Northern Cheyenne, more rebellious, came South and began raiding along the Santa Fe Trail, acts for which the Southern Cheyenne were often blamed. Secretary of War Jefferson Davis spoke out for a stern hand in dealing with the Indians, and in 1856 a peaceful, unsuspecting Cheyenne camp near Fort Kearny was attacked by G. H. Stewart, for no reason whatsoever. In their fierce anger the Cheyenne retaliated by killing two white women and some children, the first time they had committed such an act. But their own women and children were being slaughtered without feeling and with no regret on the part of the white soldiers and settlers. Their fury at the murdering and raping of their own could no longer be held in check. Perhaps if white women were killed the white soldiers would understand the agony of such cowardly attacks and would leave them alone.

But by 1857 the rumor was spread that a Colonel Edwin Sumner was organizing four hundred cavalry and infantry and hauling along four mountain Howitzers in a planned "search and destroy" mission against the Northern Cheyenne, using Fall Leaf, a Delaware Indian, as a guide. The result was a major confrontation in which the brave and angry Cheyenne rode straight into the guns of the soldiers, putting up a heroic battle but losing to the superior weapons of the United States Army. The huge Indian village was deserted and Sumner promptly destroyed everything in it, building one huge bonfire of food and tipis, including a whole winter's supply of buffalo meat. The destruction of the food supply was the biggest blow the Cheyenne could have suffered.

It seemed Zeke was always gone during those terrible months, sitting in on peace talks, helping his red brothers find food, acting as interpreter, often pleading with Indian agents to understand the plight of the Cheyenne. But it was a losing battle, and to further "starve out" the Cheyenne, Colonel Sumner himself rode to Bent's Fort to confiscate that summer's government issue of guns, flint and powder, food and clothing. Most of it was either destroyed or given away to others.

Four Southern Cheyenne chiefs who wanted only peace, White Antelope, High-Back-Wolf, Tall Bear, and Starved

Bear, gathered at Bent's Fort in October of 1857 to plead with William Bent to speak for them, again emphasizing that it was not the Southern Cheyenne who made trouble, but rather the Northern Cheyenne and the Sioux, who were much more rebellious. The Southern Cheyenne had remained, for the most part, peaceful, constantly trying to stay at peace in spite of the invasion of their land by whites who did not belong there. In spite of cruel and uncalled-for attacks on their women and children, in spite of the vicious and deliberate torture of one of their warriors at Fort Kearny that summer, and in spite of another of their men being starved to death in a guardhouse, they still wanted peace and had never wanted anything else—just to be left alone. William Bent, always in sympathy with his good Southern Cheyenne friends, pleaded their case to their new agent Robert Miller. Since agents seemed to change as fast as the days went by, it seemed the Cheyenne were constantly repleading their case, explaining all over again to each new agent who came along their fear of loss of land and game, their desire for peace if only the whites and the soldiers would stop attacking innocent bands and villages.

Early in 1858 it seemed that there might be a softening in the government's attitude toward the Southern Cheyenne, and that new efforts would be made to keep the whites out of their territory. But then came the devastating news that was to drive the first nail into the coffin that would hold the bodies of dead Cheyenne for years to come. Gold was discovered at Pike's Peak.

It was not the miners who angered the Indians, even though they invaded Indian lands by the thousands. For most of the miners were friendly, handing out gifts and whiskey, trading for robes, even having huge cookouts with neighboring tribes and holding horse races. The Indians were for the most part friendly to the miners, for they came only to take their gold and leave again. But the miners were followed by settlers, whites who came to lap up the money that could be made off the miners, suppliers and speculators, prostitutes and land-hungry dealers who sent word back East about the vast and beautiful land in "gold country." The greed that follows any discovery of gold quickly arrived, and soon Cheyenne country was flooded even more by emigrants, so many that the soldiers stopped trying to keep them out as they had first been instructed to do. The whites wanted their way, and the government was not about to opt for the Indian. Those whites who lusted after rich Indian territory plotted their course, sending home tales of "wild Indians" who were murderous and savage, calling them "instinctive thieves" and doing everything they could to make them look bad so that the government would be less prone to hand the Indians any rights.

New trails separated the Northern and Southern Cheyenne into even more distinctive factions, and there was no longer just one Cheyenne nation. Zeke and Abbie did not see Swift Arrow during those years of turmoil, and they both prayed for the rebellious brother who led raids in the North. William Bent predicted a "smoldering passion" in the Indians, a building rage over white infiltration and over the loss of game that would build into bloody conflict, both North and South, a conflict that could mean nothing but the extinction of the Indian.

"Come to Denver," Anna read in the senator's letter. "I have come here to see what is happening. Gold everywhere, which means men. You'll make more money than ever here in Denver. Leave someone else in charge of your place in Santa Fe and come start a new one here. I have already claimed several properties and am having a house built. We'll make twice as much here in Denver as we did in Santa Fe. Get here as quickly as you can, and bring your best girls. The miners are hungry for women, and the price that can be charged for a good prostitute would set your head reeling. I am making a fortune on supplies I've had shipped here from St. Louis. See if you can get some of your youngest girls to come with you, Anna. It's a prostitute's heaven here.
Winston."

Anna folded the letter, wondering if she would ever be

able to climb out of the pit of debt Winston Garvey kept her in so that she could truly be her own businesswoman. Always he had a hold on her, ever since he had first set her up in Santa Fe, after she fled Washington, D.C. in the wake of a rampage of the law against prostitution. Winston Garvey had helped her, and he had held her under his thumb ever since. Somehow she would get out from under that thumb someday. But for now he had ordered her to Denver.

She shrugged and put the letter away. She would go. Perhaps if prostitution was as lucrative there as he said, she could see her way out of debt and no longer have to answer to the fat old senator.

Abbie was busier than ever just feeding and cleaning up after her several children, as well as insisting that they sit for two hours every morning for lessons. All of those old enough to understand were taught, and all were obedient and easy to work with, except Little Rock. When he was ten years old the boy's lessons stopped completely, for Abbie was tired of forcing him to sit still and study, tired of watching the agony on his face and seeing him constantly wiggle and squirm and gaze out the window. The boy was a distraction to his brothers and sisters who tried to study, and finally Abbie told him he no longer needed to take lessons, that he knew enough of reading and writing to get by on.

Never had Little Rock displayed more joy at an announcement, and never had he hugged her more tightly. It seemed only seconds before he was outside and mounted, charging past the cabin giving out war whoops and riding off to practice more with the lance, a skill at which he was becoming amazingly adept. Four-year-old Little Wolf, now called Jeremy, who was always a little awed by his big brother, glanced up and watched the elder Monroe son ride past the doorway. Jeremy had no desire to ride horses. He was afraid of horses, a fear which he sensed displeased his father.

"He'll want to ride when he's bigger," Abbie was always

telling a scowling Zeke, who remained patient with his second son. He loved the boy as deeply as any of his children, but there was a certain friction between the towering half-breed and his small second son, for Zeke expected more of Jeremy than the boy could give. He was not anything like Little Rock, not as broad and strong, not as daring and wild, not even as dark. In fact, he did not look Indian at all, and he sometimes wondered if Little Rock was really his brother and if Zeke was really his father. He was a bright boy, surprisingly adept at his lessons, and at four years old he already knew all of his letters and could spell some words and even read simple sentences. He also knew his numbers, and at times when he studied he looked more like a grown man perusing his ledgers. The boy was a true "student," often asking Abbie questions that were very difficult to answer.

There was love and affection between Jeremy and his father, whom Jeremy worshipped but also feared, for he was such a big man, so physically vital, so dark and strong, always urging Jeremy to learn to ride the way Little Rock could ride. But Jeremy was afraid—afraid of horses, afraid of violence, afraid of blood. It was the boy's fear and timidity that disappointed Zeke, creating the invisible wall between father and son that worried Abbie, for no matter how much they loved each other, the friction over their vastly different characters would always be there, creating the worst kind of pain for a woman, the pain of motherhood.

That pain was eased somewhat when Jeremy finally mastered the art of staying on a horse's back. The boy's joyful smile of victory and the loving embrace from his father warmed her heart. She knew Zeke loved this second son as deeply as his firstborn and that he only feared their differences would someday drive Jeremy away from him. She saw it in his eyes that day when he clung to the boy longer than necessary, praising him and telling him how much he loved him. From that day on they drew a little closer, and Abbie no longer held her own tiny resentment against Zeke for getting upset with Jeremy. It was Zeke's own old fear of being deserted by someone he loved that caused him to react as he did, but after the day Jeremy rode a horse, Zeke seemed to relax and accept his second son more readily, even sitting and listening to Jeremy read to him. Jeremy in turn began listening to his father's stories of riding with the Cheyenne in the days of Indian freedom, stories of the buffalo hunt and the raids against enemy tribes.

Abbie pulled off her tunic, breathing deeply of the rich smell of the fresh wood being used to add a room onto the little cabin. Its walls were bursting with children and another room was needed. Zeke watched her lovingly as she brushed out her hair before coming to the bed of robes, the place where they had both found so much happiness and strength, joy and sweet sharing. He studied her lovely form, her body still amazingly trim for a woman with six children; but he was worried. She was pregnant again, only two months along but not feeling as well and as strong as usual, and again too thin. He was still haunted by Jeremy's birth and her terrible bleeding. He wished there were some way to stop the pregnancies other than to stop their lovemaking, but she would not hear of it again. She would take the risks.

"My body will stop on its own," she always said. But she was still very young and had a lot of childbearing years ahead of her. She never complained, never denied him in the night, never seemed too busy for any one child, and never ran out of patience, either with the children or with her own untamed husband. Sometimes he loved her so much that it actually hurt to ponder the matter.

"Zeke, I got another letter today," she was telling him now. "You were out rounding up strays all day. I didn't have a chance to tell you."

"From Bonnie?"

"Yes." She sighed deeply and lay down beside him. "Crooked Foot has had his fifth operation, and they think he'll be able to walk almost normally after this one. She says this will probably be the last one until he's about eighteen and his bones are finished growing. I can hardly believe he's four years old now."

He smiled and rubbed a big hand lightly across her belly. "Taking him to those people was the best thing we could have done for him."

She turned her eyes to meet his, and he could see tears in them by the light of a bright moon that peeked through the window that still had no glass in it. He frowned and kissed her lightly.

"What's wrong, Abbie girl?"

She sniffed and pressed her face against his chest and he could feel wet tears against his skin. "They want to keep him, Zeke. Adopt him officially."

There was a long moment of silence. He kissed her hair and drew her into his arms. "That's the best thing for him, Abbie. You know that. You'll have a time keeping up with our own brood. I worry about you all the time as it is. I think it's a godsend that they want to adopt him. He's been with them a long time now—long enough to consider them his parents."

"I know," she replied with a sigh. She wiped at her eyes. "It's just that . . . I don't know . . . I feel like I'm giving one of my own children away."

He smiled and pressed her tight against himself. "Abbie, Abbie. What am I going to do with you? You can't be mother to every baby who was ever orphaned. You have six of your own to think about and another on the way. Crooked Foot has folks who love him and who can give him everything he needs. What is there to be sad about?"

She sniffed again. "Do you think, perhaps some day we can go North again and see him?"

He ran a hand over her bare back and her hips. "Maybe we can figure out a way. But with all the trouble between soldiers and settlers and Indians, I don't want to risk my family, Abbie. The fact remains that half of us look Indian. We'll have to be careful."

"You think it's all right then? We have to send them written permission."

"I think it's best."

She pulled back and studied his dark eyes in the moon-

367

light. "Kiss me, Zeke. Sometimes I get so scared, and I don't even know what I'm afraid of."

He kissed her lightly. "It's the future, Abbie girl. It's the future we're all afraid of. Seems like everything is exploding all around us. I even heard a man at Bent's Fort talking about a possible civil war. I don't think such a thing would ever come about—something about the North telling the South to free the black slaves. But still, I can't imagine all this trouble with the Indians being added to by a civil war."

They studied each other, and she felt her old fear of having to be separated from him creeping back into her veins. "I don't like it, Zeke. It seems like whatever happens, you get mixed up in it and you're gone again."

He kissed her eyes. "I'm not going anywhere, Abbie girl."

She moved her mouth to meet his, kissing him hungrily, almost desperately, wrapping her arms around his neck like a little child clinging to her father. "Don't go away again, Zeke, ever, ever!" she whimpered.

He moved on top of her, touching familiar places that still fed his manly desires, for this woman fed his emotional needs as no other person would ever do, and therein lay the beauty of their lovemaking. Her sweet love made the sex very exciting, always satisfying. "I'm not going to leave you, Abbie," he whispered. *"Ne-mehotatse."*

His big, strong hands slid under her small hips, while his lips tasted her mouth, instilling in her the peace only he could bring her, assuring her he was there and would not leave her. She was lost beneath the familiar, dark figure that loomed over her then, his masculine needs filling the very air, his lips tenderly caressing her neck, her full breasts, her belly, his big frame bending over to lightly awaken every part of her to his love.

She wondered if this part of their relationship would ever become less passionate, less fulfilling, and she was certain it would not. For the love that brought them together would never become less passionate or less fulfilling, and because of that their mating would always be as necessary and as emotionally vibrant as it had always been, for love erased the years, erased the hurts, erased the bad times. Love went beyond all those things. They were one, not just in body, but in spirit and mind and heart.

His lips met hers again, and he moved between her slim thighs. She could feel the rock-hard muscle of his legs as he pushed against her thighs as she willingly opened herself to him as she had always done in these moments. In the next instant he surged inside of her, as strong and demanding as he had always been, and in that moment of ecstasy and quiet lovemaking, her mind floated back once again to that night deep in the foothills of the Rockies, when Abigail Trent, desperate and alone, lay beneath a Cheyenne scout named Zeke Monroe, and let him change her from child to woman in one moment of desperate need and the passions of young love.

There was a rumbling north of the Arkansas River in Kansas and Nebraska Territory, a rumbling like that of thunder in the distance warning of an impending storm. Senator Stephen A. Douglas of Illinois managed to get a bill into Congress calling for a vote by citizens of Kansas and Nebraska Territories on whether or not slavery should be allowed in those territories. The Douglas Kansas-Nebraska Bill passed, bringing havoc to those territories, and bringing a surge of new emigrants westward, as backers of slavery and those against slavery both began heading into Kansas Territory to try to beef up their numbers and outvote one another. Senator William H. Seward of New York declared: "We will engage in competition for the virgin soil of Kansas, and God give the victory to the side which is stronger in numbers as it is in right."

No bill could have done more damage for the struggling, weary Cheyenne. Massachusetts quickly formed the Emigrant Aid Company, an organization designed to encourage antislavery citizens to head for Kansas.

As bits and pieces of news filtered down to Zeke and Abbie about the bitter fighting taking place in Kansas Territory over slavery, Abbie struggled to shut out the thought of what this new turn of events would mean for the Cheyenne, let alone for herself and Zeke. It seemed ironic to her that white citizens and their white government were suddenly hell-bent on freeing slaves, and at the same time were most assuredly doing everything in their power to either murder or enslave every Indian. She wondered at the antislavery speakers' words about "equality." There was no equality for the Indian, and things were getting even worse as thousands more emigrants filtered into Indian lands. She was not against freeing the slaves, for she remembered hearing about some of the atrocities committed against black slaves in Tennessee. Her own family had been too poor to own slaves, and she had no firsthand, eye-witness experiences of how the wealthy plantation owners treated their slaves. But she knew enough from hearsay and from the knowledge of the way many pious whites looked on anyone with darker skin that the stories she had heard were probably true. But she could not help but wonder why those speaking out about freeing slaves were not also speaking out on behalf of the starving, dispossessed Indians.

It was not long before more stories of outrageous atrocities between proslavery and antislavery factions were carried to Zeke and Abbie by way of travelers and traders through Bent's Fort. Now the territory to the north of them was nicknamed "Bleeding Kansas," and an antislavery extremist by the name of John Brown was apparently dealing out his own form of justice against those who believed in owning slaves. Abbie was relieved that the skirmishes had not made their way into New Mexico Territory; still, they were too close for comfort, and she was grateful for every morning that she awoke to the peaceful sound of birds singing and the gentle flowing of the river not far away.

Zeke continued to be involved only in the problems of the Cheyenne, but she could see by his eyes when they spoke of the slavery issue that if he were not tied down to family, he would run off to Kansas to find out what was going on. Being from Tennessee, he also knew something of the treatment of the slaves. In his youth he had been so involved with finding his Cheyenne mother and with the atrocities

370

being committed against the Creeks and Cherokees that he had not concerned himself with the issue of slavery; nor had he ever been involved directly in the issue, for his family, like Abbie's, was simple and poor. But it became more and more evident that the issue of slavery had become a heated debate in Washington, dangerously volcanic, and the rumors of civil war did not seem so ridiculous any longer.

More troops were brought into Kansas Territory to keep order in that bloody land, and Zeke found more business than ever from army representatives who came down to his ranch on the Arkansas to purchase his horses. It seemed Zeke was already involved indirectly in the bloody confrontation to come, and he was already involved up to his neck in the problems of his Cheyenne family. He was a proud man, apt to fight for what he believed in. Abbie could only bury her fears and pray each night that her God would keep her man at home.

Abbie was glad about her seventh pregnancy, for it kept her worried husband home and prevented him from riding off too often to lend his services to others. Eoveano, Yellow Hawk, whose Christian name was Jason Trent, was born in December of 1858. Abbie had finally given birth to another son, to whom she could give the name of her deceased father. But Zeke's worst fear was realized when she again bled heavily, although not quite as dangerously as she had bled with Jeremy. Zeke made up his mind she must see a doctor, and the only place where a good doctor might be found was Denver, for the discovery of gold had brought out people of all walks of life, and doctors services were in demand there.

"My mind is made up for certain this time, Abbie," he told her. "No more lovemaking until you've seen a doctor. Maybe a good doctor can come up with an answer for us. And you ought to see one anyway. You haven't been to a good doctor since you left Tennessee, and any woman who has birthed seven kids with no help ought to have a good checkup."

"I won't have you leaving my bed again!" she wept. "I won't let us grow apart again!"

He bent over her and took her hands, his heart torn at her pale, drawn face. This seventh birth had been very hard on her. "Look up here, Abbie girl." She met his eyes. "I never said I'd leave your bed," he told her gently. "But I love you too much to be animal enough to lose control of my own needs and risk your health by it. We won't grow apart this time, Abbie. I intend to sleep right here every night like always, holding you just as much as you need to be held. I won't leave you that way again." He kissed her cheek. "It's all right. I'm going to be right here. We'll just let your body rest up and come spring we'll go to Denver. I'd take you to Bonnie's father, but that's too far to go now and the trip is too dangerous. We'll find a doctor in Denver. After the doctor tells us how you are, we'll decide on other things then. Agreed?"

She pulled his hands to her lips and kissed them. "As long as I have you close to me." He studied her lovingly. Sometimes she still seemed like the frightened little girl he had helped on the wagon train West.

"I'll be right here, Abbie. Just like I have always been."

She smiled through her tears and he squeezed her hands. It was decided. They would go to Denver in the spring.

Twenty-One

Zeke waited outside the doctor's office with little Lillian and Jason. The two babies had been brought along on the trip because they were still breast feeding. All the other children, except Little Rock, obediently accepted the fact that there were simply too many Monroe children for all of them to parade along on a trip to Denver, especially when Zeke and Abbie had no idea what a doctor might tell them and how long they might be gone. Twelve-year-old Little Rock promptly informed his parents that he would most certainly go along also, for his father might need help in some way with his mother and the babies, especially since Zeke planned to take a supply of robes, several sacks of potatoes they had kept buried that winter and which were still in excellent shape, and some of the horses. Rumor was that miners paid well for such supplies, and with nine mouths to feed, Zeke decided it wouldn't hurt to sell some supplies and extend his horse trading. His Appaloosas were becoming widely known and admired, from St. Louis in the East, north to Sioux country and south to Santa Fe, for he had been raising and selling his fine steeds since even before he'd married Abbie.

Zeke could not argue with Little Rock's reasoning, for the boy was quite dependable, strong and fearless, good with the lance and excellent at herding horses. And so it was decided that Little Rock should also go to Denver.

Now Zeke waited anxiously while Abbie was examined, while Little Rock stood outside guarding the gear. The horses they had brought along were quickly sold, as well as the other supplies, and Zeke had an ample roll of money hidden inside his weapons belt. Lillian and Jason both slept quietly in their cradleboards next to Zeke on the crude wooden floor of the hastily erected log building that served as temporary offices for the new doctor from the East, who had almost more business than he could handle in the booming new town of Denver. Mining accidents, firearms accidents, fights, diseases of all sorts, as well as a variety of mishaps that occurred to greenhorns from the East who knew nothing about the mountains or the dangers of living in an untamed land, kept the only physician in Denver running night and day.

Zeke shifted uncomfortably on the wooden bench, anxious to know about Abbie's health and anxious to get out of civilization and back to their peaceful home on the Arkansas. Hopefully, there would be some good word from the doctor so that their painful nights of abstaining could be over with. Both realized Abbie's health had to come first, and the pain had been lessened at least by Zeke's gentle understanding and their determination not to let abstinence build a wall between them as it had done before. He had been there to hold her when she needed him, and he in turn took comfort in the holding.

Outside, Little Rock gazed again with utter amazement at the busy and hurried life of the white man who had so quickly built up this town from the tiny tent city that had been erected when gold was discovered at Cherry Creek. The town of Denver had sprung up as the result of the combining of two separate settlements, St. Charles and Auraria. That very spring gold had been discovered also at Clear Creek, thirty miles west of Denver. As a result, an astonishing one hundred thousand people had headed for Denver, and already the town boasted assay offices, drugstores, carpenters, and even a newspaper called *Rocky Mountain News*. Fifteen guidebooks to the Pike's Peak region were published in the East, and the town of Denver had mushroomed into neat rows of cabins, hotels, brothels, land offices, and supply stores.

Little Rock, like his father, preferred the peace of the

Monroe ranch on the Arkansas, and he looked forward anxiously to their return home. He sat beside their horses, peeking between the horses' legs at the myriad of people, reporters, miners, bankers, merchants, prostitutes and mountain men, all seeming to be in a hurry to get wherever it was they intended to go. Little Rock was astounded to see just how many white people had flocked to the area, and he began to worry about how many more there might be in the East to come into Indian lands. Perhaps they would turn all the land into a place like Denver, even his father's ranch. The thought frightened him, and he longed to ride as fast as he could back to the Arkansas to make sure the whites had not already invaded there.

A boy of about sixteen kicked a tin cup ahead of him as he walked down the boardwalk toward Little Rock. He was tall and thin, his face pocked with acne, but his clothes were obviously expensive, and too fashionable for a boy so young. Little Rock rose and stood beside his horse, watching the boy curiously, wondering why he dressed in cumbersome long pants and high, hard boots in such hot weather, and why he had nothing better to do than to stroll down the boardwalk kicking the tin cup. The boy's eyes were oddly glassy, his face hard set, and he looked bored. Little Rock had never been around a white boy even close to his age, and he could not help staring, until the boy stopped in front of him and glanced over at him. His eyes were immediately full of hatred.

"What are you staring at, little brown boy?" he sneered.

Little Rock straightened, his pride immediately wounded. "I do not stare. I only wondered why you kick the cup. Is it a game?"

The white boy chuckled. "Yeah. It's called 'Kick the Indian.' I'm pretending the cup is the scummy Indian that killed my mother," he said with an odd grin. Little Rock wondered for a moment if he was mad, for his eyes were ugly and wild.

"Your mother was killed by Indians?" he asked.

The boy's smile faded and his lip curled. "Yeah, redskin. An Indian, just like you! You're all stinking, dirty murder-

375

ers. I bet you've already killed a white person, haven't you? Maybe a woman, huh? You rape a white woman yet, little brown boy?"

Little Rock was instantly embarrassed and humiliated, his fierce pride deeply wounded. He smashed into the older boy, caring little about the fact that the other boy was much bigger than he. He was too young to know how to ignore insults, too proud to let them go by without a fight, and too full of a wild desire for action to pass up an opportunity to see just how much skill and muscle he had.

In seconds Little Rock had the white boy on his back and was pommeling him with his fists, while the white boy just lay there yelling for help. Zeke frowned at all the commotion and started outside, where by then two men had come along to pull Little Rock off the older boy, who was crying like a baby.

It all happened in seconds. Just as Zeke exited the doctor's office, one of the white men called Little Rock a name and slammed a fist into his face, sending the boy flying into the street, where a passing rider could not stop his horse in time to keep from stepping on the boy's ribs. Zeke's rage knew no bounds. His mind reeled at the sight of Little Rock's flying body and the horror of the horse trampling over it, and in the next second a roaring half-breed was ramming into the man who had hit Little Rock, charging the man like a bull and pushing him through a hitching post, snapping the post in half with the man's back. They landed hard on the ground and Zeke immediately yanked the man back up to his feet, blasting a big fist into the man's ribs several times over, then rending a smashing blow to the man's jaw and sending him flying backward again. Then the big blade was out.

Several men were there by then, as well as a lovely woman in a red satin dress, who watched curiously as the Indian man warded off the efforts of four men to seize him, whirling and slashing with his knife, frightening all of them away from him, his long black hair flying, his face the picture of human fury and vengeance. Three men were bleeding profusely from the wicked blade, and the man Zeke

376

had beaten groaned and tried to rise. Zeke whirled, while the men who had tried to grab him, now afraid of him, watched him approach his would-be victim. One of those watching decided to be the hero of the day. He picked up a large rock and bravely walked up behind the stalking half-breed, slamming the rock into the back of Zeke's head. Zeke stumbled forward, falling to his knees and missing his mark as everything went black. He sank his blade into his victim's thigh, then slumped over unconscious.

Abbie was just exiting the examination room when she heard the shouted words. "Arrest him!" "No, just hang him now! He ain't nothin' but a goddamned Indian anyway!" "Get that knife out of his hand 'fore he wakes up and uses it on somebody else!" "Get Lew into the doctor's office before he bleeds to death!"

Abbie noticed with a pounding heart that Zeke was not sitting in the outer office. "Oh, dear God!" she whispered, hurrying to the door. The doctor frowned and followed her out.

Abbie froze on the boardwalk, seeing the bodies of her husband and little boy lying in the street. "Little Rock!" she screamed. No one seemed eager to help the boy or Zeke, but several men were already carrying the wounded white man into the doctor's office. The doctor stared after Abbie for a moment, aching at the poor woman's plight while the white men shouted at him to hurry up and go inside and help their bleeding friend.

Abbie bent over Little Rock's unconscious body, her body racked with sobs at the sight of the boy's bloody lip and bleeding teeth and the dark bruise already showing itself on his cheek, as well as a purple swelling on his ribs where the horse's hoof had done its damage. She checked frantically for a pulse, unsure of what to do for him, afraid to pick him up, while at the same time several more men were picking up Zeke's body to carry it off to jail. Abbie looked up at them and screamed Zeke's name, leaving her son's side for a moment to run after the men.

"No! No! Where are you taking my husband?" she screamed at them.

The men stopped and stared at her for a moment, shocked to see a white woman pleading on behalf of an Indian. They looked her over as though she were a prostitute. "Who the hell are you, lady?"

"I am Abigail Monroe!" she sobbed. "That man is Zeke Monroe, my husband. Where are you taking him? What has happened?"

The men just grinned and looked her over again. "White squaw, huh?" one of them sneered. "Well your stud Indian husband is gonna hang, lady, for attacking one of our friends and pullin' a knife on him. You'd best go tend to your little maggot over there."

They walked off with Zeke, and Abbie stared after them, feeling helpless and frightened now for her own person and her children. She turned and stumbled blindly back to Little Rock who still lay alone with no one even trying to help him. She kicked something with her foot and looked down to see Zeke's knife. She picked it up, hugging it to her breast as she knelt down beside Little Rock, taking the child's hand and crying out his name, begging him to wake up and speak to her. But the boy lay seemingly lifeless, while the white boy who had picked on him stood at a distance staring and laughing to himself.

"That will teach the little worm to pick on the son of Winston Garvey!" the boy sneered. He turned and walked away.

The woman in the red dress waited until the older boy had left, then hurried to Abbie's side, signaling another woman who had been walking with her to follow. The other woman knelt down and carefully picked up Little Rock in her arms, while Abbie glanced up at her with wide, frightened eyes.

"What are you doing?" she asked.

"You come with us, honey. We'll help him," came the reply. In the brief glance Abbie knew right away the woman was a prostitute, for her face was heavily painted and her hair was bleached, and the dress she wore was fashionable but exposed a great deal of her bosom. The woman in the red dress put a hand on Abbie's upper arm and helped her to her feet.

"Stay with us and you'll be all right," came the comforting words. For some reason, in spite of what these women obviously were, Abbie trusted them. She turned to look into the face of the one in the red dress. She saw a beautiful woman who was just about her own age. The woman's blue eyes were wide, their lashes long and dark. Her dark hair was expertly coifed, with curls dancing over her lily-white shoulders. "I'll get the doc over to my place and he'll look at your boy, Mrs. Monroe," the woman told her. "And don't you worry about Zeke. I have connections in this town. He won't be hung. If he is, there are a hell of a lot of wives here and back East who are going to find out just who visits my place every night."

Abbie watched after the woman, her mind racing with confusion. She had called her Mrs. Monroe, yet Abbie had never met this woman. The woman put a hand to her waist and urged her to follow, but Abbie stopped.

"My babies. My babies are still in the doctor's office," she told the woman with a shaking voice. "And our horses and gear are here. Someone will steal them."

"No one will steal them. I'll take care of it. Go and get your babies." She led the shaking Abbie to the doctor's door. "How many children do you have?" she asked.

"Seven," Abbie answered as they both hurried inside, each picking up a cradleboard while some of the men waiting there watched curiously as the prostitute in the red dress picked up a papoose and carried it out.

"Seven," the woman muttered to herself. "I might have known." she sighed and shook her head. "Where are the rest of them?" she asked.

"Home. Over a week's ride from here," Abbie answered absently, following the woman back out the door, her mind torn between husband and son, her heart hurting from fear and the pain of seeing them hurt. She wanted to go to Zeke, but with a mother, the child always comes first, and she followed the lady in red. The news the doctor had given her would have to wait. It was even more cause for her terrible agony, for it was possible she would produce no more children for Zeke Monroe. But if he did not live, it would

379

not matter.

"Who are you?" she asked in a shaking voice as they hurried down the street after the woman who carried Little Rock.

The woman stopped and turned, meeting Abbie's eyes boldly. "My name is Anna Gale," she replied.

Their eyes held, and Abbie felt faint. This was the woman who had lured Zeke into her bed before she would give him information about Yellow Moon. Her face paled, and it was impossible to hide her shock and jealousy.

"What's past is past," the woman spoke up. "Judging from these two little papooses, you apparently forgave your husband. Knowing Zeke, he most assuredly told you about me. He's too damned honest to do otherwise. Right now there is no time for jealousy or hatred, Mrs. Monroe. We have to help your husband and son. Follow me now. It will be all right."

She turned and kept walking. Abbie stared after her a moment, watching the sway of her walk. She closed her eyes and said a quick prayer, asking God to help her forgive this woman and not hate her. For at this moment Anna Gale was apparently the only person who was going to help her.

Abbie stood nervous and shaking in the gawdy room of one of Anna Gale's prostitutes, feeling awkward and conspicuous in her plain tunic. She was standing on thick oriental carpeting and was surrounded by the color red—the wallpaper, the curtains, the lampshades. There was a rich aroma of expensive perfume in the room, and the bed on which her wounded son lay was a grand brass bed with satin sheets. She had barely spoken two words to Anna Gale, who stood to the side while the doctor studied Little Rock. There had not yet been time for conversation. But Abbie could feel Anna watching her, and she wondered if Anna was just as curious about her as she was about the wicked prostitute who had forced her husband into her bed. Abbie's mind was torn between gratefulness to the woman and a desire to scratch her eyes out and scream at her that she had

380

no right touching Zeke Monroe. But the fact remained that if not for Anna Gale, Abbie would have had no place to turn and there would be no bed now for poor Little Rock, who was at the moment her greatest worry, for he lay lifeless and bruised. If this boy died, Zeke Monroe would also die, if not physically then at least on the inside. He would be a walking dead man without this son whom he loved to the point of worship. Abbie wanted desperately to go to Zeke; she was not even certain how badly he was wounded. But she was forced to make a choice and could not be two places at once. Zeke would understand. The son must come first. She would get a message to him as soon as the doctor told her what condition Little Rock was in.

Watching her son lying injured would not be so painful if only Zeke could be there also. But now there was the added burden of not knowing what was going to happen to Zeke. All of their fear of what could happen to them in a town full of whites had become reality. Perhaps what might have happened to him in Tennessee would happen to him now in this crazy town called Denver. This was no place for men like Zeke, who knew only one kind of justice. Right was right and wrong was wrong, but oddly enough, where there was supposed to be law it didn't seem to work that way. The man Zeke had attacked had not been killed, only injured; and yet Abbie was well aware that Zeke could hang for it. They should never have come. She felt it was her fault. If she hadn't needed a doctor, they wouldn't be here at all; and therein lay even more of a burden, for the doctor's news had not been good. But there was no time to think about that now. First there was Little Rock to tend to—and the matter of keeping Zeke from getting hung.

"He'll be all right," came the wonderful words from the doctor, as he stood up and removed his stethoscope from his ears. "He's a good strong boy. Couple of broken ribs maybe. He'll heal in a couple of weeks—maybe a month for the ribs. I'll wrap them for you."

Abbie closed her eyes and sank into a chair, putting her hands over her face, breaking into the tears she had been holding back. The doctor frowned and came around the bed

381

to her side, carrying a small bottle.

"Now you get hold of yourself, Mrs. Monroe. Everything will be all right," he told her. "I have something here I want you to take and then I want you to lie down and get some sleep. You'll be no good to your son and your husband this way, let alone your babies."

She sniffed and nodded, wiping at her eyes and taking the bottle from him. "I . . . thank you . . . for tending to my son," she said brokenly. "Some doctors won't treat Indians."

He patted her shoulder. "Well, I treat anyone who needs it. You get some rest and we'll do something about your son and your husband. Then we'll worry about the other problem. You just take it easy and keep your strength."

Abbie nodded again and wiped at her eyes while the doctor returned to Little Rock, preparing to wrap the boy's ribs. Abbie sniffed, and in the next moment a lovely hand was in front of her, holding out a feminine handkerchief. "Need this?" came the lilting voice.

Abbie looked up at Anna Gale and their eyes held, challenging at first, until Abbie's softened. The woman was right. What was past was past, and she must struggle to bury her jealousy of this woman who was now being kind to her.

"Thank you," she told Anna quietly, noticing a sweet scent on the handkerchief when she put it to her nose.

Anna glanced at the doctor, then touched Abbie's shoulder. "Come with me into the next room, Mrs. Monroe."

Abbie shook her head. "I . . . don't want to leave my son."

"He'll be all right for a few minutes. Please. I want to talk to you alone."

Abbie glanced at Little Rock. The doctor was still with him and the boy was still unconscious. She looked up at Anna, constantly overwhelmed by the woman's beauty and the thought of how pleasant it had to have been for Zeke to bed her. The unwanted wave of jealousy swept over her again. She had made a promise when she had put on her wedding band when Zeke first returned that they would not speak of Anna Gale again. But now the woman was standing before her, and the reality of it was difficult to bear. She saw an oddly pleading look in Anna's eyes, and she nodded, rising and following her out of the room and across the hall to another room, this one even more elegant, everything decorated in a lush orchid color. Abbie walked inside and clung to the thick poster of a grand four-poster bed, feeling weak. Anna closed the door.

"Sit down, Mrs. Monroe. I'll get you a drink."

"I . . . don't drink," Abbie protested.

"Your husband might get himself hung and your son is badly wounded. I'd say that calls for something stiff, whether you drink or not," Anna replied, going to a cabinet in the corner and taking out a crystal bottle, pouring something into a small glass. She came to Abbie and held it out, and again their eyes held. This time Anna's softened. "You're one hell of a lucky woman, Abigail Monroe," she told her. "Just plain one hell of a woman—period—to capture and hold that wild animal sitting in jail down the street. How did you do it?"

Abbie's emotions were again mixed, for she could see the admiration in Anna Gale's eyes and had to appreciate the compliment. "I . . . don't really know," she answered, taking the glass. She sipped it and made a face.

"Drink it quick. It will burn, but then you'll feel better, I guarantee."

Abbie closed her eyes and took a deep breath, then swallowed it quickly, shuddering afterward with the bitterness and heat of the drink. Anna grinned, then chuckled.

"Sit down on the bed, honey. It won't bite you."

Abbie swallowed and sat down slowly, wondering with renewed raging jealousy if this was the kind of bed Zeke had shared with this ravishing prostitute. Anna sat down in a chair close by.

"I'll tell you how you captured that savage," she told Abbie. "Just by being yourself. You're all goodness and honesty and loyalty. It's written all over your face. You're just the kind of woman a man like Zeke would want. I'll bet if he told you to jump off a mountain for him you'd do it.

And I'll bet it didn't take you long to forgive him for being with me, did it?"

Abbie blushed, looking at the floor. "You gave him little choice." Then she raised her eyes to meet Anna's, unable to read the woman just then, except that there was a strange longing in Anna's eyes. "It was easy to forgive him," she continued. "Because I know he would never willingly be untrue to me. And because he . . . he made a sacrifice . . . to show me how it pained him to cheat on me. He thought that being a white woman, I would not understand and would turn him away. You should know that because of what you made him do, he cut off the end of his little finger, wanting to suffer because he would make me suffer."

Anna paled slightly and leaned forward. "You're joking!"

Abbie blinked back tears. "No, Miss Gale. It's the Cheyenne way—to suffer for having caused a loved one pain."

Anna let out a long sigh and rose to pour herself a drink. "I'll be damned," she muttered. "This calls for a stiff one for me." She slugged down the burning booze easily, then turned and walked over to kneel in front of Abbie. "Look, Mrs. Monroe, I called you in here to talk so the doctor wouldn't know about me and Zeke. I figured maybe you wouldn't want him to know. But I just wanted to tell you I . . . uh . . . I admire you, believe it or not. Ever since I was with your husband I had this funny feeling. I don't know why, but after he left I couldn't get my mind off of you— what you might be like and all. And that man," she shook her head, "he was absolutely devastated—walked out of that room looking like a little boy who had done something bad and would have to go home and tell his mother about it. If it weren't so pitiful, it would be humorous, him being such a big, mean varmint and all. Ever since then he's been on my mind often, mainly because I wanted him to like me—because I wanted to do something to show him I wasn't all bad. When I saw him standing there in the street, I couldn't believe my eyes—Zeke Monroe." She breathed deeply and shook her head. "I never thought I'd see him again. Then when I saw you running out there, I knew who you had to be, and I couldn't fight the sudden urge to help you."

Abbie looked down at the hanky, twisting it in her fingers and feeling more relaxed from the small drink. "You're helping because of Zeke, not for my sake. I've been married to him a long time, Miss Gale. I'm not blind to the effect a man like Zeke can have on a woman," she continued boldly, feeling braver because of the whiskey. "I am aware that women find him appealing. But Zeke and I have . . . something very special." She swallowed back new tears that wanted to come. "We've been through hell more than once, Miss Gale . . . saved each other's lives, fought side by side. Zeke delivered all of our children himself. He has been my friend and lover, father and provider since I was fifteen years old and he was a scout for my father's wagon train. I lost my family, and Zeke . . ." she turned away and rose, walking to a window, "Zeke is the only man who has ever touched me. He's never touched another woman since he gave himself to me. You had no right doing what you did. I'd rather you'd have taken all our money, than to have touched my husband." Her voice broke and she swallowed hard, forcing herself not to cry. "You . . . have me in a strange position, Miss Gale," she continued after a moment. "It isn't easy for me to . . . look at you . . . to talk to you. But you have helped me and my son, and I must thank you for that."

Anna sighed and rose herself, coming to stand behind her. "Mrs. Monroe, I was raised an orphan back East. I was beat on, kicked around, and raped by my factory boss when I was only twelve years old. I took the only road that is open to someone like me. It made me what I am, and I make no apologies now." Abbie turned to face her, finding a tiny bit of pity in her heart at the words. "Oh, I could change," Anna went on, "but once a whore always a whore—at least that's the way any good man would think of it. So I'll stay what I am and get rich. But I'd rather be dirt poor and have a man like Zeke Monroe any day. You have a part of him women like me could never have. In a way I never touched that man at all. Don't you understand that?"

Their eyes held for a long moment. "I think I do," Abbie

told her quietly.

"You know you do. Because you know Zeke Monroe better than anybody. You know why he cut off his finger for you. Do you know what I would give to have a man who would do something like that for me?" She shrugged again. "But such a thing will never be. What would be nice is to think that a woman like yourself might consider calling me her friend."

Abbie frowned, surprised at the statement. She saw the strange pleading look in Anna Gale's eyes again, and suddenly they were both simply women, understanding women's feelings and needs. She saw that behind the painted Anna Gale in the red dress lay a woman no different from herself, a woman whose life had turned out very differently through the simple matter of fate. Her jealousy and dislike of the woman suddenly drained from her.

"You have helped me," she told the woman. "How can I not call you friend? It is as you said. The past is past. Zeke and I settled it years ago and have not spoken of it since. I guess that means I should include not speaking with you about it. Fate often deals us a cruel hand, Miss Gale. It has dealt many blows to me and to Zeke. But at least we had each other. With Zeke . . ." Her eyes teared and she turned away again, then felt Anna's hand on her arm.

"Look, I think I can get Zeke out of this."

Abbie turned back, her eyes wet and pleading. "How?"

Anna just winked. "Trust me. I can be a very scheming lady, as you already know. There are a few men in this town who will have a hand in deciding Zeke's fate. I happen to know some of them . . . intimately." She smiled a crooked smile. "I'll be leaving soon to go and do some dirty work. I'm very good at it, you know."

Abbie felt a smile passing her own lips. "I'll be forever grateful, Miss Gale, if you can help him."

Anna patted her arm. "Call me Anna. You go back in there with your son and I'll go see how Zeke is doing. You'd best not go to that jail. Some of the men might not treat you kindly, honey. You know how they can be. That's why Zeke stays around his own people." She frowned. "What on earth brought you to Denver in the first place? This is dangerous territory for men who don't live by white man's law."

Abbie's eyes clouded again. "I . . . had to see the doctor." She turned away again. "I . . . my last baby brought . . . heavy bleeding. It happened once before. Zeke is afraid if I have any more—" She swallowed. "He wanted me to see a doctor before we . . . before . . . you know." She looked down at the twisted hanky again.

Anna smiled and shook her head at the woman's bashfulness at talking about such things, secretly loving Zeke Monroe more for being so thoughtful of his wife. "What did the doctor tell you, Mrs. Monroe?"

"You can call me Abbie," Abbie replied. She swallowed again. "The doctor wants to operate on me . . . something about little growths . . . inside me . . . that should be removed. He said . . . I wouldn't be able to have any more children." Her voice broke and Anna frowned.

"Is that so bad? My goodness you told me you have seven! How wonderful that you've given Zeke seven children."

Abbie put a hand to her face. "But I'm only twenty-eight!" she sobbed. "What will Zeke think? How . . . will he feel . . . knowing I can't have any more children?"

Anna shook her head. "Don't be a fool, Abbie. The only thing that man cares about is having you for the rest of his life. What good would three or four more children do him if his wife dies having one of them? In heaven's name, woman, you've given him seven children! Count them! Seven! Maybe somebody upstairs is saying enough is enough and the good Lord wants you to rest now and enjoy the children you already have . . . time to enjoy your man without always having to worry about getting pregnant again. Zeke will probably be relieved. Maybe what you have will kill you if you don't have the operation. Then who would take care of your babies and your husband? Is that what you want? To die and leave them all alone with no wife and no mother?"

"No, of course not," Abbie sniffed.

Anna hesitantly put a hand lightly on Abbie's shoulder. "Look, honey, Doc Bartlett is good—real good. I've been to him myself. We prostitutes have female problems just like anybody else. He knows what he's doing and you'll be all right, and that's all that is important. Don't you be afraid of a thing."

Abbie wiped at her eyes. "I won't be afraid, if Zeke is with me. But if he isn't there—"

"Don't you worry. He'll be there. You just go on back in there with your son and stay with him and rest. I have some fast work to do. I'll go see Zeke and tell him you and his son and the babies are all right."

Abbie turned to meet her eyes once more, a trace of doubt still there. Anna grinned. "Don't worry. I'll keep my hands off him. For once in my life I'll be a decent woman, but that's a real hard thing for a woman like me."

Their eyes held. "I don't think it is, Anna," Abbie replied.

Anna's grin faded and she suddenly turned away, not wanting Abbie to see the trace of tears in her eyes. "Let's get you back across the hall. The doc must be done by now."

"Anna," Abbie spoke up. The woman stopped at the door. "Tell him . . . I love him. But . . . don't tell him what I just told you . . . about what the doctor said. I . . . want to tell him myself. He'll just worry, and he has enough to worry about."

The woman nodded. "Sure." She went through the door and Abbie hurried after her.

"Let me in there, Jack, or you'll never do business at my place again!" Zeke heard the female voice in the outer office. It sounded familiar, but he was too upset to try to place it. He remained standing at the jailhouse window, gripping the bars to the tiny open square and wondering if he could rip the bars out and crawl through. The excruciating pain in his head was only made worse by his terror over what might have happened to his family, and not knowing if his son was alive.

The door from the outer office opened and closed, but he did not turn to look. It was probably a visitor for someone

388

else. With Little Rock hurt, Abbie would not be able to come. But then the keys rattled to his own cell door. He turned to look, stunned to see Anna Gale coming inside his cell.

"You're taking your life in your hands going into a cell with an Indian," the sheriff was telling her.

Anna just grinned, looking Zeke up and down as he stared back at her in surprise. "Oh, I don't think so, Jack," she replied. "Now get out of here and leave me alone with him for a few minutes."

The man called Jack shook his head and relocked the door before leaving. Zeke and Anna stood staring at each other, he with mere confusion and surprise; she with reawakened passions she had not felt since Zeke Monroe left her bed.

"Your son is all right, Zeke," she told him quickly. "His eyes are open but he isn't talking yet. The doc says he'll be okay, though. He has a couple of broken ribs and a badly bruised jaw, but he's a tough little devil, just like his father."

She saw the incredible relief on his face, and he turned away, grasping the bars and looking out the window again. He threw his head back and breathed deeply, as though struggling not to weep.

"I . . . don't understand," he said in a strained voice. "What are you doing in Denver, and how do you know . . . about my boy?"

"I saw the whole thing. Your son made the fatal mistake of pouncing on the son of one Winston Garvey, who is also in Denver now."

Zeke turned, frowning. "Garvey?" He ran a hand through his hair. "His boy must be three or four years older than Little Rock."

"He is. But your son is probably twice as strong. Frankly, I enjoyed seeing Garvey's crazy brat get licked. I don't like him. He frightens me. He isn't all there upstairs, know what I mean?"

Zeke remembered the young boy who had kicked at him and shouted obscenities when he had gone to Winston Garvey's to get Yellow Moon. He nodded. "My wife. What

389

about my wife?"

"She's fine. She's with your son and the two young ones."

"Where?"

She grinned. "At my place." She saw the instant fear and disgust in his eyes. "Look, my Cheyenne lover, I know she's too good for the likes of a brothel, but right now it's the safest place for her. I'll not let anything happen to her. My place is clean and quite comfortable. She'll get a good rest and your son can recover there. I've come here to tell you they're all right and that I intend to help you out of this mess. The man you attacked is alive and will do okay."

He studied the blue eyes. "Why are you doing this? What do you want in return this time?"

She actually reddened slightly. "Believe it or not I want to show you that I can do something decent once in a while," she replied. "And I am also doing it because you are the only man who has left my bed whom I missed afterward, the only man who has ever harassed my mind and heart after he was gone. I've thought about you often, Zeke Monroe, wondered about the woman you were so against betraying. Now I've met her. That's quite a wife you have there. She knows who I am, but she's been nice to me; and considering all the children she says the two of you have, she apparently forgave you for our little liaison." She stepped closer and took his left hand, lifting it to look at the stub of his finger. "Well, I'll be damned. You really did go and cut it off."

"She told you that?"

She raised her eyes to meet his. "We had a lot of time to talk." She studied the dark eyes and the hard lines of his face. "She said to tell you she loves you, as if you didn't know." She sighed. "What a lucky woman she is," she added almost wistfully. The softness in her eyes surprised him. For a brief moment the hard shell she usually donned to guard against her hard life was gone. "I could almost love a man like you myself," she told him. Then she smiled a crooked smile and let go of his hand. "But women like me aren't supposed to love a man. Bad for business, you know."

She folded her arms and turned to look out the cell door. "Right now we have to get you out of here. That is our number one problem. I can tell you what they'll do. There will be an investigation." She turned to look at him again. "Under normal circumstances, meaning if you were white, you would automatically get a light sentence at the investigation. If you had committed murder, you would get a trial. But you are half Indian, so there will definitely be no trial, murder or not. Indians are not allowed such things. What would normally happen is that you would probably be hung after a quick mock hearing, even though you didn't kill the man."

He frowned. "The son-of-a-bitch hit my son! My boy might have died! What the hell was I supposed to do, stand there and shake his hand?"

She smiled a little and came closer, putting her hands at his sides. "Calm down, Indian. I'm just explaining what will probably happen. But I intend to see that you go free—that the excuse that you were defending your little boy gave you the right to go after the man, that you acted out of grief and a father's protectiveness."

He sighed and turned back to the window. "You just said Indians don't get any justice. What makes you think you can get me freed?"

She laughed lightly. "Come now, Zeke, not *all* men tell their wives about their visits with me the way you did."

He turned back around, and after a moment of thought he suddenly grinned a little. The handsome smile warmed her heart.

"That's blackmail," he told her.

Her full lips were still smiling. "That's right. You leave it all to me, Zeke," she told him. "And if it doesn't work, I'll come up with a way to help you escape. If the worst should happen, I'll see that your wife and family get safely back to wherever it is you live."

He came closer and put his hands on her shoulders. "I don't know what to say, Anna. I've never been in a position like this, where I couldn't go to my family and help them." He looked around the cell and let go of her, walking to the

391

bars. "I have to get out of here, Anna! I'll go crazy in here. I have to see my son and hold my woman and feel the wind in my face."

She stepped up and ran a gentle hand over his back. "I know. I'll do what I can. Just don't do anything foolish, Zeke. I can get you out of here without risk. But if you try to escape on your own, you'll be shot down on sight. By the way, I have your weapons and your gear. Everything is safe."

He turned to study her eyes, and he saw no deceit there. He unbuckled his weapons belt and unlaced the inside of it, pulling out the money he had made from selling his horses and supplies. "See that Abbie gets this. If anything happens to me, she'll need it. If the sheriff and those men find it on me, they'll keep it."

She took the roll of bills and shoved it into her handbag. "She'll get it."

"What about Winston Garvey? The man is rich and powerful, and we had a run-in when I went to his place down in Santa Fe to get Yellow Moon. If he knows it's me in here, he might do his best to get me hung, just to get rid of me."

"Winston just made a trip to Washington on business—probably cooking up a way to steal some more Indian land, I don't doubt. You're lucky. He isn't in town. He'll never know Zeke Monroe was here." Her face clouded. "I wish it were as easy for me to get out from under that fat slob's thumb." She shrugged. "But then we all get ourselves into our own messes, don't we?" She looked up at him and smiled sadly.

"Why are you under his thumb?" Zeke asked. "Do you owe him money?"

She laughed lightly. "A considerable amount. It seems my threat to go to his new and very proper wife isn't good enough." She shrugged again. "The bitch probably wouldn't believe it anyway. I have no proof."

He put a hand on her arm, and her blood felt warmer at his very touch. "Anna, what if you did have proof, of something much more damaging than his being associated with

392

you—something that to his wife would be much more degrading—something he would never want his son to know?"

She looked up at him hopefully. "What are you talking about?"

He squeezed her arm. "Winston Garvey has another son—a half-breed."

She studied his eyes in confusion, then her eyes began to light up with incredible but evil joy. "Yellow Moon?"

He nodded. "She gave birth to a crippled half-breed boy. There is no doubt whose it is because she never flowed after leaving Garvey's home. Yellow Moon is dead now. She was killed when her village was attacked by soldiers. But the boy lives, and only Abbie and I know where he is and who he is, other than the people who have him now. I'll not give you their names. Suffice it to say that he does exist, and you can tell Winston Garvey you know he exists. Abbie and I can put something in writing that you could put someplace safe. We could simply say that if you die under any unusual circumstances, the law is to contact us for some vital information. That would protect Garvey from harming you, because if he does, we will have some very interesting things to tell the investigators. We could not only reveal that Garvey has a half-breed son, but we could probably hang Garvey himself. You don't need to give him any names at all. Just tell him you know the boy exists and all you want is to be let off the hook and to be independent of him."

She smiled the crooked smile again. "Well, well. If you wanted to repay me for helping you, Zeke Monroe, you couldn't have thought of a better way." Her eyes actually teared with relief, and she could not resist giving him a quick hug. "Thank you for the information," she said quietly.

He put his arms around her for a brief, hesitant moment. "Thank you . . . for helping my son and my wife."

She pulled back from him and smiled, blinking back tears, then turned and shouted for the sheriff. Zeke stepped back as the man came in and unlocked his cell door.

"You all right?" the man asked Anna. Anna glanced back at Zeke once more and smiled.

"I'm fine," she answered. She hurried out and the sheriff slammed the door shut again, glaring at Zeke.

"I could use a drink," Zeke told the man.

The man grunted a laugh. "You could also go to hell!" he sneered.

Twenty-Two

Little Rock opened his eyes to see his mother sitting beside him and holding his hand. "Mother?" he muttered, his lips swollen and painful.

Abbie was immediately bending over him. She kissed his forehead gently. "You must lie very still, Little Rock," she told him, overjoyed that he had spoken and his eyes were brighter now. "You have a couple of broken ribs, sweetheart."

The boy's dark eyes quickly glanced all around the bed. "Where is he? Where is . . . my father?"

Her chest tightened. "He'll be along," she lied.

His breathing quickened. "A man . . . hit me. Did Father hurt the man?"

She closed her eyes. He was as difficult to lie to as Zeke was. She picked up the boy's hand, its knuckles raw from hitting the Garvey boy. She kissed the sore knuckles. "Yes, son. Your father is all right, though. Some men are just questioning him, that's all. He'll be along soon."

The boy swallowed and sniffed. "But . . . the man . . . hit me. It was all right . . . for Father to hit him back."

"Darling, we are in a city. They have laws here. You can't just attack a man at will."

"Those are . . . stupid laws!" the boy choked out, struggling not to cry. "I . . . do not like . . . this place! The boy I hit . . . said dirty things . . . to me. He called me . . . names . . . bad names. He was . . . bad. And now . . . men have taken my father. I know it . . . or he would be here now."

She gently stroked the thick dark hair back from his face. "Please stay calm, Little Rock. A nice woman is helping us, and the doctor has been very nice also. Everything will work out."

A tear slipped down the side of his face into his ear. "I . . . hate . . . white men! I hate them!" the boy choked out. "I want . . . to go back . . . and see Black Elk. I want to . . . go ride my horse . . . and hunt the buffalo. I never want—"

She struggled against her own tears. "I know, my darling. We'll go home just as soon as you can ride. But you shouldn't hate all whites, Little Rock. I am white, you know. And the woman who is helping us and the doctor who examined you are white. They aren't all like that boy who called you names."

The boy shook his head. "I . . . cannot help it. They all . . . look at me and my father . . . the same way. I . . . hate them all."

Her heart felt shattered. He was slipping even further away from her. This incident would only make matters worse.

"Look at me, Little Rock. Am I like that?"

He met her eyes, this white mother of his who was so good to him. "You are . . . different."

She shook her head. "I am not so different. There are many others like me. You forget that there are also Indians who are bad, like Dancing Moon."

Another tear slipped down the side of his face. "Not so many. Not like the whites. I do not care what you say. I do not like them. I will . . . never say that I have white blood in my veins!"

She hung her head, wanting to scream out the pain of his words. Then his brown hand, now as big as his mother's, squeezed her hand.

"I am . . . sorry," he told her. "I have hurt you."

She shook her head. "It's all right, Little Rock."

He swallowed. "I . . . love you, Mother. I do not care . . . what you say about the others. No other white woman . . .

is as good as you."

Abbie sipped her tea, watching Anna Gale position her feathered hat several different ways, searching for the most provocative position. She intended to do her very best job of intimidating a few men this day. It was time for the hearing on Zeke Monroe. Anna had done some visiting the day before, and had had some notes delivered to a few she could not reach. She had every confidence that the hearing would result in Zeke's dismissal, or a few men would have some explaining to do to their wives.

"Don't you worry about a thing, honey. I'll make those bastards so uncomfortable they'll be shaking Zeke's hand and telling him to come back to Denver any time."

Abbie smiled softly. "I'm very grateful. I just hope your idea works."

Anna turned and winked, and Abbie again had to bury her burning jealousy at the sight of the remarkably beautiful woman. "You bet it will work," she answered. "I have already paid a private visit to each and every one of those pious gents and told them exactly what I will do about any one of them who says Zeke should be jailed or hung. I'm going to that hearing today and plop myself right where they can all see me. I said I'd go to their wives if they don't let Zeke go, and they know I'll do it. They'll free him, all right." She fused with a hat pin. "You just sit tight here and we'll be back in no time. Besides, Denver is too damned busy a town to waste time on a needless hanging. There are men in this town who want to show how civilized and advanced we're becoming. Hanging an innocent man wouldn't help their image." She studied herself in the mirror once more.

"You're very beautiful," Abbie told her.

Anna shrugged. "I wish I had your kind of beauty. Mine is painted on. Yours is natural. You're a very lovely woman, Abbie Monroe. You don't need a damned thing to make you pretty. I envy you. How you've kept yourself so well living out there among savages I can't imagine."

Abbie smiled softly. "Thank you, Anna—for the room and all—and for trying to help Zeke."

The woman smiled the crooked smile and stood up, scanning Abbie's fine figure with her eyes. "Don't thank me yet, honey. Thank me when I bring that crazy savage of yours back with me. And do me a favor after this. Keep that wild man down on the farm, will you? He shouldn't be in places like Denver. Civilization is dangerous for his kind."

Abbie had to smile more. "I don't think I'll have any trouble once we leave. He'll be ready to ride in open spaces again."

Anna nodded. "I can just imagine." She picked up a parasol that matched her dress and hat. "Say your prayers, honey. I'm sure they do more good coming from you than from me." She winked again and strutted through the door.

It seemed hours while Abbie waited. The noise of every-day business in the streets below met her ears and she wondered at how quickly a once desolate spot could fill up with emigrants. It was almost frightening to think of all the changes that had taken place since first she had come West with her father. This place called Denver hadn't even existed three years earlier. She glanced at her son. Freedom for those such as he was fast fading. What would the Indians do without their freedom? She shuddered at the thought. Gold, greed, hunger for land, all these seemed to be taking precedence over everything else. If the Indian had to die or be moved, then so be it. It seemed the whole country was in an upheaval, for news continued to spread of even worse fighting in Kansas, and the even stronger possibility of civil war. Such a war seemed incredibly impossible. Too many things were happening too fast. It was frightening to think about. Yet she knew she could handle it all as long as she had Zeke to hold her. That was the important thing. She could even bear the operation, if she had Zeke there, and as long as he didn't mind that she could be barren.

A mantel clock ticked away in the red-curtained harlot's room. It seemed strange to be sleeping in this house of sin, and she wondered at women like Anna Gale. Were they truly so different from someone like herself? So much of life seemed to be guided by fate alone, as though one's destiny was already mapped out from the day one was born. Perhaps that was the way it was after all. Perhaps no one really had total control over his destiny. She looked at Little Rock again, who lay sleeping. What would be his destiny? With the impending Indian problems and the threat of a civil war, his destiny could only be a savage one. Perhaps even her own would be savage.

Then she heard the familiar voice outside the door as he came up the stairs. She heard Anna laugh, and again her chest felt heavy with the agony of knowing he had slept with the beautiful prostitute, and the irony of the fact that the very woman she should hate had been their only help. The door opened, and Abbie stood there frozen for a moment at the sight of them together. But the remnants of jealousy vanished as their eyes held and he quickly walked closer, enveloping her in his arms. He was free.

"Zeke," she whispered, reassuring herself that he was really there by breathing deeply of the familiar scent of man and leather, feeling his hair brush against her face, feeling the strength of the powerful arms that held her so tightly now, himself not even speaking. Neither of them noticed the door close softly as Anna Gale left them alone and went to her own room, her own body aching to be held by Zeke Monroe. Still, she was totally surprised at how good it could feel to do something decent. But there was still a certain wickedness about her, as well, that made her smile slyly at the thought of how uncomfortable she had made the men at the meeting, at how she knew most of them intimately. An even more pleasing thought was how pale Winston Garvey's face would get when she told him he had a half-breed son.

Abbie opened her eyes to pain and the blurred red paisley wallpaper of the room at Anna Gale's whorehouse. Almost immediately her mind rushed to reality, finding it almost cruelly humorous to be lying in a harlot's bed, the mother of seven children by one man, now possibly unable to give him any more. Any prostitute would be happy to know she was safe from pregnancy, but such a thought only made Abbie feel hollow and useless.

She moved only her eyes, afraid to move anything else yet; and she saw Zeke at the window, standing and gazing at the sky. Surely he longed to escape from this prison that was called civilization, just as his son also longed to go home, to the Arkansas, to the wide plains, to the People. But as always, she came first. Perhaps if the worst had been done, and the doctor had been forced to make her barren, it was best after all. For Zeke had been tortured by the fear of her having any more babies. If that fear was always to be present, perhaps they could never fully and joyfully perform that act that was most vital to their great love.

"Zeke?" she spoke up weakly.

He turned, his hollow, circled eyes telling her how worried he had been about her even surviving the operation. In two long strides he was beside her bed, bending over her, placing a big hand to the side of her face. Somehow his touch always gave her the reassurance and the strength she needed when she thought all was lost. She closed her eyes and a tear slipped down the side of her face. He caught it with his finger before it could go into her ear.

"It's all right, Abbie girl," he told her softly. "The doctor says everything went real well and that you're very strong and everything he left looks good and healthy. Soon as you're strong enough we can get out of this place and go home."

She only nodded slightly. "I need . . . to cry . . . but it hurts to cry," she whispered.

"Then don't cry, Abbie. You've nothing to cry about." He bent down and kissed her forehead. "Look here at me."

She met his eyes and knew her worst fear had been met. "I'm . . . barren," she said quietly.

He studied her a moment, gently pushing the lustrous dark hair back from her face, loving her for being upset over such a thing after already giving him seven children. There would be eight now, if not for the child Dancing Moon had

400

caused her to lose.

"It's better than death, Abbie. The doctor said you never would have survived another pregnancy. Is that what you would have wanted, to leave me alone with seven youngsters?"

She closed her eyes again. "No," she squeaked.

"We all need you, Abbie girl. Need you bad. There's no more room, no more time and no more money for any more children. You have all you can handle, and if you want the truth, I'm glad I don't have to worry about it anymore."

She opened her eyes and met the gentle dark eyes of this man who had been her dearest friend and only lover for thirteen years. "Are you sure?"

He smiled softly. "Sure I'm sure." He ran his hand gently through her hair. "Now we can enjoy each other all we want. Our love can be more free and unplanned." He gave her a wink. "That doesn't sound so bad, does it?"

She swallowed. "Some men . . . think . . . I mean, especially Indian men . . . don't want a barren wife. Sometimes they take a second wife . . . a younger one who—"

He laughed lightly, taking her hands. "Abigail Monroe, you amaze me." he knelt beside the bed. "Sometimes you talk as silly as that fifteen-year-old girl who chased me all over the place a few years back on that wagon train till she wore me down and got me to make a woman out of her."

Her eyes widened. "I did not chase you, Zeke Monroe!"

He smiled the handsome smile. "Then why was I so out of breath all the time?" She reddened and he chuckled, studying her lovingly. He gently grasped her chin in one hand. "Abbie, I'll tell you once and then I don't want to talk about it anymore. I don't want you fretting over not having any more children. I love you, and your life is worth more to me than any number of children. If this had happened after only one child, it wouldn't have mattered. What matters is having you beside me in the night, having you around to talk to, knowing you're my woman and that you love me. A man like me needs your kind of quiet, loyal love. You've given me seven children, Abbie, three of them fine sons. I couldn't ask for more, and I wouldn't if I could. I have more

401

than I ever dreamed could be possible a few years back after I lost Ellen and our son. I never imagined I could ever be happy again. But you changed all that just by the touch of your hand that first night we met at your pa's campfire. Now just knowing you'll live and probably be healthier than you've been in a long time makes me a happy man. The doctor did what he had to do for your health, and he asked my permission first. I told him to go ahead. He would have tried something less drastic, but I didn't want to risk it. Do you understand what I'm telling you?"

She watched the firm conviction in his eyes. "I . . . think so."

"It was my decision, Abbie. Mine. It was what I wanted because it was the only way to be sure we'd grow old together." His eyes teared. "I don't want to grow old alone, Abbie. There's so much sorrow ahead for the People. I can see it already. I can't handle that, help them, without the strength I get from you."

She reached up and traced a finger over the thin scar on his cheek from the old Crow knife wound. "But you're such a strong man, Zeke . . . always so sure about everything."

He took her hand and kissed the back of it. "There's different kinds of strength, Abbie girl. You know that as well as I, after that time we grew apart when Jeremy was born. We've done what was best, and I don't want you shedding one tear over it. You be proud of the fact that you've borne seven beautiful children for your man, risked your life doing it. You're still my lovely Abbie, my woman, my friend, the mother of my children, the prettiest girl I ever set eyes on. I've been so afraid for you, Abbie, living away from civilization, giving up a whole way of life just for me. At least now there's one less thing I have to worry about you dying from out there all alone."

"I promised you . . . I'd give you lots of children . . . to make up for the son you lost."

He smiled. "And you did just that. You kept your promise."

"I never minded, Zeke. I never minded . . . the pain of birth. You were . . . always there . . . and I was never afraid

402

when you were there. You . . . made a good midwife."

She smiled lightly and he grinned more, but she quickly bit her lip as a few more tears trickled from her eyes. "Hold me, Zeke," she whimpered. "I don't care . . . if it hurts. Just . . . bend over and hold me for a little while."

He carefully sat down on the bed, leaning over and moving one arm under her neck and gently drawing her close so that she could nestle her head against his side. He took a leather pouch from his belt. "Put out your hand, Abbie," he told her quietly, as she struggled against the sobs that brought so much pain. She asked no questions but did as he asked. She felt something smooth and round in her palm as he emptied something from the little pouch into her hand. "Remember these?" he asked her.

She blinked through tears at the lovely blue stones. "The crying stones!" she exclaimed, staring at the first gift Zeke Monroe had ever given her when she was but a child of fifteen. She remembered how he'd used them to calm a small girl on the wagon train who had been bitten by a rattler, putting the child in a virtual spell as he spun a tale about letting the stones cry for her; and they had seemed to do just that as they began to sweat when he laid them in front of the little girl's eyes. Later he had given the stones to Abbie, a token of friendship at the time, telling her to always let the stones cry for her.

"I . . . had these in my parfleche . . . at home," she sniffed, "with all my other souvenirs."

"I know. But I had a feeling . . . considering the reason we were coming here . . . that maybe you'd need them." He folded her fingers around them and wrapped his own big hand around her small fist. "My first gift of friendship. I didn't know then we would be much more than friends. I loved you even then, Abbie, as I love you now." He placed her hand against his heart. *"Ne-mehotatse."*

She raised her eyes to meet his and knew what had happened was best. "This reminds me . . . of the time you sewed me up . . . from that arrow wound," she told him.

He nodded and their eyes held, each remembering so much. How could so many things have happened in only

403

thirteen years? Indians and outlaws, the sad death of her family. So many were gone now, Zeke's gracious and patient Cheyenne mother, Red Eagle and Yellow Moon, the little girl Abbie had saved from drowning, her whole family and many of her Cheyenne friends. Gone. But there were the children now . . . the children would take the place of loved ones lost. At least God had given her seven before she was made barren, and she still had their father, scarred from his many battles, but alive and well, virile and handsome and rock-hard strong as he was the first time she set eyes on him.

"*Ne-mehotatse*," she whispered, pressing the crying stones tightly in her hand.

Abbie walked to the door again. How many times a day did she stand there, watching for her son?

"It's October, Zeke. It's cold in the mountains."

"He'll be along."

"But he's only twelve years old. He's just a baby."

Zeke sighed and rose from the table where he had been cleaning his rifle. He came up behind her and put strong, reassuring arms around her, hugging her tightly. How frail she still seemed, but her color was good. She had spent eight weeks recuperating in Denver from the operation. It was done. There would be no additional children for Zeke and Abbie Monroe, and he was glad of it. He no longer had to worry about her dying in childbirth.

On their journey home, Little Rock, still injured physically and emotionally from the scrap in Denver, had made the announcement that he would go to the mountains alone to seek a vision and find himself, where he would decide if he was to forever be an Indian and nothing more.

"Twelve years old is only a baby to a white woman," Zeke told her, kissing the top of her head. "To an Indian it's close to being a man. He's strong and independent and willful. He knows how to survive, Abbie. He knows how to hunt and he's afraid of nothing. This is something he must do." He sighed. "You knew when you married me, Abbie girl, that it might be this way for one or more of our children. But I understand how hard it is for you—harder than you thought it would be."

She turned and wept against his chest, the bitter tears of a mother losing her son. In this case it was even more painful, for Little Rock had grown up much too fast. Sometimes it seemed he had never really been a child.

"Oh, Zeke, it seems like nothing is the same," she sobbed, taking some comfort in the familiar broad chest and the manly, earthy scent that belonged only to Zeke Monroe. "Sometimes I wish . . . I wish it could be . . . like the old days. I wish I still had . . . the old tipi . . . and we could migrate with the People freely. I wish . . . there were no cities . . . no gold, no soldiers and forts and fences! I wish it could be . . . like that first year . . . when they were so free and happy . . . and Swift Arrow and Red Eagle . . . and Yellow Moon were with us . . . and your mother. How I miss Gentle Woman!"

Her tears came like a waterfall, for she had not wept over being barren since that first day she awoke after the operation; and that, more than anything else, was something she needed to cry about and get out of her system, even though she had promised not to cry about it. It brought on the terrifying feeling of something being over, finished. He held her tightly for several minutes, his heart aching for her.

"Those old days are gone," old Deer Slayer spoke up. He had come to live with them, where he could be more assured of food and warmth. His old bones were always hurting now, and with soldiers constantly harassing the People, he could not keep up with all the constant migrating. There seemed to be no real peace for them. The old man rose and limped to the door. "I am glad my days are numbered," he mumbled.

He walked outside and was immediately surrounded by his several grandchildren. Zeke urged Abbie to look out at them. "Look there, Abbie girl. There goes an old man, surrounded by his grandchildren. Life goes on, Abbie. And things seem to work out. There are always things to cry about. Sometimes there are so many that we forget what we have to be glad about. How many times have we almost lost each other to death, Abbie? Our children are healthy, the

405

ranch is doing well, and we haven't even heard any more about a railroad coming through here. Did I tell you that a trader who came through here to water his horse told me he'd heard they'd decided to build a railroad way to the north of us?"

She wiped at her eyes. "No."

"Well, he did. So we can rest easy over that one. All our kids are healthy, and the doctor said your operation went real well and you'll be just fine. And look at me—all scarred up from old wounds but still strong and meaner than hell."

She looked up at him and he grinned, bending down to kiss her cheek. "He'll be okay, Abbie. He'll be back."

He urged her to a chair and poured her some coffee. She studied the broad shoulders and the fringed buckskin shirt he wore. She wondered if she would spend the rest of her life waiting for some member of her family to return from danger. He brought her the coffee and sat down to the table to pick up the rifle again. Nearby lay the infamous blade. It seemed violence followed Cheyenne Zeke everywhere. She did not want to think about violence just then.

"Zeke, will you do something for me?" she asked, pulling out a handkerchief and blowing her nose.

"Whatever my woman asks," he answered.

"Do you realize it's been years since you played the mandolin for me? Sometimes I almost forget you ever played it at all. Remember when we first met how you used to play it and sing? I need to see the mandolin in your hands instead of a gun."

He studied her eyes and put the rifle down. "I'd be rusty as hell, Abbie."

"I don't care. Remember that Tennessee mountain song you used to sing?"

He smiled. "I made that up. I used to sit and play back in Tennessee, when I'd go to the swamps alone to get away from the white kids."

Their eyes held. She wanted to remind him he still had a father in Tennessee, but he would only get upset at the subject, and she did not want to spoil the moment. Perhaps one day he would choose to see his white father again, but it was not likely. Whether he did or not, it was his decision.

"Go and get the mandolin," she told him. "It's probably awfully dusty. It's been sitting in the corner of the bedroom for ever so long."

He sighed and shook his head. "If it will make you happy, I'll get it," he told her. He rose and ambled into the bedroom, returning with the long unused instrument and blowing dust from it. He sat down and strummed it a little, tuning the cords to his musical ear. She thought about how beautiful his voice used to be, a surprisingly mellow, soothing voice for such a big and violent man. Now he hummed a little, trying to remember some songs, and the voice was still there. It warmed her heart to hear it again, and in moments all the children were swarming through the door to stare at the strange instrument and listen to its mysterious, haunting tones.

Zeke looked at Abbie, and she was fifteen again as he began the song.

> "See the mist a-risin'
> Out there upon the hill.
> The mornin' sun's a-comin' up,
> And dawn is bright and still."

The children all quickly hushed. The frail little Lillian climbed up on her mother's lap, and the others sat in a circle around their father.

> "I've lived on this here mountain
> Since I was freshly born.
> And there ain't nothin' nicer
> Than a misty mountain morn'.

> "Lord, I know heaven's pretty,
> And death I do not fear.
> But I hope that heaven's mornin's
> Are like the ones down here.

> "I've lived on this here mountain

407

Since I was freshly born.
And there ain't nothin' nicer
Than a misty mountain morn'."

He stopped, and the children stared, some of them never having heard their father sing.

"Your father used to sing and play for me when we first met," Abbie told them.

"How did you meet?" Jeremy asked them.

Abbie blinked back more tears. "On a wagon train, Jeremy. Your father was the scout." She sighed deeply and hugged Lillian. "I was only fifteen. I lost my whole family."

Zeke watched her lovingly. "Your mother was wounded by a Crow arrow," Zeke went on. "It was when I thought she'd die that I decided I couldn't go on without her. I was going to take her on to Oregon and try to forget her. But she never got to Oregon. She stopped right here in Cheyenne country and went no further."

Their eyes held. "And I've never regretted it," she told him.

"But look at how much you've suffered, Abbie girl. You could have had a lot better life."

She looked around at her children. He was right about remembering what there was to be thankful for. She looked back at Zeke. "Look at what is sitting around you. How could we have had it any better than this?" she replied.

He grinned and winked and returned to his playing for the children, strumming out a funny tune about a mountain made of candy.

It was two more weeks before Little Rock came riding up to the cabin. It was Zeke who charged out the door first, having been much more worried than he would let on. His heart leaped with joy to see that the boy looked fine, actually more healthy than ever. He started to run to the boy's mount and grab him off, but there was a look of manliness on Little Rock's face that told Zeke his son did not want to be hugged like a baby. He reined his mount to a

408

halt while Abbie stayed on the porch and watched hesitantly, her heart pounding with happiness that her son had come back safely to her. She forced back tears, sensing he would not want to see her crying. He must know they had every confidence he was manly enough to go off alone and take care of himself.

Little Rock met his father's eyes boldly, putting out a hand which Zeke gripped firmly with both his hands. "Hello, son."

The boy smiled a little. "I am glad to be home, Father. I missed you. But I had to go."

Zeke nodded. "I understand."

The boy picked up something that had been riding across his lap. It was a baby wolf. He handed it out to Zeke. "This is my friend. I call him Smoke."

Zeke held the animal close and it licked at his chin as Little Rock urged his horse closer to the cabin, then slid off it. The other children stood gawking through the doorway, quietly whispering at the return of their "big" brother. Abbie met the boy's eyes, her own chin held proudly, her chest feeling tight and painful.

He wanted to go and hug his mother, but somehow he could not do it. Not yet. There would be an easier time. He sensed that if he hugged her now, she would weep, and he was not ready for her weeping. Zeke walked up beside Abbie, holding the baby wolf in one arm while he put the other arm around Abbie. Little Rock studied both of them, standing tall and straight.

"I lived in a cave with Smoke's family," he told them. "I talked with them, and they told me the secrets of survival. They told me about how we need no more than the air and the land and the free things the Spirits give us to survive, that nothing else matters. Smoke's mother told me I should take her son with me when I left, so that he will always remind me of the things that are free and wild. And she told me I am to be called Wolf's Blood. I ask that you call me this name from now on. I am no longer Little Rock." He moved his eyes only to his father's. "When I am fifteen, I am to go North for the Sun Dance, no matter what the danger might

409

be. I must do this."

Zeke nodded. "Then I shall see that you get there."

Abbie wanted to scream out that she would not allow her son to undergo the bloody ritual. But it would be of no use, and he would only be insulted. It was the Cheyenne way, and she had always accepted that in Zeke. She must now accept it in her son. He moved his eyes to hers questioningly, afraid she would refuse to allow it. But she met his eyes squarely and nodded herself.

"Make me proud, Wolf's Blood, and don't cry out when you feel the pain," she told him.

The boy smiled brightly, and for a brief moment she saw him as he once was, a tiny brown boy who had once fed at her breast.

Epilogue

The October morning was cool and crisp, one of those days when everything seemed alive and bright and perfect. The smell of Abbie's freshly baking bread wafted through the windows and over the meadow where autumn wildflowers bloomed. Abbie hummed as she removed the bread from the ovens, then checked on little Jason, who had fallen asleep on a stack of robes in the corner of the kitchen, the warmth from the oven making her little ten-month-old boy sleepy.

She smiled and walked out onto the porch. She felt stronger and healthier than she had since Jeremy had been born six years before. Perhaps she had needed the operation for many years and had not known it. She watched the children playing and chasing one another, Lillian, two; Ellen, four; Jeremy, six; blond-haired LeeAnn looking so out of place amid them all, seven; and the dark, strikingly beautiful Margaret who still looked all Indian, ten.

Wolf's Blood, her firstborn and the only child without a Christian name, was off again hunting for more game to help feed his sisters and brothers. His pet wolf was with him, as always. Boy and wolf were never apart. Zeke worked in the corral with the Appaloosas, his faithful friend and helper Dooley working at his side. Abbie watched them for a moment, wondering what her life might have been like if she had never left Tennessee. No one could say it had not been exciting—to say the least. But could she have turned away from Zeke Monroe those many years ago and done things any differently?

411

No. She still remembered how she had felt the first time Cheyenne Zeke walked into the light of her father's campfire and she had offered him coffee. His hand had lightly touched hers, and in that moment the magic had started. She was under the spell of his dark eyes and his powerful command, and things could not have been different for her. It was destined, as all things seemed to be.

Old Deer Slayer, walking with a cane, also headed for the corral. Watching him made her think of another destiny yet to unfold: the destiny of the Cheyenne. It was unlikely the ending would be a happy one, but she knew that she must accept this growing and changing nation and do her own small part in helping make the terrible changes come easier for the People. What else was there to do? They would always be her friends, her family. Life was no more difficult for her than it was going to be for poor Danny, who was still at Fort Laramie and doing his best to keep the peace; and no more difficult than it was for Swift Arrow, who now rode the bloody trail of raiding. People did what they chose to do. She could not live their lives for them. She could only pray for them.

Little Crooked Foot, now called Joshua Lewis, was walking quite well and doing very well in his schooling, according to Bonnie Lewis. It was comforting to know the poor little crippled half-breed would have a good home. The thought reminded Abbie of Bonnie's secret love for Zeke, which brought to mind Swift Arrow's secret love for herself. Perhaps it was as Zeke had told her. There are many others who can love and admire a person, and who that person can in turn love and admire. But there is only one person who can be special, only one who brings out one's passion even after years of being together; only one person who comes along in one's lifetime who is so special that one seemingly could not survive without the other. That was how it was with herself and Zeke. It was comforting to know there was one man on whom she could rely for all things; one man who would never desert her, not for any reason; one man who would die for her a thousand times over. There was never any need to fear when Cheyenne Zeke was around, her friend, her protector, her lover.

To her surprise she saw an eagle sail over the distant meadow. There was no mistaking its magnificent wing span and wild screeching call. It was rare to see an eagle this far from the mountains. Was it trying to tell her something? She remembered Zeke's words, years ago when he had first asked her to marry him. He had told her he had seen her in a dream, her hair graying, her skin wrinkled. She stood at the top of a mountain alone and he came to her, but he was an eagle. His spirit was in the eagle. He warned her that the dream meant he would probably die before she did. But she would not worry about that now. She must not worry about it. If one spent one's life worrying about such things, one would miss out on what was going on around one today, this very moment. And today she could smell the baking bread and watch her children play. She was still young and strong, her skin still supple and her figure still trim. Zeke was as hard and vital and strong as he had ever been, with only an ache or a pain at times from old wounds. But he still wore the infamous knife at his side, and he could still use it with all the fierceness that had earned him his reputation with the knife. He was a warrior at heart, a warrior who ignored his need to ride free because of one small woman he could not leave.

She watched the eagle for a few minutes until it finally disappeared. Then she went back inside.

How peaceful everything was that day on the little ranch along the Arkansas. How odd that on that very day the abolitionist John Brown was leading a raid against the U.S. arsenal at Harper's Ferry, Maryland, in an effort to steal arms and ammunition to aid in his fight against those who believed in owning slaves. The bloodiest conflict the United States was ever to experience had begun. But Abigail Monroe didn't know such things were taking place. She walked to the oven to take out the bread.